REBEL ANGELS

⌇⌇⌇⌇

REBEL ANGELS

Libba Bray

DELACORTE PRESS

Published by
Delacorte Press
an imprint of
Random House Children's Books
a division of Random House, Inc.
New York

Visit us on the Web! www.randomhouse.com/teens
Educators and librarians, for a variety of teaching tools, visit us at www.randomhouse.com/teachers

Library of Congress Cataloging-in-Publication Data

Bray, Libba.
    Rebel angels / Libba Bray.
        p. cm.
    Summary: Gemma and her friends from the Spence Academy return to the realms to defeat her foe, Circe, and to bind the magic that has been released.
    ISBN 0-385-73029-2 (trade) — ISBN 0-385-90257-3 (glb)
    [1. Magic—Fiction. 2. Supernatural—Fiction. 3. Boarding schools—Fiction. 4. Schools—Fiction. 5. England—Social life and customs—19th century—Fiction.] I. Title.
    PZ7.B7386Reb 2005
    [Fic]—dc22

                                                                    2005003805

The text of this book is set in 13-point Adobe Jenson.
Book design by Trish Parcell Watts
Printed in the United States of America
August 2005
10 9 8 7 6 5
BVG

For Barry and Josh, of course

And for my much-loved friends,
proof that we somehow manage to find our own tribe

⌇⌇⌇

ACKNOWLEDGMENTS

Books do not write themselves. If they did, I'd have a lot more time to spend at Target. Nor are books written without the sage counsel, honest input, and occasional cheerleading of others. That's why I have so many fabulous people to thank.

My wonderful editor, Wendy Loggia, without whom I would be lost. My sassy and savvy publisher, Beverly Horowitz; talented designer Trish Parcell Watts; copyediting goddess Colleen Fellingham; the much-missed Emily Jacobs; publicity wenches Judith Haut and Amy Ehrenreich; Adrienne Waintraub and Tracy Bloom, for keeping me in fries; the deliciously puckish and zany Chip Gibson; and everybody else for everything else. Random House rocks.

My terrific agent, Barry Goldblatt, and not just 'cause he cuts my checks and talks me off the ledge when I think my writing is so bad it might cause someone internal injury.

The Strapping Gods of Victoriana: Colin Gale, senior archivist at Royal Bethlem Hospital, who tirelessly answered my questions and whose book, *Presumed Curable*, was a godsend. Mark Kirby, of the London Transport Museum, who was unfailingly polite and incredibly detailed even when I said stuff like, "Okay, but if she took the Underground from Piccadilly . . . ," as if I were staging a scene out of *Monty Python and the Holy Grail*. And the delightful Lee Jackson—the one-stop-shopping source for *anything*, and I do mean anything, about the Victorian age. Smart, funny, incredibly knowledgeable, fast with the e-mail answers, and an Elvis Costello fan. My heart swells with love. These men know their stuff. Any mistakes made or liberties taken are solely the fault of the author.

Laurie Allee, reader extraordinaire, who once again nailed it. I'm not worthy.

Holly Black, Cassandra Claire, and Emily Lauer, who know more about fantasy and magic systems on an off day than I could ever begin to know.

Nancy Werlin, for asking all the right questions.

The Right Honorable Kate Duffy of Kensington Books, who is without peer when it comes to peerage.

My pals at YAWriter for just about everything.

The barista staff of the Tea Lounge in Brooklyn—Brigid, Ben, Mario, Ali, Alma, Sherry, Peter, Amanda, Jonathan, Jesse, Emily, Rachel, Geoffrey—for caffeine, making me laugh, playing amazing music, letting me sit for hours, and generally making my work experience a happy one. Can't wait till they finish building me that cubicle near the outlet. . . .

The passionate booksellers and librarians I have met. You are my heroes.

BookDivas, long may they read and reign.

All the readers I've met on this crazy ride. Thanks for the inspiration and encouragement.

And last but certainly not least, thanks to my son, Josh, for being so patient. Yes, honey, now we can play Clue.

All that we see or seem / Is but a dream within a dream.

—Edgar Allan Poe

✦✦✦✦✦

Who first seduc'd them to that foul revolt?
Th' infernal Serpent; he it was, whose guile
Stir'd up with Envy and Revenge, deceiv'd
The Mother of Mankinde, what time his Pride
Had cast him out from Heav'n, with all his Host
Of Rebel Angels, by whose aid aspiring
To set himself in Glory above his Peers,
He trusted to have equal'd the most High,
If he oppos'd; and with ambitious aim
Against the Throne and Monarchy of God
Rais'd impious War in heav'n and Battel proud
With vain attempt. Him the almighty Power
Hurl'd headlong flaming from th' Ethereal Skie
With hideous ruine and combustion down
To bottomless perdition, there to dwell. . . .

O Prince, O Chief of many Throned Powers,
That led th' imbattell'd Seraphim to Warr
Under thy conduct, and in dreadful deeds

Fearless, endanger'd Heav'n's perpetual King;
And put to proof his high Supremacy,
Whether upheld by strength, or Chance, or Fate,
Too well I see and rue the dire event,
That with sad overthrow and foul defeat
Hath lost us Heav'n, and all this mighty Host
In horrible destruction laid thus low,
As far as Gods and Heav'nly Essences
Can Perish: for the mind and spirit remains
Invincible, and vigour soon returns,
Though all our Glory extinct, and happy state
Here swallow'd up in endless misery. . . .

To reign is worth ambition though in Hell:
Better to reign in Hell, than serve in Heav'n.
But wherefore let we then our faithful friends,
Th' associates and copartners of our loss
Lye thus astonisht on th' oblivious Pool,
And call them not to share with us their part
In this unhappy Mansion, or once more
With rallied Arms to try what may be yet
Regain'd in Heav'n, or what more lost in Hell?

—John Milton, *Paradise Lost*, Book 1

REBEL ANGELS

PROLOGUE

DECEMBER 7, 1895

HEREIN LIES THE FAITHFUL AND TRUE ACCOUNT OF
my last sixty days, by Kartik, brother of Amar, loyal son of the
Rakshana, and of the strange visitation I received that has left
me wary on this cold English night. To begin at the beginning,
I must go back to the middle days of October, after the misfortune that occurred.

It was growing colder when I left the woods behind the
Spence Academy for Young Ladies. I'd received a letter by fal-
con from the Rakshana. My presence was required immediately in London. I was to keep off the main roads and be
certain I was not followed. For several miles, I traveled under
cover of the Gypsy caravan. The rest of the way I made on
foot, alone, shielded by trees or the broad cape of night.

The second night, exhausted by my travels, half dead with

cold and hunger—for I had finished my meager portion of meat two days prior—my mind made strange by isolation, the woods began to play tricks on me. In my weakened state, every whippoorwill became a haunt; each twig broken under a fawn's hooves a threat from the unquiet souls of barbarians slaughtered centuries before.

By the light of the fire, I read several passages from my only book, a copy of *The Odyssey*, hoping to gain courage from the trials of that hero. For I no longer felt brave or certain of anything. Finally, I drifted into sleep and dreams.

It was not a restful sleep. I dreamed of grass gone black as kindling. I was in a place of stone and ash. A lone tree stood outlined against a bloodred moon. And far below, a vast army of unearthly beings clamored for war. Above the din, I heard my brother, Amar, screeching out a warning: "Do not fail me, brother. Do not trust . . ." But here the dream changed. She was there, bending over me, her golden red curls a halo against the bright sky.

"Your destiny is joined to mine," she whispered. She leaned close; her lips hovered near my own. I could feel the slightest heat from them. I woke quickly, but there was nothing, save the smoldering ash from my campfire and the night sounds of small animals scurrying for cover.

When I arrived in London I was half starved and unsure where to go next. The Rakshana had not given me instruction as to where to find them; that was not their way. They always found me. As I stumbled among the crowds of Covent Garden, the smell of eel pie, hot and salty, nearly drove me mad with hunger. I was about to risk stealing one when I spotted him. A man stood against a wall, smoking a cigar. He was not remarkable: of medium height and build, wearing a dark suit and hat, the morning's newspaper folded neatly under his left arm. He sported a well-groomed mustache, and along his cheek was a wicked smile of a scar. I waited for him to look away so that I could lift the pie without consequence. I feigned interest in a pair of street performers. One juggled knives while the other charmed the crowd. A third man, I knew, would be slipping about, relieving people of their wallets. I looked toward the wall again, and the man was gone.

Now was the time to strike. Keeping my hand hidden beneath the cover of my cloak, I reached toward the pile of steaming buns. The hot pie was barely in my grasp when the man from the wall sidled up to me.

"The Eastern Star is hard to find," he said in a low but cheery voice. It was only then that I noted the pin on his lapel—a small sword emblazoned with a skull. The symbol of the Rakshana.

I answered excitedly with the words I knew he expected, "But it shines brightly for those who seek it."

We clasped right hands then, placing the left over the fist as brothers of the Rakshana.

"Welcome, novitiate, we've been waiting for you." He leaned forward to whisper in my ear. "You have much to account for."

I cannot say exactly what happened next. The last sight I remember was of the meat pie woman pocketing coins. I felt a sharp pain at the back of my head, and the world swirled into blackness.

When I came to, I found myself in a dank, dark room, blinking against the sudden light of many tall candles arranged in a circle around me. My escorts had vanished. My head ached like the devil, and now awake, my terror was sharpened against the whetstone of the unknown. Where was I? Who was that man? If he was Rakshana, why the club on the head? I kept my ears open, listening for sounds, voices, some clue as to where I was.

"Kartik, brother of Amar, initiate of the brotherhood of the Rakshana . . ." The voice, deep and powerful, came from somewhere above me. I could see nothing but the candles, and behind that, utter darkness.

"Kartik," the voice repeated, most definitely wanting an answer.

"Yes," I croaked, when I could find my voice.

"Let the tribunal begin."

The room began to take shape in the dark. Twelve feet or more above the floor was a railing running the circumference of the circular room. Behind the railing, I could just make out the ominous deep purple robes of the highest ranks of the Rakshana. These were not the brothers who had trained me my whole life, but the powerful men who lived and ruled in the shadows. For such a tribunal to take place, I had either done something very good—or very bad.

"We are dismayed by your performance," the voice continued. "You were supposed to watch the girl."

Something very bad. A new terror seized me. Not the fear that I might be beaten or robbed by hooligans, but the fear that I had disappointed my benefactors, my brothers, and that I would face their justice, which was legendary.

I swallowed hard. "Yes, brother, I did watch her, but—"

The voice rose sharply. "You were supposed to watch her and report to us. That is all. Was this mission too difficult for you, novice?"

I could not speak, so great was my fear.

"Why did you not report to us the moment she entered the realms?"

"I—I thought I had things well in hand."

"And did you?"

"No." My answer hung in the air like so much smoke from the candles.

"No, you did not. And now the realms have been breached. The unthinkable has happened."

I rubbed my sweaty palms against my knees, but it did not help. The cold, metallic taste of fear worked its way into my mouth. There was much I didn't know about the organization to which I'd pledged myself, my loyalty, my very life, as my brother had before me. Amar had told me stories of the Rakshana, of their code of honor. Their place in history as protectors of the realms.

"If you'd come to us immediately, we could have contained the situation."

"With all due respect, she is not what I expected." I paused to think of the girl I'd left behind—headstrong, with startling green eyes. "I believe that she means well."

The voice boomed. "That girl is more dangerous than she knows. And more of a threat than you realize, boy. She has the potential to destroy us all. And now, between the two of you, the power has been unleashed. Chaos reigns."

"But she defeated Circe's assassin."

"Circe has more than one dark spirit at her disposal." The voice continued. "That girl shattered the runes that have housed the magic and kept it safe for generations. Do you understand that there is no control? The magic is loose inside the realms for any spirit to use. Already, many are using it to corrupt the spirits who must cross. They will bring them to the Winterlands and fortify their strength. How long before they weaken the veil between the realms and this world? Before they find a way to Circe or she finds a way in? How long before she has the power she covets?"

A slick, icy fear spread through my veins.

"Now you see. You understand what she has done. What you have helped her do. Kneel . . ."

From nowhere came two strong hands, forcing me to my knees. My cloak was loosened at my neck and I felt cold hard steel against the frantic throbbing of the vein there. This was it. I had failed, brought shame on the Rakshana and my brother's memory, and now I would die for it.

"Do you bow to the will of the brotherhood?" asked the voice.

My voice, pressed tight in my throat by the flat of the knife, sounded frantic, strangled. A stranger's voice. "I do."

"Say it."

"I . . . I bow to the will of the brotherhood. In all things."

The blade retreated. I was released.

When I realized my life would be spared, I am ashamed to say that I felt near to crying tears of relief. I would live, and I'd have a chance yet to prove my worth to the Rakshana.

"There is still hope. Has the girl ever made mention to you of the Temple?"

"No, my brother. I have never heard of such a place."

"Long before the runes were constructed to control the magic, the Order used the Temple. It is rumored to be the source of all power in the realms. It is the place where the magic can be controlled. Whosoever claims the Temple rules the realms. She must find it."

"Where is it?"

There was a moment's pause. "Somewhere inside the realms. We do not know for certain. The Order kept it well hidden."

"But how . . ."

"She must use her wits. If she is truly one of the Order, the Temple will most likely call to her in some fashion. But she must be careful. Others will seek it as well. The magic is unpredictable, wild. Nothing from the other side can be trusted. This is most important. Once she finds the Temple, she must say these words: *I bind the magic in the name of the Eastern Star.*"

"Won't that give the Temple to the Rakshana?"

"It will give us our due. Why should the Order have it all? Their time is past."

"Why do we not ask her to bring us in with her?"

The room fell silent for a moment, and I feared I would have the knife to my throat again. "No member of the Rakshana may enter the realms. That was the witches' punishment on us."

Punishment? For what? I had heard Amar say only that we were guardians to the Order, a system of checks and balances for their power. It was an uneasy alliance, but an alliance nonetheless. These things being spoken now made me wary.

I was afraid to speak out but knew I must. "I do not think she will work for us willingly."

"Do not tell her your aim. Gain her trust." There was a pause. "Woo her, if necessary."

I thought of the strong, powerful, stubborn girl I'd left behind. "She is not so easily wooed."

"Any girl can be wooed. It is merely a question of finding the right tool. Your brother, Amar, was quite skilled at keeping the girl's mother on our side."

My brother wearing the cape of the damned. My brother using a demon's war cry. Now was not the time to mention my unsettling dreams. They might think me a fool or a coward.

"Gain her favor. Find the Temple. Keep her from any other dalliances. The rest shall be ours."

"But—"

"Go now, Brother Kartik," he said then, using the title of honor that might one day be conferred upon me as a full member of the Rakshana. "We shall be watching you."

My captors came forward then to place the blindfold over my eyes once more. I jumped to my feet. "Wait!" I cried out. "Once she has found the Temple, and the power is ours, what is to become of her?"

The room was silent save for the flickering of the candles in the slight draft. At last the voice echoed down into the chamber.

"Then you must kill her."

CHAPTER ONE

DECEMBER 1895
SPENCE ACADEMY FOR YOUNG LADIES

AH, CHRISTMAS!

The very mention of the holiday conjures such precious, sentimental memories for most: a tall evergreen tree hung with tinsel and glass; gaily wrapped presents strewn about; a roaring fire and glasses filled with cheer; carolers grouped round the door, their jaunty hats catching the snow as it falls; a nice fat goose resting upon a platter, surrounded by apples. And of course, fig pudding for dessert.

Right. Jolly good. I should like to see that very much.

These images of Christmas cheer are miles away from where I sit now, at the Spence Academy for Young Ladies, forced to construct a drummer boy ornament using only tinfoil, cotton, and a small bit of string, as if performing some diabolical experiment in cadaver regeneration. Mary Shelley's monster could not be half so frightening as this ridiculous thing. The figure will not remind a soul of Christmas happiness. More likely, it will reduce children to tears.

"This is impossible," I grumble. I elicit no pity from any quarter. Even Felicity and Ann, my two dearest friends, which is to say my only friends here, will not come to my aid. Ann is determined to turn wet sugar and small bits of kindling into an exact replica of the Christ child in a manger. She seems to take no notice of anything beyond her own two hands. For her part, Felicity turns her cool gray eyes to me as if to say, *Suffer. I am.*

No, instead, it is the beastly Cecily Temple who answers me. Dear, dear Cecily, or as I affectionately refer to her in the privacy of my mind, She Who Inflicts Misery Simply by Breathing.

"I cannot fathom what is giving you such trouble, Miss Doyle. Really, it is the simplest thing in the world. Look, I've done four already." She holds out her four perfect tinfoil boys for inspection. There is a round of oohing and aahing over their beautifully shaped arms, the tiny woolen scarves—knit by Cecily's capable hands, but of course—and those delicate licorice smiles that make them seem overjoyed to be hanging by the neck from a Christmas tree.

Two weeks until Christmas and my mood blackens by the hour. The tinfoil boy seems to be begging me to shoot him. Compelled by a force larger than myself, I cannot seem to keep from placing the crippled ornament boy on the side table and performing a little show. I move the ugly thing, forcing him to drag his useless leg like Mr. Dickens's treacly Tiny Tim.

"God bless us, every one," I warble in a pathetic, high-pitched voice.

This is greeted by horrified silence. Every eye is averted. Even Felicity, who is not known as the soul of decorum, seems cowed. Behind me, there is the familiar sound of a throat being cleared in grand disapproval. I turn to see Mrs. Nightwing, Spence's frosty headmistress, staring down at me as if I were a leper. *Blast.*

"Miss Doyle, do you suppose that to be humorous? Making light of the very real pain of London's unfortunates?"

"I—I . . . why . . ."

Mrs. Nightwing peers at me over her spectacles. Her graying pouf of hair is like a nimbus warning of the storm to come.

"Perhaps, Miss Doyle, if you were to spend time in service to the poor, wrapping bandages as I once did in my own youth during the Crimean War, you would acquire a healthy and much-needed dose of sympathy."

"Y-yes, Mrs. Nightwing. I don't know how I could have been so unkind," I blabber.

Out of the corner of my eye, I can see Felicity and Ann hunched over their ornaments as if they were fascinating relics from an archeological dig. I note that their shoulders are trembling, and I realize that they are fighting laughter over my terrible plight. There's friendship for you.

"For this you shall lose ten good conduct marks and I shall expect you to perform an act of charity during the holiday as penance."

"Yes, Mrs. Nightwing."

"You shall write a full account of this charitable act and tell me how it has enriched your character."

"Yes, Mrs. Nightwing."

"And that ornament needs much work."

"Yes, Mrs. Nightwing."

"Have you any questions?"

"Yes, Mrs. Nightwing. I meant, no, Mrs. Nightwing. Thank you."

An act of charity? Over the holiday? Would enduring time with my brother, Thomas, count toward that end? Blast. I've done it now.

"Mrs. Nightwing?" The sheer sound of Cecily's voice could make me froth at the mouth. "I hope these are satisfactory. I do so want to be of service to the unfortunate."

It's possible that I shall lose consciousness from holding back a very loud *Ha!* at this. Cecily, who never misses an opportunity to tease Ann about her scholarship status, wants nothing to do with the poor. What she does want is to be Mrs. Nightwing's lapdog.

Mrs. Nightwing holds Cecily's perfect ornaments up to the light for inspection. "These are exemplary, Miss Temple. I commend you."

Cecily gives a very smug smile. "Thank you, Mrs. Nightwing."

Ah, Christmas.

With a heavy sigh, I take apart my pathetic ornament and begin again. My eyes burn and blur. I rub them but it does no good. What I need is sleep, but sleep is the very thing I fear. For weeks, I've been haunted by wicked warnings of dreams. I cannot remember much when I awaken, only snatches here and there. A sky roiling with red and gray. A painted flower dripping tears of blood. Strange forests of light. My face, grave and questioning, reflected in water. But the images that stay with me are of her, beautiful and sad.

"Why did you leave me here?" she cries, and I cannot answer. *"I want to come back. I want us to be together again."* I break away and run, but her cry finds me. *"It's your fault, Gemma! You left me here! You left me!"*

That is all I remember when I wake each morning before dawn, gasping and covered in perspiration, more tired than when I went to bed. They are only dreams. Then why do they leave me feeling so troubled?

"You might have warned me," I protest to Felicity and Ann the moment we are left alone.

"You might have been more careful," Ann chides. From her sleeve she pulls a handkerchief gone gray with washing and dabs at her constantly leaking nose and watery eyes.

"I wouldn't have done it had I known she was standing directly behind me."

"You know that Mrs. Nightwing is like God—everywhere at once. In fact, she may be God, for all I know." Felicity sighs. The firelight casts a golden sheen upon her white-blond hair. She glows like a fallen angel.

Ann looks around, nervous. "Y-y-you oughtn't to talk about"—she whispers the word—"*God* that way."

"Why ever not?" Felicity asks.

"It might bring bad luck."

Quiet descends, for we are all too well and too recently

acquainted with bad luck to forget that there are forces at work beyond the world we see, forces beyond all reason and comprehension.

Felicity stares at the fire. "You still assume there is a God, Ann? With all we've seen?"

One of the noiseless servants flits down the dim hallway, the white of her apron outlined by the somber gray of her uniform so that all that is seen against the darkness is the apron; the woman disappears entirely into shadow. If I follow her movement as she rounds a corner, I can see the happy, firelit hall from whence we've just come. A swarm of girls of varying ages, from six to seventeen, breaks out into spontaneous caroling, entreating God to rest ye merry gentlemen. No mention of God's resting gentlewomen, merry or not.

I long to join them, to light the candles on the grand tree, to pull at the strings on the bright Christmas crackers and hear the paper pop with a satisfying, jolly sound. I long to have no concerns other than whether Father Christmas will be kind this year or I shall find coal in my stocking.

With arms linked like paper dolls cut from the same paper, a trio of girls sways back and forth; one places her soft, curly head on the shoulder of the girl next to her, and she in turn gives a tiny kiss to that one's forehead. They have no idea that this world is not the only one. That far beyond the formidable, castle-like walls of Spence Academy, far beyond the barrier of Mrs. Nightwing, Mademoiselle LeFarge, and the other instructors here to mold and shape our habits and characters like so much willing clay, beyond England itself, there is a place of such beauty and fearsome power. A place where what you dream can be yours, and you must be careful what you dream. A place where things can hurt you. A place that has already claimed one of us.

I am the link to that place.

"Let's gather our coats," Ann says, moving for the immense, coiling staircase that dominates the foyer.

Felicity regards her curiously. "What ever for? Where are we going?"

"It's Wednesday," Ann says, turning away. "Time to visit Pippa."

CHAPTER
TWO

We make our way through the barren trees behind the school until we reach a familiar clearing. It is frightfully damp, and I'm glad for my coat and gloves. To our right lies the pond where we lay lazily in a rowboat under early September skies. The rowboat sleeps now on the frostbitten rocks and the bitter, dead grass of winter at the water's edge. The pond is a smooth, thin sheet of ice. Months ago, we shared these woods with an encampment of Gypsies, but they are long gone now, headed for warmer climes. In their party, I suppose, is a certain young man from Bombay with large brown eyes, full lips, and my father's cricket bat. Kartik. I cannot help wondering if he thinks of me wherever he is. I cannot help wondering when he will come looking for me next, and what that will mean.

Felicity turns to me. "What are you dreaming about back there?"

"Christmas," I lie, my words pushing out in small, steam engine puffs of white. It is miserably cold.

"I have forgotten that you've never had a proper English Christmas. I shall have to acquaint you with it over the holiday. We'll steal away from home and have the most splendid time," Felicity says.

Ann keeps her eyes trained on the ground. She'll stay here at Spence over the holiday. There are no relations to take her in, no presents to shake or memories to warm her till spring.

"Ann," I say too brightly. "How lucky you are to have the run of Spence while we're away."

"You needn't do that," she answers.

"Do what?"

"Try to paint a bright face on it. I shall be alone and unhappy. I know it."

"Oh, please don't go and feel sorry for yourself. I shan't be able to bear the hour with you if you do," Felicity says, exasperated. She grabs a long stick and uses it to whack at the trees as we pass them. Shamed into silence, Ann trods on. I should say something on her behalf, but more and more, I find Ann's refusal to speak up for herself an annoyance. So I let it go.

"Will you be attending balls over Christmas, do you think?" Ann asks, biting her lip, torturing herself. It is no different from the small cuts she makes on her arms with her sewing scissors, the ones her sleeves hide, the ones I know she has begun again.

"Yes. Of course," Felicity answers, as if the question is tedious. "My mother and father have planned a Christmas ball. Everyone shall be there."

Everyone except you, she might as well say.

"I shall be confined to close quarters with my grandmama,

who never misses an opportunity to point out my faults, and my infuriating brother, Tom. I promise you, it shall be a very taxing holiday." I smile, hoping to make Ann laugh. The truth is that I feel guilty for abandoning her, but not guilty enough to invite her home with me.

Ann gives me a sideways glance. "And how is your brother, Tom?"

"The same. Which is to say impossible."

"He hasn't set his hopes on someone, then?"

Ann fancies Tom, who would never look twice at her. It's a hopeless situation.

"I do believe he has, yes," I lie.

Ann stops. "Who is it?"

"Ah . . . a Miss Dalton. Her family is from Somerset, I believe."

"Is she pretty?" Ann asks.

"Yes," I say. We press on, and I hope that is the end of it.

"As pretty as Pippa?"

Pippa. Beautiful Pip, with her dark ringlets and violet eyes.

"No," I say. "No one is as beautiful as Pippa."

We've arrived. Before us stands a large tree, its bark mottled with a thin coat of frost. A heavy rock sits at its base. We remove our gloves and push the rock out of the way, revealing the decaying hollow there. Inside is an odd assortment of things—one kid glove, a note on parchment secured by a rock, a handful of toffees, and some desiccated funeral flowers that the wind takes the moment it whips through the old oak's ancient wound.

"Have you brought it?" Felicity asks Ann.

She nods and pulls out something wrapped in green paper. She unfolds the paper to reveal an angel ornament constructed of lace and beads. Each of us has had a hand in sewing bits of it. Ann wraps the gift in the paper again and places it on the makeshift altar with the other remembrances.

"Merry Christmas, Pippa," she says, speaking the name of a girl who lies dead and buried these two months some thirty miles from here. A girl who was our dearest friend. A girl I might have saved.

"Merry Christmas, Pippa," Felicity and I mumble after.

No one says anything for a moment. The wind's cold here in the clearing with little to block it. Sharp pellets of mist cut through the wool of my winter coat, pricking my skin into gooseflesh. I look off to the right where the caves sit, silent, the mouth closed off by a new brick wall.

Months ago, the four of us gathered in those caves to read the secret diary of Mary Dowd, which told us of the realms, a hidden, magical world beyond this one that was once ruled by a powerful group of sorceresses called the Order. In the realms, we can make our fondest wishes come true. But there are also dark spirits in the realms, creatures who wish to rule it. Mary Dowd discovered the truth of that. And so did we when our friend Pippa was lost to us forever.

"Frightfully cold," Ann says, breaking the silence. Her head is down and she clears her throat softly.

"Yes," Felicity says halfheartedly.

The wind pulls a stubborn brown leaf from the tree and sends it skittering away.

"Do you suppose we'll ever see Pippa again?" Ann asks.

"I don't know," I answer, though we all know she's gone.

For a moment, there's nothing but the sound of the wind scuttling through the leaves.

Felicity grabs a sharp stick, pokes it at the tree aimlessly. "When are we going back? You said . . ."

". . . that we'd go back once we've found the other members of the Order," I finish.

"But it's been two months," Ann whines. "What if there are no others?"

"What if they refuse to allow Ann and me to enter? We're not special, as you are," Felicity says, giving "special" a nasty tone. It's a wedge between us, the knowledge that I alone can enter the realms; that I have the power, and they do not. They can enter only if I take them.

"You know what my mother told us: The realms decide who shall be chosen. It isn't left to us," I say, hoping that is the end of it.

"When, pray, will these ladies of the Order make contact, and how?" Felicity asks.

"I've no idea," I admit, feeling foolish. "My mother said they would. It isn't as if I can simply take an advert in the newspaper, is it?"

"What of that Indian boy sent to watch you?" Ann asks.

"Kartik? I haven't seen him since the day of Pippa's funeral." Kartik. Is he out there even now in the trees, watching me, preparing to take me to the Rakshana, those men who would stop me from ever going back into the realms?

"Perhaps that's it, then, and he's gone away for good."

This thought makes my heart ache. I can't stop thinking of the last time I saw him, his large, dark eyes filled with some new emotion I couldn't read, the soft heat of his thumb brushed across my lip, making me feel strangely empty and wanting.

"Perhaps," I say. "Or perhaps he's gone to the Rakshana and told them everything."

Felicity mulls this over as she scrapes her name into the dry tree bark with a pointed stick. "If that were the case, don't you think they would have come for us by now?"

"I suppose."

"But they haven't, don't you see?" She pushes too hard on the stick and it breaks off on the *Y* so that her name reads FELICITV.

"And you still haven't had any visions?" Ann asks.

"No. Not since I smashed the runes."

Felicity regards me coolly. "Nothing at all?"

"*No-thing*," I answer.

Ann folds her hands under her arms to keep warm. "Do you suppose that was the source of it, then, and when you destroyed the runes you stopped your visions for good?"

I hadn't considered this. It makes me uneasy. Once, I was afraid of my visions, but now, I miss them. "I don't know."

Felicity takes my hands in hers, giving me the full seductive powers of her charm. "Gemma, think of it—all that lovely magic going to waste. There's so much we haven't tried!"

"I want to be beautiful again," Ann says, warming to Felicity's plan. "Or perhaps I could find a knight as Pippa did. A knight to love me true."

It isn't as if I haven't argued with myself over these very things. I ache to see the golden sunset over the river, to have all the power that I am denied in this world. It's as if Felicity can sense my resolve weakening.

She gives me a kiss on the cheek. Her lips are cold. "Gemma, darling, just a quick look around? In and out, with no one the wiser."

Ann joins in. "Kartik is gone and no one is watching us."

"What about Circe?" I remind them. "She's still out there somewhere, just waiting for me to make a mistake."

"We'll be very careful," Felicity says. I can see how this will go. They will push me until I agree to take them in.

"The truth of it is that I can't enter the realms," I say, looking off toward the woods. "I tried."

Felicity steps away from me. "Without us?"

"Just once," I say, avoiding her eyes. "But I couldn't make the door of light appear."

"What a pity," Felicity says. Her tone whispers, *I don't believe you.*

"Yes, so you see, we shall have to find the other members of the Order before we can return to the realms. I'm afraid there doesn't seem to be any other way."

It's a lie. For all I know I could enter the realms again at any time. But not yet. Not until I've had time to understand this strange power I've been given, this gift-curse. Not until I've had time to learn to master the magic, as my mother warned me I must. The consequences are too grave. It's enough that I will live with Pippa's death on my conscience for the rest of my days. I won't make the same mistake twice. For now, it's best that my friends believe I have no power left. For now, it's best that I lie to them. At least, that is what I tell myself.

In the distance, the church bell tolls, announcing that it is time for vespers.

"We'll be late," Felicity says, walking toward the chapel. Her tone has turned cold as the wind. Ann follows dutifully, which leaves me to roll the heavy stone back in place over the altar.

"Thank you for your help," I mumble, straining against the rock. I catch sight of the parchment again. Strange. I don't remember any of us putting it there, now that I think of it. It wasn't there last week. And no one else knows of this place. I take the torn paper from under the rock and unfold it.

I need to see you immediately.

There is a signature, but I don't need to read it. I recognize the handwriting.

It belongs to Kartik.

CHAPTER
THREE

KARTIK IS HERE, SOMEWHERE, WATCHING ME AGAIN.

This is the thought that consumes me during vespers. He is here and needs to speak to me. Immediately, his note said. Why? What is so urgent? My stomach is a tight fist of fear and excitement. Kartik is back.

"Gemma," Ann whispers. "Your prayer book."

I've been so absorbed that I've forgotten to open my prayer book and pretend to follow along. From her position in the front pew, Mrs. Nightwing turns to glare at me as only she can. I read a bit more loudly than is necessary so as to seem enthusiastic. Our headmistress, satisfied at my piety, faces forward again, and soon I am lost in new, troubled thoughts. What if the Rakshana have finally sent for me? What if Kartik is here to take me to them?

A shudder travels the length of my spine. I shan't let him do that. He shall have to come for me, and I won't go down without a solid fight. *Kartik.* Who does he think he is? *Kartik.* Perhaps he'll try to take me unawares? Sneak up behind me and wrap his strong arms about my waist? A struggle would ensue, of course. I would fight him, though he is quite strong, as I recall. *Kartik.* Perhaps we would fall to the ground, and he would pin me with the weight of his body, his arms holding mine down, his legs atop mine. I'd be his prisoner then, unable to move, his face so very near my own that I could smell the sweetness of his breath and feel its heat on my lips. . . .

"Gemma!" Felicity whispers sharply from my right side.

Flushed and flustered, I snap to attention and read aloud the first line of the Bible that I see. Too late I realize that mine is the only voice in the silence. My outburst startles everyone, as if I have had a sudden religious conversion. The girls giggle in astonishment. My cheeks grow hot. Reverend Waite narrows his eyes at me. I daren't look at Mrs. Nightwing for fear that her withering glare will reduce me to ash. Instead, I do as the others and bow my head for prayer. In seconds, Reverend Waite's reedy voice drifts over our heads, nearly putting me to sleep.

"What ever were you thinking about?" Felicity whispers. "Your expression was very strange."

"I was lost in prayer," I answer guiltily.

She attempts to say something to this, but I lean forward, my gaze intent on Reverend Waite, and she cannot reach me without invoking the ire of Mrs. Nightwing.

Kartik. I have missed him, I find. Yet I know that if he is here, the news cannot be good.

The prayer has ended. Reverend Waite gives a benediction

to us, his flock, and turns us out into the world. Dusk has rolled in, quiet as a ghost ship, and with it has come the familiar fog. In the distance, the lights of Spence beckon. An owl hoots. Strange. There haven't been many owls about lately. But there it is again. It's coming from the trees to my right. Through the fog, I can see something glowing. A lantern rests at the base of a tree.

It's him. I know it.

"What's the matter?" Ann asks, seeing that I've stopped.

"I've a pebble in my boot," I say. "You carry on. I won't be a moment."

For a second, I stand perfectly still, wanting to see him, wanting to be sure he is no haunt of my mind. The owl sound comes again, making me jump. Behind me, Reverend Waite closes the chapel's oak doors with a boom, cutting off the light. One by one, the girls disappear into the fog ahead, their voices growing faint. Ann turns around, half swallowed by gray.

"Gemma, come along!" Her voice drifts over the mist in echoes before it is gobbled completely.

. . . ma . . . come . . . long . . . ong . . . ong . . .

The owl's call comes from the trees, more insistent this time. The dark has come down hard in the last few minutes. There is only the glow from Spence and this one lonely light in the woods. I am alone on the path. In a flash, I pull up my skirt hem and rush headlong after Ann with a most unladylike shout.

"Wait for me! I'm coming!"

CHAPTER
FOUR

THIS IS WHAT I KNOW OF THE STORY OF THE ORDER.

They were once the most powerful women imaginable, for they were the keepers of the magical power that ruled the realms. There, where most mortals came only during dreams or after death, it was the Order who helped spirits cross over the river into the world beyond all worlds. It was the Order who helped them complete their souls' tasks, if need be, so that they could move on. And it was the Order who could wield that formidable power in this world to cast illusions, to shape lives, and to influence the course of history. But that was before two initiates who were attending Spence, Mary Dowd and Sarah Rees-Toome, brought destruction to the Order.

Sarah, who called herself Circe after the powerful Greek sorceress, was Mary's dearest friend. While Mary's power continued to grow, Sarah's began to fade. The realms had not chosen her to continue on the path.

Desperate to hold on to the power she craved, Sarah made a pact with one of the dark spirits of the realms in a forbidden place called the Winterlands. In exchange for the power to enter the realms at will, she promised it a sacrifice—a little Gypsy girl—and she convinced Mary to go along with her plan. With that one act, they bound themselves to the dark spirit and destroyed the power of the Order. To keep the spirits from entering this world, Eugenia Spence, the founder of Spence and a high priestess of the Order, stayed behind, sacrificing herself to the creature, and the Order lost their leader. Her last act was to toss her amulet—the crescent eye—to Mary and bid her to close the realms for good so that nothing could escape. Mary did, but she struggled with Sarah over the amulet, knocking over a candle. A terrible fire raged through the East Wing of Spence, and indeed, the damaged wing is still locked and unused today. It was assumed that both girls died in the fire, along with Eugenia. No one knew that as the fire raged, Mary escaped into the caves behind the school, leaving behind the diary we would eventually discover. Sarah was never found. Mary went into hiding in India, where she married John Doyle and was reborn as Virginia Doyle, my mother. Unable to enter the realms, the members of the Order scattered, looking and waiting for a time when they could claim their magical world and their power once more.

For twenty years, nothing happened. The story of the Order faded from legend to myth—until June 21, 1895, my sixteenth birthday. That is the day that the magic of the Order began to come alive again—in me. That is the day that Sarah Rees-Toome, Circe, finally came for us. She had not died in that horrible fire after all, and she had been using her corrupt bond with that dark spirit of the Winterlands to plot her revenge. One by one, she hunted down the members of the Order, looking for the daughter who was being whispered about, the girl who could enter the realms and bring back the glory and the power. That is the day that I had my first vision, when I saw my mother die, hunted by Circe's assassin—that supernatural creature who also brutally murdered Amar of the Rakshana, a cult of men who both protect and fear the power of the Order. It was the day I first met Kartik, Amar's younger brother, who would become my guardian and tormentor, bound to me by duty and sorrow.

It was the day that would come to shape the rest of my life. For afterward, I was sent here to Spence. My visions led me to enter the realms with my friends, where I was reunited with my mother and learned of my birthright to the Order; where my friends and I used the magic of the runes to change our lives; where I fought Circe's assassin and smashed the Runes of the Oracle—those stones that hold magic; where my mother died at last, and our friend Pippa, also. I watched her choose to stay, watched her walk hand in hand with a handsome knight into a place of no return. Pippa, my friend.

In the realms, I learned of my fate: I am the one who must form the Order once again and continue their work. That is my obligation. But I have another, secret mission: I shall face my mother's old friend—my foe. I shall face Sarah Rees-Toome, Circe, at last, and I shall not waver.

A steady rain lashes at the windows, making sleep impossible, though Ann is certainly snoring loudly enough. But it is not the rain that has me up, my skin prickly, my ears attuned to every small sound. It is that every time I close my eyes, I see those words on parchment: *I must see you immediately.*

Is Kartik out there, now, in the rain?

A gust blows against the windows, rattling them like bones. Ann's snoring rises and falls. It is pointless to lie here fretting. I light my bedside lamp and adjust the flame to a low flicker, just enough to find what I need. Rummaging through my wardrobe, I find it: my mother's social diary. I run my fingers over the leather and remember her laugh, the softness of her face.

I turn my attention back to the diary I know so well and spend half an hour scouring my mother's words for some guidance, but I find none. I haven't the vaguest idea of how to go about reforming the Order or how to use the magic. There is no useful information on the Rakshana and what they may have planned for me. There is nothing more to tell me about Circe and how I might find her before she finds me. It feels as if the whole world is waiting for me to act, and I am lost. I wish my mother had left me more clues.

The pull of my mother's voice, even on a page, is strong. Missing her, I stare at her words until my eyes feel heavy, pulled down by the late hour. Sleep. That is what I need. Sleep without the terror of dreams. Sleep.

My head snaps up suddenly. Was that a knock at the front door? Have they come for me? Every nerve is alive, every muscle taut. There is nothing but the rain. No bustling in the hallways to suggest someone rushing to answer a call. It is far too late for visitors, and surely Kartik would not use the front door. I am beginning to think that perhaps I dreamed it when I hear the knock again—louder this time.

Now there is movement below. Quickly I put out my lantern. Brigid, our garrulous housekeeper, mutters as she thunders past on her way to answer the door. Who could be calling at so late an hour? My heart is keeping fast time with the rain as I creep down the hall and perch near the staircase. Brigid's candle streaks the wall with shadows as she takes the stairs nearly two at a time, her long braid flying wildly behind her.

"By awl the saints," Brigid mutters. She huffs and puffs and reaches the door just as another knock descends. The door swings wide, letting the driving rain in with it. Someone has arrived in the dead of night. Someone dressed entirely in black. I feel as if I shall be sick with fright. I am frozen in place, not sure whether to make a dash down the stairs and out the door or run back to my room and bolt the door. In the dark of the hall, I cannot make out a face. Brigid's candle moves closer, casting a glow on the figure. If this is a member of the Rakshana come for me, then I am most confused. For this is a woman. She gives her name, but as the door is still open I cannot hear it over the howling of the rain and wind. Brigid nods and bids the coachman come in and leave the woman's trunk in the hallway. The woman pays him and Brigid closes the door against the press of night.

"I'll just wake the parlormaid to get you set'led," Brigid grouses. "No sense wakin' Missus Nightwing. She'll see you in proper come mornin'."

"That will be satisfactory," the woman says. Her voice is deep with a hint of a burr, an accent I cannot place.

Brigid turns up the lights to a low glow. She can't resist giving one final harrumph on her way to the maid's quarters. Left alone, the woman peels off her hat, revealing thick, dark hair and a severe face framed by heavy brows. She looks about the place, taking in the snake chandelier, the ornate carvings of nymphs and centaurs here and there. No doubt she has already noted the gargoyle collection dotting the roof and is likely wondering what sort of place this may be.

She glances up the expanse of the staircase, and stops, cocking her head. She squints as if she sees me. Quickly I duck into the shadows, pushing myself flat against the wall. In a moment, I hear Brigid's sharp voice barking out orders to the sleepy parlormaid.

"This is Miss McCleethy, our new teacher. See to her things. I'll show her to her room."

Mimi, the parlormaid, yawns and reaches for the lightest of the luggage, but Miss McCleethy takes it from her.

"If you don't mind, I should like to take this. My personal effects." She smiles without showing any teeth.

"Yes, miss." Mimi curtsies in deference and, sighing, directs her attention to the large trunk in the foyer.

Brigid's candle turns the staircase into a dance of shadow and light. I fly on tiptoe down the hall and take refuge behind a potted fern resting on a wooden stand, watching them from the cover of those mammoth leaves. Brigid leads the way, but Miss McCleethy stops at the landing. She gazes at everything as if she has seen it before. What happens next is most curious indeed. At the imposing double doors that lead to the fire-damaged East Wing, the woman stops, flattening her palm against the warped wood there.

In straining to see, my shoulder bumps the potted fern. The stand wobbles precariously. Quickly, I put out a hand to steady it, but already, Miss McCleethy peers into the darkness.

"Who's there?" she calls out.

Heart pounding, I tighten myself into a ball, hoping the fern will disguise me. It won't do to be caught sneaking about the halls of Spence in the dead of night. I can hear the creaking of the floorboards signaling Miss McCleethy's approach. I'm done for. I shall lose all my good conduct marks and be forced to spend an eternity writing out Bible passages in penance.

"This way, Miss McCleethy, if you please," Brigid calls down.

"Yes, coming," Miss McCleethy answers. She leaves her perch by the doors and follows Brigid up and around the staircase till the hall is dark and silent once again save for the rain.

⌁⌁⌁⌁⌁

My sleep, when it comes, is fitful, poisoned by dreams. I see the realms, the beautiful green of the garden, the clear blue of the river. But that is not all I see. Flowers that weep black tears. Three girls in white against the gray of the sea. A figure in a deep green cloak. Something's rising from the sea. I cannot see it; I can see only the faces of the girls, the cold, hard fear reflected in their eyes just before they scream.

I wake for a moment, the room fighting to take shape, but the undertow of sleep is too powerful and I find myself in one last dream.

Pippa comes to me wearing a garland of flowers on her head like a crown. Her hair is black and shining as always. Strands of it fly about her bare shoulders, so dark against the paleness of her skin. Behind her, the sky bleeds red into thick streaks of dark clouds, and a gnarled tree twists in on itself, as if it's been burned alive and this is all that remains of its once proud beauty.

"Gemma," she says, and my name echoes in my head till I can hear nothing else. Her eyes. There's something wrong with her eyes. They're a bluish white, the color of fresh milk, circled by a ring of black with one small dot of black in the center. I want to look away, but I can't.

"It's time to come back to the realms . . . ," she says, over and over, like the gentlest lullaby. "But careful Gemma, my darling . . . they're coming for you. They're all coming for you."

She opens her mouth with a terrible roar, exposing the sharp points of her hideous teeth.

CHAPTER
FIVE

WHEN MORNING FINALLY COMES, I AM SO TIRED that my eyes feel as if they are coated in sand. I've a foul taste in my mouth, so I gargle a bit of rosewater, spitting it as delicately as possible into the washstand. What I cannot rid myself of is the horrible image in my head, the one of Pippa as a monster.

It was only a dream, Gemma, only a dream. It is your remorse come to haunt you. Pippa chose to stay. It was her choice, not yours. Let it go.

I give my mouth one more rinse, as if that could possibly cure me of my ills.

In the dining room, the long rows of tables have been set for breakfast. Winter floral arrangements of poinsettias and feathery ferns in silver vases dot every fourth place setting. It is lovely, and I find myself forgetting the dream and remembering that it is Christmas.

I join Felicity and Ann as we stand wordlessly at attention

behind our chairs, waiting for Mrs. Nightwing to lead us in grace. There are bowls of preserves and great slabs of butter beside our plates. The air is perfumed with the wood-sweet smell of bacon. The waiting is torture. At last, Mrs. Nightwing stands and asks us to bow our heads. There is a mercifully short prayer and we are allowed to take our places at the table.

"Have you noticed?" Martha says in a stage whisper. She is one of Cecily's loyal followers and has begun to dress like her and even to resemble her a bit. They share the same practiced, coy laugh and a tendency to smile in a way that is meant to look demure but only seems as if they have bitten off too much bread and cannot swallow.

"Noticed what?" Felicity asks.

"We've a new teacher," Martha continues. "Do you see? She's sitting beside Mademoiselle LeFarge."

Mademoiselle LeFarge, our plump French instructor, sits with the other teachers at a long table set apart. She has been seeing a detective from Scotland Yard, an Inspector Kent whom we all like very much, and since their courtship began, she has taken to wearing brighter colors and more fashionable dresses. Her newfound gaiety, however, has not extended to excusing my deplorable French.

Heads swivel in the direction of the new teacher, who is seated between LeFarge and Mrs. Nightwing. She wears a suit of gray flannel, a sprig of holly pinned to one lapel. I recognize her instantly as the woman who arrived in the dead of night. I could share this information. It might make me quite popular at the table. Most likely, it would cause Cecily to run immediately to Mrs. Nightwing and inform her of my nighttime activities. I decide to eat a fig instead.

Mrs. Nightwing rises to speak. My fork, which was so very close to tasting happiness, must be stilled at my plate. I utter a silent prayer that she will be brief, though I know this is very much like asking for snow in July.

"Good morning, girls."

"Good morning, Mrs. Nightwing," we answer in unison.

"I wish to present Miss McCleethy, our new instructor in the arts. In addition to drawing and painting, Miss McCleethy is knowledgeable in Latin and Greek, badminton, and archery."

Felicity flashes me an excited smile. Only Ann and I know how happy this makes her. In the realms, she proved to be quite a skilled archer, a fact that would no doubt startle those who think she is concerned only with the latest fashion from Paris.

Mrs. Nightwing drones on. "Miss McCleethy comes to us from the very esteemed Saint Victoria's School for Girls in Wales. I am fortunate indeed, for I've known her as a dear friend for many a year."

At this Mrs. Nightwing gives Miss McCleethy a warm smile. It is astonishing! Mrs. Nightwing has teeth! I have always assumed that our headmistress hatched from a dragon's egg. That she is in possession of a "dear friend" is beyond me.

"I've no doubt she will prove an invaluable asset to us here at Spence, and I ask you to welcome her warmly. Miss Bradshaw, perhaps you'd be willing to sing a song for our Miss McCleethy? A carol would be nice, I should think."

Ann rises dutifully and walks between the long tables

toward the front. As she goes there is a bit of whispering, a snicker or two. The other girls never seem to tire of tormenting Ann, who keeps her head down and endures their cruelty. But when she opens her mouth to sing "Lo, How a Rose E'er Blooming," her voice, clear and beautiful and powerful, silences every critic. When she finishes, I want to stand and cheer. Instead, we give a round of brief, polite applause as she walks back to the table. Cecily and her friends make a point of not acknowledging Ann at all, as if she hasn't just sung for the whole room. It's as if she doesn't exist for them. She's no more than a ghost.

"That was splendid," I whisper to her.

"No," she says, blushing. "It was terrible." But a sheepish smile lights up her face anyway.

Miss McCleethy stands to address us. "Thank you, Miss Bradshaw. That was a nice start to our day."

A nice start? It was lovely. Perfect, in fact. Miss McCleethy has no passion at all, I decide. I shall be forced to give her two bad conduct marks in my invisible ledger.

"I look forward to meeting each of you and hope to be of service. You may find that I am an exacting teacher. I expect your very best at all times. But I think you will also find that I am fair. If you put forth effort, you shall be rewarded. If not, you shall suffer the consequences."

Mrs. Nightwing beams. She has found a kindred spirit, which is to say, someone devoid of all human joy. "Thank you, Miss McCleethy," she says. She sits, which is our blessed cue to begin eating.

Ah, grand. Now to the bacon. I lift two thick slices onto my plate. They are like heaven.

"She sounds a jolly sort," Felicity whispers naughtily, nodding toward Miss McCleethy. The others titter behind closed mouths. Only Felicity can get away with such outright cheek. If I were to make such a remark, I'd be greeted with stony silence.

"What a strange accent she has," Cecily says. "Foreign."

"Doesn't sound Welsh to me," Martha adds. "More Scottish, I should think."

Elizabeth Poole drops two lumps of sugar into her brackish tea and stirs daintily. She's wearing a delicate bracelet of golden ivy, no doubt an early gift from her grandfather, who is rumored to be wealthier than the Queen. "She could be Irish, I suppose," she says in her tight, high voice. "I do hope she isn't a Papist."

It wouldn't be worth my time to point out that our own Brigid is Irish and Catholic. For people like Elizabeth, the Irish are fine—in their place. And that place is living under stairs, working for the English.

"I certainly hope she is an improvement on Miss Moore." Cecily takes a bite of jam on toast.

At Miss Moore's name, Felicity and Ann go silent, eyes down. They haven't forgotten that we were responsible for the dismissal of our former art teacher, a woman who took us into the caves behind Spence to show us the primitive goddess paintings there. It was Miss Moore who told me about my amulet and its connection to the Order. It was Miss Moore who told us stories about the Order, and that, in the end, was what led to her fall. Miss Moore was my friend, and I miss her.

Cecily wrinkles her nose. "All those stories about magical women . . . what was it?"

"The Order," Ann says.

"Oh, yes. The Order," Cecily says. She gives the next bit a dramatic flair. "Women who could create illusions and change the world." This makes Elizabeth and Martha laugh and draws the attention of our instructors.

"Utter nonsense, if you ask me," Cecily says in a quiet voice.

"They were only myths. She told us that," I say, trying not to meet the eyes of either Ann or Felicity.

"Exactly. What purpose did she have in telling us stories about sorceresses? She was supposed to teach us how to draw lovely pictures, not take us into a damp cave to see primitive scratchings by some old witches. It's a wonder we didn't all take a chill and die."

"You needn't be so melodramatic," Felicity says.

"It's true! In the end, she got what she deserved. Mrs. Nightwing was right to dismiss her. And you were absolutely right to put the blame where it belonged, Fee—on Miss Moore. If it hadn't been for her, perhaps dear Pippa . . ." Cecily doesn't finish.

"Perhaps what?" I say icily.

"I shouldn't say," Cecily demurs. She is rather like a cat with a small mouse in her mouth.

"It was epilepsy that killed Pippa," Felicity says, fiddling with her napkin. "She had a fit. . . ."

Cecily lowers her voice. "But Pippa was the first to tell Mrs. Nightwing about that wretched diary you were all reading. She was the one who confessed that you'd been out to the caves at night, and that you had gotten the idea from Miss Moore herself. I think that a strange coincidence, don't you?"

"The scones are exceptionally good today," Ann says, trying to change the subject. She cannot bear conflict of any kind. She fears that it will always be her fault somehow.

"What are you accusing her of?" I blurt out.

"I think you know what I'm saying."

I can contain myself no longer. "Miss Moore was guilty of nothing but sharing a bit of folklore. I suggest we refrain from speaking of her altogether."

"Well, I like that," Cecily says, laughing. The others follow her lead. Cecily is an idiot, but why is it that she still has the power to make me feel foolish? "Of course, you would defend her, Gemma. It was that strange amulet of yours that began the conversation in the first place, as I recall. What is it called again?"

"The crescent eye," Ann answers, crumbs sticking to her bottom lip.

Elizabeth nods, adding kindling to the fire. "I don't think you ever told us exactly how you came to be in possession of it."

Ann stops eating mid-scone, her eyes large. Felicity jumps in. "She did say. A village woman gave it to her mother for protection. It was an Indian custom."

It is an amulet of the Order, given to me by my mother before she died. My mother, Mary Dowd, who with her friend, Sarah Rees-Toome, committed a vile act of sacrifice here at this very school more than twenty years ago and shattered the Order.

"Yes, that's correct," I say softly.

"They were most likely in league," Cecily says to her followers in a whisper that is meant to be overheard. "I wouldn't be at all surprised if she were a . . ." Cecily stops suddenly for effect. I shouldn't take the bait, but I do.

"A what?"

"Miss Doyle, do you not know that it's rude to eavesdrop on others' conversations?"

"A what?" I press.

A cruel smirk spreads across Cecily's face. "A witch."

With the back of my hand, I knock the bowl of preserves onto Cecily's plate. Some of the raspberry splatters across her dress so that she will have to change before Mademoiselle Le-Farge's class. She'll be late and lose marks.

Cecily stands in outrage. "You did that on purpose, Gemma Doyle!"

"Oh, how clumsy of me." I make a diabolical face, baring my teeth. "Or perhaps it was witchcraft."

Mrs. Nightwing rings a bell. "What is happening there? Miss Temple! Miss Doyle! Why are you creating such a scene?"

"Miss Doyle deliberately knocked the preserves onto my dress!"

I stand. "It was an accident, Mrs. Nightwing. I don't know how I could have been so clumsy. Dear Cecily, here, let me help you." Giving my best well-mannered smile, I swipe at her dress with my napkin, infuriating her.

She pushes my hand away. "She's lying, Mrs. Nightwing! She did it on purpose, didn't she, Elizabeth?"

Elizabeth, the obedient dog, comes to Cecily's aid. "She did, Mrs. Nightwing. I saw it."

Felicity's up now. "That is a lie, Elizabeth Poole. You know very well that it was an accident. Our Gemma would never do such an unkind thing."

Well, that *is* a lie, but I'm grateful for it.

Martha stands for Cecily. "She's always had it in for our Cecily. She is a most uncivilized girl, Mrs. Nightwing."

"I resent that!" I say. I look to Ann for help. She sits meekly at the table, still eating and unwilling to enter the fray.

"That is enough!" Mrs. Nightwing's harsh voice silences us. "This is a fine welcome for our Miss McCleethy. She will probably pack her things and head for the hills rather than stay amongst the savages. I cannot possibly loose you upon an unsuspecting London like the hounds of Hades. Therefore, we shall spend the day perfecting our manners and reflecting in prayer until what emerges is the sort of young lady Spence would be proud to call her own. Now, let us finish our break-fast in peace without any further unseemly outbursts."

Reprimanded, we sit and resume our meal.

"If I weren't a Christian, I should tell her exactly what I think of her," Cecily says to the others as if I can't hear her clearly.

"Are you a Christian, Miss Temple? I couldn't be sure," I say.

"How would you know about Christian charity, Miss Doyle, raised among the heathens in India?" Cecily turns to Ann. "Dear Ann, you should take care not to be associated with such a girl," she says, flicking her glance to me. "She might do great harm to your reputation, and, truly, that is all you have to recommend you as a governess."

I have met the devil, and her name is Cecily Temple. The evil frog knows just how to sow fear and doubt in Ann—poor, orphaned Ann, a scholarship student who is only here at a distant cousin's largesse, so that she might work for them when she leaves. Cecily and her ilk will never accept her, but they make sport of using her when it suits them.

If I'd hoped that Ann would rise to the occasion, I was sadly mistaken.

Ann does not say, "Why, Cecily, you really are a toad of a girl." "Why, Cecily, thank heavens you've a fortune, for with that face you'll need it." "Why, Cecily, Gemma is my good, dear, true friend, and I should never speak against her."

No. Ann sits silently, letting Cecily think she's won by her refusal to go against her. And so Cecily does, making Ann feel, for the moment, as if she has been accepted into their circle, though nothing could be further from the truth.

The potatoes are cold and tasteless now, but I eat them anyway, as if I have no feelings to hurt and the snickers of the other girls are nothing more than the patter of rain.

⌇⌇⌇⌇⌇

When the dishes have been cleared away, we're forced to sit at the long tables and endure a lesson on manners. It has been snowing all morning. I've never seen snow, and I long to walk out into the lush whiteness, feel the cold, wet crystals on my fingertips. Mrs. Nightwing's words drift in and out of my wandering mind.

"*You would not wish to find yourself snubbed by good society and crossed off the visiting lists of the best households . . .*"

"*Never ask a gentleman to hold your fan, bouquet, or gloves during a dance unless he is your escort or a relative. . . .*"

As I know no gentlemen besides my father and brother, this shan't be a concern. That isn't entirely true. I know Kartik. But we are unlikely to see each other in the ballrooms of London. What news has he for me? I should have gone to him on the way back from vespers. What a foolish girl he must think me.

"The lady of the highest rank shall enter the dining room first. The hostess shall enter last. . . ."

"Talking loudly or laughing on the street shows ill-breeding. . . ."

". . . Association with a man who drinks, gambles, or engages in other ills is to be avoided at all costs, lest he should bring disgrace upon your reputation. . . ."

A man who drinks. Father. I want to push the thought away. I see him as I saw him in October, eyes glazed with laudanum, hands trembling. Grandmama's few letters since have made no mention of his health, his addiction. Is he cured? Will he be the father I remember, the jolly man with the gleam in his eye and a quick wit to make us all laugh? Or will he be the father I've known since Mother's death—the hollow man who doesn't seem to see me anymore?

"Ladies may not leave a ballroom unattended. To do so could invite gossip."

The snow piles against the windowpanes, creating tiny hilly villages there. The white of the snow. The white of our gloves. Of Pippa's skin. Pippa.

They're coming for you, Gemma. . . .

A chill passes through me. It has nothing to do with the cold and everything to do with what I do not know; what I am afraid to discover.

CHAPTER
SIX

ALL THE MORNING'S DIFFICULTIES ARE FORGOTTEN once we are let out. The sun, strong and bright, reflects off the fresh white in dazzling sparkles. The younger girls squeal in delight as the wet snow spills over the tops of their boots and down inside. A group has already begun work on a snowman.

"Isn't it glorious?" Felicity sighs. She's got her new fox-fur muff to show off, so she is quite happy. Ann follows gingerly, her mouth set in a grimace. The snow is a marvel to me. I grab a handful and am surprised to find it so pliable. "Ah, it sticks!" I shout.

Felicity regards me as if I've grown two heads. "Yes. Of course." Now it dawns on her. "You've never seen snow!"

I want to fall back and bathe in it, such is my joy. I bring a mound to my mouth. It seems as if it should taste creamy as custard, but instead it is merely cold. The flakes dissolve instantly, melting into the heat of my tongue. I'm giggling like a fool.

"Here, let me show you something," Felicity says. She scoops the snow in both gloved hands, patting and shaping till she's got a hard ball of it, which she shows to me. "Behold: the snowball."

"Ah," I say, not understanding in the least.

Without warning, she hurls the packed snow at me. It hits me hard on the sleeve, sending a spray of wet crystals into my face and hair till I'm sputtering.

"Isn't snow marvelous?" she says.

I should be angry, I suppose, but I find I am laughing. It *is* marvelous. I love the snow and wish it would go on forever.

Huffing and puffing, Ann finally reaches us. She slips and plops down into a large puff of white with a squeal, which makes Felicity and me laugh uncharitably.

"You might not laugh if you were the one soaked through," Ann grumbles, struggling to her feet in a very ungraceful fashion.

"Don't be such a ninny," Felicity scoffs. "It isn't the end of the world."

"I haven't ten pairs of stockings at the ready, as you do," Ann says. It's meant to sound clever but it comes out dreary and petulant.

"I shan't bother you further, then," Felicity says. "Oh, Elizabeth! Cecily!" And with that, she marches off to the other girls, abandoning us to the cold.

"But I *don't* have a wealth of stockings," Ann says, defending herself.

"You sounded very sorry for yourself is all."

"I can't seem to say anything right."

My happy afternoon in the snow is fading. I don't think I can bear an hour of Ann's whining. I am still a bit angry with her for not coming to my defense at breakfast. The snow is in my hand before I can think. I hurl it at Ann and it splats across her surprised face. Before she can react, I throw another snowball.

Ann splutters, "I—I—I . . ."

Another hits across her skirt.

"Come on, then, Ann," I say, taunting her. "Are you going to allow me to keep punishing you? Or are you going to take your revenge?"

The answer is a spray of snow across my neck. The ice trickles down my collar and into my dress and I squeal from the sudden freeze. I reach for another handful of snow and Ann's next snowball finds my head. My hair drips with the wet ice.

"That isn't fair!" I shout. "I've no ammunition."

Ann stops, and I hit her with a snowball I've hidden behind my back. Her face is the picture of outrage. "You said—"

"Ann, do you always do as you're told? This is war!" I throw one that misses, but Ann's next snowball finds my face again. I'm forced to find higher ground while wiping the ice pellets from my eyes.

Beneath the snow, the land has turned to thick mud due to all the rain. The heels of my boots have sunk in, and with nothing to brace myself against—no tree or bench—I'm afraid I'm stuck fast. I lift my boot and pitch forward, nearly toppling face-first into the muck. Someone grasps my wrist hard, pulling me up and over behind a tree. When my eyes clear, I am face to face with him.

"Kartik!" I exclaim.

"Hello, Miss Doyle," he says, smiling at my soggy appearance. Melting snow drips from my hair onto my nose. "You look . . . well."

I'm a fright.

"Why didn't you respond to my note?" he asks.

I feel foolish. And happy to see him. And wary. So many thoughts I cannot name them all. "It is difficult to get away. I . . ."

Beyond the trees, I hear Ann calling my name, looking for me in order to exact her snowball revenge.

Kartik's grip tightens. "No matter. We've little time and I've much to say. There is trouble in the realms."

"What sort of trouble? When I left, all seemed well. Circe's assassin had been defeated."

Kartik shakes his head. Beneath his hood, his long, dark curls sway. "Do you remember when you smashed the Runes of the Oracle and set your mother free?"

I nod.

"Those runes were the Order's ancient binding on the great power inside the realms. A sort of safe for their magic. It was a way to ensure that they alone could draw on it."

Ann calls again. She's getting closer to our hiding spot.

Kartik speaks in an urgent whisper. "When you smashed the runes, Miss Doyle, you destroyed the binding."

"I released the magic into the realms," I finish. A slick dread seeps into my bones.

Kartik nods. "Now it is loose, free for anyone to use for any purpose, even if they do not know how. This magic is extremely powerful. And to release it into the realms with no control . . ." He trails off, then continues. "Certain elements could seek to have dominion over all the realms. They could be in league with each other—and with Circe."

"Circe . . ." Oh, God. What have I done?

"Gemma, come out, come out wherever you are!" Ann giggles.

Kartik puts a finger to my lips, flattens himself against me. He smells of campfire, and there is a hint of shadow along his jaw. I can scarcely breathe for his closeness.

"There is a way to bind the magic again. A hope," Kartik says. Ann's voice trails off in another direction, and he steps away from me. The air rushes between us to fill the void. "Did your mother ever make mention of a place called the Temple?"

I'm still reeling from the feel of his chest against mine. My cheeks are pink from more than the cold. "N-no. What is it?"

"It is the source of the magic inside the realms. We need you to find it."

"Is there a map? A marker?"

Kartik exhales, shakes his head. "No one knows where it is. It is well hidden. Only a few members of the Order knew where to find it at any given time. That was the only way to keep it safe."

"How am I to find it, then? Am I to rely on the creatures?"

"No. Trust no one. Trust nothing."

Nothing. *No thing.* It makes me shiver.

"What about my visions? May I rely on them?" Not that I've had any of late.

"I don't know. Their source is the realms." He shrugs. "I cannot say."

"And when I find the Temple?"

Kartik's face pales as if he's frightened. I've never seen him this way. He does not look at me as he says, "Use these words: *I bind the magic in the name of the Eastern Star.*"

"The Eastern Star," I repeat. "What does it mean?"

"It is a powerful binder, a spell of the Order, I think," he says, looking off.

Ann's voice comes closer. I can see the blue of her coat through the bars of trees. Kartik sees her too. He's up and ready to run.

"I shall be in touch," he says. "I don't know what you shall find in the realms, Miss Doyle. Be careful. Please." He turns to go, stops, makes to leave again, rushes back, and gives my hand a quick kiss like a proper gentleman. Like a shot, he is gone, running fast through the snow as if it's no trouble at all.

I do not know what to think. The magic is loose in the realms. It is all my fault. I must find the Temple and restore order before the realms are lost. And Kartik just kissed me.

I've barely had time to consider it all when without warning, I'm gripped by a sharp, surprising pain that has me doubling over, grabbing a tree for balance. I'm woozy, and everything looks very strange. In fact, I feel suddenly very ill. I'm aware that someone is watching me. I'm horrified to think that anyone could see me at such a vulnerable moment. Gasping, I look up, trying to gain my bearings.

At first I think it must be the snow in my eyes. I blink, but the image doesn't fade. I see three girls dressed all in white. But they are not familiar to me. I have never seen them at Spence, and they look to be my age. Despite the frigid air, they have no coats.

"Hello," I call to them. They do not answer. "Are you lost?"

They open their mouths to speak but I can't hear them, and then a curious thing happens. The girls flicker and fade until there's no trace of them in the snow. And just as quickly, the pain passes. I feel fine.

A hard ball of snow hits me square on the jaw. "Aha!" Ann shouts in victory.

"Ann!" I cry, angry. "I was not prepared!"

She gives me a rare triumphant smile. "You were the one who said this was war." And with that, she bounds awkwardly over the snow, in hasty retreat.

CHAPTER
SEVEN

"LADIES, MAY I HAVE YOUR FULL ATTENTION? WE ARE most privileged to have with us tonight the Pantomime Players of Covent Garden. They have prepared a most satisfactory bill of the story of Hansel and Gretel, by the brothers Grimm."

I was hoping that after vespers and dinner I'd have time alone with Felicity and Ann to tell them about Kartik's warning. But, just my luck, tonight Mrs. Nightwing has arranged a special evening of pantomime for us. My news shall have to wait. The younger girls are enthralled to bear witness to a grisly fairy tale complete with menacing woods and evil witch. The players of the company are introduced to us by the impresario, a tall, heavyset man with a powdered face and enormous whiskers waxed into fine curlicues. One by one, the players file out onto the ballroom's small stage. The men bow and the women curtsy. Or rather, the characters bow and curtsy. In truth, the pantomime troupe is comprised entirely of men. Even the poor soul playing Gretel is a boy of about thirteen.

"Players, to your places," the impresario bellows in a loud, deep voice. The stage empties. A pair of stagehands maneuvers a flat of wooden trees downstage. "Let us begin our tale where it should begin—in a house at the edge of a very dark forest."

The lights are lowered. A hush falls over the crowd. There is no sound but the incessant tapping of cold rain against the martyred windows.

"Husband," the shrewish wife cries, "there is not enough for all of us to eat. We must take the children into the forest, where they shall have to fend for themselves."

Her husband, a huntsman, replies with wild gestures and a voice so melodramatic it is as if he is mocking truly horrid actors. When it becomes clear he is not, it is all I can do to keep my composure.

Felicity whispers in my ear, "I must confess: I've fallen madly in love with the poor huntsman. I believe it is his subtlety that woos me."

I put a hand to my mouth to stop the laugh there. "I find I am strangely besotted with his wife. Perhaps something about her beard . . ."

"What are you whispering about?" Ann says, drawing a sharp "shhhh" from Mrs. Nightwing, who comes to stand behind us. We sit tall and silent as gravestones, feigning interest. I can only pray that tonight's plum pudding was dressed with arsenic, and I have only moments left to endure this spectacle of men in garishly colored folk costumes parading as women.

The mother pushes Hansel and Gretel into the woods.

"That's it, children. Walk out a little farther. All you wish for is just beyond that forest."

Hansel and Gretel disappear into the woods and come upon the house of sweets. With wide eyes and exaggerated smiles, they pretend to gnaw at the painted gumdrop shutters.

The impresario struts about the edge of the stage. "The more they ate, the more they wanted," he intones gravely. A few rows away, some of the younger girls gossip behind raised hands. A giggle erupts. When more giggles follow, Mrs. Nightwing leaves her shepherd's station with us to watch over her flock elsewhere.

I want to tell Felicity and Ann about Kartik, but we are too closely watched to have this conversation now. Onstage, the hapless Hansel and Gretel have been lured into the witch's house of sweets.

"Poor children, abandoned by the world, I shall give you sustenance. I shall give you what you seek!" The witch turns to the audience with a knowing wink and we boo and hiss on cue.

The boy playing Gretel cries, "And will we be like your very own children then, dear Auntie? Will you love us and teach us so very well?" His voice breaks on the last part. There are titters from the audience.

"Yes, child. Fear not. For now that you are here, as I so often prayed you would be, I shall clutch you to my bosom and keep you in my grasp forever!" The witch pulls Hansel hard into her enormous false bosom, nearly suffocating him. We laugh merrily at this bit of foolery. Encouraged, the witch stuffs a piece of pie in Hansel's mouth, eliciting more laughter from the audience.

The lights flicker. There is a chorus of sudden gasps and a few tiny shrieks from some of the more high-spirited girls. It's only a stagehand at work, but it has had the desired effect. The witch rubs her hands together and confesses her diabolical plan to fatten the children and roast them in her grand oven. This gives everyone the chills, and I do have to wonder what sort of childhood the Grimm brothers endured. They are not a merry bunch of storytellers, what with their children roasted by witches, maidens poisoned by old crones, and whatnot.

There is a sudden nip in the air, a damp cold that works its way into the marrow. Has someone opened a window? No, they are all shut tight against the rain. The draperies don't move to suggest a draft.

Miss McCleethy walks the perimeter of the room, her hands folded in front of her like a priest in prayer. A slow smile spreads across her face as she takes in the whole of us. Something amusing has happened on the stage. The girls laugh. It sounds distorted and faraway to me, as if I am underwater. Miss McCleethy puts a hand on the back of a girl sitting on the end; she bends to hear the child's question with a smile, but beneath those thick, dark brows her eyes find mine. Though it is cold, I have begun to perspire as if I am feverish. I have a mad desire to run from the room. In fact, I'm feeling ill.

Felicity's whispering something to me but I can't hear the words. The whisper itself has a horrible din, like the dry wings and scratching legs of a thousand insects. My eyelids flutter. A roaring fills my ears, and I am falling hard and fast through a tunnel of light and sound. Time stretches out like a band. I am aware of my own breathing, the flow of blood in my veins. I'm caught in the grip of a vision. But this is like no vision I've ever had. It is much more powerful.

I'm near the sea. Cliffs. Smell the salt. Sky's a reflection, whitecap clouds churning above, an old castle on a hill. Happening fast. Too fast. Can't see . . . Three girls in white jump about the cliffs absurdly fast. The salt, tangy on my tongue. Green cloak. A hand raised, a snake, sky churning, clouds braiding black and gray. Something else. Something's—oh, God—something's rising. Fear, at the back of my throat like the sea. Their eyes. Their eyes! So afraid! Open now. See it rising from the sea. Their eyes a long, silent scream.

Feel my blood pull me back, away from the sea and the fear.

I hear voices. *"What is it? What happened?" "Stand back, give her air." "Is she dead?"*

I open my eyes. A cluster of concerned faces looms over me. Where? What are they? Why am I on the floor?

"Miss Doyle . . ."

My name. Should answer. Tongue's thick as cotton.

"Miss Doyle?" It's Mrs. Nightwing. Her face swims into focus. She waves something foul beneath my nose. Horrible sulfur odor. Smelling salts. Makes me groan. I roll my head to escape the smell.

"Miss Doyle, can you stand?"

Like a child, I do as I'm told. I see Miss McCleethy across the room. She hasn't moved from her spot.

Startled gasps and whispers float by. "*Look. There. How shocking.*"

Felicity's voice rises over the others. "Here, Gemma, take my hand."

I see Cecily whispering to her friends. Hear the whispers. "How appalling." See Ann's troubled face.

"What . . . what happened?" I ask. Ann looks down shyly, unable to answer.

"Here now, Miss Doyle, let's see you to your room." Only when Mrs. Nightwing helps me to my feet am I able to see the cause of the gossip—the large red stain spreading across my white skirt. I have begun to menstruate.

CHAPTER
EIGHT

BRIGID TUCKS THE HOT WATER BOTTLE BENEATH the covers against my belly. "Poor dear," she says. "It's always such a bother. I've 'ad me troubles with the curse. And 'avin' to be on about my duties through it all. No rest for the weary, I can tell you that."

I am in no humor to hear about our long-suffering house-keeper's aches and pains. Once she starts, there's no stopping her. And I'll be hearing about her rheumatism, her poor eye-sight, and the time she once nearly worked for the household of the Prince of Wales's twelfth cousin four times removed.

"Thank you, Brigid. I think I'll rest now," I say, closing my eyes.

"Of course, lamb. Rest is wha' you need. Rest is the thing. Why, I remember when I was to work for a very fine lady— she'd once been lady's maid to the cousin of the Duchess of Dorset, oo was as respec'able a lady as could be foun', I tell you . . ."

"Brigid." It's Felicity, trailed by Ann. "I believe I saw the parlormaids slipping belowstairs for a game of cards. I thought you might want to know."

Brigid places her fists on her meaty hips. "They've no leave from me. These new girls—they don't know their place. In my day, the 'ousekeeper was the law." Brigid harrumphs past us, muttering under her breath the while. "Off to cards. We'll see abou' that!"

"Were they really off to cards?" I ask Felicity once Brigid is gone.

"Of course not. I needed to dispatch her somehow."

"How are you feeling?" Ann asks, blushing.

"Wretched," I answer.

Felicity sits on the edge of my bed. "Do you mean to say that this is the first time you've been . . . inconvenienced by your monthly illness?"

"Yes," I snap, feeling a bit like an exotic, misunderstood animal.

In addition to the hot water bottle, I've been packed off to bed with some strong tea and a tiny bit of brandy, compliments of Mrs. Nightwing, who insisted that in this case the brandy was medicinal and not licentious. The tea has gone cold and bitter. But the brandy is soothing. It dulls the pulsing throb in my belly. I have never felt more ridiculous. If this is what it means to be a woman I am not the slightest bit interested.

"Poor Gemma," Ann says, patting my hand. "In public, no less. How embarrassing for you."

I could not be more humiliated than I am now. "If I may be so bold, may I ask, when did you commence with . . . ?" I trail off.

Felicity moves to my table, where she examines my things. She runs my brush through her white-blond hair. "Years ago."

Of course she did. How silly of me to ask. I look to Ann, who blushes the color of a radish instantly.

"Oh, I, we sh-sh-shouldn't t-t-talk of such things."

"Quite right," I say, fingering the edge of my bed linen with great care.

"She's probably not yet a woman," Felicity says coolly.

Ann is up in protest. "I am! For six months now!"

"Six months! There you are. She's practically an expert on the subject."

I try to get out of bed, but Ann pushes me back down. "Oh, no. You mustn't move about. It isn't good for you in your present state."

"But . . . how am I to go about my life?"

"You simply have to endure this. It's our punishment as daughters of Eve. Why do you think they call it the curse?"

A low rumble pulls across my stomach, making me feel heavy and irritable. "Really? And what curse befalls the Adams of the world?"

Ann opens her mouth and, presumably thinking of nothing to say, closes it again.

It is Felicity who answers, her eyes steely. "They are weak to temptation. And we are their temptresses."

The word *temptation* conjures Kartik in my mind. Kartik and warnings. The magic loose in the realms. The Temple.

"There's something I need to tell you," I begin. I tell them about Kartik's visit, about my task and the strange vision I saw during the pantomime. When I finish, they are wide-eyed.

"I've gooseflesh. Just think of it, all that magic loose for anyone to use," Felicity says. I cannot say whether she is frightened or thrilled at this prospect.

Ann's troubled. "But how can you find the Temple when you can't enter the realms?"

I'd forgotten my lie. There is no way around it now. I shall have to confess. I pull the linens to my neck, make myself small in the bed. "The truth is, I haven't actually tried to enter. Not since Pippa."

Felicity's glare could shatter glass. "You lied to us."

"Yes, I know. I'm sorry. I wasn't ready."

"You could have said as much," Ann mutters, hurt.

"I *am* sorry. I thought it best."

Felicity's gray eyes are like the sharpest flint. "Do not lie to us again, Gemma. It will be a betrayal of the Order."

I don't like the way she says this, but I'm in no mood to argue now. I nod and reach for the brandy.

"When shall we go into the realms?" Ann asks.

"Shall we meet at midnight?" Felicity half begs. "Oh, I cannot wait to see it all again!"

"I'm in no condition tonight," I say. They can hardly argue with that.

"Very well, then," Felicity says, sighing. "Rest."

"What is it?" Ann asks, reading my expression.

"It's probably nothing, really. I was just thinking that the last thing I remember before falling under was Miss McCleethy's face. She was looking at me in the most curious way, as if she knew all my secrets."

A devilish grin lights up Felicity's full mouth. "You mean the fairrr but exacting Miss McCleethy," she says, imitating our new teacher's strange brogue. This makes me laugh in spite of everything.

"If she's an old friend of Nightwing's, she's doubtless a hideous prig who will make our lives a misery," I say, still giggling.

"I am glad to see that you seem in better spirits, Miss Doyle." It's Miss McCleethy herself at my door. My heart falls through the floor of my stomach. Oh, no. How long has she been standing there?

"I'm feeling much better, thank you," I say in a squeak of a voice.

I am almost certain she's overheard everything, for she holds my gaze a moment too long, till I'm forced to look away, and then she says simply, without any enthusiasm, "Well, I am glad to hear it. You should take some exercise. Exercise is the key. Tomorrow I shall take all my girls out to the lawn for archery."

"What a splendid idea! I cannot wait to begin," Felicity says too brightly, hoping to cover any overheard unpleasantness with a fresh coat of charm.

"Have you some experience with the bow and arrow, Miss Worthington?"

"A trifling amount," Felicity demurs. In truth, she is excellent.

"How marvelous. I'd wager you ladies have all manner of surprises ready for me." A curious half smile tugs at the corners of Miss McCleethy's taut mouth. "I look forward to our becoming friends. My previous pupils have found me to be rather jovial, despite my reputation as a hideous prig."

She's heard everything. We're done for. She shall hate us forever. No, she shall hate me forever. *Jolly good start, Gemma. Bravo.*

Miss McCleethy inspects my desk, lifting my few belongings there—the ivory elephant from India, my hairbrush—for closer examination. "Lillian—Mrs. Nightwing has told me of your unfortunate involvement with your former teacher Miss Moore. I am sorry to hear that she misused your trust so."

She gives us that penetrating stare again. "I am not Miss Moore. There will be no stories, no impropriety. I will not tolerate disruption in the ranks. We shall follow the letter of the law and be the better for it." She takes in our pale faces. "Oh, come now, you all look as if I've sentenced you to the guillotine!"

She attempts a laugh. It is not winning or warm. "Now, I do believe we should allow Miss Doyle to rest. They're serving eggnog in the parlor. Come and tell me of yourselves and let's be good friends, hmmm?"

Like a great bird spreading her gray wings, she puts her hands on Felicity's and Ann's backs, ushering them toward the door. I'm left to suffer the curse alone.

"Good night, Gemma," Ann says.

"Yes, good night," Fee echoes.

"Good night, Miss Doyle. Sleep well," Miss McCleethy adds. "Tomorrow dawns ere we know it."

"I'm sorry I shall miss the archery," I say.

Miss McCleethy turns back. "Miss it? You'll do no such thing, Miss Doyle."

"But, I thought . . . given my condition . . ."

"There'll be no time for weakness on my watch, Miss Doyle. I shall see you tomorrow on the range, or you shall lose conduct marks." It feels less like a statement than a challenge.

"Yes, Miss McCleethy," I say. I have decided: I do not like Miss McCleethy.

⌁⌁⌁⌁

I can hear happy laughter floating up from the parlor. No doubt Felicity and Ann have told Miss McCleethy their entire histories by now. They're probably all thick as thieves, sitting round the fire, sipping the froth from the eggnog, while I'll still be known as the ghastly, ill-mannered girl who called Miss McCleethy a prig.

My stomach aches anew. Blasted inconvenience. What do young men have to mark their entry into adulthood? Trousers, that's what. Fine, new trousers. I despise absolutely everyone just now.

In time, the brandy makes me warm and drowsy. The room grows narrower with each heavy blink. I slip into sleep.

I am walking through the garden. The grass is sharp and

prickly, scratches my feet. I'm near the river, but it is shrouded in mist.

"*Closer*," comes a strange voice.

I inch forward.

"*Closer still.*"

I am at the river's edge, but I can see no one, only hear that eerie voice.

"So it's true. You have come. . . ."

"Who are you?" I say. "I can't see your face."

"No," comes the voice. "But I have seen yours. . . ."

CHAPTER
NINE

THE FOLLOWING AFTERNOON AT TEN MINUTES TO three o'clock, we report to the great lawn. Six targets have been placed in a line. The brightly colored eyes in the center seem to mock me—*Go on, hit us if you think you can.* All during breakfast, I had to endure tales of the *splendid* night I missed with the *absolute dearest* Miss McCleethy, who wanted to know *simply every little thing* about the girls.

"She told me that the Pooles were descendants of King Arthur himself!" Elizabeth trills.

"Gemma, she tells the most wonderful stories," Ann says.

"Of Wales and the school there. *They* had dances practically every other week, with actual *men* present," Felicity says.

Martha speaks up. "I pray that she will prevail upon Mrs. Nightwing to let us do the same."

"Do you know what else she said?" Cecily asks.

"No. For I was not there," I answer. I'm feeling rather sorry for myself.

"Oh, Gemma, she did ask about you as well," Felicity says.

"She did?"

"Yes. She wanted to know all about you. She didn't even seem to mind that you'd called her a prig."

"Gemma, you didn't," Elizabeth says, wide-eyed.

"I wasn't the only one," I say, glaring at Felicity and Ann.

Felicity is undisturbed. "I'm sure you'll become friends in time. Oh, here she is now. Miss McCleethy! Miss McCleethy!"

"Good afternoon, ladies. I see we are ready." Miss McCleethy strides across the lawn like the Queen herself, giving us clipped instructions on the proper technique for holding the bow. The girls clamor for her attention, begging to be shown correct form. And when she gives a demonstration, her arrow finding the center of the target straightaway, everyone applauds as if she has shown the path to heaven itself.

Arrows are given out to the first group of girls.

"Miss McCleethy," Martha calls out, worried. "Are we to use real arrows, then?"

She holds the arrow's sharp metal tip away from her as if it were a loaded pistol.

"Yes, shouldn't we use rubber-tipped ones?" Elizabeth asks.

"Nonsense. You will be perfectly fine with these, so long as you don't aim at each other. Now, who is first?"

Elizabeth steps up to the line that has been chalked in the dead grass. Miss McCleethy coaxes her into position, guiding her elbow back. Elizabeth's arrow falls with a thud, but Miss McCleethy has her practice again and again, and on the fourth try, she manages to graze the bottom of the target.

"That's progress. Keep trying. Who is next?"

The girls jockey to be second. I confess that I also want Miss McCleethy to like me. I vow to do my very best, to win her over and erase last night's unfortunate encounter. As Miss McCleethy makes her way down the line, moving from girl to girl, I silently practice my approach.

This is very exciting, Miss McCleethy, for I've long wanted to be an archer. How clever you are, Miss McCleethy, to have thought of this. I do so like your suit, Miss McCleethy. It is the epitome of taste.

"Miss Doyle? Are you with us?" Miss McCleethy is standing beside me.

"Yes, thank you," I say. Nervously, I take my bow and arrow in hand and take my stand at the line. The bow is much heavier than I anticipated. It pulls me forward into a hunch.

"Your form needs work, Miss Doyle. Stand tall. Don't slouch. There. Arm back. Come now, you can pull harder than that."

I strain to draw the string back till I'm forced to let it go with a grunt. The arrow does not sail so much as it whimpers in the air before lodging itself straight in the ground.

"You must aim higher, Miss Doyle," she says. "Retrieve!"

My arrow is covered in muddy snow. Arrows puncture the ground everywhere—except for Felicity's. Hers manage to strike some portion of the target most of the time.

"Got it," I say, stating the obvious with a smile that is not returned. *Use your charm, Gemma. Ask her something.* "Where do you come from, Miss McCleethy? You're not English," I say, attempting a conversation.

"I am a citizen of the world, I suppose. Bring it up like so."

I struggle to raise my arrow into position. It will not cooperate. "I am from Bombay."

"Bombay is very hot. I could scarcely breathe while there."

"You've been to Bombay?"

"Yes, briefly, to visit friends. Here, keep your elbow close to your side."

"Perhaps we have friends in common," I say, hoping for a way into Miss McCleethy's good graces. "Do you know the Fairchilds—"

"Hush, Miss Doyle. Enough talk. Concentrate on your mark."

"Yes, Miss McCleethy," I say. I let go. The arrow skitters across the soggy grass.

"Ah, you had it, but then you hesitated. You must strike without hesitation. See the target, the objective, and nothing else."

"I do see the target," I say impatiently. "I simply can't hit it."

"Are you going to walk away wounded and prideful or are you going to practice until you can accomplish your task?"

Cecily beams to see me upbraided. I raise the bow again. "I am not *wounded*," I mutter under my breath.

Miss McCleethy puts her hands over mine. "Very good. Now, concentrate, Miss Doyle. Listen to nothing but yourself, your own breathing. See the center until you cannot see it at all. Until you and the center are joined and there is no center."

My breath comes out in cold puffs. I'm trying to think only of the target, but my mind will not be quiet. When was she in India? Whom did she visit? Did she love it as I do? And why doesn't she like me? I stare at the center of the target until it's blurry.

See the objective and nothing else.

Do not hesitate.

Until there is no center.

The arrow flies with a sharp, whipping sound. It strikes the very bottom of the canvas and lodges there, quivering.

"Better," Miss McCleethy allows.

To the right of me, Felicity aims, pulls back, and shoots a perfect bull's-eye. The girls cheer wildly. Felicity stands beaming, a warrior princess.

"Excellent, Miss Worthington. You are very strong. I am an admirer of the strong. Why do you think you are able to shoot so well?"

Because she trained under a huntress in the realms, I think.

"Because I expect to win" is Felicity's solid answer.

"Well done, Miss Worthington." Miss McCleethy marches across the green, pulling wayward arrows from the grass and the bottoms of the targets as she addresses us all. "Ladies, you cannot waver in your dedication to anything. What you want can be yours. But you must first know what it is you want."

"I don't want to be an archer," Cecily whines quietly. "My arm aches."

Miss McCleethy continues her lecture. "Let Miss Worthington be an example to us all."

"Fine, then," I mumble. I'll be like Felicity—all action and very little thought. Angry, I raise my bow and let go my arrow.

"Gemma!" Ann shouts. In my haste, I didn't notice Miss McCleethy passing before my target. Quick as a fly, she puts up a hand to stop the arrow that would surely penetrate her skull. She gasps in pain. Blood pools on her white glove. The girls drop their quivers and arrows and rush to her aid. I follow dumbly behind. She's on the ground, pulling at her glove. There's a neat hole in her palm. It isn't deep but it is bloody.

"Give her a handkerchief!" someone yells.

I offer mine. Miss McCleethy takes it, shooting me a cold, angry look.

"I—I am so sorry," I stammer. "I didn't see you."

"Do you see anything, Miss Doyle?" Miss McCleethy says, wincing.

"Should I fetch Mrs. Nightwing?" Felicity asks, putting her back to me.

Miss McCleethy fixes me with a glare. "No. Continue with your practice. Miss Doyle may help me dress the wound. As penance."

"Yes, of course," I say, helping her to her feet.

We walk in silence. When we reach the school, she has me fetch bandages from Brigid, who can't resist a lecture about how it's God's punishment on Miss McCleethy for teaching us something as "unnatural" as archery.

"She ought to be teachin' skill with the needle or those luvly li'l wa'ercolors, if you ask ol' Brigid, though no one ever does, and more's the pity. Here's your bandages. Mind you put 'em on tight."

The dressing in hand, I race back to Miss McCleethy, who has washed her hand and is using a tea towel to stop the bleeding.

"I've brought the bandages," I say, offering them. I don't know what to do.

Miss McCleethy regards me as if I'm the village idiot. "I shall need you to dress the wound, Miss Doyle."

"Yes, of course," I say. "I'm sorry. I'm afraid I've never—"

Miss McCleethy interrupts. "Place it across my palm and wrap it completely around my hand, that's it. Now cross over and repeat. Ahhh!"

I've pushed too hard on the wound. "Sorry. I'm sorry," I say. I continue, securing the bandage by tucking in the edge.

"Now, Miss Doyle, if you would be so good as to fetch me another glove to replace this one. They are in my wardrobe in the top drawer on the right," she orders. "No dawdling, Miss Doyle. We've a lesson to resume."

⌁⌁⌁⌁

Miss McCleethy's room is modest and clean. Still, it feels strange to be beyond the baize door where the teachers live. I feel as if I am trespassing on sacred ground. I open the mahogany doors of the large wardrobe and find the top right drawer. The gloves are where she said they'd be, in a neat line, orderly as soldiers. I make a selection and take one last look around the room to see if there are any clues to the mystery that is our new teacher. What is notable is how little there is. No personal touches. Nothing to suggest anything about her. Hanging in the wardrobe are tasteful suits, skirts, and blouses in gray, black, and brown, nothing that would draw attention. Her bedside table holds two books. One is the Bible. The other is poetry by Lord Byron. There are no photographs of family or friends. No paintings or sketches—odd for an artist.

It is as if Miss McCleethy has come from nowhere and belongs to no one.

I am just about to leave when I spy it: the case that Miss McCleethy insisted upon carrying herself the night she arrived. It's sleeping there, just under the bed.

I shouldn't. It would be wrong.

I close the door to her room quietly and pull the case from its hiding place. There's a latch. Most likely it is locked and so that will be the end of it. My fingers tremble at the latch, which opens, I'm surprised to discover, quite easily. There is very little inside: an advert for a bookseller's, the Golden Dawn, in London. An odd ring of gold and blue enamel with two serpents intertwined round the band. Stationery and a pen set.

A scrap of paper falls to the floor and beneath the bed. Panicked, I am down on all fours looking for it. I reach my hand under the bed skirt, pull it out. It is a list: *Miss Farrow's Academy for Girls. The MacKenzie School for Girls in Scotland. Royal College of Bath. Saint Victoria's. Spence Academy for Young Ladies.* They've all been crossed off save for Spence. I slip the paper back into the case as best I can, hoping that nothing looks amiss, and tuck the whole thing under the bed again, safe and sound.

"If that is your idea of not dawdling, Miss Doyle, I should hate to see you when you are less than quick," Miss McCleethy admonishes when I return.

I do not anticipate that Miss McCleethy and I shall ever become friends now. She pulls the new glove on quickly, wincing as it slides over her injured hand.

"I am sorry," I offer again.

"Yes, well, do try to be more careful in the future, Miss Doyle," she snaps in her strange burr.

"Yes, Miss McCleethy," I say, unable to stifle a yawn. Miss McCleethy's eyes narrow at my rudeness. "Forgive me. I've not been sleeping well."

"More exercise is what you need. Moving about in the brisk air is wonderful for the constitution and for sleep. At Saint Victoria's, I insisted my girls take walks and breathe in the sea air no matter what the weather. If it rained, we wore our macintoshes. In the snow, we wore our coats. Now, let's return to the lawn, if you please."

It is possible that Miss McCleethy hasn't a bone of humor in her body. And I have just become her least favorite pupil. Suddenly, Christmas cannot come soon enough.

CHAPTER
TEN

THE EVENING STARTS WITH A TRADITIONAL CHRIST-
mas pageant in the ballroom. It is less a formal play than it is a
dramatic reading of Christmas stories in costumes pulled from
trunks stored in one of Spence's many unused rooms. Rushing
through the halls, laughing on the stairs is an odd assortment of
high-spirited girls of all ages dressed as shepherds, angels,
fairies, fauna, and flora. One little girl has gotten into the wrong
trunk. She flits about like a ballerina, all the while wearing a
threadbare pirate's coat and ragged trousers. Ann is Christmas
Past in a long brown tunic tied at the waist with a silver sash.
Felicity looks like a medieval princess in a lovely red velvet gown
with gold braid on the sleeves and hem. She insists she's Christmas Yet to Come, but really, I think she's found the best gown of
all and decided to call it whatever she wishes. I am Christmas
Present in a green robe, a crown of holly atop my head. I feel a
bit like a lumbering tree, though Ann assures me that I look "ap-
propriately seasonal."

"It's a wonder Miss McCleethy didn't take your head today. She looked as if she could have," Ann says as we make our way to dinner past a clump of gossiping fairies and a wise man or two.

"I didn't do it intentionally," I protest, straightening my mother's amulet—my amulet—at the base of my throat. I've polished the hammered metal until it gleams. "She's strange. I don't care for her at all," I say. "Don't you think she's odd?"

Felicity glides across the rugs like the princess she is. "I think she is just what Spence needs. Refreshingly frank. I quite like her. She asked all sorts of things about me."

"Just because she paid you a compliment, you've decided she's your friend," I protest.

"*You're* jealous because she singled me out."

"That isn't true," I scoff, though I suspect it is a bit. Felicity seems to have become Miss McCleethy's favorite already with very little effort, while I shall be lucky if she says good morning to me. "Do you know that she has a list of schools in a secret case she keeps hidden beneath her bed?"

Felicity raises an eyebrow. "And how would you know about that?"

I'm going pink. "It was open."

"Nonsense! You were snooping!" Felicity taunts. She hooks her arm through mine; Ann takes the other. "What else was there? Tell!"

"Not much. A ring with snakes on it; it looked very old. An advert for a bookseller's called the Golden Dawn. The list."

Two younger girls try to push past. They've got wicked

smiles and angel dresses. Felicity yanks the soft wings of the closer girl, nearly toppling her. "We've got rank. To the back of the line with you."

Terrified, the younger girls scamper behind us.

"What else was in the case?" Ann demands.

"That is all," I say.

"That is all?" Felicity echoes in disappointment.

"You've not heard everything about the list," I say. "Every school on it had been crossed off except for Spence. What do you make of that?"

Felicity dismisses it. "Nothing. She has an accounting of the schools where she's sought employment. Nothing terribly odd about that."

"You're out of sorts because she doesn't like you," Ann says.

"Did she say she doesn't like me?" I ask.

Felicity twirls, letting the hem of her gown sweep out. "She doesn't have to. It's obvious. And you did try to impale her. That didn't help your case much."

"I tell you, it was an accident!"

The two young angels are back. They manage to squeak into the dining room ahead of us. "Why, you little demons!" Felicity growls. The girls shriek as they run, thrilled by their newfound audacity.

⁂

It is a Christmas tradition for Mrs. Nightwing to hold a last supper before the girls drift away for the holidays. Apparently, it is also a tradition for there to be a celebration in the great hall afterward, with sherry for the teachers and warm cider for the rest of us. I could become drunk on the beauty of the room alone. A fire blazes in the huge stone hearth. Our tree, a fat, jolly evergreen, sits in the center of the room, branches outstretched like a welcoming host. Mr. Grunewald, our music teacher, has been pressed to play the cello for us, which he does with surprising agility for a man of nearly eighty.

We've Christmas crackers to pull. A quick tug on the ribbons and they burst open with a sharp popping sound, startling everyone half to death. I've not quite figured out why this is considered such fun. Carols are sung. The candles on the tree are lit and admired. Gifts are presented to our teachers. There's a French recitation for Mademoiselle LeFarge. A song for Mr. Grunewald. There are poems and cookies and toffees. But for Mrs. Nightwing, we girls have emptied our pockets. The room clears as Cecily walks through the room carrying a large hatbox. As eldest girl, she has the honor of bringing the gift to our headmistress.

"Merry Christmas, Mrs. Nightwing," she says, presenting the box.

Mrs. Nightwing places her glass on a small side table. "My, what ever can this be?"

She removes the top and pushes aside the stiff paper, pulling out a marvelous felt hat festooned in shiny black plumage. It was Felicity who arranged for the gift, naturally. Heartfelt "aahs" escape from our mouths. There is a sense of wonder and merriment in the room as Mrs. Nightwing places the elaborate hat upon her head.

"How do I look?" she asks.

"Like a queen!" one girl shouts.

We applaud and raise our cups. "Merry Christmas, Mrs. Nightwing."

For a long moment, Mrs. Nightwing seems undone by sentiment. Her eyes are moist, but her voice, when it finally comes, is sure as always. "Thank you. It is a most sensible gift and I'm sure I shall enjoy it greatly," she says. With that, she removes the hat and tucks it gingerly into its paper cradle. She secures the lid and pushes the box under the table, out of sight.

Our cups refilled, Ann, Felicity, and I steal away, crouching on the floor beside the tree. The earthy smell of the branches makes my nose run, and the warm cider brings a flush to my cheeks.

"For you," Felicity says, placing a small velvet pouch in my hand.

Inside is a lovely tortoiseshell comb. "It's beautiful," I say, embarrassed by the extravagance. "Thank you."

"Oh!" Ann exclaims, opening hers. I recognize it. It is a brooch of Felicity's that Ann has admired. No doubt Felicity has a new one to take its place, but Ann is thrilled. She pins it to her costume immediately.

"Here," Ann says shyly. She passes us two gifts wrapped in newspaper. She's made us each an ornament, delicate lace angels like Pippa's.

It is my turn now. I've no skill with the needle, as Ann has, and I haven't the funds to match Felicity. But I can offer something special.

"I've something as well," I say.

"Where is it?" Ann asks. Behind her, the lamps do their dance, sending will-o'-the-wisps of light to haunt the walls.

I lean forward, whispering, "Meet me here at midnight."

They are on me at once, squealing with delight, for we are going back to the realms at last.

A loud cackle erupts. It's a laugh I've never heard. Perhaps that is because it belongs to Mrs. Nightwing. She sits among the teachers, who are all quite merry by now.

"Oh Sa—Claire, you have undone me," Mrs. Nightwing says, hand patting her chest as if to stop the laugh there.

"As I recall, it was you who started the trouble," Miss McCleethy says, smiling. "You were quite bold then, I remind you."

Girls rush in like water through a split log, their busy questions pushed along by the current of their insatiable curiosity. "What is it?" they demand. "Do tell us!"

"Did you not know your headmistress was quite the mischief maker?" Miss McCleethy says, dangling the carrot. "And a romantic, as well."

"Now, now," Mrs. Nightwing chides, sipping another glass of sherry.

"Do tell us," Elizabeth implores. The others join in a chorus of "Yes, please!"

When Mrs. Nightwing offers no protest, Miss McCleethy continues her tale. "We were at a Christmas dance. Such glorious favors they had. Do you remember, Lillian?"

Mrs. Nightwing nods, eyes closed. "Yes. Cards with thick red tassels. Lovely, lovely."

"There were many gentlemen in attendance, but of course,

we all had our hearts set on a particular man with dark hair and the most elegant figure. He was so very handsome."

Mrs. Nightwing says nothing, only has more sherry.

" 'That is the man I shall marry,' your headmistress announced to all of us, bold as you please. We laughed, but in a moment, she took my arm and paraded past—"

"I did not *parade*. . . ."

". . . and dropped her dance card very artfully at his feet, pretending not to notice. Of course, he came after her. And they danced three in a row till the chaperones intervened."

We are delighted by this.

"What happened then?" Felicity asks.

"She married him," Miss McCleethy answers. "That very Christmas."

Mr. Nightwing? I forget that Mrs. Nightwing was once married, was once a girl herself. I try to picture her young and laughing, talking with her friends. Nothing comes. I can only see her as she is now, the pouf of graying hair, the spectacles, the severe manner.

"That is terribly romantic," Cecily says, swooning.

"Yes, terribly," we all agree.

"It was quite bold of you, Lillian," Miss McCleethy says.

A cloud passes over Mrs. Nightwing's face. "It was folly."

"When did Mr. Nightwing die?" I whisper to Felicity.

"I don't know. I'll pay you a pound to ask about him," she whispers back.

"Not on your life."

"Don't you want to know?"

"Not that badly."

"A pound, you say?" It's Ann.

Felicity nods.

Ann clears her throat. "Mrs. Nightwing, has Mr. Nightwing been gone from us long?"

"Mr. Nightwing has been with the angels for twenty-five years," our headmistress says, without looking up from her glass. Mrs. Nightwing is a woman of but forty-eight, fifty perhaps. That she's been a widow for half her life seems a pity.

"He was a young man, then?" Cecily prods.

"Yes. Young, young," she says, staring into the pale red sherry. "We'd been married for six very happy years. One day . . ." She trails off.

"One day?" Ann prompts.

"One day, he left for work at the bank." She stops, takes a sip. "And I never saw him again."

"What happened?" Elizabeth gasps.

Mrs. Nightwing seems startled, as if we've asked her a question she doesn't understand, but then the answer comes slowly. "He was run down by a carriage on the street."

A terrible silence descends, the kind that accompanies the sort of unexpected bad news you can do nothing to change or improve. I think of Mrs. Nightwing as the impenetrable fortress that is our headmistress. Someone who can control anything. It's hard to think that she cannot.

"How awful for you," Martha says at last.

"Poor Mrs. Nightwing," Elizabeth chimes in.

"That is so very sad," Ann says.

"Let's not become sentimental. It was a very long time ago. Forbearance. That is the thing. One must learn to lock unpleasant thoughts away and never think on them. Else we should spend our lives crying 'Why?' into our handkerchiefs and accomplish nothing." She drains her glass. The chink in the armor has been mended. She is Nightwing again. "Now. Who has a Christmas story to share with us?"

"Oh, I do," Elizabeth trills. "It is a chilling tale about a ghost named Marley with a long chain—"

Miss McCleethy interrupts. "Do you mean *A Christmas Carol* by Mr. Dickens? I believe we are all familiar with that one, Miss Poole."

There is giggling at Elizabeth's expense. "But it is my favorite," she says, pouting.

Cecily chirps, "I've a lovely story, Mrs. Nightwing." Of course she does.

"Ah, splendid, Miss Temple."

"Once there was a girl who was as good a girl as could be found. Her character was above reproach. In all matters, she was discreet and kind and genteel and mannerly. Her name was Cecile."

I believe I know where this story leads.

"Unfortunately, Cecile was tormented by a cruel savage of a girl named Jemima." She has the nerve to look at me when she says this. "Hateful as she was, Jemima taunted the poor sweet Cecile, speaking falsehoods and turning some of her dearest friends against her."

"How terrible," Elizabeth tuts.

"Through it all, Cecile remained kind and virtuous. But the strain proved too great for her, and one day, the dear girl fell deathly ill, driven to her sickbed by Jemima's relentless cruelty."

"I do hope that Jemima gets her just deserts," Martha says with a sniff.

"I hope that Cecile meets an untimely end," Felicity whispers to me.

"What happened then?" Ann asks. It is very much her sort of story.

"Everyone came to know what a horrible girl Jemima was at heart, and they shunned her ever after. When the prince heard of Cecile's kindness, he brought his doctor to make her well and fell madly in love with her. They were married, while Jemima wandered the countryside as a sightless beggar, her eyes having been torn out by wild dogs."

Mrs. Nightwing looks confused. "I don't quite see how this is a Christmas story."

"Oh," Cecily adds quickly. "It takes place during the season of our Lord's birth. And Jemima comes to realize the error of her ways, begs for Cecile's forgiveness, and goes to work in a country parish, sweeping floors for the vicar and his wife."

"Ah," Mrs. Nightwing says.

"Must be difficult seeing to the sweeping, as she's lost her eyes," I grumble.

"Yes," Cecily says brightly. "Her suffering is great. But that's what makes it such a fine Christian story."

"Splendid," Mrs. Nightwing says, her tongue a bit thick. "Shall we have a song? It is Christmas, after all."

Mr. Grunewald sits at the piano and plays an old English tune. Some of the teachers sing along. Several girls get up to dance. Miss McCleethy doesn't. She's staring right at me.

No, she's looking at the amulet. When she catches me watching her, she gives me a broad smile, as if we've never had a quarrel and are old friends.

"Miss Doyle," she calls, beckoning me with her hand, but Ann and Felicity are upon me.

"Come on, let's dance," they insist, pulling me to my feet and far away.

The evening passes like a happy dream. The excitement proves too much for many of the younger girls. Nestled against each other, they sleep by the fire, angel wings crushed under the limp, plump arms of their dear friends, sugarplum and holly crowns askew in the tangle of their hair. In a far corner sit Mrs. Nightwing and Miss McCleethy, heads bent in conference. Miss McCleethy speaks in an intent whisper, and Mrs. Nightwing shakes her head.

"No," our headmistress says, her voice made louder by the sherry. "I cannot."

Miss McCleethy places her hands gently over Nightwing's, murmuring things I can't hear.

"But think of the cost," Mrs. Nightwing answers. Her eyes catch mine for a moment, and I look quickly away. In a moment, she rises unsteadily to her feet, placing a hand on the back of her chair till she finds her footing.

Long after the lamps have been dimmed, the fires have fizzled out, and all are safely in bed, Ann and I meet Felicity down in the great hall. The last glowing embers in the enormous stone hearth cast an eerie glow over the cavernous room. The Christmas tree seems an ominous giant. In the center stand the marble columns decorated with fairies, centaurs, and nymphs. The sight gives me a shudder, for we know they are more than carvings. They are living things imprisoned there by the magic of the realms, the place we are ready to see and feel and touch once more—if we can.

"Don't forget that you owe me a pound," Ann tells Felicity. Her teeth are chattering.

"I shan't," Felicity answers.

"I'm afraid," Ann says.

"So am I," I say.

Even Felicity has lost her usual bluster. "Whatever happens, we do not leave without each other." She doesn't say the rest: *like you left Pip . . . left her to die.*

"Agreed," I say. I take a deep breath, trying to steady my nerves. "Give me your hands."

We join hands and close our eyes. It has been so long since we've entered the realms. I'm afraid I shan't be able to make the door of light appear. But soon, I feel the familiar tingle on my skin, the warmth of the light. I open one eye, then the other. There it is, shimmering before us: the glorious portal into the other world.

Felicity and Ann wear their awe on their faces.

"I don't know what we'll find there," I say before we start.

"There is only one way to find out," Felicity answers.

I open the door and we step through into the realms.

The trees rain flowers that tickle our noses. The grass is still the green of eternal summer. To our right lies the gurgling river. I can hear the faint song that floats up from its depths and forms silver rings on the surface. And the sky! Like the most gorgeous sunset on the happiest of days. My heart feels as if it shall burst. Oh, I have missed this place! How could I ever have thought of leaving it?

"Oh!" Felicity cries. Laughing, she twirls round and round, her palms out and open to the orange sky. "It's so beautiful!"

Ann steps to the river. She stoops and gazes at her reflection, smiling. "I'm so beautiful here." And indeed she is. She is Ann as Ann would look with no cares, no fear or meekness, no need to fill her emptiness with cakes and scones.

Felicity runs her fingers over a willow tree that shifts, like water rippling, and becomes a fountain. "That's extraordinary. We can do anything here. Anything!"

"Watch!" Ann calls. She cups a blade of grass in her palms, closes her eyes. When she opens her hands, a ruby pendant lies glittering there. "Help me put it on!"

Felicity locks the clasp. The thing shines against Ann's skin like a rajah's treasure.

"Mother?" I call, wondering if she will walk out to greet me. There is nothing but the river's song and my friends' delighted laughter as they turn flowers to butterflies, rocks to jewels. I suppose I knew she was gone for good, but I could not help hoping.

Beyond the trees lies the silver arch leading into the heart of the garden. It was there that I fought with Circe's assassin, one of the dark spirits from the Winterlands. It was there that I smashed the Runes of the Oracle, freeing my mother but also setting loose the magic. Yes, the magic is loose. That is why we've come. And yet, everything seems as it was. Nothing seems amiss.

"Follow me," I say. We pass beneath the shiny arch and find ourselves in a familiar circle. Where the crystal runes once rose tall and powerful there are now only charred patches of earth and an odd assortment of tiny toadstools.

"Gracious," Ann says. "Did you really do that, Gemma?"

"Yes."

"But how?" Felicity asks. "How were you able to break something that stood for centuries?"

"I don't know," I say.

"Ugh," Ann says. She's stepped on one of the toadstools. It splits open, black and wet.

"Mind your step," Felicity warns.

"Where do we look for this temple?" Ann asks.

I sigh. "I've no idea. Kartik said there's no map. I only know that it is somewhere inside the realms."

"We don't know how large this place is," Ann says. "Or how many realms there could be."

"You've nothing to go on?" Felicity asks.

"No. We know it can't be here in the garden or else we'd have seen it already. I suppose we should pick a direction and . . . What is it?"

Felicity's face has gone white. Ann's too. Whatever it is, it's behind me. Every muscle taut, I turn slowly to face my doom.

She steps out from behind a grove of olive trees, a garland of flowers wound into her dark hair. The same violet eyes. The same pale skin and dazzling beauty.

"Hello," Pippa says. "I was hoping you'd come back."

CHAPTER
ELEVEN

FELICITY RUNS TO HER.

"Wait!" I yell, but there's no holding her back. She runs to Pippa and embraces her tightly. Pippa kisses Felicity's cheeks.

"It's you!" Felicity says. She's laughing and crying at the same time. "Pip, Pip, darling Pip, you're here!"

"Yes! I'm here. Ann! Gemma! Oh, please don't stand staring so."

"Pippa!" Ann cries, running to her. I can scarcely believe it. Pip, our Pip, is here, as lovely as ever. Something in me gives way. I fall to the grass, sobbing, my tears bringing up small lotus blossoms where they fall.

"Oh, Gemma, darling, don't cry," Pippa says. Swift as a deer, she's by my side. The cold hands I've seen in my dreams are brushing through my hair, and they are as warm as summer rain. "Don't cry."

I look up at her. She gives me a smile. "If you could see your face, Gemma. Really, so serious!"

This makes me laugh. And cry a bit more. Soon, we're all laughing through tears, our arms around each other. It feels like coming home after a long, dusty journey.

"Let me look at you," Pippa says. "Oh, I have missed you so. You must tell me everything. How is Mrs. Nightwing? Are Cecily and Martha still the most unbearable snobs?"

"Positively hideous," Ann says, giggling.

"Gemma spilled jam on Cecily's dress just the other morning to keep her quiet," Felicity says.

Pippa's mouth opens. "You didn't!"

"I'm afraid I did," I admit, feeling foolish for my bad behavior.

"Gemma!" she cries, smiling brightly. "You are my hero!"

We fall back in the grass laughing. There is so much to say. We tell her everything—about Spence, the girls, her funeral.

"Did everyone cry awfully much?" Pippa asks.

Ann nods. "Terribly."

She blows at a dandelion. The fluff spreads out on the wind, where it becomes a swarm of fireflies. "I am glad to hear it. I'd hate to think of people sitting stony-eyed round my casket. Were the flowers lovely? There were flowers, weren't there?"

"The loveliest, most elaborate cascade of flowers," Felicity says. "They must have cost a fortune."

Pippa nods, smiling. "I am so glad to have had such a nice funeral. Oh, do tell me more stories of home! Do they talk about me in the great hall? Do they all miss me awfully?"

"Oh, yes," Ann says in earnest. "We all do."

"Now you do not have to miss me at all," Pip says, squeezing her hand.

I don't want to ask, but I must. "Pippa, I thought that you were . . ." *Dead*. I cannot bring myself to say it. "I thought that you'd crossed over the river. To the other world beyond the realms. When I left, you and your knight . . ."

Ann sits up. "Where is your knight?"

"Oh, him. I had to let him go." Pippa yawns. "He always did whatever I asked. Frightfully dull."

"He was certainly handsome." Ann swoons.

"Yes, he was rather, wasn't he?" Pippa giggles.

"I am sorry," I say, afraid to disrupt our happiness. "But I don't understand. Why didn't you cross over?"

Pippa shrugs. "My lord, the knight, told me that I didn't have to cross after all. There are many tribes here, creatures who've lived in the realms forever. They are part of this world." She leans back on straight arms, bends her knees, and lets them sway gently against each other.

"So you just came back?" I prompt.

"Yes. And then I stopped to pick wildflowers to make a crown. Do you like it?"

"Oh, yes," Ann says.

"I shall make you one, then."

"And for me," Felicity adds.

"Of course," Pip says. "We shall all have one."

I'm terribly confused. My mother told me that souls had to cross over or become corrupted. But here is our Pippa, happy and shining, eyes the color of fresh violets, the girl we've always known.

"How long have I been here?" Pippa asks.

"Two months," I say.

"Really? Sometimes it seems like yesterday; other times, it's as if I've been here forever. Two months . . . that would make it nearly Christmas. I do think I shall miss Christmas morning."

None of us knows what to say to this.

Ann sits up. "Perhaps she hasn't completed her soul's task. Perhaps that is why she is still here."

"Perhaps she is supposed to help us find the Temple!" Felicity exclaims.

"What temple?" Pippa asks.

"When I shattered the runes, I released the Order's power into the realms," I explain. "The Temple is the source of that magic. Whoever finds the Temple and binds the magic there controls it."

Pippa's eyes widen. "How marvelous!"

Ann chimes in. "But everyone's looking for it, including Circe's spies."

Pippa links her arm through mine. "Then we must find it first. I shall do everything I can to help you. We can ask the creatures for help."

I shake my head. "Kartik said we shouldn't trust anything from the realms, not with the magic loose." *Trust no one. Trust nothing.* But surely that doesn't mean Pippa.

"Kartik?" Pippa says, as if trying to remember something from long ago. "The Indian boy? The Rakshana?"

"Yes."

She lowers her voice. "You ought to be careful with him. The Rakshana have their spies here too. They cannot be trusted."

"What do you mean?"

"I've been told that the Rakshana and the Order are not friends at all. The Rakshana only pretend to be their protectors. What they're really after is the Order's power—control of the magic and the realms."

"Who told you such a thing?"

Pippa shrugs. "It is well known here. Ask anyone."

"I've never heard that," I say. "Surely my mother would have warned me if that were true."

"Perhaps she never got the chance," Pippa says. "Or perhaps she didn't know everything. We know from the diary that she was only a novice when the fire happened." I start to object, but Pippa stops me. "Poor Gemma. Are you cross that I know more about it than you do now?"

"No, of course not," I say, though it is true. "I simply think we should be careful."

"Hush, Gemma. I want to hear all the secrets of the realms," Felicity chides, turning her back on me. Pippa breaks into a gloat of a grin, and I think of what she told me in the ballroom at Spence months ago when I replaced her as Felicity's favorite: *Be careful. It's a long way to fall.*

Pippa pulls us into one giant embrace and kisses our cheeks with fervor. Her smile is so genuine. "Oh, I have missed you!" A tear trickles over the roses of her cheeks.

I am a horrid friend. I have dearly missed Pip too. Here she is, and I'm spoiling the moment with my moodiness. "I am sorry, Pip. Please, do tell us what you know."

"If you insist!" Her smile is dazzling, and we're all laughing as if we've never been apart. The trees rain leaves that float gently down, covering our skirts in the most radiant colors.

"The realms are vast. They seem to have no end. I hear there are wonders such as you cannot imagine. A forest of light-filled trees that glow eternally. Golden mists and winged creatures like fairies. And a ship with the head of a gorgon."

"A gorgon!" Ann says, horrified.

"Oh, yes! I've seen her at night, gliding past in the mist. Such an enormous ship and such a fearsome face," Pippa says.

"How fearsome?" Ann asks, chewing her lip.

"You could die of fright to look in her eyes," Pippa says. Ann looks terrified. Pippa kisses her cheek. "Don't worry, Ann, darling. I shall be your protector."

"I don't wish to meet this gorgon."

"They say she was cursed by the Order and bound by their power never to rest and always to tell truth," Pippa says.

"Cursed? Why?" Felicity asks.

"I don't know. It is one of the legends."

"If she must tell truth, then perhaps she can tell us where to find the Temple," I say.

"I shall find her for you," Pippa says quickly.

"Must we?" Ann says.

"Here, Ann, watch this." Pippa takes up a handful of grass, presses it between her palms. When she opens them, a tiny black kitten sits blinking at us.

"Oh!" Ann nuzzles the kitten to her cheek.

"There's such fun we shall have now that we are all together again!"

A thorn of concern pricks at my insides. My mother insisted that spirits had to cross over. But what if she was wrong?

I saw her die; I saw her buried. I saw her in my dreams.

"I've been having the most atrocious dreams about you," I say, testing.

Pippa strokes the kitten, turning her orange, then red. "Really? What were they?"

"It was only the last dream I can recall. You came to me and said, 'Careful, Gemma. They're all coming for you.'"

Pippa frowns. "Who's coming for you?"

"I don't know. I thought perhaps you were sending me a message."

"Me?" She shakes her head. "I haven't done anything of the sort. Now come with me," she cries like the Pied Piper of merriment. "I want to make a Christmas tree."

We stay for what feels like hours. It could be hours, for all we know. No one wants to be the first to say goodbye, and so we keep inventing reasons to stay—more magic tinsel for the tree, another game of hide-and-seek, more searching for the gorgon, who never appears. At last, it is time. We must go.

"Can you come back tomorrow?" Pippa pleads with a pout.

"I'm leaving for London," Felicity says sadly. "And you two had best not come without me!"

"I leave the day after," I say.

Ann is quiet.

"Ann?" Pippa asks.

"I shall stay at Spence and spend Christmas with the servants, as always."

"How long till you're together again?" Pippa asks.

"A fortnight," I answer. I hadn't thought about this. How shall we look for the Temple if we are separated for so long?

"That won't do at all," Pip says. "What shall I do for two whole weeks? I shall be so bored without you." Same old Pip.

"Felicity and I will see each other," I say. "But Ann . . ."

Ann looks as if she could cry.

"You shall simply have to come home with me," Felicity says. "I'll send a telegram to Mama first thing tomorrow morning and tell her to expect us. And I shall spend the evening thinking of a very good story as to why."

Ann's beaming. "I should like that. The holiday and the story."

"Soon as we can—two days' time—we'll be back," I assure Pippa.

"I shall be waiting."

"See what you can discover on your own," I say. "Find the gorgon."

Pippa nods. "Must you go so soon? I don't think I can bear to say goodbye."

"Two days' time," Felicity assures her.

She walks with us through the place where the runes once stood.

"Watch out," Felicity calls.

Where the toadstool split open, the grass has turned to ash. A wet black snake slithers back and forth.

"Ugh," Ann says, sidestepping it.

Pippa grabs a sharp rock and drops it on the thing.

"That is that," she says, rubbing the bit of rock chalk from her hands.

"How I loathe snakes," Felicity says with a shiver.

It's surprising that Felicity is unnerved by anything. But more surprising is this: Pippa is staring at the rock she dropped with a strange smile. I cannot name the expression she wears, but it unnerves me.

With one last kiss, we make the door of light appear and are back in the great hall.

"Look!" Ann cries.

Around her neck, the ruby still shines and dazzles.

"You've brought the magic back with you," I say, touching the stone.

"I didn't try to," Ann says, as if she's in trouble for it. "It just happened."

"There's no seal on it," I say. "I suppose that's it."

"Let me try," Felicity says. She closes her eyes, and in an instant she's floating high above us.

"Felicity! Come down!" I whisper urgently.

"Not on your life! Why don't you come up?"

With a squeal, Ann rises to meet Felicity. They clasp hands midair and twirl far above the floor like ghosts.

"Wait for me!" I say, rising to meet them. My arms outstretched, my legs dangling high above the tops of chairs and the fireplace mantel, I am filled with a giddy joy, the pleasure of weightlessness.

"How splendid," Ann says, giggling. She reaches down and repositions the angel ornament at the top of the tree so that it stands tall and straight. "There."

"What are you about?" I ask Felicity, who has her eyes closed. She rubs her right palm over her left. When she pulls her hands apart, there is a dazzling diamond ring. She slips it on her third finger and holds it out for us to see.

"This is the most marvelous Christmas present ever," Felicity says, staring at her ring. "Think of the fun we shall have in London with the magic at our disposal."

"I don't think that's wise," I say. "We're to bind the magic. That is our purpose."

Felicity purses her lips. "I shan't do anything horrible with it."

This is not an argument I wish to start now. "Let's fly again," I say, changing the subject.

At long last, even Felicity is tired. We sneak off to our rooms, speaking with joy the name of the girl we've mourned for two months: Pippa. Perhaps tonight, I will sleep peacefully. No terrible dreams to leave me exhausted by morning.

It is only after an hour has passed and I am safe in my own bed that I can give a name to the look on Pippa's face as she stared at the thing she'd killed.

Hunger.

CHAPTER
TWELVE

THE CARRIAGE HAS COME TO TAKE FELICITY AND
Ann to the train station. In the grand marbled foyer, we say
our goodbyes while the servants direct the coachmen to their
trunks. Felicity looks cool and imperious in her mauve coat
and fur muff. Ann is giddy and hopeful in some of Felicity's
borrowed finery, a royal blue velvet capelet far too light for the
weather that is secured by the brooch of grapes.

"Have you any magic left?" Felicity asks.

"No," I say. "It's gone. You?"

"The same." Narrowing her eyes, she warns, "Don't you dare
go back without us."

"For the hundredth time, I shan't." The coachman takes the
last of their things. "You'd best get on. Don't want to miss your
train." It is difficult to talk with all the hustle and bustle. And I
hate goodbyes.

Ann beams. "Fee loaned me her cape."

"Lovely," I say, trying to ignore the use of Felicity's nickname.

Felicity has never let me borrow anything, and I can't help feeling a prick of jealousy that the two of them will have the holiday together.

Felicity fiddles with Ann's clothing, smoothing out wrinkles. "I shall have Mama take us to her club tomorrow for lunch. It is one of the best women's clubs, you know. We must tell Gemma of our master plan. She'll have to play her part in it."

I am already sorry for whatever is to come.

"I am taking it upon myself to reinvent Ann for the holidays. No more of this sad mouse of a girl, this scholarship student. She'll fit in as if she's to the manner born. No one will be the wiser."

Ann pipes up on cue. "I am to tell her mother that I am descended from Russian royalty, and that only recently did my great-uncle, the Duke of Chesterfield, find me here at Spence and inform me of my late parents' bequest."

Taking in the sight of pudgy, very English-looking Ann, I ask, "Do you think that wise?"

"I got the idea from the ruby last night. I thought, what if we were to spin our very own illusion?" Felicity says. "What if we play a little game?"

"What if we are found out?" Ann frets.

"We won't be," Felicity says. "I shall tell the ladies at the club that before the death of your parents, you received musical training from a world-famous Russian opera singer. They will be thrilled to hear you sing. Knowing how they are, they'll all fight to have you sing at their dances and dinners. You'll be the prize exhibit, and the whole time, they'll have no idea you're poor as a church mouse."

There is something feral in Felicity's grin.

"I shall probably disappoint them," Ann mumbles.

"You must stop that this instant," Felicity chides. "I'm not doing all this work on your behalf so that you can go and undo it."

"Yes, Felicity," Ann says.

Umbrellas opened against the rain, we step outside, where we can have a moment alone. None of us wants to say what we're really feeling, that it shall be torture to wait to enter the realms. Having tasted the magic, I cannot wait to try it again.

"Dazzle them," I say to Ann. We embrace lightly, and then the driver is calling over the cascade of rain.

"Two days," Felicity says.

I nod. "Two days."

They skitter off for the carriage, kicking up mud as they do.

Mademoiselle LeFarge is seated in the great hall when I enter. She's got on her very best wool suit and is reading *Pride and Prejudice*.

"You look lovely," I say. "Er, *très jolie!*"

"*Merci beaucoup*," she says, smiling. "The inspector is calling for me shortly."

"I see you are reading Miss Austen," I say, grateful that she has not upbraided me for my terrible French.

"Oh, yes. I do enjoy her books. They're so romantic. It's very clever of her to end always on a happy note—with a betrothal or wedding."

A maid knocks. "Mr. Kent to see you, miss."

"Ah, thank you." Mademoiselle LeFarge puts away her book. "Well, Miss Doyle, I shall see you in the new year, then. Have a happy Christmas."

"Happy Christmas to you, Mademoiselle LeFarge."

"Oh, and do work on your French over the holiday, Mademoiselle Doyle. It is a season of miracles. Perhaps we shall both be granted one."

∿∿∿

Within hours, Spence is nearly deserted. Only a handful of us remain. All day long, girls have been leaving. From my window, I've watched them step out into the cold wind for the carriage ride to the train station. I've watched their goodbyes, their promises to see each other at this ball or that opera. It's a wonder they carry on so with tears and "I'll miss you's" since it seems as if they will scarcely be apart.

I've the run of the place, and so I spend some time exploring, climbing steep stairs into thin turrets whose windows give me a bird's-eye view of the land surrounding Spence. I flit past locked doors and dark, paneled rooms that seem more like museum exhibits than living, breathing places. I wander until it is dark and past the time when I should be in bed, not that I think anyone shall be searching for me.

When I reach my own floor, I am stopped cold. One of the enormous doors to the burned remains of the East Wing has been left ajar. A key juts from the lock. In the time I've been here, I've never seen these doors unlocked, and I wonder why they should be opened now, when the school is empty.

Nearly empty.

I creep closer, trying not to make a sound. There are voices coming from inside. It takes me a moment, but I recognize them: Mrs. Nightwing and Miss McCleethy. I cannot hear them clearly. The wind pushes through like a bellows, sending puffs of words out to me: "Must begin." "London." "They'll help us." "I've secured it."

I am too afraid to peer in, so I put my ear to the crack, just as Mrs. Nightwing says, "I shall take care of it. It is my charge, after all."

With that, Miss McCleethy steps through the door, catching me.

"Eavesdropping, Miss Doyle?" she asks, her eyes flashing.

"What is it? What's the matter?" Mrs. Nightwing demands. "Miss Doyle! What on earth!"

"I—I am sorry, Mrs. Nightwing. I heard voices."

"What did you hear?" Mrs. Nightwing asks.

"Nothing," I say.

"You expect us to believe you?" Miss McCleethy presses.

"It's true," I lie. "The school is so empty and I was having trouble sleeping."

Miss McCleethy and Mrs. Nightwing exchange glances.

"Get on to bed, then, Miss Doyle," Mrs. Nightwing says. "In the future, you should make your presence known at once."

"Yes, Mrs. Nightwing," I say, nearly running to my room at the end of the hall.

What were they speaking of? Must begin what?

With effort, I remove my boots, dress, corset, and stockings, till I am down to my chemise. There are exactly fourteen pins in my hair. I count them as my trembling fingers remove each one. My coppery curls roll down my back in a sigh of relief.

It's no good. I'm far too jittery to think of sleep. I am in need of a distraction, something to ease my mind. Beneath her bed, Ann keeps a stack of magazines, the sort that offer advice and show the latest fashions. On the cover is an illustration of a beautiful woman. Her hair is adorned with feathers. Her skin is creamy perfection and her gaze manages to be both kind and pensive, as if she's staring off into the sunset while also thinking of bandaging the skinned knees of crying children. I do not know how to accomplish such a look. I find myself with a new fear: that I shall never, ever be this lovely.

I sit at the dressing table, staring at myself in the mirror, turning my face this way and that. My profile is decent. I've a straight nose and a good jaw. Turning to the mirror again, I take in the freckles and pale brows. Hopeless. It isn't as if there's something horrific about me; it's just that there's nothing that stands out. No mystery. I am not the sort one would picture on the cover of penny magazines, gazing adoringly into the distance. I am not the sort who is pined for by admirers, the girl immortalized in song. And I cannot say that it doesn't sting to know this.

When I attend dinners and balls—if I attend any, that is— what will others see in me? Will they even notice? Or will sighing brothers and dear old uncles and distant cousins of other cousins be forced to dance with me out of some sense of politeness because their wives, mothers, and hostesses have forced them into it?

Could I ever be a goddess? I brush my hair and arrange it across my shoulders as I've seen in daring posters for operas in which consumptive women die for love while looking achingly beautiful. If I squint and part my lips just so, I could be mistaken for alluring, perhaps. My reflection wants something. Gingerly, I push down the shoulder straps of my chemise, baring flesh. I shake my hair slightly so that it goes a bit wild, as if I were a wood nymph, something untamed.

"Excuse me," I say to my reflection, "I don't believe we've met. I am . . ." Pale. That's what I am. I pinch roses in my cheeks and start over, adopting a low snarl of a voice. "Who is it that roams my woods so freely? Speak your name. Speak!"

Behind me, there is the clearing of a throat, followed by a whisper. "It is I, Kartik."

A tiny yelp escapes from my throat. I jump up from my dressing table and immediately trip on the edge of it, falling on the rug and bringing the chair down with me. Kartik steps from behind my dressing screen, his palms up in front of his chest.

"Please. Don't scream."

"How dare you!" I gasp, running for my cupboard and the robe that hangs there. Oh, God, where is it?

Kartik stares at the floor. "I . . . It wasn't my intention, I assure you. I was there, but I dozed off, and then . . . Are you . . . presentable?"

I've found the robe but my fingers cannot possibly work in such a state. The robe is buttoned all wrong. It hangs at an odd angle. I cross my arms to minimize the damage. "Perhaps you do not know, but it is unforgivable to hide in a lady's room. And not to announce yourself whilst she is dressing..." I fume. "Unforgivable."

"I am sorry," he says, looking sheepish.

"Unforgivable," I repeat.

"Should I go and come back?"

"As you are already here, you may as well stay." Truthfully, I am glad to have company after my unfortunate encounter earlier. "What is it that is so urgent it requires you to scale a wall and hide behind my dressing screen?"

"Did you enter the realms?" he asks.

I nod. "Yes. But nothing seemed amiss. It was as beautiful as before." I stop, thinking of Pippa. Beautiful Pippa, whom Kartik once gazed upon with such awe. I think of her warning about the Rakshana.

"What is it?"

"Nothing. We have asked someone there to help us. A guide, of sorts."

Kartik shakes his head. "That is not wise! I told you, nothing and no one that comes from within the realms can be trusted just now."

"This is someone we can trust."

"How do you know?"

"It's Pippa," I say quietly.

Kartik's eyes widen. "Miss Cross? But I thought..."

"Yes, so did I. But I saw her last night. She doesn't know about the Temple, but she's going to help us find it."

Kartik stares at me. "But if she doesn't cross over, she'll become corrupted."

"She says that isn't the case."

"You cannot trust her. She could already be corrupted."

"There's nothing strange about her at all," I protest. "She's just as . . ." She's just as beautiful as before, I was about to say.

"She's just as what?"

"She is the same Pippa," I answer quietly. "And she knows more about the realms than we do at this point. She can help us. It's more than you've given me to go on."

If I've injured Kartik's pride, he doesn't let on. He paces, passing so near that I can smell him, a mixture of smoke, cinnamon, the wind, the forbidden. I clutch my robe tightly about me.

"All right," he says, rubbing his chin. "Proceed carefully. But I don't like this. The Rakshana expressly warned—"

"The Rakshana have not been there, so how can they possibly know what is to be trusted?" Pippa's warning seems suddenly very good to me. "I know nothing about your brotherhood. Why should I trust them? Why should I trust you? Honestly, you sneak into my room and hide behind my dressing screen. You follow me about. You're constantly barking orders at me: Close your mind! No, dreadfully sorry—open your mind! Help us find the Temple! Bind the magic!"

"I've told you what I know," he says.

"You don't know very much, do you?" I snap.

"I know my brother was Rakshana. I know that he died trying to protect your mother, and that she died trying to protect you."

There it is. The ugly sorrow that joins us. I feel as if the breath has been knocked from me.

"Don't," I warn.

"Don't what?"

"Don't change the subject. I think I shall give the orders for a while. You want me to find the Temple. I want something from you."

"Are you blackmailing me?" he asks.

"You can call it what you like. But I won't tell you anything further until you answer my questions."

I sit on Ann's bed. He sits on mine, opposite me. Here we are, a couple of dogs ready to bite if provoked.

"Ask," he says.

"I'll ask when I'm ready," I say.

"Very well, don't ask." He stands to leave.

"Tell me about the Rakshana!" I blurt out.

Kartik sighs and looks up to the ceiling. "The Brotherhood of the Rakshana has existed for as long as the Order. They rose in the East but were joined by others along the way. Charlemagne was Rakshana, as were many of the Knights Templar. They were the guardians of the realms and its borders, sworn to protect the Order. Their emblem is the sword and the skull." He says this in a rush, like a history lesson recited for the benefit of a teacher.

"That was serviceable," I say, irritated.

He holds up a finger. "But informative."

I ignore his jibe.

"How did you come to be part of the Rakshana?"

He shrugs. "I have always been with them."

"Not always, surely. You must have had a mother and a father."

"Yes. But I never really knew them. I left them when I was six."

"Oh," I say, shocked. I'd never thought of Kartik as a little boy leaving his mother's arms. "I am sorry."

He won't meet my eyes. "There is nothing to be sorry for. It was understood that I would be trained for the Rakshana, like my brother, Amar, before me. It was a great honor for my family. I was taken into the fold and schooled in mathematics, languages, weapons, fighting. And cricket." He smiles. "I'm quite good at cricket."

"What else?"

"I was taught how to survive in the woods. How to track things. Thievery."

I raise my eyebrows at this.

"Whatever it takes to survive. One never knows when picking a man's pocket will buy a day's food or create a distraction at just the right moment."

I think of my own mother, gone for good now, and how deeply I feel her loss. "Didn't you miss your family terribly?"

His voice, when it comes, is very quiet. "In the beginning, I looked for my mother on every street, in every market, always hoping I would see her. But I had Amar, at least."

"How terrible. You had no say in it."

"It was my fate. I accept it. The Rakshana have been very good to me. I have been trained for an elite brotherhood. What would I have done in India? Herded cows? Gone hungry? Lived in the shadow of the English, forced to smile while serving their food or grooming their horses?"

"I didn't mean to upset you. . . ."

"You didn't upset me," he says. "I don't think you understand how great an honor it is to be chosen for the brotherhood. Soon, I will be ready to advance to the last level of my training."

"What happens then?"

"I don't know," he says, with a sweet smile. "You must swear an oath of allegiance for life. Then you are shown the eternal mysteries. No one ever speaks of it. But first, you must complete a challenge set before you, to prove your worthiness."

"What is your challenge?"

His smile fades. "To find the Temple."

"Your fate is joined to mine."

"Yes," he says softly. "So it would seem."

He's looking at me in such an odd way that I am once again aware of how compromised I am in my robe. "You should go now."

"Yes. I should," he says, leaping up. "May I ask you a question?"

"Yes," I answer.

"Do you often talk to your mirror? Is that something young ladies do?"

"No. Of course not." I blush a shade of crimson deeper than has ever been noted on any girl's cheeks. "I was rehearsing. For a play. I—I am to perform in a chorus."

"That will certainly be a most interesting exhibition," Kartik says, shaking his head.

"I have a rather long day of traveling tomorrow and must bid you good night," I say rather formally. I'm eager for Kartik to leave so that I may suffer my embarrassment in private. He swings his strong legs over the window's edge and reaches for the rope nestled in the thick ivy running up the school's walls. "Oh, how will I contact you should I find the Temple?"

"The Rakshana have secured employment for me in London over the holiday. Somewhere close. I'll be in touch."

And with that, he is through the window and scurrying down the rope. I watch him join the night, wishing he could come back. I've barely secured the latch when there's a knock on my door. It is Miss McCleethy.

"I thought I heard voices," she says, surveying the room.

"I—I was reading aloud," I say, grabbing Ann's magazine from the bed.

"I see," she says in her strange accent. She offers me a glass. "You said you were having trouble sleeping, so I've brought you some warm milk."

"Thank you," I say, taking it. I loathe warm milk.

"I feel that you and I got off on rather the wrong foot."

"I am sorry for what happened with the arrow, Miss McCleethy. Truly, I am. And I wasn't eavesdropping on you earlier. I—"

"Now, now. It is all forgotten. You share this room with Miss Bradshaw?"

"Yes," I say.

"She and Miss Worthington are your dearest friends?"

"Yes." They are my only friends, actually.

"They are certainly fine young ladies, but not half so interesting as you, I daresay, Miss Doyle."

I am dumbfounded. "M-me? I'm not so very interesting."

"Come now," she says, moving closer. "Why, Mrs. Nightwing and I were speaking of you just this very evening, and we agreed that there is something very special about you."

I am standing before her in a misbuttoned robe. "You are too kind, I'm sure. Actually, Miss Bradshaw has an astonishing voice, and Miss Worthington is frightfully clever."

"See how loyal you are, Miss Doyle? Quick to come to the defense of your friends. It is a commendable trait."

She means to compliment me, but I feel uncomfortable, as if I am being studied.

"What a most unusual necklace." Bold as you please, she traces the curve of the crescent moon with her finger. "Where did you get this?"

"It was my mother's," I say.

She gives me a penetrating look. "It must have been hard for her to part with something so precious."

"She is dead. It is my inheritance."

"Does it have some meaning?" she asks.

"No," I lie. "None that I am aware of."

Miss McCleethy stares at me till I have to look away. "What was she like, your mother?"

I force a yawn. "Forgive me, but I believe I am tired after all."

Miss McCleethy seems disappointed. "You should drink

the milk while it's still warm. It will help you sleep. Rest is so very important."

"Yes, thank you," I say, holding the glass.

"Go on. Drink it."

There's no way around it. I force down a few mouthfuls of the chalky liquid. It tastes strangely sweet.

"Peppermint," Miss McCleethy announces, as if reading my mind. "It aids sleep. I'll take the glass back to Brigid. I don't think she much likes me, do you?"

"I am sure you are mistaken," I say, because it is the polite response.

"She looks at me as if I am the devil himself. Do you think I am the devil, Miss Doyle?"

"No," I croak. "Of course not."

"I am glad we have decided to be friends. Sleep well, Miss Doyle. No more reading aloud tonight."

〜〜〜〜〜

My body feels warm and heavy. Is it the warm milk? The peppermint? Or has Miss McCleethy poisoned me? *Don't be ridiculous, Gemma.*

I open both windows, letting in the freezing air. Must stay awake. I move about the room in large paces. I bend at the waist and touch my toes. At last, I sit on the bed, singing Christmas carols to myself. It's to no avail. My song trails off, and I slide into twilight dreaming.

The crescent moon glows in my hand. My hand becomes a lotus blossom on a trail. Thick green vines push through cracks, their tiny buds blooming into magnificent roses. I see my face staring back at me, reflected in a wall of water. I push my hand through the wall until I'm falling through it entirely.

I fall deeper and am swallowed by the black cloak of dreamless sleep.

I do not know what time it is when I am startled awake by something. I listen for it, but there is nothing. The milk has left a thin coating on my tongue. It seems to grow in my mouth. Much as I wish I didn't, I have to go downstairs for a drink.

With a heavy sigh, I push back the blanket and light a candle, cupping the flame with my hand as I travel the darkened hall, which seems a mile long. I'm the only soul who remains on this floor. The thought lends quickness to my steps.

When I'm near the stairs, the flame sputters and dies. No! I shall have to go back to light it. A sudden dizziness overtakes me. My knees buckle, and I manage to grip the top of the banister to steady myself. In the darkness, there's a faint, sharp scratching sound, like chalk pulled too hard across a slate.

I am no longer alone. There's someone here with me.

I barely manage a whisper. "Hello? Brigid? Is that you?"

The scraping sound moves closer. In my hand, the candle flares to life, filling the hall with a tight sphere of light. There they are, shimmering about the edges. Not quite real, yet more solid than the vision I saw in the snow. Three girls, all in white. The pointed toes of their boots scrape against the wooden floor with the most awful sound as they float closer and closer. They move their mouths to speak. I cannot hear them. Their eyes are sad, and there are great dark circles beneath them.

Don't scream, Gemma. It's only a vision. It can't hurt you. Can it?

They are so close I have to turn my head and close my eyes. I am near to vomiting with fright and the smell. What is it? The sea and something else. Decay.

There is that sound again, like the scratching of thousands of insect wings. They're speaking so softly it takes me a moment to make out the message, but when I do, it chills me to the bone.

"Help us."

I don't want to open my eyes, but I do. They are so close, these flickering bright things. One reaches out a hand. *Please. Please don't touch me. I'm going to scream. I'm going to scream. I'm going to . . .*

Her hand's like ice on my shoulder, but there is no time to scream because my body goes rigid as I'm pulled under. Images flood my mind. Three girls hop along craggy cliffs. The sea splashes up and over, leaving thin strands of foam across their feet. The clouds are darkening. A storm. A storm is coming. Wait, there's a fourth girl. She lags behind. Someone calls to them. A woman comes. She wears a green cloak.

The girls' syrupy voices slip into my ear. "Look . . ."

The woman takes the hand of the fourth girl. And then comes the terror from the sea. The sky darkening. The girls screaming.

We're back in the incandescent hall. The girls fade, pulling back into the darkness. "She lies . . . ," the girls whisper. "Don't trust her. . . ." And then they are gone. The pain disappears. I'm on my knees on the cold, hard floor, alone. The candle hisses suddenly, spitting out a wayward spark.

That's all it takes. I'm up and scurrying, pell-mell, like a frightened mouse, and I don't stop running until I'm back in my room with the door shut tight—though what I think I'm shutting out, I cannot say. I put on all the lamps in the room. When the room is bright, I feel a bit better. What sort of vision was that? Why have they become so much stronger? Is it because the magic is loose? Does that somehow make it bolder? I felt her hand on my shoulder. . . .

Stop it, Gemma. Stop frightening yourself.

Who are these girls and what do they want with me? What did they mean, "Don't trust her"? It doesn't help that the school is so empty, or that tomorrow I shall be in London with my family, and who knows what real horrors await me there.

I've no answers to any of it. And I'm afraid of sleep. By the time the first light presses its nose against my windowpanes, I am already dressed, my trunk is packed, and I am ready to see London if I have to drive the horses there myself.

CHAPTER
THIRTEEN

Tom is late, as usual.

I've arrived at Victoria Station on the twelve o'clock train from Spence as expected, but my brother is nowhere to be found. Perhaps he's been in a horrible accident and lies dying on the street, begging with his last breath that one of the crying bystanders rush to the train station to rescue his most innocent and virtuous sister. It is the only charitable explanation I can muster. Most probably, he is at his club, sharing laughs and cards with his friends, and has forgotten all about me.

"My dear, are you sure your brother is coming for you?" It is Beatrice, one of the seventy-year-old spinster sisters who sat beside me on the train, talking incessantly of rheumatism and the joys of cabbage roses till I thought I should go mad. Unlike my brother, they are concerned for my welfare.

"Oh, yes. Quite sure, thank you. Please don't worry on my account."

"Oh, dear, Millicent, I don't believe we can leave her here alone, do you?"

"No, quite right, Beatrice. She must come with us. We shall send word to her family."

That decides it. I am going to murder Tom.

"There he is!" I say, looking off into the distance, where my brother is not.

"Where?" the sisters ask.

"I see him just over there. I must have been looking in the wrong direction. It was lovely to meet you. I hope we shall meet again," I say, offering my hand and sending them on their way. I march off purposefully and hide behind the ticket booth. When all is clear, I take a seat on a bench far down the platform.

Where could he be?

Another train whooshes into the station and unloads its passengers. They are embraced by smiling relations. Packages are handed over; flowers are given. Tom is a half hour late. Father shall hear about this.

A man in a fine black suit comes to sit next to me. What must he think of me sitting here by myself? An angry scar mars the left side of his face, stretching from above his ear to the corner of his mouth. His suit is expertly tailored. I spy his lapel pin and my mouth goes dry, for I know what it is. It is the sword and skull of the Rakshana. Is it coincidence that he has sat beside me? Or has he come with a purpose? He gives me a slight smile. Quietly, I rise and walk away. When I've gone halfway down the platform, I turn back. He's left the bench as well. His newspaper tucked beneath his arm, he follows me. Where is Tom? I stop at a flower seller, pretending to inspect the blooms and buds there. The man comes as well. He selects a red carnation for his buttonhole, tips his hat in thanks, and drops a coin in the vendor's hand without so much as a word.

Fear makes my legs weak as a newborn kitten's.

What if he tries to take me? What if something has gone wrong with Kartik? What if Pippa is right and these men cannot be trusted at all?

I can feel the man in the black suit closing in. If I were to scream, who would hear me above the hiss and snarl of the trains? Who might help me?

I spy a young man standing alone, waiting.

"There you are!" I say, striding quickly toward him. He looks about to see whom I'm addressing. "You're late, you know."

"I'm . . . late? I'm terribly sorry, but have we . . ."

I lean in, whispering urgently. "Please help me. That man is following me."

He looks confused. "What man?"

"*That* man." I look behind me, but he is gone. There is no one. "There was a man in a black suit. He had a hideous scar on his left cheek. He sat beside me on the bench, and then he followed me to the flower seller." I'm aware that I sound slightly mad.

"Perhaps he wanted a flower for his lapel," the young man says.

"But he followed me over here."

"We are near the way out." He points to the doors that lead to the street.

"Oh. So we are," I say. I am such a fool. "I'm terribly sorry. I am jumping at shadows, it seems. My brother was to meet my train. He is late, I'm afraid."

"Then I shall stay and keep you company until he arrives."

"Oh, no, I couldn't possibly . . ."

"You could be of help to me, actually," he says.

"What sort of help could I give?" I ask warily.

From his coat pocket, he pulls out a beautiful velvet box the size of a cracker tin. "I need a lady's opinion about a gift. Will you help me?"

"Of course," I say, relieved.

He places the box on his open palm and lifts the top. There is nothing inside.

"But it is empty," I say.

"So it seems. Watch." He pulls at what appeared to be the floor of the box. It comes up to reveal a secret compartment, and inside this hidden space sits a beautiful cameo.

"It's lovely," I say. "And the box is very clever."

"So you approve?"

"I'm sure she'll be pleased," I say. I blush instantly.

"It's for my mother," the young man explains. "I've come to meet her train."

"Oh," I say.

We stand uncertainly. I don't know what to say or do. Should I continue to stand here like an idiot or should I salvage what's left of my pride, bid him good day, and find a place where I can hide until my brother comes for me?

I open my mouth to say goodbye just as he extends a hand.

"I am Simon Middleton. Oh, I'm terribly sorry. What were you about to say?"

"Oh, I, I was only . . . How do you do?"

We shake hands.

"Very well, thank you. How do you do, Miss . . . ?"

"Oh, dear. Yes, I am—"

"*Gemma!*" My name rings out. Tom has arrived at last. He rushes over, hat in hand, that annoying lock of hair flopping into his eyes. "I thought you said Paddington Station."

"No, Thomas," I say, forcing a smile for politeness' sake. "I distinctly said Victoria."

"You're mistaken. You said Paddington!"

"Mr. Middleton, may I present my brother, Mr. Thomas Doyle. Mr. Middleton has been kind enough to wait with me, Thomas," I say pointedly.

Tom's face pales. If he's feeling ashamed, then I am glad for it.

Simon smiles broadly. It makes his eyes dance. "Good to see you, Doyle, old boy."

"Master Middleton," Thomas says, offering his hand. "How fare the Viscount and Lady Denby?"

"My mother and father are well, thank you."

Simon Middleton is a viscount's son? How could someone as kind and charming and titled as Mr. Middleton be on familiar terms with my disagreeable brother?

"You are acquainted with each other?" I ask.

"We were together at Eton," Simon says. That would make Simon—the Honorable Simon Middleton—my brother's age, nineteen. Now that I'm past my shock, I see that Simon is also handsome, with brown hair and blue eyes. "I'd no idea you'd such a charming sister."

"Nor did I," Tom says. I take his arm, but only so that I can pinch the inside of it without being seen by Simon. When Tom gasps, I feel better and stop pinching. "I do hope she hasn't pestered you too much."

"Not at all. She was under the impression that someone was following her. A man in a dark suit with a, what was it? A hideous scar upon his left cheek."

I feel very foolish about that now.

A flush rises up Tom's pale neck. "Ah, yes. The famous Doyle imagination. She's likely to become a writer of mystery novels, our Gemma."

"I am sorry to have bothered you," I say.

"Not at all. It was the most exciting part of my day," he says with such a winning smile that I believe him. "And you were most helpful with this," he adds, holding up the velvet box. "Our carriage is just outside. If you care to wait, I could offer you a ride."

"We've our own carriage waiting," Tom says smugly.

"Of course."

"It was a most generous offer," I say. "Good day to you."

Simon Middleton does the most extraordinary, daring thing. He takes my hand and gives it a courtly kiss. "I do hope we shall meet again over the holiday. You must come to dinner. I shall see to it. Master Doyle, carry on." He gives Tom a grand tip of the hat, and Tom returns it as if they are two old friends playacting together.

Simon Middleton. I cannot wait to tell Ann and Felicity.

Outside the station, the streets are alive with noise, horses, omnibuses, and people who've come into London for a day's shopping or entertainment. It is a mad, merry scene, and I'm happy to be part of the beating heart of the city. The moment the foggy air and clanging bells of the churches greet me, I feel sophisticated and mysterious. I could be anyone here—duchess or witch or conniving fortune hunter. Who is to say? After all, I've already had a most wonderful encounter with a viscount's son. I'm feeling very optimistic. Yes, this will be a pleasant visit with dances and gifts and perhaps even a dinner at the home of a handsome viscount's son. Father loves Christmas. The Christmas spirit will make him merry, and he will not need the laudanum so much. Together, Ann, Felicity, and I shall find the Temple and bind the magic and it will all turn out right in the end.

A man bumps me on his busy way without so much as an apology. But that is all right. I forgive you, busy man about town with the sharp elbows. Hail and farewell to you! For I, Gemma Doyle, am to have a splendid Christmas in London town. All shall be well. God rest us merry gentlemen. And gentlewomen.

Tom's trying desperately to secure a hansom cab among the throng.

"But where is the carriage?" I ask.

"There is no carriage."

"But you said—"

"Yes, well, I wasn't about to let on to Middleton and suffer that humiliation. We've a carriage at home, to be sure. But we've no driver. Old Potts left rather suddenly two days ago. I wanted to put in an advert but Father says he's found someone. Oh, I say . . ."

With a bit of finagling, we find a cab and set off for the London home I've never seen.

"I cannot believe you ran into Simon Middleton of all people," Tom says as the cab pulls away from the station. "And now we are to have dinner with his family."

It hardly seems worth noting that the Honorable Simon Middleton invited *me* to dinner, not Tom. "Is he really a viscount's son, then?"

"Indeed. His father is a member of the House of Lords and a highly influential patron of the sciences. With his help, I could go far indeed. Pity they've no daughters to marry."

"Pity? I was just thinking it was a mercy."

"So, my own sister will not promote me? Speaking of which, weren't you supposed to find me a beautiful future wife with a small fortune? Have you had any success on that front?"

"Yes—I have warned them all."

"And a merry Christmas to you, too!" Tom says, laughing. "I understand we'll be attending your friend Miss Worthington's Christmas ball. Perhaps I'll find a suitable—which is to say wealthy—wife among the ladies attending."

And perhaps they will all run screaming for the convent.

"How is Father?" I ask at last. That question, burning a hole inside me.

Tom sighs. "We're making progress. I've locked away the laudanum bottle and given him one that I've diluted with water. He's getting less. I'm afraid it's made him quite disagreeable at times, plagued by horrible headaches. But I'm certain it's working." He looks at me. "You're not to give him more, do you understand? He's clever, and he'll press you for it."

"He wouldn't do that," I argue. "Not to me. I know it."

"Yes, well . . ."

Tom doesn't finish his thought. We ride in silence, the noise of the streets our only chatter. Soon my worries fade as the excitement of the city takes over. Oxford Street is a fascinating place. All these grand buildings side by side. They stand so tall and proud, and at the bottom story, their awnings stretch out over the sidewalks like ladies coyly lifting their skirt hems to reveal temptation. Here is a stationer's shop, a furrier, a photographer's studio, and a theater, where several patrons have congregated at the box office to see about the day's program.

"Blast!"

"What?" I ask.

"I was to pick up a cake for Grandmama, and we've just passed the shop." Tom calls to the driver, who stops by the curb. "I won't be a minute," Tom says, though I suspect he says this less to reassure me and more to convince the driver not to charge him an egregious amount for this unscheduled stop.

For my part, I am happy to sit and watch the world in all its glory. A young boy weaves his way through the passersby, a large goose resting precariously on his shoulder. Amidst a chorus of French horns and oboes, a happy throng of carolers makes its way to each establishment, hoping for a handful of nuts or a bit of drink. They walk on, their song drifting behind them. In the window of the shop where Tom has gone, there are all sorts of delicious confections on display: plump currants and candied lemons; mountains of pears, apples, and oranges; colorful piles of spices. It makes my mouth water. A tall woman in a smart hat and tweed suit approaches. She seems familiar, but it is not until she passes that I recognize her.

"Miss Moore!" I shout from the window, forgetting my manners entirely.

Miss Moore stops, no doubt wondering who could be calling to her on the street in such a rude fashion. When she sees me, she comes over to the carriage. "Why, Miss Doyle! You're looking well. Merry Christmas to you."

"Merry Christmas."

"Are you in London long?" she asks.

"Until after the new year," I say.

"What a happy coincidence! You must come to call."

"I should like that very much," I say. She looks quite radiant.

She hands me her card. "I have taken lodgings in Baker Street. I am at home all day tomorrow. Do say you'll come."

"Oh, yes, of course! That would be grand. Oh . . ." I stop.

"What is it?"

"I'm afraid I have a previous engagement tomorrow, with Miss Worthington and Miss Bradshaw."

"I see." She doesn't need to say anything else. We both know that we girls were responsible for her dismissal.

"We're all terribly sorry for what happened, Miss Moore."

"What's done is done. We can only move forward."

"Yes. You are right, of course."

"Though, given the chance, I should enjoy torturing Miss Worthington," Miss Moore says with a gleam in her eye. "She has more cheek than should be reasonably tolerated."

"She is quite saucy," I say, smiling. Oh, I have missed Miss Moore!

"And Miss Cross? Will you not be seeing my accuser over the holidays?" Miss Moore's smile falters when she sees my shocked expression. "Oh, dear. I've upset you. I am sorry. Despite my feelings toward Miss Cross, I know you are friends. That was rude of me."

"No, it isn't that. It's . . . Pippa's dead."

Miss Moore covers her mouth with her hand. "Dead? When?"

"Two months now."

"Oh, Miss Doyle, forgive me," Miss Moore says, placing her hands on mine. "I had no idea. I've been away these two months. I only just returned last week."

"It was her epilepsy," I lie. "You remember her difficulty." Something in me wants to tell Miss Moore the truth about that night, but not yet.

"Yes, I remember," Miss Moore says. "I am sorry. Here it is the season of forgiveness and I've shown nothing but a hard heart. Please do invite Miss Bradshaw and Miss Worthington. They are welcome."

"That is very generous of you, Miss Moore. I'm sure we should all like to hear of your travels," I say.

"Then I shall tell you. Shall we say tomorrow at three o'clock? I shall prepare a very strong tea and Turkish delight."

Blast. There is the difficulty of getting my grandmother to allow me to pay a call without her. "I should like that very much, if my grandmother will agree to it."

"I understand," she says, stepping away from the carriage. A beggar boy with one leg limps to her side.

"Please, miss? A ha'penny for the crippled?" he says, lip trembling.

"Nonsense," she says. "You've tucked your leg up inside your trousers there, haven't you? Don't lie to me."

"No'm," he says, but now I can see the outline of the other leg clearly.

"Run along with you before I call the constable."

Quick as a flash, the leg comes down and he's off running on two able feet. I laugh at this. "Oh, Miss Moore, I am happy to see you."

"And I you, Miss Doyle. I am home most afternoons from three until five o'clock. You have an open invitation to call any-time."

She heads off blending back into the throng of Oxford Street. Miss Moore was the one who first told us about the Order, and I wonder what more she could tell us—if we dare ask her. She'd probably send us packing if we did, and right-fully so. Still, there must be something on which she can shed a bit of light, if we are very careful in our inquiries. And if not, at the very least it is a way out of my grandmother's house. Miss Moore just may be my best hope for sanity this holiday.

Tom's back from the shop. He drops the box, wrapped artfully in brown paper and string, into my lap. "One hideous fruitcake. Who was that woman?"

"Oh," I say, "no one. A teacher." As the carriage jostles to life, I add, "A friend."

CHAPTER FOURTEEN

GRANDMAMA HAS LET AN ELEGANT HOUSE IN FASHionable Belgrave Square bordering Hyde Park. She usually stays at Sheep's Meadow, her country home, coming into London only for the season, May through mid-August, and for Christmas. That is to say, she comes only when she wants to see and be seen by London society.

It is very strange to walk into the unfamiliar front hall and see the coat rack and the side table with its accompanying mirror, the burgundy paper on the walls, the tasseled velvet drapes, as if I should find comfort in these strange things, as if this were a place I should know and love when I've never set foot in it. Though it is filled with cushioned chairs, a piano, a Christmas tree festooned with popcorn and ribbon, and though every room is warmed by a blazing fire, this does not feel like home. For me that place is India. I think of our housekeeper, Sarita, and see her lined face and gap-toothed smile. I see our house with the open porch and a bowl of dates sitting on a table draped in red silk. Mostly, I think of Mother's presence and Father's booming laugh, back when he did laugh.

As Grandmama is still out paying a call, the housekeeper, Mrs. Jones, is there to greet me. She asks if I've had a pleasant journey, and I answer yes, as is expected. We've nothing more to say to each other, so she leads me up two flights of stairs to my bedroom. It is a back room that looks out onto the carriage houses and stables of the mews, the small lane behind us where the coachmen and their families live. It is a dingy little place, and I wonder what it must be like mucking about in the hay with the horses, always staring up at the lights of these grand, towering white ladies where we have everything we could ask for.

When I have changed clothes for dinner, I make my way downstairs again. At the second-floor landing, I stop. Father and Tom are having an argument behind the closed doors of the library, and I move closer to listen.

"But, Father," Tom says. "Do you think it wise to hire a foreigner to be your driver? There are plenty of good Englishmen for the job, I daresay."

I peek through the sliver of light at the door. Father and Tom stand opposite each other, a couple of coiled springs.

Some part of the old Father flares to life. "We had many loyal Indian servants in Bombay, may I remind you, Thomas."

"Yes, Father, but that was India. We're here now, amongst our peers, who all use English drivers."

"Are you questioning my decision, Thomas?"

"No, sir."

"Good man."

There is a moment of uncomfortable silence, and then Tom says carefully, "But you must admit that the Indians have habits that have led to trouble for you before, Father."

"That is enough, Thomas Henry!" Father barks. "There shall be no more discussion of it."

Tom barrels through the door, nearly knocking me over.

"Oh, dear," I say. When he doesn't respond, I add, "You might apologize."

"You might not want to listen at keyholes," he snaps back. I follow him to the stairs.

"You might not want to tell Father how to run his affairs," I whisper tersely.

"That's all well and fine for you to say," he growls. "You're not the one who's spent the better part of a fortnight weaning him off the bottle only to see that he could easily be led astray again by some carriage driver."

Tom takes the stairs at an angry clip. I struggle to keep up.

"You don't know that. Why must you aggravate him so?"

Tom whirls around. "I aggravate *him*? I do nothing but try to please him, but I can do no right in his eyes."

"That isn't true," I say.

He looks as if I've hit him. "How would you know, Gemma? It's you he adores."

"Tom . . . ," I start.

A tall butler appears. "Dinner is served, Mr. Thomas, Miss Gemma."

"Yes, thank you, Davis," Thomas says tightly. With that, he turns smartly on his heel and walks away.

⌇⌇⌇⌇⌇

Dinner is a dismal affair. Everyone is trying so very hard to be bright and smiling, as if we are posing for an advert. We're all trying to erase the fact that we do not live here, together, and that this is our first Christmas without Mother. No one wants to be the one who brings truth to the table and spoils the evening, and so there is a lot of forced polite talk of holiday plans and doings at school and gossip about the town.

"How are things at Spence, Gemma?" Father asks.

Well, you see, my friend Pippa is dead, which is my fault, really, and I'm trying desperately to locate the Temple, the source of the magic in the realms, before Circe—the evil woman who killed Mother, who was also a member of the Order, but you wouldn't know about that—finds it and does diabolical things, and then I'm to bind the magic somehow, though I haven't the vaguest idea how. And that is how things are.

"Very good, thank you."

"Ah, splendid. Splendid."

"Did Thomas tell you he's become a clinical assistant at Bethlem Royal Hospital?" Grandmama says, taking a generous portion of peas on her fork.

"No, I don't believe he did."

Tom gives me a smirk. "I've become a clinical assistant at Bethlem Royal Hospital," he parrots smartly.

"Really, Thomas," Grandmama chides without enthusiasm.

"Do you mean Bedlam, the lunatic asylum?" I ask.

Tom's knife scrapes his plate. "We do not call it that."

"Do eat your peas, Gemma," Grandmama says. "We've been invited to a ball hosted by Lady George Worthington, the admiral's wife. It is the most coveted invitation of the Christmas season. What sort of girl is Miss Worthington?"

Ah, an excellent question. Let's see. . . . She kisses Gypsies in the woods and once locked me in the chapel after asking me to steal the communion wine. By the light of a pale moon, I saw her kill a deer and climb from a ravine naked and splattered with blood. She is also, strangely, one of my best friends. Do not ask me to explain why.

"Spirited," I say.

"I thought tomorrow we would call upon my friend Mrs. Rogers. She is to have a program of music in the afternoon."

I take a deep breath. "I've been invited to pay a call tomorrow."

Grandmama's fork stops midway to her mouth. "To whom? Why was no card left here for me? Absolutely not. Out of the question."

This is going well. Perhaps next I could hang myself with the table linens.

"It is Miss Moore, an art teacher at Spence." There is no need to mention her dismissal from that same institution. "She is tremendously popular and beloved, and of all her students, she has invited only Miss Bradshaw, Miss Worthington, and me to visit her at home. It is quite an honor."

"Miss Bradshaw . . . Didn't we meet her at Spence? She's the scholarship student, is she not?" Grandmama says, scowling. "The orphan?"

"Did I not tell you?" My newly discovered penchant for lying is fast becoming a skill.

"Tell me what?"

"It was discovered that Miss Bradshaw has a great-uncle, a duke, who lives in Kent, and she is actually descended from Russian royalty. A distant cousin to the czarina."

"You don't say!" Tom exclaims. "That is lucky indeed."

"Yes," Grandmama says. "It's rather like those stories they print in the halfpenny papers."

Exactly. And please dig no further or you're likely to see the startling similarities.

"Perhaps I shall have to take another look at Miss Bradshaw now that she is in possession of a fortune," Tom jokes, though I suspect he may be in earnest.

"She is wise to fortune hunters," I warn Tom.

"Do you suppose she'd find me so disagreeable?" Tom sniffs.

"As she has both ears and eyes, yes," I snap back.

"Ha! You've been called down, my good man," Father says, laughing.

"John, don't encourage her. Gemma, it is not becoming to be so unkind," Grandmama chides. "I do not know this Miss Moore. I don't know that I can allow this visit."

"She gives excellent instruction in drawing and painting," I offer.

"And charges handsomely for it, no doubt. That sort always does," Grandmama says, taking a bite of potatoes. "Your drawing will not suffer during these few weeks. Your time is better spent at home or accompanying me on calls so that you may become better acquainted with people who matter."

I could kick her for that comment. Miss Moore is worth ten of her "people who matter." I clear my throat. "Of course, we will be making ornaments to brighten the hospitals this time of year. Miss Moore stresses that one cannot perform enough charitable acts."

"That is quite admirable," Grandmama says, cutting her pork loin into tiny pieces. "Perhaps I shall go with you and see this Miss Moore for myself."

"No!" I practically shout. "What I mean is . . ." What do I mean? "Miss Moore would be terribly embarrassed to have her good works so publicly known. She advises discretion in all matters. As the Bible says . . ." I pause. Having never read much of the Bible, I haven't the vaguest idea what it says. "Let thine ornaments be only for God's ears—fingers. God's fingers."

Hurriedly, I take a sip of tea. Grandmama seems perplexed. "The Bible says that? Where?"

Too much hot tea fills my mouth. I choke it down. "Psalms," I rasp out, coughing.

Father gives me a curious look. He knows I'm lying.

"Psalms, you say? Which psalm?" Grandmama asks.

Father's wry smile seems to say, *Aha, now you're caught in a trap, my girl.*

The tea burns its way to my stomach in instant penance. "The Christmas psalm."

Grandmama resumes her noisy chewing. "I think it best if we visit Mrs. Rogers."

"Mother," Father says, "our Gemma is a young lady with interests of her own."

"Interests of her own? Nonsense! She's not yet out of the schoolroom," Grandmama harrumphs.

"A bit of freedom will do her good," Father says.

"Freedom can lead to misfortune," my grandmother says. She hasn't said my mother's name out loud, but she's stabbed Father with the threat of it.

"Did I mention that Gemma had the most extraordinary luck of meeting Simon Middleton at the train station today?" The moment it's out of his mouth, Tom realizes he's made a mistake.

"And how did that happen?" Father demands.

Tom blanches. "Well, I couldn't secure a hansom, and you see, there was the most horrendous congestion of wagons at—"

"My boy," Father blasts, "do you mean to tell me that my daughter was alone at Victoria?"

"Only for a moment," Tom says.

Father's fist comes down on the table, rattling our plates and making Grandmama's hands flutter. "You've disappointed me today." And with that, he leaves the room.

"I'm always a disappointment," Tom says.

"I do hope you know what you're doing, Thomas," Grandmama whispers. "His mood blackens by the day."

"At least I am willing to do something," Tom says bitterly.

Mrs. Jones appears. "Is everything all right, madam?"

"Yes, quite," Grandmama says. "Mr. Doyle shall have his cake later," she says, as if nothing in the world is the matter.

After our thoroughly unpleasant dinner, Father and I sit at the gaming table to play chess. His hands tremble, but he's still surprisingly good. In only six moves, he's got me solidly in checkmate.

"That was terribly clever of you. How did you do that?" I ask.

He taps the side of his head with one finger. "You have to understand your opponent, how she thinks."

"How do I think?"

"You see what seems to be the obvious move, assume it's the only move, and rush in without thinking it through, without looking to see if there is another way. And that leaves you vulnerable."

"But that *was* the only move," I protest.

Father holds up a finger to shush me. He places the pieces as they were on the board two moves prior. "Now, look."

I see the same predicament. "Your queen is open."

"Hasty, hasty . . . Think a few moves ahead."

I see only the queen. "I'm sorry, Father. I don't see it."

He shows me the progression, the bishop lying in wait, luring me into a tight spot from which there's no retreat. "It's all in the thinking," he says. "That's what your mother would say."

Mother. He's said it aloud, the word that could not be said.

"You look very much like her." He buries his face in his hands and cries. "I miss her so much."

I don't know what to say. I've never seen my father cry. "I miss her too."

He takes out a handkerchief and blows his nose. "I'm so sorry, my pet." His face brightens. "I've an early Christmas gift for you. Do you suppose I'll spoil you by giving it early?"

"Yes, horribly!" I say, trying to lighten the mood. "Where is it?"

Father goes to the curio cabinet and rattles the doors. "Ah. Locked. I believe the keys are in Grandmama's room. Could you go for them, darling?"

I race to Grandmama's room, find the keys on her nightstand, and return with them. Father's hands shake so he can barely open the curio.

"Is it jewelry?" I ask.

"That would be telling, I believe." With effort, he opens the glass doors and moves things aside, looking for something. "Now where did I leave it? . . . Wait a minute."

He opens the unlocked drawer below and retrieves a package wrapped in red paper with a sprig of holly nestled into the ribbon. "It was in the drawer the entire time."

I take it to the sofa and tear away the paper. It's a copy of Elizabeth Barrett Browning's *Sonnets from the Portuguese*.

"Oh," I say, hoping I don't sound as disappointed as I feel. "A book."

"It was your mother's. They were her favorites. She used to read them to me in the evenings." He breaks off, unable to continue.

"Father?"

He pulls me to him, holding me close. "I'm glad you're home, Gemma."

I feel I should say something, but I don't know what. "Thank you for the book, Father."

He lets go. "Yes. Enjoy. And would you take the keys back, please?"

Mrs. Jones enters. "Excuse me, sir. This just arrived for Miss Gemma by messenger."

"Yes, yes," Father says a bit irritably.

Mrs. Jones hands the package and note to me. "Thank you," I say. The note is a formal invitation to dinner addressed to my grandmother. *Viscount and Lady Denby request the pleasure of the company of Mr. John Doyle, Mrs. William Doyle, Mr. Thomas Doyle, and Miss Gemma Doyle to dinner on Tuesday, the 17th, at 8 o'clock. The favor of a reply is requested.* I've no doubt Grandmama will give an enthusiastic yes.

Now to the package. Ripping open the paper, I find Simon Middleton's beautiful velvet box with a note that reads *A place to keep all your secrets.*

Curiously, Father doesn't even ask me about the gift.

"Gemma, pet," he says, sounding distracted. "Take the keys back now. There's my good girl, hmmm?"

"Yes, Father," I say, kissing his forehead. I step merrily up to Grandmama's room and replace the keys, then run to my own room, where I lie upon the bed, gazing at my beautiful gift. I stare at the note again and again, examining his handwriting, admiring the strong, fine way he makes his letters. Simon Middleton. Yesterday, I did not even know he existed. Now, he is all I can think of. Strange how life can turn like that.

I must have drifted off, for I'm awakened by a loud knock at my door. The clock shows half-past twelve. Tom bursts into my room. He's very cross.

"Did you give him this?"

"Wha—what?" I ask, wiping sleep from my eyes.

"Did you give Father this?" He's clutching a brown bottle in his hand. Laudanum.

"No, of course not!" I say, coming to my senses.

"How, pray, did he get it, then?"

He's no right to barge into my room and badger me so. "I don't know, but I didn't give it to him," I answer in a hard tone.

"I'd locked it in the curio cabinet. Only Grandmama and I had the keys."

I sink onto the bed, sick and numb. "Oh, no. He asked me to open it so that he could give me an early Christmas gift."

"I told you he's clever, didn't I?"

"Yes, so you did," I say. I simply didn't believe it. "I'm sorry, Tom."

My brother rakes his fingers through his hair. "He was doing so well."

"I'm sorry," I say again, though it seems little comfort. "Shall I throw it in the rubbish?"

"No," he says. "We can't throw it out completely. Not just yet." He hands me the bottle. "Take this and hide it—somewhere he can't find it."

"Yes, of course." The bottle feels hot in my hand. Such a small thing. So powerful.

Once Tom is gone, I open Simon's gift and pull up the false bottom.

A place to keep all your secrets . . .

I put the bottle inside and place the clever floor back into the grooves and it's as if the laudanum doesn't exist at all.

CHAPTER FIFTEEN

Grandmama will not relent and allow me to visit Miss Moore, but she does agree to let me shop for Christmas gifts along with Felicity and Ann, provided that Felicity's maid accompany us as chaperone. When Felicity's carriage pulls round to our house, I am so overjoyed to see my friends—and so desperate to escape my overbearing grandmother—that I nearly run to greet them.

Ann is very smartly dressed in some of Felicity's clothes, a new green felt hat on her head. She is beginning to look the part of the debutante. In fact, she's beginning to look like Felicity's double. "Oh, Gemma, it's so wonderful! No one knows that I'm not one of them! I've not washed a single dish or been laughed at. It's as if I truly am a czarina's descendant."

"That's won—"

Ann prattles on. "We're to attend the opera. And I shall be on the receiving line at their Christmas ball as if I were one of the family!" Ann grins at Felicity, who slips her arm through Ann's. "And later today—"

"Ann," Felicity warns quietly.

Ann gives an embarrassed smile. "Oh, sorry, Fee."

"What is it?" I ask, annoyed at their coziness.

"Nothing," Ann mumbles. "I shouldn't say."

"It's impolite to keep secrets," I answer hotly.

"Today we are to accompany Mother to her club for tea. That's all," Felicity says. There is no invitation for me. Suddenly, I'm no longer happy to see them. I wish they were far away. "Oh, Gemma, don't look so dour. I'd invite you too, but it's so very hard to bring more than one guest."

I don't think this is the case at all. "It's no trouble," I say. "I've a previous engagement myself."

"Really?" Ann asks.

"Yes, I'm to see Miss Moore," I lie. Their mouths hang open as I tell them of my encounter. I'm enjoying their astonishment very much. "I thought I would ask her about the Order. So you see I couldn't possibly . . ."

"You can't go without us," Felicity protests.

"But you're going to your mother's club without me," I say. Felicity has nothing to say to this. "Are we to go to Regent Street to the shops, then?"

"No," Felicity answers. "We're going with you to see Miss Moore."

Ann pouts. "I thought we were to find me a new pair of gloves. It is only nine days until Christmas, after all. Besides, Miss Moore must surely hate us for what happened."

"She doesn't hate you," I say. "She has forgiven us all. And she was distressed to hear about Pip."

"That settles it," Felicity says, slipping her other arm through mine. "We shall pay a call on Miss Moore. And afterward, Gemma shall come with us for tea."

Ann balks. "But what about Franny? You know she tattles over the slightest infractions."

"Franny shall be no bother at all," Felicity says.

The sun is high, the day bright and crisp when we arrive at Miss Moore's modest lodging house on Baker Street. Franny, Mrs. Worthington's lady's maid, is all ears and eyes, ready to take note of any indiscretion on our parts so that she may dutifully report to Felicity's mother and Grandmama. Franny isn't much older than we are. It can't be much fun to trail us, reminded daily of another sort of life, one denied her. If she's bitter about her lot, she wouldn't dare speak it aloud. But it is there, nonetheless, present in the tight line of her mouth, in the way she forces herself to look through us while seeing everything.

"I was to accompany you to the shops, miss," she says.

"There's been a change of plans, Franny," Felicity says coolly. "Mother asked me to look in on a friend who has taken ill. It is important to perform acts of charity, don't you think?"

"She didn't mention it to me, miss."

"You know how things slip Mother's mind. She is so very busy."

The coachman helps us from the carriage. Franny makes to follow. Felicity stops her with a cold smile. "You may wait in the carriage, Franny."

Franny's carefully trained, placid face flares to unrehearsed life for a brief moment—all narrowed eyes and half-open mouth—before settling into a hateful resignation.

"Mrs. Worthington asked me to accompany you everywhere, miss."

"And so you have. But the appointment is for three, not three and a servant."

I hate Felicity when she is like this. "It's rather cold out," I say, hoping she will take the hint.

"I'm sure Franny remembers her place." Felicity gives a smile that might pass for genteel if I didn't feel the cruelty behind it.

"Yes, miss." Franny dips her head under the carriage's top and tucks her body into the far corner of the seat to wait the hour.

"Now we can have a pleasant afternoon free of my mother's spy," Felicity says. So it isn't about being cruel to Franny; it is Felicity getting revenge on her mother for some reason that escapes me.

Ann stands uncertainly, her eyes on the carriage.

"Are you coming?" Felicity asks.

Ann marches back to the carriage, removes her coat, and hands it to the grateful Franny. Without a word, she sails past me and the astonished Felicity and rings the bell to announce our visit.

"There's gratitude for you," Felicity grumbles to me as we catch up. "I bring her home and turn her into Russian royalty and now she's living the part."

The door opens. A scowling, squinting old woman stands before us, hand on her ample hip. "Oi! Oo's there? Whatcha wont, then? 'Aven't got all day to stand 'ere lookin' at the likes of you. Got me 'ouse to run."

"How do you do?" I begin, but I am cut off by the impatient woman. She squints hard in my direction. I wonder if she can see at all.

"If yer collectin' fer the poor, you can clear off."

Felicity extends her hand. "I am Felicity Worthington. We are paying a call on Miss Moore. We are her pupils."

"Pupils, you say? Di'n't tell me nuffin' 'bout takin' in pupils," she harrumphs.

"Did I not mention it, Mrs. Porter? I was certain I did yesterday." It's our Miss Moore coming down the stairs to the rescue.

"Very odd, Miss Moore. If it's to be regular like, I'll be raisin' me fee for the rooms. Nice rooms, they is. Plen'y o' people lookin' to let them."

"Yes, of course," Miss Moore says.

Mrs. Porter turns to us, chest puffed up. "I likes to be informed as to wha' goes on in me 'ouse. A woman alone can't be too careful these days. I run a respec'able 'ouse. You ask anybody and they'll tell you, Missus Por'er's a respec'able toiype."

I fear we shall stand out here all day in the cold. But Miss Moore gives us a wink as she steers us in. "Quite right, Mrs. Porter. I shall keep you apprised in the future. How very nice to see you all again. What a lovely surprise."

"How do you do, Miss Moore?" Felicity gives our former teacher a quick handshake, as does Ann. They both have the decency to look shamed by how shabbily they once treated her. For her part, Miss Moore does not lose her smile.

"Mrs. Porter, allow me to present Miss Ann Bradshaw, Miss Gemma Doyle, and Miss Felicity Worthington. Miss Worthington, of course, is the daughter of our own Sir George Phineas Worthington, the admiral."

Mrs. Porter gasps and straightens. "You don't mean it? 'Ow do you like that? The admiral's daugh'er in me own 'ouse?" Mistaking me for Felicity, the nearsighted Mrs. Porter clasps my hands in hers, shaking the life out of them. "Oh, miss, wha' an honor this is, I can tell you. The late Mr. Por'er were a seagoing man 'imself. That's 'im on the wall."

She points to a very bad painting of a terrier dressed in an Elizabethan ruff. The dog's pained expression seems to implore me to look away and allow him to bear his humiliation alone.

"Oh, this calls for port! Don't you agree, Miss Moore?" Mrs. Porter exclaims.

"Perhaps another time, Mrs. Porter. I must get to our lesson or the admiral shall be very put out with me indeed," Miss Moore says, spinning a smooth lie.

"Mum's the word, then." Mrs. Porter smiles conspiratorially, revealing large teeth as chipped and yellow as old piano keys. "Missus Por'er can keep a secret. Don't you douw' it."

"I never would, Mrs. Porter. Thank you for your trouble."

Miss Moore ushers us up the stairs to the third floor and into her modest rooms. The velvet settee, flowery rugs, and heavy draperies must reflect Mrs. Porter's taste in furnishings. But the overstuffed bookshelves and the desk awash in drawings are pure Miss Moore. In one corner stands an old globe nestled in its wooden cradle. Paintings, mostly landscapes, crowd one wall. On another is a collection of exotic masks, gruesome in their fierce beauty.

"Oh, my," Ann says, peering at them.

"Those are from the East," Miss Moore says. "Do you like my masks, Miss Bradshaw?"

Ann shivers. "They look as if they could eat us up."

Miss Moore leans close. "Not today, I think. They've been fed." It takes Ann a moment to realize that Miss Moore is making a joke. There is an awkward silence, and I fear I've made a terrible mistake in bringing my friends here. I should have come alone.

"This looks like Aberdeen," Felicity says at last, taking in a painting of hills and purplish pink heather.

"Yes, it is. You've been to Scotland, Miss Worthington?" Miss Moore asks.

"On holiday once. Just before my mother went to France."

"Lovely country," Miss Moore says.

"Is your family in Scotland?" Felicity asks coyly.

"No. I'm afraid both my parents are long dead. I have no family left to me now, save for some distant cousins in Scotland who are so dull as to make one wish to be an orphan."

We laugh at this. It is so grand not to have to play at piety all the time.

"Have you traveled very much, Miss Moore?" Ann asks.

"Mmmm," Miss Moore says, nodding. "And these are my mementos of those lovely visits." She gestures to her many drawings and paintings that line the walls—a desolate beach, an angry sea, a pastoral English field. "Travel opens your mind as few other things do. It is its own form of hypnotism, and I am forever under its spell."

I recognize one of the places in the paintings. "Are these the caves behind Spence?"

"Indeed," Miss Moore says. The awkwardness is back, for we all know that our visit to those caves was one of the reasons for Miss Moore's dismissal.

Miss Moore brings tea, crumpets, bread, and a slab of butter. "Be it ever so humble, here is tea," she says, placing the tray on a small table. The clock ticks off nervous seconds as we peck at our food. Felicity clears her throat repeatedly. She's waiting for me to ask about the Order, as I'd promised. Now I'm not sure it's a good idea.

"Is the room too warm, Miss Worthington?" Miss Moore asks when Felicity clears her throat a fourth time. Felicity shakes her head. She brings her boot down on mine with a slight pressure.

"Ouch!"

"Miss Doyle? Are you all right?" Miss Moore asks.

"Yes, fine, thank you," I say, moving my feet away.

"Tell me, ladies, how are things at Spence?" Miss Moore asks, saving me.

"We've a new teacher," Ann blurts out.

"Oh?" Miss Moore asks, buttering a thick slice of crusty bread. Her face is a mask. Does it hurt to hear she's been replaced?

"Yes," Ann continues. "A Miss McCleethy. She comes to us from Saint Victoria's School for Girls in Wales."

Miss Moore's butter knife slips, leaving a thick cap of butter on her thumb. "That shan't make me sweet enough to eat, I should think." She smiles and we all laugh at her wit. "Saint Victoria's. I can't say as I've heard of it. And is your Miss McCleethy a very fine teacher?"

"She's teaching us archery," Felicity says.

Miss Moore raises an eyebrow. "How very unusual."

"Felicity is quite good," Ann says.

"I'm sure she is," Miss Moore says. "Miss Doyle, what do you think of this Miss McCleethy?"

"I can't say as yet." Felicity and I exchange glances that do not go unnoticed by Miss Moore.

"Do I sense dissatisfaction?"

"Gemma is convinced she's a witch," Felicity confesses.

"Really? Did you spy her broomstick, Miss Doyle?"

"I never said she was a witch," I protest.

Ann jumps in, nearly breathless. She loves demonic intrigue. "Gemma told us she arrived at Spence in the dead of night—just as a terrible storm raged!"

Miss Moore's eyes go wide. "Heavens! Extreme rain? In December? In England? A sign of witchery, to be sure." They all share a laugh at my expense. "Do go on. I want to hear the part where Miss McCleethy feeds children into her oven."

There's a fresh wave of giggles from Felicity and Ann.

"She and Mrs. Nightwing went into the East Wing," I say. "I overheard them talking about securing something in London. They were making plans together."

Felicity narrows her eyes. "You didn't tell us this!"

"It happened the night before last. I was the only one

there. They caught me outside the doors and were angry with me. And Miss McCleethy brought me warm milk with peppermint."

"Peppermint?" Miss Moore says, furrowing her brow.

"She said it would help me sleep."

"It is an herb known to soothe. Curious that she should know it."

"She has a strange ring, with two snakes intertwined."

"Snakes, you say? Odd."

"She asked about my amulet, too!" I say. "And about my mother."

"And what did you tell her?" Miss Moore asks.

"Nothing," I reply.

Miss Moore sips her tea. "I see."

"She is an old friend of Mrs. Nightwing's, though she looks to be several years younger," Felicity muses.

Ann shudders. "Perhaps she's not. Perhaps she's made a pact with the devil!"

"Not a very good one if she's still teaching at a finishing school in England," Miss Moore notes wryly.

"Or perhaps she's Circe," I say at last.

Miss Moore's teacup halts halfway to her lips. "You've lost me."

"Circe. Sarah Rees-Toome? She was the one from Spence who caused the fire and destroyed the Order, or at least that's what we read in the diary of Mary Dowd. Do you remember?" Ann says breathlessly.

"Remember? How could I forget? That little book was instrumental in my dismissal."

An uncomfortable silence descends. Had Miss Moore not

discovered us reading that diary, had she not read aloud to us from its pages, she might never have been dismissed from Spence. But she did, and that sealed her fate with Nightwing.

"We are so sorry, Miss Moore," Ann says, staring at the Turkish rug.

Felicity adds, "It was mostly Pippa's doing, you know."

"Was it?" Miss Moore asks. We sip our tea guiltily. "Careful with blame. It's a boomerang. Anyway, it's done now. But this Sarah Rees-Toome—Circe—if she did exist . . ."

"Oh, she did!" I insist. I know it for a fact.

". . . didn't she die in the fire at Spence?"

"No," Felicity adds, wide-eyed. "She only wanted people to *think* she'd died. She's still running about."

My heart's hammering away in my chest. "Miss Moore? We were wondering, that is, we rather hoped you might tell us more stories of the Order?"

Her glare is stony. "We've been down that road, haven't we?"

"Yes, but it can't possibly lead to trouble now that you've already been let go from Spence," Felicity says bluntly.

Miss Moore gives a half laugh. "Miss Worthington, your gall astounds me."

"We thought, perhaps, you might know certain things. About the Order. Yourself," I say haltingly.

"Myself," Miss Moore repeats.

"Yes," I say, feeling foolish in one hundred different ways, but there is no chance to stop and take it back now, so I might as well continue. "We thought perhaps you . . . had even been counted among their ranks."

It's been said. My teacup shakes in my hand. I wait for Miss

Moore to scold us, throw us out, admit she knows all, anything. I am not prepared for her laugh.

"You thought . . . ? That I . . . ? Oh, great heavens!" She's laughing so hard, she can't finish.

Ann and Felicity begin laughing too, as if they thought it ridiculous from the start. Traitors.

"Oh, dear me," Miss Moore says, wiping her eyes. "Yes, it's true. I am a grand sorceress of the Order. Living here in these three rooms, taking pupils to pay the rent—it's all an artful ruse designed to keep my true identity hidden."

My cheeks go hot. "I am sorry. *We*," I say, emphasizing the word, "simply thought that since you know so very much about the Order . . ."

"Oh, dear. What a disappointment I must be to you all." She takes a long look around the room, her gaze moving from the drawings of the seaside to those of the caves behind Spence and to the masks on the opposite wall. I fear we've really upset her. "Why such interest in the Order?" she says at last.

"They were women who had power," Felicity says. "It isn't like how it is here."

"We have a woman on the throne," Miss Moore offers.

"By divine right," Ann mutters.

Miss Moore smiles bitterly. "Yes. True."

"I suppose that's why the diary intrigued us so," I say. "Imagine a world—these realms—where women rule, where a girl could have whatever she wished."

"That would be a fine place indeed." Miss Moore takes a sip of her tea. "I confess that the idea of the Order, the stories of them, has been a great fascination to me since girlhood. I suppose that I, too, liked the idea of a magical place when I was a girl of your age."

"But . . . but what if the realms really existed?" I ask.

Miss Moore regards us for a moment. She places her tea on the side table and sits back in her chair, thumbing the pocket watch she keeps pinned at her waist. "Very well, I'll play. What if the realms really existed? What would they look like?"

"Beautiful beyond all imagining," Ann says dreamily.

Miss Moore points to a sketch she's done. "Ah. Like Paris, then?"

"Better!" Ann says.

"How would you know? You've never been to Paris," Felicity mocks. Ignoring Ann, she continues, "Imagine a world where whatever you wish can come true. Trees rain flowers. And dew becomes butterflies in your hand."

"There is a river, and when you look into it, you are beautiful," Ann says. "So beautiful that no one would ever ignore you again."

"Sounds very lovely," Miss Moore says gently. "And is it all like this? You said realms, plural. What are the other realms like?"

"We don't know," I say.

"We haven't been . . . imagined the rest," Ann says.

Miss Moore offers the plate of crumpets. "Who lives in these realms?"

"Spirits and creatures. Some of them aren't very nice," Ann says.

"They want control of the magic," I explain.

"Magic?" Miss Moore repeats.

"Oh, yes. There is magic. Lots of it!" Felicity exclaims. "The creatures would do anything to get it."

"Anything?"

"Yes, *anything*," Ann says, with a dramatic flair.

"*Can* they get to it?" Miss Moore asks.

"Now they can. The magic used to be protected inside the runes," Ann continues, between bites. "But the runes are gone and the magic is wild, there for anyone to use as they like."

Miss Moore looks as if she wants to ask a question, but Felicity rushes in. "And Pippa's there, beautiful as ever," she says.

"You must miss her terribly," Miss Moore says. She turns the pocket watch over and over between her fingers. "These stories are a lovely way of remembering her."

"Yes," I say, hoping my guilt does not show.

"And now that the magic is free, as you say, what is it like? Do you commune with the other members of the Order there and work your hocus-pocus?"

"No. They've all been killed or gone into hiding," Felicity says. "And it isn't good at all that the magic has been unleashed."

"Really? Why not?"

"Some of the spirits can use it for dark purposes. They could use it to break through to this world or to bring Circe in," Felicity explains. "That is why we must find the Temple."

Miss Moore is confused. "I fear I shall have to take notes to keep up. What, pray tell, is the Temple?"

"That is the secret source of the magic inside the realms," I say.

"A secret source?" Miss Moore repeats. "And where is this place, this Temple?"

"We don't know. We've not discovered it yet," I say. "But once we do, we can bind the magic again and form a new Order."

"*Bon courage*, then. What a fascinating story," Miss Moore says. The mantel clock chimes four o'clock. Miss Moore checks the time on her watch against it. "Ah, unfailingly accurate."

"Is it four already?" Felicity says, leaping up. "We're to meet Mother at half past."

"What a shame," Miss Moore says. "You must come back for another visit. As a matter of fact, there is an excellent exhibit at a private gallery in Chelsea on Thursday. Shall we go?"

"Oh, yes!" we exclaim.

"Very well," she says, rising. She helps us into our coats. We don our gloves and secure our hats.

"So there is nothing further you can tell us about the Order?" I ask tentatively.

"Have you an aversion to reading, ladies? If I wanted to learn more about any subject, I should find a good book or two," she says, ushering us down the stairs, where Mrs. Porter is waiting for us.

"Where are yer luv'ly drawings?" the landlady asks, inspecting us for paper or chalk. "Don't be shy, now. Show old Por'er."

"We've nothing to show, I'm afraid," Ann says.

Mrs. Porter's face darkens. "'Ere now, I run a respec'able establishment, Miss Moore. You said the admiral was payin' fer lessons. Whatchoo been abou' up there all this time, then?"

Miss Moore leans toward Mrs. Porter till the old woman has to take a step back. "Witchcraft," she whispers saucily.

"Come along, ladies. Button up. The wind is brisk and takes no prisoners."

Miss Moore ushers us out the door as Mrs. Porter shouts from the vestibule. "I don't like tha', Miss Moore. I don't like tha' a' awl."

Miss Moore never looks back or loses her smile. "I shall see you Thursday," she says, waving goodbye. And with that, we are dismissed.

CHAPTER
SIXTEEN

"THAT WAS AN AFTERNOON WASTED. MISS MOORE knows nothing more about the Order and the realms. We should have gone to the shops instead," Felicity announces as we arrive at her mother's women's club.

"I didn't force you to go with me," I say.

"Perhaps Pippa has had luck in finding the Temple," Ann says brightly.

"It has been two days," Felicity says, looking to me. "We promised to return as soon as we could."

"How can we come by any privacy together?" I ask.

"Leave that to me," Felicity answers.

The doors are held open for us by a white-gloved attendant. Felicity offers her mother's card, and the spindly man examines it.

"We are guests of Lady Worthington, my mother," Felicity says with disdain.

"Begging your pardon, miss, it is not the custom of the

Alexandra to admit more than one guest. I am sorry, but rules are rules." The attendant does his best to look sympathetic, but in his smile, I see the slightest hint of satisfaction.

Felicity gives the man in his crisp uniform a steely gaze. "Do you know who this is?" she says in a mock whisper that draws the attention of all standing near. I'm on my guard, for I know Felicity is hatching some plan. "This is Miss Ann Bradshaw, the recently discovered grand-niece of the Duke of Chester-field." She bats her eyelashes as if the servant is an idiot. "She is a descendant of the czarina herself. Surely you read about it."

"I'm afraid I have not, miss," the attendant says, less sure now.

Felicity sighs. "When I think of the hardships Miss Brad-shaw has endured, living as an orphan, thought dead by those who loved her best, oh, it breaks my heart to know how she is being mistreated here at this very moment. Oh, dear, Miss Bradshaw. I am very sorry for this trouble. I've no doubt Mother will be quite put out when she hears of it."

One of the society matrons comes near. "Dear me, Miss Worthington, is this really the long-lost grand-niece of the czarina?"

We've never said that, actually, but it serves us well.

"Oh, yes," Felicity says, wide-eyed. "As a matter of fact, Miss Bradshaw has come to sing for us today, so you see, she is not really a guest of Mother's, but rather, she is a guest of the Alexandra."

"Felic—Miss Worthington!" Ann says, panicked.

"She is exceedingly modest," Felicity adds.

There is whispering among the society matrons. We are on

the verge of creating a scene. The attendant is ill at ease. If he admits us all, he is breaking the rules in view of everyone; if he turns one of us away, he risks angering a member and perhaps being dismissed for it. Felicity has played her hand masterfully.

The matron steps forward. "As Miss Bradshaw is a guest of the Alexandra, I cannot see that it shall be any trouble at all."

"As you wish, madam," the man says.

"I look forward to hearing you sing this afternoon," the woman calls after.

"Felicity!" Ann whispers as the attendant escorts us into an oak-paneled dining room filled with lovely tables covered in white damask cloths.

"What is it?"

"You shouldn't have said that, about my singing today."

"You can sing, can't you?"

"Yes, but . . ."

"Do you want to play this game or don't you, Ann?"

Ann says nothing more. The room is nearly filled with elegant women sipping tea and picking at watercress sandwiches. We are seated at a table in a far corner.

Felicity's face falls. "My mother has arrived."

Lady Worthington cuts a swath through the room. All eyes are upon her, for she is a handsome woman—fair as a china cup and seemingly as delicate. She exudes an air of fragility, like someone who has been cared for her entire life. Her smile is cordial without being too inviting. I could practice for a thousand years and not give such a smile. And her brown silk dress is sumptuous and cut in the latest fashion. Ropes of pearls hang round her slender neck. An enormous hat with peacock feathers on the band frames her face.

"*Bonjour*, darling," she says, kissing Felicity's cheeks as I've heard the Parisians do.

"Mother, must you make such a display?" Felicity chides.

"Very well, darling. Hello, Miss Bradshaw," Lady Worthington says. She looks at me, and her smile falters a bit. "I don't believe we are acquainted."

"Mother, may I present Miss Gemma Doyle."

"How do you do, Lady Worthington?" I ask.

Mrs. Worthington gives Felicity a tight smile. "Felicity, darling, I do wish you would let me know when you've invited a guest to tea. The Alexandra is quite strict about its guests."

I want to die. I want to sink through the floor and disappear. Why must Felicity do these things?

A maid appears like a shadow at Mrs. Worthington's side and pours tea for her.

Mrs. Worthington places a napkin in her lap. "Well, no matter now. I am happy to meet Felicity's friends. It's so nice that Miss Bradshaw could spend Christmas with us as her dear great-uncle, the duke, is detained in Saint Petersburg."

"Yes," I say, trying not to choke at this outrageous lie. "How fortunate we all are."

Lady Worthington asks a few polite questions and I give a dull but somewhat accurate autobiography; in return Lady Worthington seems to hang on every word. She makes me feel as if I'm the only person in the room. It's easy to see why the admiral would fall in love with her. When she speaks, her stories are exceedingly entertaining. But Felicity sits sullenly, playing with her spoon, until her mother puts a hand on hers to stop her.

"Darling," she says. "Must you?"

Felicity sighs and looks around the room as if hoping to see someone to rescue her.

Lady Worthington gives one of her dazzling smiles. "Darling, I've some wonderful news. I had wanted to surprise you, but I don't think I can wait a moment longer."

"What is it?" Felicity asks.

"Papa has taken a ward. Little Polly was his cousin Bea's daughter. Bea died of consumption, we are told, though I daresay she died of a broken heart. The father was always useless and signed her away without so much as a care. His own daughter."

Felicity has gone pale. "What do you mean? She's to live with us? With you and Papa?"

"Yes. And Mrs. Smalls, the governess, of course. Your father is so happy to have a little princess in the house again. Felicity, dear, not too much sugar in your tea. It isn't good for the teeth," Lady Worthington chides without losing her smile.

As if she hasn't heard, Felicity drops two more lumps of sugar into her tea and drinks it. Her mother pretends she hasn't noticed.

A woman as soft and overstuffed as a settee waddles to our table. "Good afternoon, Mrs. Worthington. Is it true that your distinguished guest is to sing for us today?"

Lady Worthington looks startled. "Oh. Well, I can't say . . . I . . ."

The woman prattles on. "We were just discussing how extraordinary it is that you've taken Miss Bradshaw under your wing. If we might borrow you for a bit, please do come and tell Mrs. Threadgill and me how the czarina's long-lost relation has come to be with us."

"If you'll excuse me," Lady Worthington says, gliding to the other table like a swan.

"Are you all right, Fee?" I ask. "You look pale."

"I'm fine. I simply don't like the idea of some little beast underfoot while I'm at home."

She's jealous. Jealous of someone named little Polly. Felicity can be so incredibly petty at times.

"She's just a child," I say.

"I know that," Felicity snaps. "It isn't worth discussing. We have more important matters at hand. Follow me."

She leads us through tables of elegant ladies in grand hats sipping tea and gossiping. They glance up but we are unimportant, and they resume their discussions of who has done what to whom. We follow Felicity up wide, carpeted stairs, past ladies in stiff, fashionable dresses who seem to take a keen, if discreet, interest in these brash young ladies storming the barricades of their genteel club.

"Where are you taking us?" I ask.

"The club has private bedchambers for members. One of them will surely be empty. Oh, no."

"What is it?" Ann asks, panicked.

Felicity's peering over the banister to the foyer below. A solid-looking woman in a purple dress and a fur stole is holding court. She's a commanding presence; the others hang on her every word. "One of my mother's former friends, Lady Denby."

Lady Denby? Could this be Simon's mother? A lump forms in my throat. I can only hope that I will be able to slip away undetected, so that Lady Denby will not form an unfavorable opinion of me.

"Why do you say former friend?" Ann asks, looking worried.

"She has never forgiven my mother for living in France. She doesn't like the French, as the Middleton family can be traced to Lord Nelson himself," she says, mentioning Britain's great naval hero. "If Lady Denby likes you, you are set for life. If she finds you wanting in any way, you are shunned. Mind, she's still cordial, but very cold. And my foolish mother is too blind to see it. She continues to try to win Lady Denby's favor. I shall never be like that."

Felicity moves slowly, daringly, along the balcony, watching Lady Denby. I'm doing my best to keep my head down.

"Is she Simon Middleton's mother, then?" I ask.

"Yes," Felicity answers. "How do you know Simon Middleton?"

"Who is Simon Middleton?" Ann asks.

"I met him just yesterday at the train station. He and Tom are acquainted."

Felicity's eyes widen. "When had you planned to tell us about it?"

Ann tries again. "Who is Simon Middleton?"

"Gemma, you're keeping secrets again!"

"It is not a secret," I say, blushing. "It is nothing, really. He has invited my family to dinner. That is all."

Felicity looks as if someone has dropped her in the middle

of the Thames. "You've been invited to dinner? That is certainly something."

"It is bad manners to discuss people I've never met," Ann says, pouting.

Felicity takes pity on her. "Simon Middleton is not only a viscount's son but exceedingly handsome. And he seems to have taken an interest in Gemma, though she doesn't wish us to know about it."

"It is nothing, truly," I protest. "He was simply being charitable, I'm sure."

"The Middletons are never charitable," she says, looking down. "You must take great care around his mother. She scrutinizes people for sport."

"You've not put me at ease," I say.

"Forewarned is forearmed, Gemma."

Below us, Lady Denby says something merry that makes her companions laugh in that restrained way women learn somehow when they pack away their girlish selves. She doesn't seem to be the monster Felicity makes her out to be.

"What will you wear?" Ann asks dreamily.

"Horns and the pelt of a large animal," I say. Ann takes this in for a moment, as if she believes it wholeheartedly. What shall I do with her? "I shall wear a proper dress. Something that meets with my grandmother's approval."

"You must give us every detail after," Felicity says. "I shall be most interested to hear about it."

"Do you know Mr. Middleton well?" I pry.

"I've known him for ages," Felicity says. Standing there, with loose tendrils of golden hair curving under her chin, she looks a picture, her strange beauty at its most seductive.

"I see. And have you set your sights on him?"

Felicity makes a face. "Simon? He is like a brother to me. I can't possibly imagine a romance with him."

I am relieved. It's silly of me to pin my hopes on Simon so early, but he is charming and handsome and he seems to like me. His attention makes me feel beautiful. It is only a small string of excitement, but I find I do not want to let go of it so soon.

One of Lady Denby's companions looks up, sees us staring. Lady Denby follows her gaze.

"Let's go," I whisper. "Come on!"

"Must you push?" Felicity snipes as I practically fall over her. We duck down a hall. Felicity pulls us into an empty bed-chamber and closes the door.

Ann glances around nervously. "Should we be in here?"

"You wanted privacy," she says. "Now we have it."

There is a dressing gown draped across a chair, and several hatboxes in a corner. The room may be empty—for the moment—but it is most definitely not unoccupied.

"We'll have to work fast," I say.

"Precisely," Felicity says, grinning.

Ann looks as if she could be ill. "We shall be ruined. I know it."

But once we hold hands and I make the door of light appear, all discomfort is forgotten, swallowed whole by our awe.

CHAPTER
SEVENTEEN

WE'VE BARELY STEPPED INTO THE BRIGHT GLOW OF the realms when everything goes dark; cold fingers press against my eyes. I slide out of the embrace, whirling around quickly to see Pippa standing behind me. She still wears her garland, though it's begun to droop some. She's added nettle and a pink narcissus to brighten it a bit.

She giggles to see me gasping so. "Oh, poor Gemma! Did I frighten you?"

"N-no. Well, a little, perhaps."

Felicity and Ann run to Pip with a shout and throw their arms around her.

"What is the matter?" Ann asks me.

"I gave our poor Gemma a start. Don't be cross with me," Pippa says, taking my hand. She speaks in a whisper. "I've a surprise. Follow me."

Pip leads us through the trees. "Close your eyes," she calls. At last she stops. "Open them."

We're at the river. On the water is a ship the likes of which

I've never seen before. I'm not entirely sure that it is a ship, for it more resembles a dragon's body, black and red, with great wings that stretch up on the sides. It is certainly of a monstrous size, curved at both ends, with one giant mast rising near the bow and a sail as thin as onionskin. Large ropes of seaweed hang over the sides, as do sparkling silver nets that float on the surface of the water. But the most extraordinary thing of all is the massive head attached to the front of the ship. It is green and scaly, with snakes as long as tree branches slithering about its fearsome, motionless face.

"I've found her!" Pippa says excitedly. "I've found the gorgon!"

That thing is the gorgon?

"Quickly! Let's ask her about the Temple before she gets away," Pippa says, stepping closer to the intimidating ship. "Ahoy, there!"

The gorgon swivels her face in our direction. The snakes of her head hiss and twist as if they'd like to eat us for disturbing their peace. Surely they would if they were not attached to that thing. I am not at all prepared when the creature opens her large yellow eyes.

"What do you wish?" she asks, in a dark slither of a voice.

"Are you the gorgon?" Pippa asks.

"Yessss."

"Is it true that you are bound by the Order's magic to do no harm and speak only truth?" she continues.

The gorgon closes her eyes for the briefest moment. "Yesssss."

"We are looking for the Temple. Do you know it?" Pip demands.

The eyes open again. "All know of it. None knows where it

may be found. None but the Order, and they have not come for many years."

"Is there anyone who may know where to find it?" Pippa asks. She's annoyed that the gorgon is proving so unhelpful.

The gorgon looks to the river again. "The Forest of Lights. Philon's tribe. Some say they were once allies to the Order. They may know where to look for this Temple."

"Very well, then," Pippa says. "We wish to go to the Forest of Lights."

"Only one of the Order may bid me," the gorgon says.

"She is one of the Order," Pippa says, pointing to me.

"We shall see," the gorgon hisses.

"Go on, Gemma," Felicity presses. "Try."

I step forward, clear my throat. The snakes fan out around the gorgon's head like a writhing mane. They hiss at me, revealing their sharp, pointed fangs. Looking into that horrible face, it is hard to find my voice.

"We wish to go to the Forest of Lights. Will you take us, gorgon?"

In answer, one of the boat's grand wings lowers slowly to shore, allowing us passage. Pippa and Felicity can barely contain their joy. They grin like happy fools as they step onto the plank.

"Must we go on this?" Ann asks, hanging back.

"Don't be scared, Ann, darling. I'll be with you," Pippa says, pulling her forward.

The wing creaks and sways as we make our way across it. Felicity reaches out and touches one of the nets hanging from the side of the barge.

"These are light as cobwebs," she says, fingering the delicate fibers. "What fish can you possibly catch with them?"

"They are not for catching," the gorgon says in her syrupy thick voice. "They are for warning."

Below us, the water swirls, sending a shimmer of pinks and violets to the surface.

"Look how pretty," Ann says, putting a hand to the water. "Wait, do you hear that?"

"Hear what?" I ask.

"There it is! Oh, that is the most beautiful sound I have ever heard," Ann says, putting her face near the water. "It's coming from the river. Something's there, just below the surface."

Ann's fingers touch the shimmery water, and for an instant, I think I see something moving very near her hand. Without warning, the great wing that has been lowered for us lifts quickly, forcing us to scurry onto the ship.

"That was sudden," Ann says. "The music's stopped. Now I'll never know where that lovely song came from." She pouts.

"Some things are best not known," the gorgon says.

Ann shivers. "I don't like this. We've no way off now."

Pippa gives Ann a kiss on the cheek like a mother soothing all fears. "We must be brave girls now. We must go to the Forest of Lights if we are to find the Temple."

The gorgon speaks again. "You are my mistress and must bid me go."

I realize she's waiting for me. I look out at the twists and turns of the river, not knowing where it goes from here. "Very well," I say, taking a deep breath. "Down the river, if you please."

The great boat purrs into motion. Behind us, the garden

fades from view. We take a bend and the river widens. Immense stone beasts with long fangs and elaborate headdresses guard the distant shores. Like the gargoyles of Spence, they are unseeing but ominous, ancient guardians of what lies within. The water is rough here. Whitecaps rock the boat, making my stomach lurch.

"Gemma, you look positively green," Pippa says.

"My father says if you can see where you are headed, it helps," Felicity offers.

Yes, anything. I'll try anything. I leave my companions to their laughter and stories and step out onto the bow of the boat, sitting on the long, pointed end near our strange navigator.

The gorgon senses me there. "Are you well, Most High?"

That slithery black tongue catches me off guard. "I am indisposed. I shall be fine in a moment."

"You must breathe deeply. That is the way."

I take several deep breaths. It seems to work, and soon both the river and my belly are calm. "Gorgon," I ask, when I find my courage, "are there more creatures like you?"

"No," comes the reply. "I am the last of my kind."

"What happened to the others?"

"They were destroyed or banished during the rebellion."

"The rebellion?"

"It was long, long ago," the gorgon says, sounding weary. "Before the Runes of the Oracle."

"There was a time before the runes?"

"Yesss. It was a time when the magic was loose inside the realms for all to use. But it was also a dark time. There were many battles as the creatures fought each other for more power. And it was a time when the veil between your world and ours was thin. We were able to come and go as we pleased."

"You could come into our world?" I ask.

"Oh, yes. Such an interesting place."

I think of the stories I've read, stories of fairy sightings, ghosts, mythical sea creatures luring sailors to their deaths. Suddenly, they do not seem like mere stories.

"What happened?"

"The Order happened," the gorgon says, and I cannot tell whether her tone is one of anger or relief.

"Hadn't the Order always existed?"

"In a fashion. They were one of the tribes. Priestesses. Healers, mystics, seers. They ferried spirits across to the world beyond. They were the master makers of illusion. Their power was always great, but it grew stronger over time. It was rumored that they had found the source of all magic inside the realms."

"The Temple?"

"Yesss," comes the gorgon's slithery reply. "The Temple. It was said the Order drank of its waters, and thus the magic became part of them. It lived in them, getting stronger with each generation. Now, they had more power than anyone else. What they did not like they sought to correct. They began to limit the creatures' visits to your world. No one could enter without their permission."

"Is that when they built the runes?"

"No," the gorgon replies. "That was their revenge."

"I don't understand."

"Several creatures from every tribe banded together. They resented the power the Order held over them. They did not want to ask permission. One day, they struck back. As several of the Order's young initiates played in the garden, they caught them unaware, carrying them off to the Winterlands, where they slaughtered them all. And that was when the creatures discovered a horrible secret."

My mouth has gone dry with the tale. "What secret was that?"

"The sacrifice of another granted enormous power."

Water rushes under us in a *whoosh-whoosh*ing, carrying us forward.

"In their rage and grief, the Order built the runes as a seal on the magic. They closed the border between worlds so that only they could enter. Whatever remained on either side of the border remained imprisoned there forever."

I think of the marble columns of Spence, the creatures caught in stone there.

"It remained thus for many years. Until one of your own betrayed the Order."

"Circe," I say.

"Yesss. She offered a sacrifice and gave power to the dark spirits of the Winterlands once more. The more spirits they brought to their side, the more powerful they became, the more the seal of the runes began to weaken."

"So that is why I was able to shatter them?" I ask.

"Perhaps." The gorgon's answer is like a sigh. "Perhaps, Most High."

"Why do you call me Most High?"

"That is who you are."

The others are leaning against the side of the boat. They take turns holding on to the ropes of the sails, letting their bodies push against the force of the wind. Pippa's merry laugh drifts above the shooshing of the water. I have a question I want to ask, but I am afraid to say it aloud, afraid of what the answer might be.

"Gorgon," I start. "Is it true that the spirits of those from our world must cross over?"

"That is the way it has always been."

"But are there some spirits who remain forever?"

"I know of none who did not become corrupted and go to live in the Winterlands."

The wind's caught Pippa's garland. She chases it, laughing, before clutching it tightly in her hands.

"But everything is different now, isn't it?"

"Yesss," the gorgon hisses. "Different."

"So perhaps there is a way to change things."

"Perhaps."

"Gemma!" Pippa calls. "How are you feeling?"

"Much better!" I shout back.

"Come back, then!"

I leave my perch beside the gorgon and join the others.

"Isn't the river beautiful?" Pippa says, grinning widely. Indeed, it is a glorious teal blue here. "Oh, I've missed you all so very much. Did you miss me terribly?"

Felicity runs to embrace her. She holds Pip fiercely. "I thought I should never see you again."

"You saw us not two days ago," I remind her.

"But I can scarcely bear it. It is nearly Christmas," she says wistfully. "Have you been to any dances yet?"

"No," Ann reports. "But Felicity's mother and father will have their Christmas ball."

"I suppose it will be very grand," Pippa says, pouting.

"I'm to wear my first gown," Ann continues. She describes the gown in detail. Pippa asks us questions about the ball. It is as if we are back at Spence, sitting in the great hall in Felicity's tent, gossiping, making plans.

Smiling, Pippa twirls Felicity around as the boat creaks slowly down the river. "We are together. And we never have to part."

"But we have to go back," I say.

The hurt in Pippa's eyes wounds me. "But when you form the Order again, you'll come for me. Won't you?"

"Of course we will," Felicity says. She's fallen into step with Pippa again, happy to be near her.

Pippa wraps her arms about Felicity and places her head on her shoulder. "You are my dearest friends in all the world. Nothing will ever change that."

Ann joins in the embrace. At last, I too put my arms about Pippa. We surround her like petals, and I try not to think about what shall happen to us all once we find the Temple.

Around a sharp bend, the river opens, giving the most majestic view of the shore and the cliff caves that rise high above us. Goddesses have been carved into the rock. They stand, possibly fifty feet tall, adorned with elaborate coned headdresses. Their necks are strung with jewels. Save for that, they are naked and quite sensual, hips cocked at an angle, an arm placed behind the head just so, lips curved into a smile. Decency tells me I should look away, but I find I keep stealing glances.

"Oh, gracious," Ann says, looking up and immediately down.

"What are those?" Felicity asks.

The gorgon opens its mouth. "The Caves of Sighs. They are but abandoned ruins now, inhabited only by the Hajin, the Untouchables."

"The Untouchables?" I ask.

"Yesss. There is one." The gorgon's head lolls to the right. Something scurries in the brush along the shore. "Filthy vermin."

"Why are they called Untouchables?" Ann asks.

"They've always been thus. The Order banished them to the Caves of Sighs. No one goes there now. It is forbidden."

"Well, that isn't fair," Ann says, her voice rising. "It isn't fair at all." Poor Ann. She knows what it is to be an untouchable.

"What was it used for before?" I ask.

"It was the place where the Order took their lovers."

"Lovers?" Felicity asks.

"Yes." The gorgon pauses before adding, "The Rakshana."

I don't know what to say to this. "The Rakshana and the Order were lovers?"

The gorgon's voice sounds far away. "Once."

Felicity gives a shout. "Look at that!" She points to the horizon, where a heavy mist falls from the sky like shavings of gold, obscuring our view of what lies ahead. It roars like a waterfall.

"Are we going through there?" Ann asks, worried.

Pippa pulls Ann close. "Don't fret so. It will be all right, I'm sure, else the gorgon wouldn't bring us through it. Isn't that right, Gemma?"

"Yes, of course," I say, trying not to seem as truly terrified as I feel. For I've no idea what will become of us. "Gorgon, you are bound to do us no harm. Is that so?"

But my question is drowned out by the relentless pounding of the golden waterfall. We huddle together on the floor of the ship. Ann closes her eyes tightly. As we push forward, I shut my eyes too, afraid to know what's going to happen next. With the roar thick in our ears, we pass through this damp curtain and emerge on the other side, where the river becomes like an ocean with no land in sight, save for a verdant island in the distance.

"We're alive," Ann says, both surprised and relieved.

"Ann," Pippa says, "look—now you are a golden girl!"

It's true. Golden flakes coat our skin. Felicity turns her hands this way and that, laughing joyfully as she watches them shimmer. "Oh, we're fine, aren't we? No trouble at all!"

Pippa laughs. "I told you not to be afraid."

"The magic is strong," the gorgon says. Whether it's a statement or a caution I cannot tell.

"Gemma," Pippa asks, "why must we bind the magic?"

"What do you mean? Because it is loose inside the realms."

"What if that's not such a terrible thing? Why shouldn't anyone be allowed to use this power?"

I do not like where this is going. "Because they could use it to come into our world and create havoc. There'd be no sense of order or control upon it."

"You don't know that the inhabitants of the realms would use it unwisely."

She hasn't heard the gorgon's story, else she might think otherwise. "Don't we? Do you remember that creature that enslaved my mother?"

"But it was joined to Circe. Perhaps they're not all like that," Pippa muses.

"And how would I decide who should have it, who can be trusted?"

No one has an answer to this.

I shake my head. "It is out of the question. The longer the magic is loose, the greater the danger that those spirits here can become corrupted. We must find the Temple and bind the magic once again. Then we shall reform the Order and maintain the balance of the realms."

Pippa pouts. She has the irritating good fortune of looking beautiful while she does this. "Very well. We're almost there anyway."

CHAPTER
EIGHTEEN

THE RIVER HAS NARROWED AGAIN. WE'RE ENTER-
ing a spot where the trees grow tall, thick, and green. Thousands
of lanterns hang from their branches. It reminds me of Diwali,
the festival of lights in India, when Mother and I would stay up
late to watch the streets bloom with candles and lanterns.

The ship comes to rest in the soft, wet sand of the island.
"The Forest of Lights," the gorgon says. "Be on your guard.
State your business to Philon and Philon only."

The winged plank lowers and we step off into a soft carpet
of grass and sand that disappears into thick brush dotted by
fat white double lotuses. The trees are so tall they disappear
into a ceiling of dark green. Looking up at them makes me feel
dizzy. The lights sway and move. One darts across my face,
making me gasp.

"What was that?" Ann whispers, eyes wide.

"What's happening?" It's Felicity. Several of the lights have
descended on her head. Her rapturous face is illuminated by
the glowing crown.

The lights congregate into a ball that floats ahead of us, showing the way.

"It seems they want us to follow them," Pippa says in wonder.

The luminous little sprites, if that's what they are, take us into the forest. The air has a rich, earthy smell. Moss grows on the enormous trees like soft green fur. Looking back, I can no longer see the gorgon. It's as if we've been absorbed into the forest. I've the urge to run back, especially when I hear the soft rhythm of hooves coming closer. The ball of light bursts, the tiny illuminations flying away pell-mell into the forest.

"What is that?" Felicity squeaks, looking around wildly.

"I don't know," Pippa says.

The pounding seems to come from all sides. Whatever it is, we are surrounded. It grows closer and just as suddenly stops. A band of centaurs emerges one by one from the trees. They pace uneasily on their strong horse legs, their thick arms crossed over bare man chests. The largest of the clan comes forward. His chin sports a wisp of beard.

"Who are you? What business have you here?" he demands.

"We've come to see Philon," Pippa asserts. She's being quite brave, for I'd like to run.

The centaurs exchange suspicious glances. "The gorgon brought us," I say, hoping it will open doors.

The largest of them comes forward till his hooves are inches from my own feet. "The gorgon? What game does she play with us? Very well, then. I shall take you to Philon and let our leader decide your fate. Climb on, unless you care to walk."

His grip is strong as he swings me with one hand up onto his broad, smooth back.

"Oh," I say, for there is no bridle as on a horse. In fact, there is no decent place for me to hold on, and I am forced to wrap my arms around his thick waist and rest my head against the broad expanse of his back.

Without so much as a by-your-leave, he takes off at a gallop, with me holding on for dear life as we dart through trees whose branches come dangerously close. Some of them leave scratches along my face and arms, and I suspect he's doing this on purpose. The centaurs carrying Felicity, Pippa, and Ann ride up beside me. Ann has her eyes closed and her mouth set tightly in a grimace. But Felicity and Pippa seem almost to enjoy the strange ride.

At last, we reach a clearing of thatched huts and mud houses. The centaur gives me his hand and flings me to the ground, where I fall on my backside. He puts his hands at his hips, towering over me, grinning. "Shall I help you to your feet?"

"No, thank you." I jump up, brushing the grass from my skirt.

"You're one of them, aren't you?" he says, pointing to my amulet, which has worked free from beneath my blouse during the bumpy ride. "The rumors are true!" he shouts to his friends. "The Order is returning to the realms. And here they are."

The clan moves in, surrounding our little band of girls.

"What should we do about that?" the centaur asks, rage snarling around his words. I no longer care about seeing Philon or asking him about the Temple. I only want to escape.

"Creostus!" comes a new and strange voice.

The centaurs part, back away. They bow their heads. The large one, Creostus, dips his but does not keep it down.

"What is that?" Ann whispers, clinging to me.

Before us is the most magnificent creature I have ever seen. I do not know whether it is a man or a woman, for it could be both. It is slight, with skin and hair the dusty color of a lilac bloom and a long, trailing cape made of acorns, thorns, and thistle. Its eyes are vivid green and turned up at the corners like a cat's. One hand is a paw; the other a talon.

"Who comes?" the creature asks in a voice that is like three-part harmony, the tones distinct but inseparable at the same time.

"A witch," the defiant centaur says. "Brought to our shores by the cursed gorgon."

"Hmmm," the creature says, staring at me till I feel like a naughty child facing the belt. The sharp edge of its talon lifts my amulet for inspection. "A priestess. We have not seen one of your kind in many years. Are you the one who broke the runes, the seal on the magic?"

I pull my necklace out of its reach and tuck it into my blouse again. "I am."

"What is it you seek from us?"

"I'm sorry, I can only speak with Philon. Do you know where I might find—"

"I am Philon."

"Oh," I say. "I've come to ask your help."

Creostus interrupts. "Do not aid her, Philon. Do you remember what it has been like for us all these years?"

Philon silences him with a glance. "Why should I help you, priestess?"

I have no ready answer for this. "Because I've undone the seal on the magic. Order must be restored."

Laughing erupts among the centaurs. "Then let us be the ones to restore—and control it," one yells. The others cheer.

"But only the Order can bind the magic and rule the realms," Felicity says.

Philon speaks again. "That is the way it was for generations, but who is to say it must always be so? Power is fleeting. It shifts like sand."

There are more cheers from the others. A crowd has gathered. In addition to the centaurs, the creatures of light have grown to about one foot tall. They hover like overgrown fireflies.

"Would you rather Circe find it first?" I say. "Or the dark spirits of the Winterlands? If they control it, do you imagine they would be generous with you?"

Philon considers this. "The priestess has a point. You may come with me."

Creostus shouts after us. "Promise them nothing, Philon. Your loyalty is to your people first! Remember!"

Philon settles us in a grand hut and pours a goblet of red liquid. None is offered to us, which makes me trust the strange creature a bit more. For if we were to eat or drink anything here, we would have to stay, as Pippa did. Philon swirls the liquid in the goblet and swallows it. "I agree that the magic must be contained. It is too powerful this way. Some have never been exposed to its full force, and they are giddy with it. They want more and more. There is unrest. I am afraid they will enter into ill-advised alliances and doom us to enslavement. It is a threat to our ways."

"Then you will help me find the Temple?" I ask.

"And what will you promise us if we help you?" When I do not speak, Philon smirks. "Just as I thought. The Order isn't interested in sharing the power of the realms."

"The gorgon said you and the Order were allies once."

"Yes," Philon says. "Once." The creature circles the room with an elegant, feline grace. "The centaurs were their messengers; I, the weapons master. But after the rebellion, they kept the magic from us just as they did from all the others, though we had remained loyal. That was their thanks to us."

I do not know what to say to this. "Perhaps there was no other way." The creature stares at me for a long moment till I'm forced to look away.

"They're not going to help us, Gemma. Let's be on our way," Felicity says.

Philon refills the goblet. "I cannot tell you where to find the Temple, because in truth, I do not know where it is. But I can offer you something. Come with me."

We emerge into the foggy day again. Creostus stops the magnificent leader, speaking low in a language we cannot understand. But I do understand the anger in his voice, the wariness in his eyes each time he looks our way. Philon dismisses him with a curt "Nyim!"

"You cannot trust them, Philon," the centaur spits out. "Their promises are like glamour—in time, they fade."

Philon takes us into a low hut. The walls shimmer with an array of shining weaponry, some of which I've never seen. Silver lariats hang from hooks. Jeweled goblets and exquisitely wrought mirrors stand side by side.

"While the magic is loose, we are using it to return to the old ways. If we do not know the outcome, we must be prepared. You may take one weapon for your journey."

"These are all weapons?" I ask.

"With the right spell, anything can become a weapon, priestess."

There are so many. I don't know where to begin.

"Oh," Felicity gasps. She's found a featherlight bow and a quiver of silver-tipped arrows.

"It seems the choice is made," Philon says, handing them to her. The arrows are well crafted but unremarkable save for the strange markings on the silver tips, a series of numbers, lines, and symbols I cannot begin to understand.

"What are these?" Felicity asks.

"That is the language of our elders."

"Magic arrows?" Ann asks, peering at the tips.

Felicity raises the bow and closes one eye against an imaginary target. "They are arrows, Ann. They shall work like any other."

"Perhaps," Philon says. "If you have the courage to aim and shoot."

Felicity glowers. She turns the bow to Philon.

"Felicity!" I hiss. "What are you doing?"

"I've plenty of courage," Felicity snarls.

"Will you have it when it counts most?" Philon asks coolly.

Pippa pushes the bow down and away. "Fee, stop it."

"I've plenty of courage," she says again.

"Of course you do," Pippa soothes.

Philon regards them curiously. "We shall see." To me it says, "Priestess, these arrows, then, are they your choice of weapon?"

"Yes," I answer. "I suppose they are."

"We should be leaving," Felicity says. "Thank you for the arrows."

Philon dips that magnificent head. "You are most welcome. But they are not a gift. They are a marker against a debt to be paid."

I feel as if I am falling into a hole, and the more I try to dig my way out, the deeper it gets. "What sort of payment?"

"A share of the magic is what we ask, should you find the Temple first. We do not intend to live in the dark again."

"I understand," I say, making a promise I do not know if I can honor.

⌁⌁⌁⌁⌁

Philon walks us to the edge of the forest, where the strange glowing lights wait to take us back to the ship.

"They will all try to keep you from the Temple. You must know that. How will you protect yourselves? Have you any alliances?"

"We have the gorgon," I say.

Philon nods slowly. "The gorgon. The last of her kind. Imprisoned on a ship for all time as punishment for her sins."

"What do you mean?" I ask.

"I mean there is much you do not know," Philon says. "Tread carefully, priestess. There is no hiding here. Your fondest wishes, your deepest desires or greatest fears can be used against you. There are many who would want to keep you from your task."

"Why are you telling me this? Are you loyal to the Order after all?"

"This is war," Philon says, long purplish hair blowing across sharp cheekbones. "I am loyal to the victor."

The lights circle and dart about Pippa's head. She swats at them playfully. I've one last question before we go, though.

"The gorgon is our ally, isn't she? She is bound to tell us truth always."

"Bound by what? The magic is no longer reliable." With that, the tall, thin creature turns away, its thistle cape trailing like a chain.

When we reach the shore, Creostus is there waiting for us, his arms crossed. "Did you find what you were after, witch?"

Felicity pats the quiver of arrows on her back.

"So Philon's given you a token. What will you give us in return? Will you grant us power? Or will you deny us?"

I do not answer but climb aboard the gorgon's winglike plank, listening as it creaks closed behind us. The wind catches the wide, translucent sail, and we move away from the tiny island till it is only a spot of green behind us. But the centaur's raw cry follows me on the breeze, catching my breath in its fist.

"What will you give us in return, witch? What will you give us?"

We sail once more through the golden curtain and down the river. When we come again to the statues in the cliffs, to the Caves of Sighs, I see colorful smoke—reds, blues, oranges, purples—rising from high above, and I am fairly certain that I spy a figure behind the smoke. But when the wind blows, the smoke changes direction, and I see nothing but wisps of color.

A silvery fog rolls in. Hints of the shore peek through here and there, but it is difficult to see. Ann runs to the side of the ship.

"Listen, do you hear it? That lovely song is back!"

It takes a moment, but now I hear it. The song is faint but beautiful. It seeps into my veins and runs through me, making me feel warm and light.

"Look! In the water!" Ann shouts.

One by one, three bald heads emerge. They are women like none I've ever seen before. Their bodies shimmer faintly with luminescent scales that glow pink, brown, and peach. When they lift their hands from the water, I can see the faint webbing between the long fingers. They are mesmerizing, and I find I can't stop staring. I feel giddy with their song. Felicity and Ann laugh and crowd the side of the boat, trying to get closer. Pippa and I join them. The webbed hands stroke the great barge as if it were a child's hair. The gorgon does not slow. The tangled mass of snakes hisses wildly.

Ann reaches a hand down, but she cannot reach. "Oh, I wish I could touch them," she says.

"Why can't we?" Pippa asks. "Gorgon, lower the plank, if you please."

The gorgon does not answer and does not slow.

The women are so beautiful; their song is so lovely.

"Gorgon," I say. "Lower the plank."

The snakes writhe as if in pain. "Is that your wish, Most High?"

"Yes, it is my wish."

The great ship slows and the plank is lowered till it hovers just above the water. Our skirts gathered in our hands, we rush out and crouch down, looking for signs of them.

"Where are they?" Ann asks.

"I don't know," I say.

Felicity's on all fours, the ends of her hair trailing in the water. "Perhaps they've gone."

I stand, trying to peer through the fog. Something cold and wet caresses my ankle. I shriek and wobble just as the creature's webbed hand curves away from my leg, leaving sparkling scales on my stocking.

"Oh, no! I've scared it away," I say. Its mermaid-like body slips under the plank and disappears.

The surface of the river is covered in a thick, oily sheen. After a moment, the creatures emerge once more. They seem as fascinated by us as we are by them. They bob in the small currents, their strange hands moving back and forth, back and forth.

Ann gets down on her knees. "Hello."

One of the creatures moves close and begins to sing.

"Oh, how lovely," Ann says.

Indeed, their song is so sweet, I want to follow them into the water and hear it forever. A crowd of them has gathered, six, then seven, then ten of them. With each addition, the song grows, becomes more powerful. I am drowning in its beauty.

One creature attaches herself to the boat. She meets my gaze. Her eyes are huge, like mirrors of the ocean itself. I look into them and see myself falling fast into the deep, where all light vanishes. She reaches up to stroke my face. Her song floats about my face.

"Gemma! Don't!" I'm vaguely aware of Pippa calling my name, but it blends into the song and becomes a melody inviting me into the river. *Gemma . . . Gemma . . . Gemma . . .*

Pippa yanks me back rudely and we fall to the plank in a pile. The nymphs' song becomes a fierce shriek that sends gooseflesh rushing up my back.

"Wh-what?" I ask, as if waking from a dream.

"That thing nearly pulled you under!" Pippa says. Her eyes widen. "Ann!" she shouts.

Ann has slipped both legs over the side of the plank. The most ecstatic smile crosses her lips as one of the things strokes her leg and sings so sweetly it would break the heart. Felicity reaches a hand out, her fingers inches from the webbed hands of two creatures.

"No!" Pippa and I shout in unison.

I grab Ann as Pippa ropes her arms round Felicity. They struggle against us, but we pull them back.

The creatures let loose another horrible screech. In a rage, they grab at the plank as if they mean to shake us into the water or rip it off completely.

Ann cowers in Pippa's arms while Felicity kicks at their hands with her boots.

"Gorgon!" I shout. "Help us!"

"Omata!" It's the gorgon's voice now, booming and commanding. "Omata! Leave them be or we shall use the nets!"

The creatures scream and back away. They look at us with disappointment before slipping slowly under the water again. There is nothing but an oily sheen on the surface to prove they've been here. I practically push the others onto the boat.

"Gorgon, lift the plank!" I shout.

"As you wish," she answers, pulling up the heavy wing. The bald, shiny women do not like this. They screech again.

"What are those things?" I say, panting.

"Water nymphs," the gorgon answers, as if I see them daily for tea. "They are fascinated by your skin."

"Are they harmless?" Ann says, rubbing at the colorful scales on her stocking.

"That depends," the gorgon says.

Felicity stares down at the water. "Depends on what?"

The gorgon continues. "On how bewitching they find you. If they are particularly enchanted, they'll try to lure you away with them to their pond. Once they have you trapped, they will take your skin."

When I realize how close I came to following them into the depths, I'm shaking all over.

"I want to go back," Ann whimpers.

So do I. "Gorgon, take us back to the garden at once," I order.

"As you wish," she says.

Behind us, I see the water nymphs poking above the churning surface, their glistening heads bobbing on the water like jewels from a lost treasure. A snippet of their beautiful song finds us, and for a moment, I drift toward the edge of the ship, wanting once again to dive under. We pull forward with a lurch, moving away from them, and their song turns to rage, a sound like birds deprived of food.

"Stop it," I say under my breath, willing it to end. "Why won't they stop?"

"They expected a gift, a token for the journey," the gorgon answers.

"What sort of gift?" I ask.

"One of you."

"That's horrible," I say.

"Yesss," the gorgon hisses. "You have made them unhappy, I'm afraid. They can be rather vicious when cross. And they hold a grudge."

The thought of those cold, wet hands pulling one of us under makes me shiver.

"Are there more of these nymphs out there?" Pippa asks, her pale face illuminated by the orange sky.

"Yesss," the gorgon says. "But I shouldn't worry too much about them. They can only come for you if you're in the water."

There's cold comfort.

The fog clears. My limbs are shaky, as if I have run for a very long time. The four of us lie on the floor of the boat, looking up at the bright sky.

"How will we find the Temple if these creatures use their own magic against us?" Ann asks.

"I don't know," I say.

This is not the beautiful garden my mother showed me. It is quite obvious now that the realms beyond that garden are no place to let down my guard.

"Gorgon," I ask when all is calm again and the garden is in sight, "is it true that you're imprisoned on this barge as punishment?"

"Yes," comes the hissing answer.

"By whose magic?"

"The Order's."

"But why?"

The great barge creaks and groans on the water. "It was I who led my people against the Order during the rebellion."

The snakes of her head writhe and reach. One ropes itself around the pointed bow, its tongue inches from my hand. I pull back to a safer distance.

"Are you still loyal to the Order?" I ask.

"Yessss," comes the answer. But it is not immediate, like a response compelled by magic. There is a moment's hesitation. She stopped to *think*. And I realize that Philon's warning is apt.

"Gorgon, did you know the water nymphs were near?"

"Yessss," she says.

"Why didn't you warn us?"

"You didn't ask." And with that, we reach the garden, where the large green beast closes her eyes.

Pippa squeezes us tightly, not wanting to let go. "Must you hurry back? When can you come again?"

"As soon as possible," Felicity assures her. "Don't let anything get you, Pip."

"I shan't," Pippa says. She takes my hands. "Gemma, I saved your life today."

"Yes, you did. Thank you."

"I suppose that binds us, doesn't it? Like a promise?"

"I suppose so," I say uneasily.

Pippa gives me a kiss on the cheek. "Come back soon as you can!"

The door of light flares to life, and we leave her waving to us like the last fleeting image of a dream before waking.

Back in the bedchamber, we take stock of ourselves. We are all fine, if a bit shaken, and ready to resume our places for tea.

"Do you feel it?" Felicity asks as we clamber down the stairs. I nod. The magic courses through me. My blood pumps faster, and every sense is keener for it. It is astonishing, like being lit from within. From behind the closed doors of the dining room, I can hear snippets of conversations, can feel the wants and desires, the petty jealousies and disappointments of every beating heart till I am forced to will them away.

"Ah, here is our Miss Bradshaw now," the ample woman says as we enter the room. "We understand that you were trained by the finest masters in all of Russia as a child, and that this is how the czarina's family knew at once you were their long-lost relative, by your lovely voice. Won't you please do us the honor of singing one song?"

This story grows as wild as the magic of the realms with each telling.

"Yes, you simply must," Felicity says, taking Ann's arm. "Use the magic," she whispers.

"Felicity!" I whisper back. "We're not supposed to . . ."

"We must! We can't just abandon Ann."

Ann gives me a pleading look.

"Just this once," Felicity says.

"Just this once," I repeat.

Ann turns back to the crowd, smiling. "I would be happy to sing."

She waits for the rustling of skirts to subside as the women take their seats. Then she closes her eyes. I can feel her concentrating, drawing on the magic. It's as if we are joined by it, working in concert to create this illusion. Ann opens her mouth to sing. She has a lovely voice quite naturally, but the music that tumbles out of her is very powerful and seductive. It takes me a moment to recognize the language. She's singing in Russian, a language she doesn't actually know. It is a very nice touch.

The women of the Alexandra are held in thrall. When Ann reaches the song's crescendo, a few dab at their eyes, so moved are they. As Ann finishes with a small, respectful curtsy, the women applaud and rush to praise her. Ann basks in their adoration.

Lady Denby strides to Ann's side and offers her congratulations. "Lady Denby, how wonderful you look," Felicity's mother says. Lady Denby nods but does not respond. The slight is noted by everyone. There is an uncomfortable silence in the room.

Lady Denby regards Ann coolly. "You say you are a relation of the Duke of Chesterfield?"

"Y-yes," Ann stammers.

"Strange. I don't believe I've ever met the duke."

I feel a tug, a change in the air. The magic. When I look over, Felicity has her eyes closed in concentration, and a faint smile curves those full lips. Suddenly, Lady Denby breaks wind with an enormous crackling sound. There is no hiding the shock and horror on her face as she realizes what she's done. She breaks wind again, and several of the women clear their throats and look away as if they can pretend not to notice the offense. For her part, Lady Denby excuses herself, muttering something about being indisposed on her way out.

"Felicity, that was terrible of you!" I whisper.

"Why?" she asks, cool as can be. "She is an old windbag, after all."

Now that Lady Denby has left, people gravitate to Ann and Mrs. Worthington, congratulating Felicity's mother for having such an esteemed guest in her home. Invitations for tea, dinner, calls are offered in abundance. The slight has been forgotten.

"I shall never be powerless again," Felicity says, though I don't know exactly what she means by it, and she doesn't offer to explain.

CHAPTER NINETEEN

BY THE TIME I RETURN HOME, NIGHT IS SETTLING over London like a balm, gaslight smoothing the rough edges into a hazy dark sameness. The house is quiet. Grandmama is off to play cards with her friends. Father's sleeping fitfully in his chair, his book open upon his lap. My father, haunted even in his dreams.

The last remnants of the magic flow through me. I close the doors and lay my hand on his brow. Just once, as Felicity said. That's all I need. I'm not using this power for a new ball gown; I'm using it to heal my father. How can that possibly be wrong?

But how to begin? Mother told me I must concentrate. I must be sure of what I want and intend. I close my eyes and let my thoughts go to my father, to curing him of his affliction.

"I wish to heal my father," I say. "I wish that he will never again have a desire for laudanum." My hands tingle. Something is happening. Fast as a swollen stream, the magic rages through me and into Father. He arches his back with it. My eyes still shut, I see clouds race across the sky, see Father laughing and healthy again. He sweeps me into a playful dance and offers Christmas boxes to all the servants, whose eyes light up in gratitude and goodwill. This is the father I knew. I did not realize how much I missed him till now. Tears wet my face.

Father stops moaning in the chair. I am ready to move my hand from him but cannot. There is one last thing, quick as a magician's trick. I see a man's face, his eyes lined in black. "Thank you, poppet," he snarls. And then I am free.

The candles on the Christmas tree burn brightly. I'm shaking, perspiring from the effort. Father is so peaceful and quiet I fear I have killed him.

"Father?" I say gently. When he does not rouse, I shake him. "Father!"

He blinks, surprised to see me so agitated. "Hello, darling. Dozed off, did I?"

"Yes," I say, watching him closely.

He touches his fingers to his forehead. "Such strange dreams I had."

"What, Father? What did you dream?"

"I . . . I can't recall. Well, I'm awake now. And I'm suddenly famished. Have I slept through tea? I shall have to throw myself upon the mercy of our dear cook." He crosses the room with an energetic stride. In a moment, I hear Father's booming voice and the cook laughing. It is such a lovely sound that I find I'm crying.

"Thank you," I say to no one in particular. "Thank you for helping me to make him well."

When I enter the kitchen, Father is seated at a small table, taking bites of roast duck and relish on bread, while thrilling our cook and a maid of all work with his adventures. "There I was, face to face with the biggest cobra you could imagine—rising up tall as a sapling with a neck fat as a man's arm."

"Gracious me," the cook says, hanging on every word. "What ever did you do, sir?"

"I said, 'Here now, my good fellow, you don't want to eat me. I'm nothing but gristle. Take my associate, Mr. Robbins.'"

"Oh, you didn't, sir!"

"I did." Father is enjoying his audience. He jumps up to act out the rest like a pantomime. "He went for Robbins straightaway. I'd only an instant to act. Quiet as a church mouse, I pulled out my machete and *sliced* through the cobra just before he would have struck old Robbins and killed him."

The maid, a girl of about my age, gasps. Beneath the bit of soot on her nose, she's quite lovely.

"He was most delicious." Father sits with a satisfied smile. I am so happy to see him this way, I could listen to his stories all night.

"Oh, sir, that was thrilling. The adventures you've had." The cook hands a plate to the maid. "Here. Take this to Mr. Kartik for me."

"Mr. Kartik?" I say, feeling as if I should faint.

"Yes," Father says, sopping up his relish. "Kartik. Our new coachman."

"I'll go, if you don't mind," I say, taking the plate from the rather disappointed-looking maid. "I should like to meet our Mr. Kartik."

Before anyone can object, I make my way to the mews, passing a charwoman covered in soot and a weary laundress, her hands pressed to her back. There are entire families living in the rooms above these stables. It is hard to imagine. The smell has me pressing my hand to my nose. Our carriage house is the fourth down on the right. A groom tends Father's two horses. Seeing me, the young boy removes his cap. "Evenin', miss."

"I'm looking for Mr. Kartik," I say.

" 'E's over there, miss, by the carriage."

I go around the side of it and there he is, shining the already clean coach with a rag. He's been given a proper uniform— trousers, shoes, a striped waistcoat, a fine shirt, and a hat. His curls have been oiled into obedience. He looks very much the gentleman. It quite takes my breath away.

I clear my throat. He turns and sees me, a wicked grin lighting up his face.

"How do you do?" I say quite formally for the benefit of the groom, who is spying on us this very instant.

Kartik catches on. "Good evening, miss. Willie!" he calls out to the boy.

"Yes, Mr. Kartik?"

"Be a good lad and stretch Ginger's legs, will you?"

The boy leads the chestnut horse from the stable.

"What do you think of my new suit?" Kartik asks.

"Don't you think it's rather bold of you to take a job as our coachman?" I whisper.

"I said that I would be close."

"So you did. How ever did you arrange it?"

"The Rakshana have their ways." The Rakshana. Of course. It is quiet. I can hear Ginger snorting softly on the other side of the stables.

"Well," I say.

"Well," Kartik echoes.

"Here we are."

"Yes. It was good of you to come see me. You look well."

I should die from politeness. "I've brought your supper," I say, offering the plate.

"Thank you," he says, pulling over a stool for me and removing the volume of *The Odyssey* that sits atop it. He perches on the steps of the carriage. "I suppose Emily isn't coming, then."

"Who is Emily?" I ask.

"The maid. She was to bring my dinner. She seems a most congenial girl."

My cheeks flush. "And you have decided her character after knowing her but a day."

"Yes," he says, peeling the flesh from a precious orange, no doubt put there by the congenial Emily. I wonder if Kartik could ever think of me as an ordinary girl, someone to hope for, to long for, to consider "congenial."

"Have you any news about the Temple?" he says, without looking up.

"We visited a place today called the Forest of Lights," I tell him. "I met a creature called Philon. It did not know where to find the Temple, but it offered help."

"What sort of help?"

"Weapons."

Kartik's eyes narrow. "It felt you would need them?"

"Yes. Philon gave us magic arrows. I'm useless with them, but Feli—Miss Worthington is rather skilled. She—"

"What did it ask in return?" Kartik's stare is penetrating.

"A share of the magic when we find the Temple."

"You refused, of course." When I do not answer, Kartik tosses the orange onto his plate in disgust. "You made an alliance with creatures from the realms?"

"I didn't say that!" I snap. It isn't the truth, but it isn't a lie, either. "If I'm not doing this to your liking, why don't you go?"

"You know we cannot enter the realms."

"So then I suppose you will have to trust that I am doing all I can."

"I trust you," he answers softly.

The small sounds of night surround us, tiny creatures scurrying here and there, looking for food and warmth.

"Did you know that the Rakshana and the Order were once lovers?" I ask.

"No, I didn't," Kartik says after a few seconds' hesitation. "How . . . interesting."

"Yes. It is."

He removes a stray white thread of pith from the orange and offers me a freshly plucked section.

"Thank you," I say, taking the fruit from his fingers and placing it on my tongue. It is very sweet.

"You're welcome." He gives me a little smile. We sit for a moment, savoring the orange. "Do you ever . . ."

"What?"

"I wondered if you have ever seen Amar there in the realms?"

"No," I answer. "I've never seen him."

Some sort of relief washes over Kartik. "He must have already crossed over then, don't you think?"

"Yes, I suppose so."

"What are the realms like?" he asks.

"Some of it is beautiful. So beautiful you don't ever want to leave it. In the garden, you can turn stones to butterflies or have a gown of silver thread that sings or . . . or whatever you wish."

Kartik smiles at this. "Go on."

"There is a ship, like a Viking vessel, with a gorgon's head attached. She took us through a wall of golden water that left sparkles of gold all over our skin."

"Like the gold in your hair?"

"Much finer," I say, blushing, for it's most unlike Kartik to notice anything about me.

"There are some parts that are not as nice. Strange creatures—horrid things. I suppose that's why I must bind the magic, so that they cannot wield it."

Kartik's smile disappears. "Yes. I suppose so. Miss Doyle?"

"Yes?"

"Do you think—that is, what if you were to stay there, in the realms, once you'd found the Temple?"

"What do you mean?"

Kartik rubs his fingers where the juice of the orange has turned them a chalky white. "It sounds like a very fine place to hide."

"That's an odd thing to say."

"I meant live. A fine place to live, don't you think?"

Sometimes I don't understand Kartik at all.

A lantern throws its light over the straw and dirt at our feet. The lovely kitchen maid appears out of nowhere, a look of astonishment on her face. "Beggin' your pardon, miss. I forgot to bring Mr. Kartik his coffee."

"I was just leaving," I say to her, practically leaping to my feet. I assume this is the aforementioned Emily. "Thank you for that, um, most, most informative, ah, instruction in . . . in . . ."

"Carriage safety?" Kartik offers.

"Yes. One cannot be too careful about such things. Good night to you," I say.

"Good night," he answers. Emily does not make any effort to leave. And as I stride past the horses, I hear her laughing gently—girlishly—at something Kartik has said.

Ginger snorts at me.

"It is impolite to stare," I say to her, before running up to my room to sulk in private.

<hr>

Simon's box sits on a table beside my bed. I pull open the false bottom and see the wicked brown bottle lying there.

"You shan't be needed again," I say. The box slides easily into a corner of my cupboard, where it is lost among petticoats and dress hems. From my window, I can see the lanterns of the mews and our carriage house. I see Emily returning from the stable, her lantern in hand. The light catches her face as she looks back to smile at Kartik, who waves to her. He glances up and I duck out of sight, quickly extinguishing my lamp. The room is swallowed in shadow.

Why should it bother me so that Kartik fancies Emily? What are we to each other but a duty? That, I suppose, is what bothers me. Oh, I should forget this business with Kartik. It is foolish.

Tomorrow is a new day, December 17. I shall dine with Simon Middleton. I will do my best to charm his mother and not make a nuisance of myself. After that, I'll go about finding the Temple, but for one evening, one glorious, carefree evening, I intend to wear a fine gown and enjoy the handsome company of Simon Middleton.

"How do you do, Mr. Middleton?" I say to the air. "No," I answer, lowering my voice, "How do you do, Miss Doyle?" "Why, I'm absolutely splendid, Mr.—"

The pain has me in its grip. I can't breathe. God! I can't breathe! No, no, no, please leave me alone, please! It's no use. I'm pulled out like the tide, slipping into a vision. I don't want to open my eyes. I know they're there. I can feel them. I can hear them.

"Come with us . . . ," they whisper.

I open one eye, then the other. There they are, those three ghostly girls. They seem so lost, so sad, with their pallid skin, the dark shadows carved into their cheeks.

"We've something to show you. . . ."

One of them puts her hand on my shoulder. I stiffen and feel myself falling into the vision. I don't know where we are. A castle of some sort, a great ruined fortress of stone. Deep green moss grows up the side of it. Bright laughter floats out, and through the tall, arched windows, I can see flashes of white. They're girls playing. Not just any girls—the girls in white. But how lovely they look, so fresh and alive and merry!

"Catch me if you can!" one shouts, and my heart aches, for that was the game my mother played with me as a child. The other two girls jump out from behind a wall, startling her. They laugh at this. "Eleanor!" all three call out. "Where are you? It's time! We shall have the power—she's promised."

They run toward the cliff's edge; the sea churns below. The girls step across rocks, outlined by the gray sky like Greek statues come to life. They're laughing, so happy, so happy.

"Come, don't dawdle!" they shout merrily to the fourth girl. I can't see her very well. But I see the woman in the dark green cloak coming fast, can see her long, wide sleeves catching the wind. The woman takes the hand of the girl who lags behind.

"Is it time?" the others shout.

"Yes," the woman in the green cloak shouts back. Holding the girl's hand fast in hers, she closes her eyes and raises both their hands toward the sea. She's muttering something. No— she's summoning something! Terror rises in me like nausea, making me gag. It's coming up from the sea, and she's calling it! The girls scream in terror. But the woman in green does not open her eyes. She does not stop.

Why are they showing me this? I want to get away! Must get away from that thing, from their terror. I'm back in my room. The girls hover near. Their pointed boots move across the floor—*scrape, scrape, scrape*. I think I shall go mad from it.

"Why?" I gasp, trying not to vomit. "Why?"

"*She lies . . . ,*" they whisper. "*Don't trust her . . . don't trust her . . . don't trust her . . .*"

"Who?" I pant, but they are gone. The pressure leaves me. I'm struggling for breath, my eyes teary, my nose running. I can't bear these horrible visions. And I don't understand them. Don't trust whom? Why shouldn't I trust her?

But there was something different about this vision, a detail I remember now. Something about the woman's hand. She wore a ring of some kind, something unusual. It takes me a moment on the floor to regain my senses. And then I think I know what it was.

The ring on the woman's hand was in the shape of two intertwined snakes.

I've seen that ring before—in the case beneath Miss McCleethy's bed.

"GEMMA, DON'T PLAY WITH YOUR HAIR SO," Grandmama tuts from her perch beside me in our carriage.

"Oh," I say. I've been so preoccupied with my thoughts that I haven't noticed I've been twirling a tiny tendril of hair round and round my finger. All day long, I've been lost, thinking of last night's vision and what it means. A woman adorned with a snake ring. Miss McCleethy has a snake ring. But what connection could she have to that cloaked woman or to the girls? These visions make no sense. Who are these girls, and why do they need my help? What are they trying to show me?

I must push these thoughts away for now. I've a party to attend, and the thought of facing the formidable Lady Denby is more frightening than any vision I could conjure.

I count three additional carriages when we arrive at Simon's house, which is a magnificent picture of brick and light. Across the lane, Hyde Park is a dark smudge, lost in the incandescent haze of the gaslights that cast us in foggy halos, making us seem brighter than we are, heaven's borrowed things. Kartik takes my hand, helping me down. I step on the front of my gown, tumbling against him. He catches me round the waist, and for a second, I'm in his embrace.

"Steady there, Miss Doyle," he says, helping me to my feet.

"Yes, thank you, Mr. Kartik."

"Old Potts never would have made such a catch, I daresay," Father teases Tom. I look back to see Kartik gazing at me in my blue gown and velvet coat as if I were someone altogether different, a stranger to him.

Father takes my arm and walks me to the door. Clean-shaven, in white tie and gloves, he is almost the father I remember.

"You look very handsome, Papa," I say.

The twinkle is back in his eyes. "Smoke and mirrors," he says with a wink. "Smoke and mirrors."

That is my fear. How long will the magic work? No, I shan't worry about that now. It has worked, and he is my own dear father again, and in a moment, I shall have dinner with a handsome young man who finds me interesting, for some reason.

We are greeted by a phalanx of footmen and maids in uniforms so pressed their creases could draw blood. It seems there is a servant for everything. Grandmama is beside herself with excitement. If she were to stand any straighter, her spine might snap. We're ushered into a very large parlor. Simon stands by the fire, deep in conversation with two gentlemen. He gives me a wolfish grin. I immediately look off into the distance, as if I have just noticed the papered walls and am fascinated beyond measure, though my heart beats out a new rhythm: *He likes me;*

he likes me; he likes me. I've little time to swoon. Lady Denby swoops through the room making introductions, her stiff skirts rustling with every step. She greets a gentleman warmly but is rather cool to his wife.

If Lady Denby likes you, you are set for life. If she finds you wanting in any way, you are shunned.

My tongue cleaves to the roof of my mouth. I cannot swallow. She gives me a solid looking-over as she approaches. Simon's beside her in an instant.

"Mother, may I present Mr. John Doyle; his mother, Mrs. William Doyle; Mr. Thomas Doyle; and Miss Gemma Doyle. Thomas is a chum from my Eton days. He's currently a clinical assistant under Dr. Smith at Bethlem Hospital," Simon adds.

His mother is smitten with Tom immediately. "Why, Dr. Smith is an old friend. Tell me, is it true you have a patient who was once a member of Parliament?" she asks, hoping for a bit of gossip.

"Madam, if we confined the lunatics of Parliament, there'd be no Parliament left," Father jokes, forgetting that Simon's father is a member himself. I may die.

Surprisingly, Lady Denby laughs at this. "Oh, Mr. Doyle! You are quite the wit." The breath leaves my body in a small whoosh that I hope cannot be detected.

The butler announces dinner. Lady Denby rounds up her guests like a seasoned general marshaling his troops for battle. I am doing my best to remember all Mrs. Nightwing has taught me about manners. I'm deathly afraid I'll commit some hideous faux pas and cast my family into enduring shame.

"Shall we?" Simon offers his arm and I loop mine through his. I've never taken the arm of a man who was not my blood relative. We keep a respectful distance between us, but that does nothing to stop the current coursing through me.

After the soup, we're given roast pork. The sight of a pig on a platter with an apple in its mouth does nothing to whet my appetite. While the others prattle on about country estates, fox hunting, and the problem of finding good help, Simon whispers, "I hear he was a very disagreeable pig. Always complaining. Never a nice word for anyone. He once bit a duckling in spite. I shouldn't feel guilty about eating him if I were you."

I smile. Lady Denby's voice breaks the moment. "Miss Doyle, there is something familiar about you."

"I—I was a guest of Mrs. Worthington's at the Alexandra yesterday, to hear Miss Bradshaw sing."

"Miss Bradshaw sang?" Tom is delighted to hear of Ann's social rise. "How delightful."

My eyes are on Lady Denby, who says, "Yes, strange business that. Mr. Middleton," she says, addressing her husband, "have you ever met the Duke of Chesterfield?"

"Can't say as I have, unless he's a hunting man."

Lady Denby purses her lips as if mulling something over, then says, "I hear you are attending Spence?"

"Yes, Lady Denby," I answer nervously.

"How do you find it?" she inquires, taking a serving of roast potatoes. I feel like an insect under the intense focus of the microscope.

"It is a most agreeable school," I say, averting my eyes.

"Of course, she had a proper English governess while in India," Grandmama interjects, ever afraid of social impropriety. "I did fear sending her away from home, but I was assured that Spence was a fine finishing school."

"What do you think, Miss Doyle? Are you inclined to believe that young ladies should be taught Latin and Greek these days?" Lady Denby asks.

It is not an innocent question. She is testing me, I am sure. I take a deep breath. "I believe it is just as important for daughters to be learned as it is for sons. Else how can we be able wives and mothers?" It is the safest answer I can muster.

Lady Denby gives a warm smile. "I quite agree, Miss Doyle. What a sensible girl you are."

I breathe a small sigh of relief.

"I can see why my boy is enchanted," Lord Denby announces.

A flush works its way into my cheeks, and I find I cannot look at anyone. I have to fight to keep a ridiculous grin from surfacing. I have only one giddy thought in my head: Simon Middleton, a boy of such perfection, likes me, the strange and vexing Gemma Doyle.

Low chuckling ripples through the assembled guests. "Now you've done it," a mustachioed gentleman quips. "She'll never come back."

"Oh, really, Mr. Conrad," Lady Denby chides playfully. I do not see why Felicity thinks so badly of Lady Denby. She seems rather nice to me, and I quite like her.

The evening passes like a happy dream. I have not felt so

peaceful and content since before Mother died. Seeing Father come alive again is heaven, and I am finally glad for this strange, beautiful power. During the dinner, he is his old charming self, entertaining Lady Denby and Simon with tales of India. Grandmama's face, usually lined with worry, is serene tonight, and Tom is actually likeable, if such a thing could be said of him. Of course, he thinks he has cured Father, and for once, I am in no mood to contradict him. It means so much to see my family enjoying themselves. I want to preserve this happy bubble of time, this feeling that I belong somewhere. That I am wanted. I want this night to go on forever.

The talk at the table turns to Bethlem. Tom is holding court with tales of his duties there. ". . . he insisted that he was the emperor of West Sussex and as such, should be allowed an extra serving of meat. When I refused, he promised he would have me beheaded."

"Dear me," Lady Denby laughs.

"You'd best keep your wits about you, young man. Wouldn't want to wake up with no head," Simon's father says. He has Simon's kind blue eyes.

"Or would that be an improvement in your case, my good man?" Simon taunts Tom, who pretends to be affronted.

"Oh, ho! *Touché!*"

"Now then, my son must keep his head," Father says, looking quite serious. "I paid a dear amount for his new hat, and I shan't get it back." Everyone erupts in laughter.

Grandmama speaks up. "Is it true that Bethlem holds public dances fortnightly, Lady Denby?"

"Yes indeed. It is ever so rejuvenating for them to be amongst the public, to remember the social niceties. My husband and I have gone on several occasions. There's another dance in a week's time. You must come as our guests."

"We'd be delighted," Grandmama says, answering for us all, as she so often does.

My face aches from trying to wear such a pleasant expression at all times. Is it time to don my gloves again? Should I eat the last of my dessert as I'd desperately like or leave half to show my delicate appetite? I do not want to make a misstep, not tonight.

"Oh, do tell us another tale," Lady Denby begs Tom.

"Yes, do," Simon says. "Else I'll be forced to talk of the time I looked into the eyes of an unhappy pheasant in the country and you'll all be bored to catatonia." Simon looks at me again. I find I like it when he looks for my reaction. I like being courted. It is rather a powerful feeling.

"Ah, let's see . . . ," Tom says, thinking. "There was Mr. Waltham, who claimed he could hear what was happening inside each house as he passed—that the very stones spoke to him. I am happy to say that he was cured and released just last month."

"Bravo!" Simon's father exclaims. "Nothing science and man can't overcome in time."

"Exactly," Tom says, thrilled to find a friend in so high a place.

"What else?" a lady in a peach silk gown asks.

"There's Mrs. Sommers, who seems to think this life is all a dream and that she sees spirits in her room at night."

"Poor dear," Grandmama says by habit.

These stories are stealing away my happiness. What would my dinner companions think if they knew that I see visions and visit other realms?

Tom continues. "There is Nell Hawkins, age nineteen. Diagnosed with acute mania while away at school."

"You see?" the mustachioed gentleman says, wagging his finger. "The female constitution cannot stand up to the rigors of a formal education. Nothing good can come of it."

"Oh, Mr. Conrad," his wife chides playfully. "Do go on, Mr. Doyle."

"Nell Hawkins suffers from delusions," Tom says, preening.

Father joins in. "Thinks she's Joan of Arc, does she?"

"No, that would be Mr. Jernigan in ward M1B. Miss Hawkins is unique. She suffers from the delusion that she is part of some mystical sect of sorceresses called the Order."

The room narrows. My heart races. From far away I hear myself ask, "The Order?"

"Yes. She claims that she knows the secrets of a place called the realms, and that a woman named Circe wants all the power. She claims she has driven herself mad in an attempt to keep her mind clouded and away from Circe's grasp." Tom shakes his head. "A most difficult case."

"I agree with you, Mr. Conrad, too much formal education is not good for our daughters. And this is the cost. I'm so grateful that Spence stresses the essentials of a lady's training." Grandmama shoves a rather large bite of chocolate cream into her mouth.

It is all I can do not to bolt from the table, for I'm trembling all over. Somewhere in Bethlem Hospital sits a girl who might be able to tell me everything I need to know, and I must find a way to get to her.

"What can be done for such a case?" Mr. Conrad asks.

"She does take some comfort from poetry. The nurses read to her when they can."

"Perhaps I could read poetry to her?" I volunteer, hoping I don't sound as desperate as I feel. I would do anything to see this girl. "Perhaps she would find some comfort in speaking with a girl of her own age, that is."

Simon's father raises his wine to me. "Our Miss Doyle is a very kind soul."

"She is our angel," Father says.

No, I'm not. I am a wretched girl for deceiving them so, but I must see Nell Hawkins.

"Very well, then," Tom says grudgingly. "I shall take you tomorrow afternoon."

CHAPTER
TWENTY-ONE

AFTER DESSERT HAS BEEN CLEARED AWAY, THE MEN are ready to have their brandy and cigars in the study while the women retire to the parlor for tea and talk.

"Mother, I believe Miss Doyle would like to see the portrait of Grandfather," Simon says, catching us on our way in. I've heard no mention of this painting.

"Yes, of course. We shall all go," Lady Denby says.

Simon's smug smile falters. "I should hate to take you away from the fire, Mother. It is a bit drafty in the library, you know."

"Nonsense, we shall bring our shawls and be fine. You really must see dear George—he was painted by a Cotswold portraitist of great renown."

I don't know what has just occurred, but I gather that Simon has lost.

"Here we are." Lady Denby leads us into a spacious room dominated by a painting as large as a door. It is a hideously ornate depiction of a barrel-chested man astride a horse. He wears a red jacket and looks every bit the country gentleman off to the hunt. At his heels sit two obedient dogs.

Simon nods to it. "Miss Doyle, may I present my grandfather, Cornelius George Basil Middleton, Viscount of Denby."

Grandmama makes a spectacle of herself fawning over it, though all she knows of art could fit inside a thimble. Still, it makes Lady Denby proud. She moves on to an objet d'art upon a mantel, forcing a maid who was cleaning a grate to stand waiting, brush in sooty hand.

"What a beautiful painting," I say diplomatically.

Simon raises an eyebrow. "If by beautiful you mean to say silly, overdone, and grotesque, then I accept your compliment."

I stifle a laugh. "The dogs are quite distinguished-looking."

Simon stands beside me, and I feel that strange current again. He cocks his head, taking in my comment and the painting. "Yes. In fact, perhaps I could claim *them* as kin instead." His eyes are so blue. And his smile is so warm. We are standing only inches apart. From the corner of my eye, I can see Grandmama and the others touring the room.

"How many of these have you read?" I ask, moving toward the bookshelves, pretending to be interested.

"Not many," Simon says, falling into step. "I've a great many hobbies. They take up much of my time. It's my duty to see after our interest in Denby, the manor and such."

"Yes, of course," I say, continuing my slow promenade.

"Are you attending Admiral and Lady Worthington's Christmas ball, by any chance?"

"Yes, I am," I say, walking to the windows overlooking the street.

"I shall be there as well." He catches up. Here we are, side by side again.

"Oh," I say. "How nice."

"Perhaps you will save me a dance?" he asks shyly.

"Yes," I say, smiling. "Perhaps I will."

"I see you're not wearing your necklace this evening."

My hand springs to my bare neck. "You noticed my jewelry?"

Seeing his mother occupied, he whispers in my ear, "I noticed your neck. The necklace happened to be there. It is very unusual."

"It was my mother's," I say, still blushing from the bold compliment. "It was given to her by a village woman in India. A charm of protection. I'm afraid it didn't work for her."

"Perhaps it isn't for protection," Simon says.

I've never thought of that. "I can't imagine what else it could be for."

"What is your favorite color?" Simon asks.

"Purple," I answer. "Why do you ask?"

"No reason," he says, smiling. "I might have to invite your brother to my club. He seems a good fellow."

Ha! "I'm sure he would enjoy that." Tom would leap through rings of fire for the chance to go to Simon's club. It is the best in London.

Simon regards me for a moment. "You're not like other young ladies my mother trots before me."

"Oh?" I say, wincing, desperate to know how I'm different.

"There's something adventurous about you. I feel as if you have a great many secrets I should like to know."

Lady Denby notes us standing at the windows so close. I pretend to take an interest in a leather-bound copy of *Moby-Dick* that sits upon a side table. The spine crackles when I lift the cover, as if it's never been read. "Perhaps you wouldn't really want to know them," I say.

"How do you know?" Simon asks, repositioning a ceramic figurine of two cupids. "Offer me a test."

What can I say? That I suffer from the same delusions as poor Nell Hawkins but that they are not delusions at all? That I'm afraid I'm one step away from the madhouse myself? It would be so nice to confide in Simon and have him say, See, that wasn't so very bad now, was it? You're not mad. I believe you. I am with you.

I let the chance pass. "I have a third eye," I say breezily. "I'm a descendant of Atalanta. And my table manners are inexcusable."

Simon nods. "I suspected as much. That is why we're going to ask you to eat in the stable from now on as a precaution. You don't mind, do you?"

"Not at all." I close the book and turn away. "What terrible secrets do you have, Mr. Middleton?"

"Besides the gambling, carousing, and pillaging?" He falls into step behind me. "The truth?"

My heart skips a beat. "Yes," I say, turning to him at last. "The truth."

He stares into my eyes. "I'm frightfully dull."

"That isn't true," I say, moving away again, looking up at the enormous bookcases.

"I'm afraid it is. I am to find a suitable wife with a suitable fortune and carry on the family name. It's what they expect of me. My wishes don't enter into it at all. I'm sorry. That was far too forward of me. You don't need to hear my troubles."

"No, truly. I'm happy to listen." I am, strangely enough.

"Shall we retire to the parlor?" Lady Denby asks. With a sigh, the maid resumes her scrubbing once the ladies have gone. Simon and I follow slowly.

"Your flower is slipping, Miss Doyle." The rose, pinned to my hair, slides to my neck. I reach for it just as he does. Our fingers touch for a moment before I turn away.

"Thank you," I say, completely flustered.

"May I?" With great care, Simon secures the flower behind my ear. I should stop him, lest he think me too permissive. But I don't know what to say. I am reminded that Simon is nineteen, three years my senior. He knows things that I do not.

There's a tap at the window, followed by another, harder tap that makes me jump. "Who is throwing rocks?" Simon peers out into the hazy dark. He opens the glass. Cold air rushes in, raising gooseflesh on my arms. There is no one below that we can see.

"I should join the ladies. Grandmama will be worried about me."

Making a hasty retreat, I nearly trip over the maid, who never even looks up from her scrubbing.

It is well after midnight when we say our goodbyes and emerge into a night alive with stars and hope. The evening has been a wild jumble for me. There is the good—Simon. His family. The warmth they've shown me. My father regained. Then there is the sobering prospect of meeting Nell Hawkins at Bedlam to see if she holds the key to finding the Temple and Circe. And there is the curious—the rocks thrown against the window.

At the carriage, Kartik seems agitated. "A pleasant evening, miss?"

"Yes, very pleasant, thank you," I answer.

"So I noted," he mutters, helping me into the carriage and pulling away from the curb with a bit too much gusto. What ever is the matter with him?

Once my family is safely to bed, I don my coat and dash across cold, hard ground to the stables. Kartik sits reading *The Odyssey* and having a cup of hot tea. He is not alone. Emily sits near, listening to him read.

"Good evening," I say, marching in.

"Good evening," he says, standing.

Emily looks stricken. "Oh, miss, I was just . . . just . . ."

"Emily, I have some business to discuss with Mr. Kartik just now, if you wouldn't mind."

Like a shot, Emily is running for the house.

"What did you mean by your comment tonight?"

"I simply asked if you had a pleasant evening. With Mr. Muddleton."

"Middleton," I correct him. "He is a gentleman, you know."

"He looks like a fop."

"I'll thank you not to insult him. You know nothing about him."

"I don't like the way he looks at you. As if you were a piece of ripe fruit."

"He doesn't do anything of the sort. Wait a moment. How do you know how he looks at me? Were you spying on me?"

Chagrined, Kartik buries his nose in his book. "He did look at you that way. In the library."

"You threw those rocks against the window!"

Kartik jumps up, the book forgotten. "You allowed him to touch your hair!"

It's true. It was much too unladylike of me. I'm embarrassed but I'm not about to let on to Kartik. "I do have something to tell you, if you can stop feeling sorry for yourself long enough to hear it."

Kartik scoffs. "I'm not feeling sorry for myself."

"A good night to you, then."

"Wait!" Kartik takes a step after me. I'm gloating. It is unattractive, but there it is. "I'm sorry. I promise to be on my very best behavior," he says. He falls to his knees dramatically and pulls an acorn from the ground, holding it to his neck. "I beg of you, Miss Doyle. Tell me or I shall be forced to kill myself with this mighty weapon."

"Oh, do get up," I say, laughing in spite of myself. "Tom has a patient at Bethlem. Nell Hawkins. He says she suffers from delusions."

"That would explain her confinement in Bethlem." He gives me a smug smile. When I do not return it, he says contritely, "Sorry. Please go on."

"She claims she's a member of the Order, and that a woman named Circe is trying to find her. She says she's driven herself mad to keep Circe from getting to her."

The smirk vanishes. "You must see Nell Hawkins straightaway."

"Yes, I've arranged it already. Tomorrow, around noon, I shall read poetry to Nell Hawkins and find out what she knows about the Temple. Was he really looking at me that way?"

"What way?"

"Like a piece of ripe fruit?"

"You'd best be on your guard with him," Kartik says.

He's jealous! Kartik is jealous and Simon finds me . . . delicious? I am a bit giddy. And confused. But no, mostly giddy, I find.

"I am quite able to look after myself," I say. I turn smartly on my heel and smack directly into the wall, raising a bump upon my forehead that will probably remain forever.

CHAPTER
TWENTY-TWO

THE FOLLOWING AFTERNOON, DRESSED IN MY GRAY flannel suit and a felt hat, I join Tom at Bethlem Royal Hospital. The building is impressive. The front has a portico supported by six white columns. A windowed dome rests on top like a bobby's hat. I can only hope that Tom cannot hear the hammering of my heart. With luck, Miss Hawkins will unlock the mystery of the Temple for me.

"You look quite presentable, Gemma, save for that bruise on your forehead," Tom says, peering at it. "How did you get that?"

"It's nothing," I say, pushing my hat lower on my forehead.

"No matter. You shall be the prettiest girl in Bethlem," Tom says.

Ah, lovely to know that I shall be prettier than all the lunatics. I've got that going for me, at least. Poor Tom. He means well. He's been much nicer to me since Simon's obvious interest. It's almost as if I'm human in his eyes. Perish the thought.

I decide to pity him and answer without an unruly tone. "Thank you. I am looking forward to meeting Miss Hawkins."

"Don't expect too much, Gemma. Her mind is tortured. Sometimes she does and says outrageous things. You're not used to such sights. You must steel yourself."

I have seen things you would not believe, my dear brother.

"Yes. Thank you. I shall take your advice to heart."

We walk through a long corridor, windows on our right and doors on our left. Ferns hang in baskets from the ceiling, giving the hallway a bright feel. I don't know what I expected a lunatic asylum to be like, but I did not imagine this. If I didn't know better, I'd swear I was entering one of London's exclusive clubs. The nurses pass us by with a quiet nod, their stiff white hats perched atop their heads like day-old meringues.

Tom ushers me into a wood-paneled parlor, where several women sit sewing. An older woman, slightly disheveled, concentrates intently on playing the piano, tapping out a childlike tune and singing along in a soft, shaky vibrato. In one corner stands a cage that houses a beautiful parrot. The bird squawks. "How are we feeling? How are we feeling?"

"They have a parrot?" I whisper. I'm trying to keep my composure, to make it seem as if I visit asylums every day.

"Yes. Cassandra is her name. She's quite the talker. She picks up a bit of everything from our patients. Botany, navigation, nonsensical ramblings. Soon we shall have to cure her as well."

As if on cue, Cassandra screeches out, "I am a great poet. I am a great poet."

Tom nods. "One of our patients, Mr. Osborne, fancies

himself a poet worth a small fortune. He is quite affronted by our efforts to keep him here and writes daily letters to his publisher and the Duke of Wales."

The older woman at the piano stops suddenly. Extremely agitated and wringing her hands, she approaches Tom. "Is this all a dream? Do you know?" she asks in a worried voice.

"I assure you this is all quite real, Mrs. Sommers."

"Are they going to hurt me? Have I been wicked?" She pulls at her eyelashes. A few come away in her hand.

A nurse in a starched white apron flits over, stops her. "Now, now, Mrs. Sommers, what happened to our lovely tune? Let's come back to the piano, shall we?"

The hand near the woman's eyelashes flutters like a wounded bird and spirals down to her side. "A dream, a dream. All a dream."

"You've just met Mrs. Sommers."

"So I see."

A tall, thin man with a neatly trimmed beard and mustache approaches. His clothes are slightly rumpled and his hair will not lie flat, but otherwise, he seems quite normal.

"Ah, Mr. Snow. How are we today, sir?" Tom asks.

"Fine, fine," the man answers. "I've sent a letter to Dr. Smith. He'll soon have my case well in hand, well in hand, well in hand. I shall attend the dance. I shall. I shall, sir."

"We shall see, Mr. Snow. First there is the matter of your conduct at the previous dance. You took quite a few liberties with the ladies. They were not appreciative."

"Lies, lies, all lies. My solicitor shall see to it, sir, eh, what? Lies, I tell you."

"We shall discuss it. Good day to you, then."

"Dr. Smith has my letter, sir! He shall rectify my reputation!"

"Mr. Snow," Tom explains as we make our way through the sitting room. "He has a habit of letting his hands wander during the dances."

"Oh," I say. I shall try to avoid dancing with Mr. Snow. As we walk on, Tom offers a polite hello to all he meets. Considering what a beast he is at home, it is quite surprising to see him here, kind and controlled. I'm proud of him. I can't believe it, but I am.

By the window sits a tiny creature. She is such a slight thing. Her face is gaunt, though I can see where she was once a pretty girl. There are dark circles beneath her brown eyes. She rakes thin fingers through her hair, which has been pulled back into a topknot. Tufts stick out all over, making her look quite a bit like the parrot, Cassandra.

"Good morning, Miss Hawkins," Tom says cheerily.

The girl says nothing.

"Miss Hawkins, may I present my sister, Miss Gemma Doyle. She would very much like to meet you. She's brought a book of poetry. The two of you could have a nice chat."

Silence again. Nell's tongue slides along her chapped lips. Tom looks at me as if to say, Are you sure? I nod.

"Very well, I'll leave you to get acquainted whilst I make my visits, eh?"

"How do you do?" I say, taking the chair directly opposite. Nell Hawkins goes on raking her hands through her hair. "I understand you've been away at school." Silence. "I am also at school. Spence Academy. Perhaps you've heard of it?" Down the room, Mrs. Sommers continues her abuse of the piano. "Shall I read some from Mr. Browning? His poetry is quite soothing, I find."

The parrot squawks. "Keep to the path. Keep to the path."

I make a great show of reading Mr. Browning.

Tom leaves the room, and I close my book. "I don't believe you are insane, Miss Hawkins. I know about the Order and Circe. I believe you."

Her hand stops for a moment. It shakes.

"You need not fear me. I want to stop Circe. But I need your assistance."

Nell Hawkins's eyes seem to see me for the first time. Her voice is high and scratchy as tree branches knocking against a pane in the wind. "I know who you are."

The bird squawks. "I know who you are. I know who you are." It sends a chill down my spine.

"You do?"

"They're looking for you. I hear them, in my head. Such terrible things." She goes back to pulling at her hair, singing softly as she does.

"Who is looking for me?"

"She is a house of sweets waiting to devour you. She has her spies," she whispers in a way that makes my skin go cold.

I don't know what to make of this. "Miss Hawkins. You may speak plainly to me. Truly, you can trust me. But I must know where to find the Temple. If you know where it is, it is imperative . . ."

Nell turns to me with wide eyes. "Follow the path. Stick to the path."

"The path? What path?"

Quick as a flash, Nell yanks the amulet from my neck so hard that my skin burns from it. Before I can protest, she flips it over, cradling it in both hands. She moves it back and forth as if she's trying to read something on the back of it. "The true path."

"Follow the true path. Follow the true path," Cassandra screeches.

"What path are you speaking of? Is it in the garden? Or do you mean the river?" I ask.

"No. No. No," Nell murmurs, rocking violently. With a swiftness I do not expect, she bangs the amulet hard against my chair, bending the eye.

"Stop it," I say, grabbing my necklace back. The eye lies at a strange angle now.

"Stay on the path," Nell says again. "They'll try to lead you astray. Show you things you cannot trust. Trust no one. Beware the Poppy Warriors."

My head reels from Nell's strange outbursts. "Miss Hawkins, please, how do I find this path? Will it take me to the Temple?" I ask, but Nell Hawkins is beyond reach, humming softly, knocking her fragile head against the wall in a desperate accompaniment until a nurse moves briskly to her side.

"Now, now, Miss Hawkins. What would the doctor say if he could see you behaving this way? Let's try a sampler, shall we? I've some lovely new thread."

The nurse leads Miss Hawkins away. The tufts of hair sticking out of her bun bob and sway. "The Temple hides in plain sight," she says. "Follow the path."

The nurse sits Nell Hawkins in a chair, guiding her hand up and down through tiny stitches. I'm more confused than ever. I peer into Cassandra's cage. "Do you understand?"

The bird blinks and blinks again, the tiny black dot of her pupil disappearing in a froth of white feathers and popping back to blackness again like a great illusionist's trick. Now you see it; now you don't. By inches, she turns on the bar of the cage, giving me her colorful back.

"No, I didn't think you did." I sigh.

I ask one of the nurses where I might find Tom, and she tells me to try the men's ward. She offers to escort me, which I know is the proper thing to do, but I assure her that I will wait for Tom instead. Then I slip out and walk toward the men's ward. Doctors pass, deep in conversation. They nod in acknowledgment and I give a congenial, close-mouthed smile in return. Their eyes linger on me for just a moment more, and I look away quickly. It is a strange feeling, to be seen like this. I both want it and fear it a little. There is such power in those fleeting glances, but I do not know what lies on the other side of them, and that scares me a bit. How is it possible to feel both ready and not yet ready for this new world of men?

Mr. Snow of the wandering hands approaches. I duck down a corridor to wait until he is gone. A man sits rubbing his fingers over and over, eyes staring straight ahead. *Please, Mr. Snow. Pass on so that I may get back to the hallway unscathed.*

"I've a message for you," the man says.

There is no one but the two of us here. "I beg your pardon?"

He turns slowly to face me. "The spirits are joining together, miss. They're coming for you."

I feel hot and light-headed. "What did you say?"

He grins and lowers his head, looking up at me through half-closed lids. The effect is chilling, as if he is a different person altogether. "We're coming for you, miss. We're all coming for you." With a fierce quickness, he snaps his jaws at me, growls, like a mad dog.

Get away, Gemma. Gasping, I run from him, rounding a corner fast and bumping directly into my astonished brother.

"Gemma! What on earth are you doing up here unescorted?"

"I—I—I . . . looking for you! That man . . . ," I say, pointing behind me.

Tom steps around the corner, and I follow. The old man is sitting once again, staring straight ahead. "Mr. Carey. Poor fellow. Completely beyond reach. I'm afraid he'll have to be moved to a county asylum soon."

"He . . . he spoke to me," I stammer.

Tom looks confused. "Mr. Carey spoke to you? That's impossible. Mr. Carey doesn't speak a word, ever. He is mute. What was it you thought he said to you?"

"We're coming for you," I repeat, realizing as I say it that it was not Mr. Carey speaking to me but someone else.

Someone from the realms.

⁂

"What happened to Nell Hawkins?" I ask as we take a cab to meet Felicity and Ann on Regent Street.

"That information is privileged," Tom replies with a sniff.

"Come, Tom. I'm not likely to share it with anyone," I lie.

Tom shakes his head. "Absolutely not. It is horrible and indelicate, not the sort of thing for a young lady's ears. Besides, you've a vivid imagination as it is. I won't add to your nightmares."

"Very well," I grumble. "Will she recover?"

"Difficult to say. I am working to that end, though I doubt she will ever return to Saint Victoria's. I would advise against it, certainly."

I sit straight up, my nerves on fire. "What did you say?"

"I said I would advise against it."

"No, before that."

"Saint Victoria's School for Girls. It's in Swansea, I believe. It's said to be a very fine school, but one does wonder. Why do you ask?"

There's a tingle in my stomach, a sense of foreboding. A snake ring. A woman in green. *Don't trust her . . .* "I believe one of our teachers comes from Saint Victoria's."

"Well, I do hope they keep better watch over the flock at Spence than they do at Saint Victoria's. That is all I can say about the matter," Tom states grimly.

I am troubled beyond words. Was Miss McCleethy at St. Victoria's when Nell Hawkins was a pupil there? What happened that is too "indelicate" for Tom to share? What happened to Nell Hawkins that drove her mad?

Whatever it was, I pray that I shall not suffer the same fate.

"Have you an address for Saint Victoria's?" I ask.

"Yes. Why?" Tom's suspicious.

I look out at the shops displaying their Christmas wares. "Our headmistress charged me—us—with performing an act of charity over the holiday. I thought perhaps I could write to them, let them know that another schoolgirl is spending time with Miss Hawkins and reminding her of happier days."

"Very commendable. In that case, I shall give you the address. Ah, here we are."

THE CAB STOPS BEFORE A STATIONER'S SHOP ON
Regent Street. Felicity and Ann rush out to meet us, trailed by
the ever-observant Franny. I want desperately to tell them
what I've learned about Nell Hawkins and wonder how I shall
possibly do so now.

Tom tips his hat to my friends. Pleasantries are exchanged.
"How are you finding London, Miss Bradshaw?" he asks.

"I like it ever so much," Ann says, giving him a ridiculously
demure smile.

"That is a very smart hat. It becomes you."

"Thank you," Ann mumbles, looking at the ground shyly. In
a moment, I shall hurl myself under a passing brougham.

"Might I escort you into the stationer's?"

Felicity smiles impatiently. "Yes, we're very grateful, I'm sure,
but you mustn't trouble yourself. Good day to you."

"That was not very hospitable of you," Ann scolds—as
much as Ann can scold—once we're inside the shop.

"I could have told him that 'very smart hat' was mine," Felicity snaps.

"I've news," I say, before Ann can retort. Now I've got their full attention.

"What is it?" Ann asks.

Franny hovers near, her eyes trained on the distance before us, her ears taking in our every word with a reporter's accuracy.

"We shan't have any fun at all with her in tow," Felicity whispers bitterly as we make a pretense of examining the sheaves of thick ivory paper bundled in colorful ribbons. "She dogs our every step as if she were Mrs. Nightwing herself. It is impossible to think that we have more freedom at Spence, but there it is."

We leave the stationer's shop and walk past a milliner's, a linen draper's, a toy shop, and a tobacconist, where gentlemen sit smoking fat cigars. The steets are crowded with people hunting for just the right pair of gloves for Aunt Prudence or the perfect toy drum for little Johnny. Franny does not lose her stride, however, and Felicity is on the verge of a full snit.

"Mama thinks she can run off to France, then come back and act as if I am to be under her heel and smile about it. Well, it won't do. I've a mind to give Franny the slip," Felicity complains, pouting.

"Oh, please don't," Ann begs. "I don't wish to cause any scandal."

"Yes, we'd be locked in our rooms for the entirety of the holiday," I agree.

We reach a confectioner's shop, where sumptuous pastries

and jellied fruits beckon to us from behind glass. A young man sweeps the sidewalk. He suddenly calls out boldly, "Franny! Come and give us a kiss!"

Franny blanches, looks away. "I'm sure you're mistaken, sir," she says.

Felicity pounces. "Sir, are you well acquainted with my servant?"

The young man doesn't know what to do or say. It's clear he knows Franny, and well, but now he may have gotten her in trouble. For a servant, the slightest whiff of impropriety can be grounds for dismissal.

"My mother should be quite interested to hear how her own maid kissed a man in broad daylight while in the company of her impressionable charges," Felicity says.

"But I never did such a thing!" Franny protests.

" 'Tis your word against ours," Felicity says, making us her accomplices whether we like it or not.

Franny balls her hands into tight fists at her side. "God sees yer wickedness, miss. It's a black mark in his ledger, to be sure."

"I think we might come to an agreement." Felicity pulls a shilling from her purse. "Here. Go on and take it. Take it and buy yourself a pastry. I'm sure this young man would be happy to help you. We'll agree to meet here again at, say, five o'clock?"

The shilling shines between Felicity's gloved fingers. If Franny takes it, she can enjoy a pastry and an afternoon with her gentleman friend. But she will also be forever in Felicity's pocket.

Franny shakes her head. "Oh, no, miss. Please don't ask me

to lie to Mrs. Worthington. Lying's a sin. I couldn't possibly, miss. Would you have me endanger my position and my immortal soul for only a shilling, miss?"

That Franny manages to deliver this blackmailing sermon with a straight face is quite a feat. I have newfound respect for her.

"I've a mind to tell my mother, anyway," Felicity snarls. It's an empty statement, and we all know it. Felicity's getting the precious freedom she craves. She hands Franny a pound, the price of her silence. Franny snatches the coin quickly, folding it tightly in her hand. Felicity isn't taking any chances. "If you should even think of confessing to my mother, we shall insist that it was you who left us to meet a gentleman friend. Poor us, lost and alone without our chaperone on the cruel streets of London, and missing a pound as well—most curious how that happened."

Franny, so triumphant a moment ago, blushes red and sets those thin lips in a grim line. "Yes, miss. Five o'clock."

As we hurry after Felicity, I turn to Franny, not sure what to say. "Thank you, Franny. You've, um, you've proved a very worthy girl." And with that, we are on our own.

Freedom tastes of a cream puff bought on Regent Street. Sweet leaves of flaky pastry dissolve on my tongue while the hansoms and omnibuses move up and down the street, muddy water mixed with dirty snow churning beneath their wheels. People bustle to and fro, armed with a sense of purpose. And we move among them with no constraints, another part of the nameless crowd colliding with chance, with destiny.

We walk to Piccadilly and duck into the great covered Burlington Arcade, striding past the beadles, who keep order with harsh glances and the weight of a stick in their hands. There are stalls selling items of all sorts here—sheet music, gloves, hosiery, cut-glass ornaments and the like—and I feel a deep longing for India again, with its bazaars and frantic markets.

"This is nearly as good as being in the realms," Ann says, happily devouring her treat.

"What is your news?" Felicity asks.

"My brother has a patient at Bethlem named Nell Hawkins. A most interesting case . . ."

"It is so noble of Tom to care for the unfortunate," Ann says, licking a dollop of pastry cream from her lips. "His betrothed must think him lovely."

"Betrothed? Tom?" I say, annoyed at the interruption. Too late, I remember my lie. "Oh. Yes, um, you meant Miss Richardson. Of course. How silly of me."

"You said her name was Dalton. And that she was beautiful."

"I . . ." I can think of nothing to say. I've really put my foot in it. "It is ended."

"Oh?" Ann asks, looking hopeful.

"Would you let her get on with the story?" Felicity chides.

"Nell Hawkins doesn't think herself Joan of Arc or the Queen of Sheba. Her particular delusion is that she thinks she's a member of the Order, and that a woman named Circe is after her."

Felicity gasps. "You've given me chills."

Ann's confused. "But I thought you said she was at Bethlem."

"Well, yes," I say, realizing how ridiculous it must all sound. Two newsboys pass, heckling us as they go. We pay them no mind.

"But you don't think she is mad. You think she's only play-acting to protect herself?" Felicity leads.

We've reached a place selling elaborate snuffboxes. I inspect one that is inlaid with ivory. It is dear, but I've nothing for my father yet, so I instruct the girl to wrap it for me. "Actually, I visited with her earlier. She is, in fact, insane. She did this," I say, showing my battered amulet.

"Oh, my," Felicity says.

"I don't see how she can possibly help us, then," Ann grumps.

"She's seen Circe. I'm sure of it. She kept mentioning the path. 'Stick to the path.' She said it several times."

"What do you suppose that means?" Felicity asks. We pass through the arcade and out to Bond Street, stopping before a glittering shop window. Claret silk cascades over the silent wax dummy of a woman. Each crease shimmers like wine in moonlight. We cannot help staring longingly.

"I don't know what it means. But I do know that Nell Hawkins was a student at Saint Victoria's in Wales."

"Isn't that where Miss McCleethy taught before she came to Spence?" Ann asks.

"Yes. But I've no idea if she was one of Nell's teachers. I shall write a letter to the headmistress there asking when Miss McCleethy left their employ. I believe that there is some terrible connection between what happened to Nell Hawkins and Miss McCleethy, something that has to do with the realms. If we can solve that riddle, it may very well lead us to the Temple."

"I don't see how," Ann grouses.

I sigh. "I don't either, but at present, it's my only hope."

The silk taunts us from its high perch behind glass. Ann sighs. "Wouldn't you adore having a dress made from that? Every head would turn."

"Mama is having my dress sent from Paris," Felicity says, as if discussing the weather.

Ann puts her hand to the glass. "I wish . . ." She can't even finish the sentence. It's too much even to wish.

A shopgirl steps up into the window, the arc of lettering that is *Castle and Sons, Dressmakers,* cutting her into two neat sections. She removes the dazzling fabric. Stripped of its finery, the dressmaker's dummy wobbles and settles upright, nothing more than a flesh-colored shell.

We walk on till we find ourselves on a small side street, where I am struck dumb. Tucked away under an awning is a tiny shop—the Golden Dawn.

"What is it?" Felicity asks.

"That shop. Miss McCleethy had an advert for it in her case. It was one of the only things she had, so it must be of some importance," I say.

"A bookseller's?" Ann asks, wrinkling her nose.

"Let's have a look for ourselves," Felicity says.

We dip into the dark cave of the shop. Dust swirls in the weak light. It isn't a very well-kept shop, and I wonder why Miss McCleethy is fond of it.

A voice comes from the darkness. "May I be of assistance?" The voice takes form in the person of a stooped man of about seventy. He hobbles over, leaning on a cane as he does. His knees creak with the effort. "How do you do? I am Mr. Theodore Day, proprietor of the Golden Dawn, bookseller since anno regni reginae eighteen hundred and sixty-one."

"How do you do," we murmur in unison.

"What are you after, then? Ah, wait! Don't tell me. I've just the thing." Cane leading the way, Mr. Day limps speedily to a tall bookcase crowded with volumes. "Something with princesses, perhaps? Or, no—haunted castles and maidens in peril?" His eyebrows, those two fat white caterpillars atop his spectacles, wiggle with obvious delight.

"If you please . . . ," I begin.

Mr. Day wags a finger. "No, no, no, don't spoil it. I shall find what you're after." We trail Mr. Day as he examines each shelf, running his knobby finger over leather spines, muttering to himself in book titles. "*Wuthering Heights . . . Jane Eyre . . . Castle of Otronto*—oh, that's a splendid book, I say."

"If you please, sir," I say, raising my voice slightly. "We were rather hoping to find a book about the Order. Have you any such books?"

I've perplexed Mr. Day. The caterpillar eyebrows collide at the bridge of his nose. "Dear, dear . . . I can't say as I've heard . . . What was that title again?"

"It isn't a title," Felicity says in such an impatient way I can practically hear the unspoken *you doddering old fool* that follows.

"It is a subject," Ann says kindly, salvaging us. "The Order.

They were a group of women who ruled the realms with magic—"

"Not real women, of course!" I break in. "It is but a story, after all."

"It's fiction you're after, then?" Mr. Day says, scratching at the bald spots between unruly white tufts of hair.

This is proving impossible. "Myths," I say after a moment's thought.

Mr. Day's face brightens. "Ah! I've some lovely books of myths. Right this way, if you please."

He leads us to a case in the back. "Greek, Roman, Celtic, the Norse—oh, I do love the Norse. Here they are."

Felicity gives me a forlorn look. This is not what we're after, but what can we do but say thank you and at least pretend to look before leaving? The bell over the door signals the arrival of another customer and Mr. Day leaves us. His cheery voice asks if he can be of assistance. The customer, a woman, answers. I know that strange brogue. It belongs to Miss McCleethy.

Peering around the case, I see her at the front.

"Look there," I whisper urgently.

"Where?" Stupidly, Ann steps out from behind the cover of the bookcase. A strong yank and she's back beside me.

"Look through here," I say, pulling two books from their places on the shelf, giving us a peephole to the other side.

"It's Miss McCleethy!" Ann says.

"What is she doing here?" Felicity whispers.

"I don't know," I whisper back. "I can't hear."

"Ah, yes. It's only just arrived," Mr. Day says, in answer to some unheard question on Miss McCleethy's part.

"What's only just arrived?" Ann asks. Felicity and I shush her with our hands over her mouth.

"I won't be a moment. Have a look about, if you wish." Mr. Day disappears behind a velvet curtain. Daylight streams through the sooty windows, bathing Miss McCleethy in a haze of dust. She removes her right-hand glove in order to better thumb through the pages of some novels stacked upon a table. The snake ring catches the light, blinding me with its brilliance. Miss McCleethy leaves the table and moves ever closer to our hiding spot.

Panicked, we crouch low on the floor as books above our heads are slid from their perches. If she should look on the lower shelves . . .

"Here we are," Mr. Day declares, pushing through the velvet curtain again. The mysterious book is wrapped, tied with ribbon, and given to Miss McCleethy. In a moment, the tinkle of the bell announces her departure. We peek through the hole we've made to ensure that she is gone and then we are scurrying to Mr. Day.

"Mr. Day, I believe that was my mother's dear friend who was just here. Would you be so kind as to tell me what book she purchased? I do so admire her taste in such matters," I say as sweetly as possible.

From the corner of my eye, I see Felicity's mouth hanging open in surprise and admiration. She is not the only one who can lie.

"Yes, it was Miss Wilhelmina Wyatt's *A History of Secret Societies*. I haven't read it myself."

"Have you another copy?" I ask.

"Certainly." Mr. Day limps to the back of the shop and returns carrying the book. "Ah, here we are. Isn't it curious? I've had no interest in this book, yet today I've sold two. Pity about the author."

"What do you mean by that?" Felicity asks.

"They say she died shortly after publication." He leans in, whispers. "They say she was involved in the occult. Wicked things. Now, we'll give it a nice ribbon and . . ."

"No thank you, Mr. Day," I say, reaching for it before he can wrap it. "We're in a dreadful rush, I'm afraid."

"Very well, that will be four shillings, if you please."

"Felicity?" I prompt.

"Me?" Felicity whispers. "Why should I pay it?"

"Because you've got it," I say, maintaining a terse smile.

"Don't look at me," Ann demurs. "I've nothing."

"It will be four shillings," Mr. Day states firmly.

In the end, we're forced to pool our money to purchase Miss Wyatt's sinister-sounding book.

"Let me look first. After all, I paid three shillings to your one," Felicity whines as we rush out into the London day.

"We'll read it together," I say, pulling on my end.

"There she is!" Ann gasps. Miss McCleethy is just ahead of us. "What should we do?"

"I say we follow her," Felicity says. Instantly, she sets off.

"Wait a moment," I say, catching up, keeping one eye on Miss McCleethy as she nears the corner. "I don't know if that's wise."

Ann takes Felicity's side, of course. "You wanted to know. This is the way to find out."

There is no fighting the both of them. Miss McCleethy stops, turns. With a collective gasp, we congregate in front of a knife sharpener. In a moment, she continues on her way.

"Well?" Felicity asks. It is less a question than a dare.

The knife sharpener's cries—"Knives! Made well sharp!"—rise above the street noise. Miss McCleethy is nearly gone from sight.

"Let's go," I say.

CHAPTER
TWENTY-FOUR

WE FOLLOW MISS MCCLEETHY FOR SOME TIME, PAST shopkeepers in shirtsleeves rushing parcels out to waiting carriages and a woman in severe black who implores us to remember the unfortunate during this Christmas season. We pay them no mind; only our quarry matters.

At Charing Cross, Miss McCleethy surprises us, entering the Underground station.

"What do we do now?" Felicity says.

I take a deep breath. "I suppose we travel by Underground."

"I've never been on the Underground before," Ann says uncertainly.

"Nor have I," Felicity says.

"No time like the present," I say, though the thought of it makes my breath hang to the bony rungs of my ribs. The Metropolitan District Railway. Right. It's just a train underground, Gemma. This is an adventure, and I'm an adventurous girl. Simon said so.

"Here, don't be frightened, Ann. Give me your hand," I say.

"I'm not frightened," she states, pushing past me, taking the stairs that lead down into the tunnels that run beneath London's busy streets as if it were no trouble at all. There is nothing to do but follow. I take a solid, deep breath and charge ahead. Halfway down, I turn to see Felicity standing at the top of the steps looking doubtful. She stares at me as if I am Eurydice being pulled back into the Underworld.

"Gemma—wait!" she cries, rushing to join me.

At the bottom of the stairs, a room opens. We're standing on a gaslit platform. The great curved wooden ceiling of the tunnel soars above us. Down the platform, Miss McCleethy waits. We stay out of sight until the train shooshes into the station. Miss McCleethy enters, and we walk quickly to the car adjacent to hers. It is difficult to know what is more exciting: the possibility of being discovered by Miss McCleethy or our first journey on the Underground. We take turns sticking our heads out into the aisle in a very unladylike fashion so that we might spy on Miss McCleethy in the next compartment. For her part, Miss McCleethy is contentedly reading Miss Wyatt's book about secret societies. I am desperate to know what she has discovered but don't dare look at our copy lest we lose sight of our teacher.

The conductor announces our departure. With a sharp pull, the train lurches into the tunnel. Felicity grips my hand. It is a strange sensation to find ourselves moving through this darkened passageway, the low glimmer of the gaslights trailing across our astonished faces like falling stars.

A conductor stands near, ready to call each stop from its platform. Miss McCleethy does not look up from her book. When the conductor announces Westminster Bridge, however, she closes her book and gets off the train with the three of us trailing at a safe distance. We come out onto the streets, blinking in the sudden light.

"She's taking that horse tram!" Felicity says.

"We're done for, then," I say. "We can't very well follow her onto it. She'll see us."

Ann grabs my hand. "We can do it. Look, there's a crowd. We'll fall in. If she should see us, we'll simply say we are sightseeing."

It's a very daring plan. Miss McCleethy moves to the back of the crowded tram. We stand near the front, keeping as many people between us as possible. At Westminster Bridge Road, Miss McCleethy alights, and we nearly trample one another trying to follow her. I know where we are. I've been here recently. We're in Lambeth, very near Bethlem Royal Hospital. Indeed, Miss McCleethy walks briskly in that direction. Within minutes, we are watching her as she strides through the iron gates and up the curved walk to the entrance's grand portico. We hide ourselves in some hedges along the walk, crouching low.

"What does she want at Bedlam?" Felicity says ominously.

A chill passes through me. "Nell Hawkins is there."

"You don't suppose Miss McCleethy would harm her, do you?" Ann asks in that inappropriately excited way that suggests she doesn't find the idea entirely distasteful if it makes the afternoon into a good story.

"I don't know," I say. "But it certainly makes me think they are known to each other, most likely from Saint Victoria's."

We stand outside in the cold for some time, but Miss Mc-Cleethy does not return, and we are in danger of missing our rendezvous with Franny. Reluctantly, we leave, and I have more questions than ever. What did Miss McCleethy want at Bedlam? What is she after? I feel certain that Miss McCleethy and Nell Hawkins are connected. What I don't know is how and why.

CHAPTER
TWENTY-FIVE

FELICITY INVITES US TO HER HOME FOR A VERY LATE tea. Our appetites stoked by adventure, we each devour several dainty sandwiches without apology.

"Well, what do you make of that? Miss McCleethy at Bedlam?" Felicity asks between bites.

"Perhaps Miss McCleethy has a lunatic relative?" Ann offers. "One who is a deep embarrassment to the family."

"Or perhaps she was there to see Nell Hawkins," I say.

"We have no answers to that at present. Let's see what Miss Wyatt has to say that is of such interest to Miss McCleethy," Felicity says, commandeering the book, as I knew she would. "Knights Templar, Fraternal Masons, Hellfire Club, the Hassassins . . . the table of contents alone is a read. Ah, here it is. Page two hundred and fifty-five. The Order." She flips to the page and reads aloud.

"*Each generation, young girls would be scrupulously trained to take their places within the Order's most privileged ranks. During the time* of their sixteenth year, they would be watched closely to see who among them was chosen by the realms to have true power and whose power was but a flickering flame, burned down to ash. Those who were not chosen would be turned away, perhaps to a life of home and hearth, nevermore to think on their time with these powerful conjurers. Still others went on to a life of service, called upon by the Order in some fashion or another when the time arose.

"There are those who say the Order never existed save as a story like the tales of fairies, goblins, and witches, princesses, and the immortal gods of Mount Olympus that mark literature so prized by impressionable girls who wish to believe in such fancies. Others say these women were Celtic pagans who vanished into the mists of time as did Merlin, Arthur, and his knights. Still others whisper a darker tale: that one of the Order's own betrayed them with a human sacrifice. . . ."

Felicity's eyes take in the page. She's reading to herself.

"You must read aloud!" I protest.

"It's only what we already know," she says.

"Here, I shall read," I say, taking the book.

"The lunatics, the addicts, the drunks, the poor, or the starving, these poor unfortunate souls required the protection of the Order, for their minds were too troubled and weak to resist the voices of the dark spirits who could speak to them at any time. . . ."

The drunk. The addict. I think of my father. But no, I've saved him. He is safe.

"If spirits are able to enter the minds of the insane, how can we be sure of Nell Hawkins?" Ann asks. "What if they are already using her for ill purposes?"

Felicity agrees. "It is a troubling thought."

There was Mr. Carey today, giving me his chilling warning, but Nell wasn't frightening. She was frightened. I shake my head. "I believe Nell is fighting very hard to keep any spirits from using her. It is why she is so difficult to reach, I'm sure."

"How long can she succeed?" Ann asks. I've no answer for this.

"Let me have another go," Felicity says, taking the book from me.

"*It is a fact,*" she reads aloud, "*though some dispute this wisdom as folly, that the Order still exists today, their members gone into hiding. They recognize one another by a variety of symbols known only to their members. Among these are the crescent eye, the double lotus blossom, the rose, two snakes intertwined . . .*"

"Just like Miss McCleethy's ring! Miss Moore said it was a symbol," I say. "And I've seen a ring such as that in my vision of the three girls."

Ann's eyes widen. "You have?"

"*But that is not all,*" Felicity continues loudly. She does not enjoy being interrupted for any reason. "*The priestesses of the Order also made use of the anagram. This device was particularly effective in concealing their identities from those who hunted them. Thus, Jane Snow could become Jean Wons, and no one, save her sisters, would be the wiser.*"

Felicity grabs a sheet of paper. "Let's make our own anagrams. I want to know what my secret name would be." She's giddy. Here in private, she's not the snob. She's not afraid of looking foolish in her enthusiasm.

"Very well," I say.

Felicity writes her name at the top of the page: *Felicity Worthington.* We stare at the letters, waiting for them to reveal a new and mysterious name.

Ann scribbles away. "Felicity Worthington becomes *City Worth Gin If Lento.*"

Felicity makes a face. "What sort of name is that?"

"A ridiculous one," I say.

"Try again, Ann," Felicity orders.

Ann takes pen to paper, concentrating as if she were a surgeon with a patient. "*Wont Left in City Groh?*" she offers.

"That makes no sense," Felicity complains.

"I'm doing my best."

I'm not faring much better. I've arranged and rearranged the letters of *Gemma Doyle* and come up with only one thing.

"How is yours coming along, Gemma?" Felicity asks.

"It isn't worth mentioning," I say, crumpling the paper.

Felicity snatches it from me, unfolding the name. "*Dog Mealy Em!*" The girls laugh uproariously at this, and I am instantly sorry they have it.

"Oh, that is perfect," Felicity says with glee. "Henceforth, you shall be known by your secret Order anagram name: Dog Mealy Em."

How delightful. "I'm going to try again," I say.

"You can if you wish," she says, grinning like a cat cornering her prey. "But I, for one, shall only address you as Dog Mealy Em."

Ann gives a sharp snort of laughter that makes her nose run. She dabs at it, mumbling "Dog Mealy Em" under her breath, which starts Felicity giggling again. I am irritated to be the lucky recipient of their annoying jibe. "Well then, what is your secret name, Ann?" I say, taunting her.

Ann's neat, tight script stretches across the white page. "Nan Washbrad."

"That is not at all fair!" I say. "That sounds like an actual name."

Ann shrugs. "Wouldn't do to have a conspicuous name, now, would it?" She smiles triumphantly, and in the silence I hear what she is holding back: *Dog Mealy Em.*

Felicity has been tapping the point of her pen against the paper, concentrating. She growls in frustration. "I cannot make heads or tails of my name. Nothing is coming."

"Do you have a middle name?" Ann asks. "That might help. More letters."

"That won't do any good," Felicity says too quickly.

"Why not?" Ann asks.

"Because it won't." Felicity blushes. It's not like Felicity to blush over anything at all.

"Very well, then. You can be known henceforth as City Worth Gin If Lento," I say, enjoying her predicament very much.

"If you must know, my middle name is Mildrade." Felicity turns back to her piece of paper as if she hasn't been saddled with possibly the worst middle name in history.

Ann wrinkles her nose. "Mildrade? What sort of name is that?"

"It is an old family name." Fee sniffs. "It can be traced all the way back to the Saxons."

"Oh," Ann says.

"Lovely," I say, trying desperately to keep the sides of my mouth from twitching.

Felicity buries her head in her hands. "Oh, it is awful, isn't it? I simply loathe it."

There is nothing polite to say to this. "Not at all." I can't resist saying it aloud. "Mildrade."

Felicity narrows her eyes. "Dog Mealy Em."

This could go on all evening. "Truce?"

She nods. "Truce."

Ann has begun to cut out the letters of Felicity's name so that they are like small squares that can be moved about on the desk until they form some semblance of a reasonable name. It is tedious work, and within a minute I am staring at the letters but thinking of what I'd like to have for supper. Felicity pronounces the task impossible and throws herself on the chaise to read more from Miss Wyatt's secret societies. Only Ann is determined to decipher the code of Felicity's name. She concentrates fiercely, moving letters left and right.

"Aha!" she cries at last.

"Let me see!" Felicity throws the book aside and rushes to the desk. I join them. Ann gestures proudly to the desktop, where the uneven squares have formed a new name, which Felicity reads aloud.

"Maleficent Oddity Ralingworth. Oh, how perfect."

"Yes," I say. "Evil and odd."

"Dog Mealy Em," Fee snaps back.

I shall have to work on my name. On one corner of the

paper, Ann has scribbled *Mrs. Thomas Doyle* several times, trying out a signature she will never own, and I am ashamed that I've crossed her off Tom's list before she's ever had a chance. I will remedy that. Ann's staring at a name.

"What is it?" I ask.

"I'm trying Miss McCleethy's name," she says.

Felicity and I crowd her. "What have you got?"

Ann shows us her work.

Claire McCleethy Let Her Claim Ccy I'm Clear Celt Hey C Ye Thrice Calm Cel The Mal Cire Leccy

Felicity laughs. "These certainly make no sense. Let Her Claim Ccy? Mal Cire?"

"Cire is a type of fabric. *Mal* means bad," Ann answers proudly.

I'm still looking at the page. There's something oddly familiar about it, something that makes the hair stand up at the back of my neck.

Ann pulls another C down. It makes *Circe.*

"Try the whole name," I say.

Once again, Ann writes out the name and cuts the letters into small squares that can be moved about. She tries several combinations—Circe Lamcleethy, Circe the Lamcley, Circe the Mal Cley, Circe the Ye Call M.

"Place the *Y* after *The*," I instruct.

Circe They E Call M.

Ann shifts the letters around till they read: *They Call Me Circe.*

We stare in astonishment.

"*Claire McCleethy* is an anagram," Ann whispers.

Felicity shudders. "Circe's come back to Spence."

"We've got to find the Temple," I say. "And quickly."

⌇⌇⌇⌇⌇

Pippa's sitting with the gorgon when we arrive in the realms. "Look, I've made you all crowns! They're my Christmas gifts to you!" Her arms are ringed with small circles of flowers, which she places on our heads. "Lovely!"

"Oh, they are perfect, Pip," Felicity coos.

"And I've kept your enchanted arrows safe and sound," Pip says, slipping the quiver onto Felicity's back. "Shall we take a trip on the river again?"

"No, I think not," I answer. The gorgon swivels her green face in my direction for a moment.

"No travels today, Most High?" she hisses.

"No, thank you," I say. I am reminded of our last voyage, of that moment of hesitation. I do not know if I can trust the great beast who once led a rebellion against the Order. There was a reason for them to imprison her.

I motion for the others to follow me to the garden. The toadstools have gotten fatter. Some of them seem near to bursting.

"We've found our teacher's name is an anagram for *They Call Me Circe*," Felicity tells Pippa, after giving her all the news of our day.

"How exciting!" Pip says. "I wish I had been there to follow her. That was quite brave of you."

"Do you suppose Mrs. Nightwing is suspect too?" Felicity asks. "They are friends."

"I hadn't thought of that," I say, troubled.

"She didn't want us to know anything about the Order! That's why she dismissed Miss Moore," Pippa says. "Perhaps Mrs. Nightwing has something to hide."

"Or perhaps she doesn't know anything about it," Ann says. Mrs. Nightwing has been the only mother she's ever known. I know what it is to have that certainty about someone you love taken from you.

"Mrs. Nightwing was a teacher at Spence when Sarah and Mary were there. What if she's been helping Sarah all the while, waiting for a time when she could return?" Felicity says.

"I d-don't like this talk," Ann stammers.

"What if—"

"Fee," I interrupt, giving a quick sideways glance to Ann. "I think for now we'd best be about finding the Temple. Nell Hawkins said we should look for a path. Have you seen any path round here, Pip?" I ask.

Pip gives me a quizzical look. "Who is Nell Hawkins?"

"A lunatic at Bedlam," Ann answers. "Gemma thinks she knows where to find the Temple."

Pippa laughs. "You're joking!"

"No," I say, going red. "Have you seen a path?"

"Hundreds. What sort of path are we looking for?"

"I don't know. The true path. That was all she said."

"That's not much help," Pippa says, sighing. "There is one that leads out from the garden that I've not taken yet."

"Show me," I say.

The one she speaks of is but a narrow lane that seems to disappear in a wall of leafy green. It is slow and arduous. With each step, we've got to push aside the broad leaves and fat beige stalks that leave thin ribbons of sap on our hands till we're sticky as treacle.

"What a chore," Pippa moans. "I hope this is the right way. I'd hate to think we've done all this work for nothing."

A stalk hits me square in the face.

"What did you say?" Felicity asks.

"Me? I've said nothing," I answer.

"I heard voices."

We stop. I hear it too. Something's moving in the heavy thicket. Suddenly, it seems a bad idea to have come this way without knowing a thing about it. I put out a hand to stop my friends. Felicity reaches for an arrow. We're tight as piano strings.

A pair of eyes appears between the fronds of the palm tree.

"Hello? Who's there?" I ask.

"Have you come to help us?" a soft voice asks.

A young woman steps out from behind the tree, making us gasp. The right side of her body is horribly burned. Her hand is gone to the bone. She sees the shock on our faces and tries to cover herself with what's left of her shawl. "It was a fire at the factory, miss. Went up like a tinderbox, and we couldn't get out in time," she answers.

"We?" I ask, when I find my voice again.

Behind her in the jungle growth are perhaps a dozen or so young girls, many of them burned, all of them dead.

"Those of us who couldn't get out. Fire got some; some jumped and the fall got 'em," she says, matter-of-factly.

"How long have you been here?" I ask.

"Can't rightly say," she answers. "Feels like forever."

"When was the fire?" Pippa asks.

"Third of December 1895, miss. Lot of wind that day, I recall." They've been here about two weeks, less time than Pippa. "I've seen you before, miss," she says, nodding to Pippa. "You and yer gen'leman."

Pippa's mouth hangs open. "I've never seen you in my life. I don't know what you're talking about."

"I am sorry for the offense, miss. I meant no harm, I'm sure."

I don't know why Pip's in such a foul temper. She's not helping matters.

The girl tugs at my sleeve, and I have to hold back the scream when I see that hand on me. "Is this heaven or hell, miss?"

"It is neither," I say, taking a step back. "What is your name?"

"Mae. Mae Sutter."

"Mae," I whisper. "Has anyone among you been acting strangely?"

She thinks for a moment. "Bessie Timmons," she says, pointing to another burned girl with a badly broken arm. "But in truth, miss, she's always been a bit strange. She's been talking to somebody off by herself, telling us we need to follow her to a place called the Winterlands, that they can help us there."

"Listen closely to me, Mae. You must not go to the

Winterlands. Soon everything will be as it should be, and you and your friends will cross over the river to what lies beyond."

Mae looks at me, scared. "And what might that be?"

"I—I don't know exactly," I say, offering no comfort. "But in the meantime, you must trust no one you meet here. Do you understand?"

She gives me a hard look. "Then why should I trust you, miss?" She walks back to her friends, and as she does I hear her say, "They can't help us. We're on our own."

"All those spirits waiting to cross . . . ," Felicity says.

"Waiting to be corrupted," Ann says.

"You don't know that," Pippa says.

We fall silent.

"Let's press on," I say. "Perhaps the Temple is near."

"I don't want to go on," Pippa says. "I don't want to see any more horror. I'm going back to the garden. Who's joining me?"

I look to the green ahead of us. The path dwindles under a heavy cover of leaves. But through them, I think I see a flash of ghostly, glowing white rustling through the brush.

Bessie Timmons steps onto the path. There's a hard look in her eye. "Why don't you clear off, then, if you can't help us? Go on—clear off. Or else."

She doesn't explain what the "or else" might be. Some of the other girls come to stand behind her, closing ranks. They don't want us here. It's not worth fighting them, not right now.

"Come on," I say. "Let's go back."

We turn back on the little path. Bessie Timmons calls out behind us.

"Don't be so proud. Soon you'll all be like we are. My friends are coming for us. They'll make us whole! They'll make us queens! And you'll be nothing but dust."

The walk back to the garden is a quiet one. We are tired and sticky and sullen, Pippa particularly.

"Now may we please have a bit of fun?" she huffs when we've reached the place where the runes used to stand. "This hunting about for the Temple is so dreary."

"I know a place for games, m'lady."

From behind a tree the knight emerges, startling us all. He has a cloth-wrapped bundle in one hand. We gasp and he falls to one knee. "Did I frighten you?" he asks, cocking his head to one side so that his curtain of straw-gold hair falls bewitchingly across his face.

Pippa flashes him a dark look. "You haven't been summoned."

"I am sorry," he says. He does not sound sorry. He sounds as if he is enjoying himself at our expense. "How shall I pay for my fault, m'lady? What would you bid me do?" He places his dagger at his throat. "Do you demand blood, m'lady?"

Pippa is oddly cool. "If you wish."

"What is your wish, m'lady?"

Pippa turns away, her long black curls bouncing against her shoulder blades. "I wish for you to leave me alone."

"Very well, m'lady," the knight says. "But I shall leave you with a gift."

He tosses the bundle to the ground and walks back into the thicket.

"I thought you said you'd gotten rid of him," Felicity says.

"Yes. I thought I had," Pippa answers.

"What did he bring you?" Ann asks. She unwraps the bundle and falls back in the grass with a small scream.

"What is it?" Felicity and I ask, rushing forward.

It is a goat's head, covered in flies and dried blood.

"How horrid!" Ann says, putting her hand to her mouth.

"If that man were to return I'd have something to say to him," Felicity says, her cheeks pink.

It was a ghastly thing to do, and I wonder that the knight, who was once dreamed of and called by Pippa's longing— a creature bound to her by the magic—could have become so cruel. Pippa's staring at the goat's head intently. She clutches her stomach, and at first, I think she is going to be ill or cry. But then she licks her lips just slightly, a look of longing in her eyes.

She sees me watching her. "I'll give it a proper burial later," she says, linking her arm through mine.

"Yes, that would be good," I say, moving away.

"Come back tomorrow!" she shouts. "We'll try another path. I'm sure we'll find it tomorrow!"

<hr />

The ornate cuckoo clock on Felicity's mantel cries the hour. It feels as though we've been gone for hours but it's been less than a second of London time. I'm still unsettled by the day's events—Miss McCleethy standing outside Bedlam, the anagram, Mae Sutter and her friends. And Pippa. Yes, especially Pippa.

"Shall we have some fun?" Felicity asks, rushing for the front door with us running behind her.

Shames, the butler, comes after us. "Miss Worthington? What is the matter?"

Felicity closes her eyes and holds out her hand. "You don't see me here, Shames. We are in the sitting room having our tea."

Without a word, Shames shakes his head as if he cannot understand why the door is standing open. He closes it behind us, and we are free.

The London fog hides the stars. They glint here and there but cannot break through the soupy sky.

"What should we do now?" Ann asks.

Felicity breaks into a broad grin. "Everything."

⌇⌇⌇⌇

Flying over London on a cold night by magic is an extraordinary thing. Here are the gentlemen leaving their clubs, the queue of carriages coming up to meet them. There are the mudlarks, those poor, grubby children, searching through the filthy banks of the Thames for a few coins and a bit of luck. We've only to dip low and we could touch the tops of the theaters in the West End or put our fingertips to the great Gothic spires of the Houses of Parliament, which we do. Ann sits upon the rooftop beside the towering clock of Big Ben.

"Look," she says, laughing. "I've a seat in Parliament."

"We could do anything! Steal into Buckingham Palace and wear the crown jewels," Felicity says, stepping across the spindly towers on her tiptoes.

"You w-wouldn't d-do that, w-would you?" Ann asks, horrified.

"No, she wouldn't," I answer firmly.

It is exhilarating to have such freedom. We fly lazily over the river, coming to rest beneath Waterloo Bridge. A rowboat passes under us, its lantern fighting the fog and losing. It's a curious thing, but I can hear the thoughts of the old gentleman in the boat, just as I have those of the fallen women in the Haymarket and the toppers driving through Hyde Park in their fancy private carriages as we were flying past. It is faint, like overhearing a conversation in another room, but nonetheless, I know what they are feeling.

The old man puts stones in his pocket, and I know his purpose.

"We've got to stop that man in the boat," I say.

"Stop him from what?" Ann asks, twirling in the air.

"Can't you hear him?"

"No," Ann says. Felicity shakes her head as she floats on her back like a swimmer.

"He means to kill himself."

"How do you know that?" Felicity asks.

"I can hear his thoughts," I say.

They're dubious, but they follow me down into the thick

fog. The man sings a mournful song about a bonnie lass lost forever as he puts the last of the stones in his pocket and moves to the edge of the rocking boat.

"You were right!" Ann gasps.

"Who goes there?" the man shouts.

"I've an idea," I whisper to my friends. "Follow me."

We push through the fog, and the man nearly topples backward at the sight of three girls floating toward him.

"You mustn't do such a desperate act," I say in a quavering voice that I hope sounds otherworldly.

The man falls to his knees, his eyes wide. "Wh-what are you?"

"We are the ghosts of Christmas, and woe to any man who does not heed our warnings," I wail.

Felicity moans and turns a flip for good measure. Ann stares at her openmouthed, but I, for one, am impressed by her quick thinking and her acrobatics.

"What is your warning?" the old man squeaks.

"If you should persist in this dreadful course, a terrible curse shall befall you," I say.

"And your family," Felicity intones.

"And their families," Ann adds, which I think is a bit much, but there's no taking it back.

It works. The man removes stones from his pocket so quickly I fear he'll turn over the boat. "Thank you!" he says. "Yes, thank you, I'm sure."

Satisfied, we fly away home, laughing at our resourcefulness and feeling quite smug indeed about saving a man's life. When we reach the elegant houses of Mayfair once again, I'm drawn to Simon's house. It would be an easy thing to fly close and perhaps hear his thoughts. For a moment, I hover, moving closer to him, but at the last moment, I change course, following Felicity and Ann into the sitting room again, where the tea is now cold.

"That was thrilling!" Felicity says, taking a seat.

"Yes," Ann says. "I wonder why Fee and I weren't able to hear his thoughts as well."

"I don't know," I say.

A little girl in immaculate dress and pinafore steals in. She can't be more than eight years old. Her fair hair has been pulled back at the crown with a fat white ribbon. Her eyes are the same blue-gray as Felicity's. In fact, she looks a good deal like Felicity.

"What do you want?" Felicity snaps.

A governess steps in. "I'm sorry, Miss Worthington. Miss Polly seems to have lost her doll. I've told her she must take greater care with her things."

So this is little Polly. I pity her for living with Felicity.

"Here it is," Felicity says, finding the doll under the Persian carpet. "Wait. Let me be certain she's all right."

Felicity makes a show of playing nursemaid to the doll, which makes Polly giggle, but when she closes her eyes and puts her hands over the doll, I feel the tug on the magic that we've brought back.

"Felicity!" I say, breaking her concentration.

She hands the doll to Polly. "There now, Polly. All better. Now you've got someone to look after you."

"What did you do?" I ask, when Polly's gone to the nursery with her governess.

"Oh, don't look at me that way! The doll's arm was broken. I only fixed it," Felicity huffs.

"You wouldn't do anything to harm her, would you?"

"No," Felicity says coolly. "I wouldn't."

CHAPTER
TWENTY-SIX

THE MOMENT I WAKE, I DASH OFF A LETTER TO THE headmistress of St. Victoria's School for Girls asking when Miss McCleethy was in their employ. I have Emily post it before the ink is completely dry.

As it is Thursday, Miss Moore takes us to the gallery as promised. We travel by omnibus through the London streets. It is glorious to sit at the top, the bracing wind in our faces, peering down at the people milling about on the streets and at the horses pulling carts filled with wares. It is less than a week until Christmas, and the weather has turned much colder. Overhead, the clouds are heavy with the coming snow. Their white underbellies sit on the chimney tops, swallowing them whole before moving on to the next and the next, resting each time as if they have such a long way to go.

"Our stop is nigh, ladies," Miss Moore calls out over the street noise. The wind has picked up so that she has to secure her hat with one hand. With careful steps, we descend the staircase that leads to the bottom of the omnibus, where a smartly uniformed conductor takes our hands and helps us into the street.

"Gracious me," Miss Moore says, adjusting her hair beneath her hat. "I thought I should blow away entirely."

The gallery is housed in a former gentlemen's club. Many people have come out today. We move from floor to floor in their close company, taking in each exquisite painting. Miss Moore leads us down a hall devoted to the works of lesser-known artists. There are quiet portraits of pensive maidens, fiery scenes of war at sea, and pastoral landscapes that make me want to run barefoot through them. I find that I am drawn to a large painting in the corner. In it, an army of angels are joined in battle. Below them lies a lush garden and a lone tree, and a great number of people turned away, moaning. Below that is a vast wasteland of black rock bathed in a fiery orange glow. A golden city sits in the clouds far above. In the center, two angels are locked in combat, arms entwined till I cannot tell where one stops and the other begins. It is as if without this struggle to keep them aloft, they might both pitch into the void.

"Did you find something you like?" Miss Moore asks, suddenly by my side.

"I cannot say," I answer. "It's . . . disturbing."

"Good art often is. What do you find disturbing about this painting?"

I take in the vibrant hues of the oils, the reds and oranges of the fire; the whites and pale grays of the angels' wings; the variations of the flesh tones that make muscles seem to come alive, straining for victory.

"It seems rather desperate, as if there's too much at stake."

Miss Moore leans forward to read the brass plate beneath the painting. "Artist unknown. Circa 1801. *A Host of Rebel Angels*." She quotes what sounds like poetry. " 'To reign is worth ambition though in Hell: Better to reign in Hell, than serve in Heav'n.' John Milton. *Paradise Lost*, Book One. Have you ever read it?"

"No," I say, blushing.

"Miss Worthington? Miss Bradshaw?" Miss Moore asks. They shake their heads. "Gracious, what is to become of the Empire when we do not read our best English poets? John Milton, born 1608, died 1674. His epic poem, *Paradise Lost*, is the story of Lucifer." She points to the dark-haired angel in the center. "Heaven's brightest and best-loved angel, who was cast out for inspiring a rebellion against God. Having lost heaven, Lucifer and his rebel angels vowed to continue fighting here on earth."

Ann blows her nose daintily into her handkerchief. "I don't understand why he had to fight. He was already in heaven."

"True. But he wasn't content to serve. He wanted more."

"He had all he could ask for, didn't he?" Ann asks.

"Exactly," Miss Moore states. "He had to ask. He was dependent upon someone else's whim. It's a terrible thing to have no power of one's own. To be denied."

Felicity and Ann flash me a glance, and I feel a surge of guilt. I have the power. They do not. Do they hate me for it?

"Poor Lucifer," Felicity murmurs.

Miss Moore laughs. "That is a most unusual thought, Miss Worthington. But you are in good company. Milton himself seemed to feel sympathy for him. As does this painter. Do you see how beautiful he's made the dark angel?"

The three of us peer through the brushstrokes at the angels' strong, perfect backs. They seem almost as lovers, oblivious to the rest of us. It's the struggle that matters.

"I wonder . . . ," Miss Moore muses.

"Yes, Miss Moore?" Ann prompts.

"What if evil doesn't really exist? What if evil is something dreamed up by man, and there is nothing to struggle against except our own limitations? The constant battle between our will, our desires, and our choices?"

"But there is real evil," I say, thinking of Circe.

Miss Moore gives me a curious look. "How do you know?"

"We've seen it," Ann blurts out. Felicity coughs and gives Ann an indelicate elbow to the ribs.

Miss Moore leans in close. "You're quite right. Evil does exist." My heart skips a beat. Is this it? Will she confess something to us here and now? "It is called finishing school." She gives a mock shudder, and we giggle. A grim, gray couple passes at that moment, giving us a sharp glance of disapproval.

Felicity stares at the painting as if she wants to touch it. "Do you think it's possible . . . that some people aren't quite right, in some way? That there is some evil in them that makes others . . ." She trails off.

"Makes others what?" Ann asks.

"Do things."

I don't know what she means.

Miss Moore keeps her eyes on the painting. "We must each be accountable for our own actions, Miss Worthington, if that is what you are asking."

If that is indeed what Felicity wants to know, she doesn't let on. I cannot tell whether her question has been answered.

"Shall we move on, ladies? We've yet to see the Romantics." Miss Moore strides purposefully on in the gallery. Ann follows, but Felicity doesn't move. She's fascinated by the painting.

"You wouldn't leave me out, would you?" she asks me.

"Leave you out of what?" I ask.

"The realms. The Order. All of it."

"Of course not."

She cocks her head to one side. "Do you think they missed him terribly when he fell? Did God cry over his lost angel, I wonder?"

"I don't know," I say.

Felicity links her arm through mine, and we stroll after the others, leaving the angels and their eternal struggle behind.

"I say, is that you, Ann? It is our Annie!"

A woman approaches us. She's quite overdressed in ropes of pearls and diamond earbobs that would be better suited to evening. It is obvious that she has money and that she wants everyone to know it. I am embarrassed for her. Her husband, a man with a neatly trimmed mustache, doffs his tall black hat to us. He carries an ornate walking stick for effect.

The woman embraces Ann gingerly. "What a surprise it is to see you here. But why are you not at the school?"

"I—I—I . . . ," Ann stammers. "M-may I present my cousin, Mrs. Wharton."

Introductions are made, and we come to understand that Mrs. Wharton is Ann's distant cousin, the one helping with her schooling so that she might become governess to her children in another year.

"I do hope the exhibit is tasteful," Mrs. Wharton says, wrinkling her nose. "We took in an exhibit in Paris that was obscene, I'm sorry to say. Paintings of savages sitting about without a stitch on."

"It certainly was dear enough," Mr. Wharton says, laughing, though it is in very bad taste to mention money.

Miss Moore stiffens beside me. "Ah. True art appreciators, I see. You simply must see the Moretti painting," she adds, mentioning the daring painting of a nude Venus, goddess of love, that made me blush with its boldness. It is certain to offend the Whartons, and I suspect she has done this on purpose.

"We shall indeed. Thank you," Mrs. Wharton chirps. "It is fortunate indeed that our paths crossed, Annie. It seems our governess, Elsa, is leaving sooner than expected. She'll be going in May, and we shall need you to begin straightaway. I know Charlotte and Caroline will enjoy having their cousin as governess, though I suspect Charlotte is looking forward to having someone call her Miss Charlotte now that she is eight. You mustn't let her boss you about too much." She laughs at this, oblivious to Ann's torment.

"We should be getting on, Mrs. Wharton," Mr. Wharton says, offering his arm. He has grown bored with us already.

"Yes, Mr. Wharton. I shall write to Mrs. Nightingale," his wife says, getting the name wrong. "So very nice to have met you," she says, letting her husband lead her away like a child.

⌁⌁⌁⌁⌁

We repair to a dark, cozy tearoom for afternoon tea. It is not like the clubs and parlors we usually visit, filled with flowers and stiff talk. This is a place for working women, and it fairly pulses with activity. Felicity and I are alive with the power of art. We discuss our favorite paintings and Miss Moore tells us what she knows about the artists themselves, which makes us feel very sophisticated, as if we are guests at some famous salon in Paris. Only Ann is silent. She drinks her tea and eats two large pieces of cake, one right after the other.

"Continue eating like that, and you'll never fit into your gown by the Christmas ball," Felicity chides.

"What does it matter?" Ann asks. "You heard my cousin. I'll be gone by May."

"Come now, Miss Bradshaw. There are always other choices," Miss Moore says crisply. "Your future hasn't been decided just yet."

"Yes, it has. They've helped to pay my way at Spence. I am indebted to them."

"What if you refused them but offered to repay your debt once you'd secured employment elsewhere?" Miss Moore asks.

"I could never repay the debt."

"You could, over time. It wouldn't be easy, but it could be done."

"But they'd be so very angry with me," Ann says.

"Yes, most likely. It shan't kill any of you."

"I couldn't bear to have someone think badly of me."

"Would you rather spend your life at the mercy of Mrs. Wharton and the Misses Charlotte and Caroline?"

Ann stares at the crumbs on her plate. The sadness is that I know Ann. Her answer is yes. She gives a weak smile. "Perhaps I'll be like the heroine in one of those schoolgirl stories, and someone *will* come for me. A rich uncle. Or I might strike the fancy of a good man who wishes to make me his wife." She says this last bit glancing nervously at me, and I know she is thinking of Tom.

"That's rather a lot to hang your hopes on," Miss Moore says. Ann sniffles. Fat teardrops fall into her tea.

"Come now," Miss Moore says, patting her hand. "There is time. What shall we do to cheer you? Would you like to tell me more of your story about all the lovely things you do in the realms?"

"I'm beautiful there," Ann says, voice thick with the ache of tears held back.

"Very beautiful," I say. "Tell her how we frightened away the water nymphs!"

A smile flickers across Ann's lips for a moment. "We did show them, didn't we?"

Miss Moore pretends to be put out. "Now then, don't keep me in suspense. Tell me about the water nymphs."

As we tell her the tale in great description, Miss Moore listens intently. "Ah, I see you've been reading after all. That is consistent with the ancient Greek tales of nymphs and sirens, who led sailors to their deaths with their song. And have you had success in finding your temple, was it?"

"Not yet. But we visited the Golden Dawn, a bookseller's near Bond Street, and found a book on secret societies by a Miss Wilhelmina Wyatt," Ann says.

"The Golden Dawn . . . ," Miss Moore says, taking a bit of her cake. "I don't believe I know it."

"Miss McCleethy had an advert for it in her suitcase," Ann blurts out. "Gemma saw it there."

Miss Moore raises an eyebrow.

"It was open," I say, blushing. "I could not help seeing it."

"We saw Miss McCleethy there at the shop. She asked for the book, so we did as well. It has knowledge about the Order!" Felicity says.

"Did you know the Order used anagrams to conceal their true identities when needed?" I ask.

Miss Moore pours tea for us. "Is that so?"

Ann jumps in. "Yes, and when we did an anagram for Miss McCleethy, it spelled out *They Call Me Circe*. That proves it."

"Proves what?" Miss Moore asks, spilling a bit of tea that she must sop up with her napkin.

"That Miss McCleethy is Circe, of course. And she's come back to Spence for some diabolical purpose," Felicity explains.

"Would that be the teaching of drawing or Latin?" Miss Moore asks with a wry smile.

"It is a serious matter, Miss Moore," Felicity insists.

Miss Moore leans in with a solemn face. "So is accusing someone of witchcraft for visiting a bookseller's."

Properly chastised, we drink our tea.

"We followed her," Ann says quietly. "She went to Bedlam, to where Nell Hawkins lives."

Miss Moore stops midsip. "Nell Hawkins. Who is she?"

"She's a girl who believes in the Order. She says that Circe is trying to get to her. That's why she went mad," Ann says with relish. She really does have a taste for the macabre.

"My brother, Tom, is a clinical assistant at Bethlem. Nell Hawkins is a patient there," I explain.

"Interesting. And you've spoken with this person?"

"Yes," I say.

"Did she tell you she was acquainted with Miss McCleethy?"

"No," I answer, somewhat embarrassed. "She is mad, and it is difficult to decipher her ramblings. But she was at Saint Victoria's School for Girls when this terrible misfortune befell her, and we've reason to believe that Miss McCleethy was in their employ at the same time."

"That is curious," Miss Moore says, pouring milk into her tea till the liquid turns a cloudy beige. "Do you know that for a fact?"

"No," I admit. "But I've sent an enquiry to their headmistress. I expect to know shortly."

"Then you know nothing, really," Miss Moore says, smoothing her napkin in her lap. "Until you do, I would advise you to be careful with your accusations. They can have unforeseen repercussions."

We look at each other guiltily. "Yes, Miss Moore."

"Ann, what have you done there?" she asks.

Ann's been scribbling on a piece of paper. She tries to cover it with her hand. "N-nothing."

That's all it takes for Felicity to pull it away.

"Give that back!" Ann whines, trying unsuccessfully to grab it.

Felicity reads aloud. *"Hester Moore. Room She Reet."*

"It is an anagram of your name. Not a very good one," Ann says hotly. "Fee, if you please!"

Felicity reads on, undaunted. *"O, Set Her More. Set More Hero."* Felicity's eyes flash. A feral grin appears. *"Er Tom? Eros He."*

It doesn't matter that it makes no sense. It is that Tom and Eros have been combined in the same sentence that has humiliated Ann to no end. She snatches it back. Others in the tearoom have noted our childish behavior, and I'm terribly embarrassed that our visit has ended on such a note. Miss Moore will probably never invite us on an outing again.

Indeed, she checks her pocket watch. "I should be seeing you girls home."

⸎

In the cab, Miss Moore says, "I do hope you have no further acquaintance with the water nymphs. They sound particularly gruesome."

"That makes two of us," Ann says, shivering.

"Perhaps you can bring me into the story. I should like to fight the nymphs, I think." Miss Moore adopts a mock heroic face. It makes us laugh. I am relieved. I've so enjoyed our day; I should hate to think there will not be another like it.

When Ann and Felicity are safely home again, we travel the

short distance to Belgrave Square. Miss Moore takes in the sight of the lovely house.

"Would you like to come in and meet Grandmama?" I ask.

"Another time, perhaps." She looks a bit worried. "Gemma, do you really distrust this Miss McCleethy?"

"There is something unsettling about her," I answer. "I cannot say what it is."

Miss Moore nods. "Very well. I shall make enquiries of my own. Perhaps it is nothing at all, and we shall laugh at how silly we've all been. In the meantime, you might do well to be wary of her."

"Thank you, Miss Moore," I say. "Thank you for everything."

CHAPTER
TWENTY-SEVEN

WHEN I COME THROUGH THE DOOR, MRS. JONES IS beside herself. "Your grandmother is expecting you in the parlor, miss. She said for you to come the moment you arrived."

Mrs. Jones sounds so dire that I am afraid something terrible has happened to Father or Tom. I burst into the parlor to see Grandmama sitting with Lady Denby and Simon. I have just come in from the cold. My nose is on the verge of dripping from the sudden warmth of the room. I will it to stop.

"Lady Denby and Mr. Middleton have come to pay us a call, Gemma," Grandmama says with a panicked smile as she takes in my rough appearance. "We shall wait for you to dress so that you can receive them."

It is not a request.

Once I am presentable, we take a stroll in Hyde Park. Lady Denby and Grandmama trail behind us, allowing Simon and me a chance to talk while also being chaperoned.

"Such a lovely day for a walk," I say, even as a few wayward snowflakes land on my coat sleeve.

"Yes," Simon agrees, taking pity on me. "Brisk. But lovely."

Silence stretches between us like an elastic garter near to snapping.

"Have you—"

"Was—"

"Forgive me," I say.

"The fault is mine. Please, do go on," Simon says, making my heart skip a beat.

"I was simply wondering . . ." What? I'd nothing to say. I was only desperate to make conversation and prove myself a witty, amusing, and thoughtful girl, the sort one cannot imagine living without. The difficulty, of course, is that I am in command of none of these qualities at present. It should prove a miracle if I can make some commentary on the state of the cobblestones. ". . . if . . . what I mean is . . . I . . . Aren't the trees so lovely this time of year?"

The trees, stripped of all leaves and ugly as gnomes, grimace in response.

"There is a certain elegance to them, I suppose," he answers.

This is not going well at all.

"I do hate to trouble you, Mr. Middleton . . . ," Grandmama says. "I'm afraid it's the damp in my bones." She limps for effect.

Simon takes the bait, offering her his arm. "Not at all, Mrs. Doyle."

I have never been more grateful for an interruption in my life. Grandmama is in heaven, walking arm in arm with a viscount's son through Hyde Park, where all can watch from their windows, feeling envious. As Grandmama prattles on about her health, the trouble with servants today, and other matters that make me feel as if I shall lose my mind, Simon gives me a sly sideways glance, and I'm smiling broadly. He has a way of making even a walk with Grandmama into an adventure.

"Do you like the opera, Mrs. Doyle?" Lady Denby asks.

"Not the Italians. I do like our Gilbert and Sullivan, though. Delightful."

I am embarrassed by her lack of taste.

"What a happy coincidence. *The Mikado* is to be performed Saturday evening at the Royal Opera House. We have a box. Would you care to join us?"

Grandmama falls silent, and at first, I am afraid she's on the verge of becoming catatonic. But then I realize that she is actually excited. Happy. It is such a rare occurrence she is undone by it.

"Why, we'd be delighted!" she answers at last.

The opera! I've never been. Hello, beautifully ugly trees! Have you heard? I am to attend the opera with Simon Middleton. The wind rustles through their empty branches, making it sound like the distant din of applause. Dried husks of leaves skitter across our path and stick to the wet cobblestones, where they are trod underfoot.

A shiny black carriage approaches slowly, drawn by two powerful steeds that gleam as if polished. The coachman wears his tall hat low on his brow. When the carriage pulls even with us, its occupant peers out from the shadows within, giving me a cruel smile. A scar marks his left cheek. It is the man I saw at the train station my first day in London, the one who followed me. There can be no mistake. As the coach passes, he tips his hat to me with a wicked smile. The carriage takes a bump in the road and wobbles on its giant wheels. A woman's gloved hand emerges, gripping the side of the door. I cannot see her face. The sleeve of her cloak catches the wind. It flutters there like a warning—a rich, dark green.

"Miss Doyle?" It's Simon.

"Yes?" I say, when I find my voice again.

"Are you quite all right? You seemed ill for a moment."

"I fear Miss Doyle has a chill. She should return home and sit by the fire at once," Simon's mother insists.

The road is quiet now. Even the wind has stopped blustering. But inside, my heart clamors so loudly it is a wonder it cannot be heard by all. For that green cloak was very like the one in my visions, the one I'm certain belongs to Circe, and it was fluttering from the window of a carriage carrying a member of the Rakshana.

<hr />

Once Simon and Lady Denby have gone, Grandmama has Emily draw me a hot bath. When I sink into the deep tub, water sluices along the sides and comes to settle in tiny waves beneath my chin. Lovely. I close my eyes and let my arms float upon the surface of the water.

The sharp pain comes swiftly, nearly pulling me under. My body goes rigid, out of my control. Water rushes into my mouth till I'm coughing and sputtering. Panic has me gripping the side of the bathtub, desperate to get out. I hear the dreaded whisper, like a swarm of insects.

"Come with us. . . ."

The pain subsides, and now my body is light as a snowflake, as if I were in a dream. I do not want to open my eyes. I do not want to see them. But they may have answers to my questions, so I turn my head slowly. There they are, ghoulish and haunting, with their ragged white dresses and dark circles beneath soulless eyes.

"What do you want?" I ask. I'm still coughing up water.

"Follow us," they say, and they slip through the closed door as if it were nothing.

Hurriedly, I reach for my dressing gown and open the door, searching for sign of them. They hover just outside my bedroom, casting a false light at the end of the darkened hall. They motion for me to follow as they slip into my room.

I'm shaking and wet, but I follow them, working up the courage to speak. "Who are you? Can you tell me anything about the Temple?"

They do not answer. Instead, they float to the cupboard and wait.

"My cupboard? There's nothing in there. Just my clothing and shoes."

They shake their pale heads. "The answers you seek are here."

In my cupboard? They're as mad as Nell Hawkins. Carefully as I can, I step around them and begin pushing aside dresses and coats, tearing through hatboxes and shoes, looking for what it is I'm supposed to find, though what that is I can't begin to imagine. Finally, I explode in frustration.

"I told you, there's nothing here!"

It's the horrible sound of those pointed boots scraping my floors that has me scrambling backward. Oh, God, I've done it now, made them angry. They advance, arms out, coming for me. I can move no farther; I'm trapped by the bed.

"No, please," I whisper, curling into a ball, shutting my eyes tight.

Those fingers of ice are on my shoulders and here it comes, a vision of such fury I can scarcely breathe, let alone think of crying for help. A field of green leading from the old stone ruins to the cliffs by the sea. In their white dresses, the girls run and laugh. One snatches the hair ribbon from another.

"Will she give us the power today?" the girl with the ribbon asks. "And will we at last see the realms that are so beautiful?"

"I hope so, for I should like to play with magic," another says.

The girl whose hair has fallen free of her ribbon calls, "Eleanor, did she promise that it would be today?"

"Yes," the girl answers in a tight, high voice. "She will come soon. We shall enter the realms and have it all, everything we've ever wished for."

"And she thinks this time you can take us in?"

"She says so."

"Oh, Nell, that is wonderful!"

Eleanor. *Nell.* The name pushes the air from my lungs. For the first time, I see her, walking toward the others. She is heavier, and her hair is curled and shining, the face untroubled, but I recognize her instantly: It is Nell Hawkins, before she was touched by madness.

There is the coarse sound of insect wings near my ear. "Watch. . . ."

It is like being pulled by a fast train, everything moving so quickly past the windows of my eyes. The girls on the rocks. The woman in green, face hidden. The hand taking Nell's. The sea rising like the terror in their eyes.

It stops. I'm panting on my floor. They point to the cupboard. What could it possibly be? I've been through it all, and there's nothing . . . My mother's red diary peeks out from a pocket of a coat. I reach for it.

"This?" I ask, but they are already fading into a mist that disappears completely. The room comes back to itself. The vision has ended. I've no idea what they could mean. I've been through this diary again and again, looking for clues, and there is nothing. I turn each page till I reach the place where I've saved my mother's creased newspaper clippings. When I read the first line this time, I do not find it to be a melodramatic story badly told. No, this time it chills me through and through.

A trio of girls in Wales went out walking and were never heard from again. . . .

I read on, feeling my blood run fast as I do.

Young ladies who were the angels of Saint Victoria's School for Girls . . . fair, shining daughters of the Crown . . . loved by all . . . walked gaily to the cliffs by the sea, never knowing the tragic fate that awaited them . . . lone survivor . . . went mad as a hatter . . . bears some resemblance to the story of a bonnie lass from the MacKenzie School for Girls . . . Scotland . . . the tragic dagger of suicide . . . claimed to see visions, frightening the other girls . . . fell to her death . . . other disquieting tales . . . Miss Farrow's Academy for Girls . . . Royal College of Bath. . . .

The names of these schools are familiar. I know them. Where have I heard them before? And then it comes to me with a cold, hard chill: Miss McCleethy. I saw them on the list she kept inside her case beneath the bed. She'd marked through them all. Only Spence remained.

CHAPTER
TWENTY-EIGHT

NELL HAWKINS AND I TAKE A STROLL THROUGH
Bethlem's cheerless airing yards. The day is brisk, but if Nell
wants to walk, then I shall walk. I shall do anything to try to
unlock this mystery, for I'm sure that somewhere inside Nell's
tortured mind lie the answers I need.

Only a few of the bravest souls have come out today. Nell's
refusing to wear her gloves. Her tiny hands blotch purple in
the cold but she doesn't seem to mind. When we are a safe distance from Bethlem's doors, I give Nell the scrap of newspaper.

Nell lets it rest in her hands, which shake. "Saint Victoria's . . ."

"You were there, weren't you?"

She settles onto a bench like a balloon floating to earth, de-
flated. "Yes," she says, as if remembering something. "I was
there."

"What happened that day by the sea?"

Nell's eyes, full of pain, find mine as if they hold the answers.
She closes hers tightly. "Jack and Jill went up the hill to fetch a

pail of water," she says. "Jack fell down and broke his crown, and . . ." She stops, frustrated. "Jack and Jill went up the hill to fetch a pail of water. Jack fell down and broke his crown, and . . ."

She says it faster. "JackandJillwentupthehilltofetchapailofwaterJackfelldownandbrokehiscrownand . . . and . . ."

I can't bear it. ". . . Jill came tumbling after . . . ," I finish for her.

She opens her eyes again. They are teary with the cold. "Yes. Yes. But I didn't tumble after."

"What are you saying? I don't understand."

"We went up the hill . . . up the hill . . ." She rocks. "To fetch a pail of water. From the water. It came up from the water. She made it come."

"Circe?" I whisper.

"She is a house of sweets waiting to devour us."

The odd Mrs. Sommers has been walking nearby, tearing at her eyebrows when no one watches her. She hovers closer and closer to us, trying to hear.

"What did Circe want from you? What was she looking for?"

"A way in." Nell giggles in such a way that a chill races up my spine. Her eyes glance left and right, like those of a child with a naughty secret. "She wanted in. She did. She did. She said she'd make us her new Order. Queens. Queens with a crown. Jack fell down and broke his crown . . ."

"Miss Hawkins, look at me, please. Can you tell me what happened?"

She seems so sad, so far away. "I could not take her in after all. I could not enter. Not wholly. Only here." She points to her head. "I could see things. Tell her things. But it wasn't enough. She wanted in. She tired of us. She . . ." Mrs. Sommers moves closer. Nell turns on her suddenly, screaming till the woman, undone, races away. My heart beats wildly, unsettled by Nell's outburst.

"She's looking for the one who can bring the magic back to its full glory. The one with the power to take her in, to take her to the Temple. That is what she has always wanted," she whispers. "No, no, no, no!" she shouts to the air.

"Miss Hawkins," I ask, trying to lead her back to the subject at hand. "Was it Miss McCleethy? Was she there? Is she Circe? You can tell me."

Nell bends my head to hers till our foreheads touch, her tiny hand surprisingly strong on the back of my neck. The skin of her palm is rough as burlap. "Don't let her in, Lady Hope." Is that an answer? Nell continues in hushed tones. "The creatures will do anything to control you. Make you see things. Hear things. You must keep them out."

I want free of that tiny hand that frightens me with its hidden strength. But I am afraid to move. "Miss Hawkins, please, do you know where I can find the Temple?"

"You must follow the true path."

Here we are again. "There are hundreds of paths. I don't know which one you mean."

"It is where you least expect it. It hides in plain sight. You must look and you will see it, see it, see, sea, it came up from the sea, from the sea." Her eyes widen. "I saw you! I'm sorry, sorry, sorry!"

I'm losing her again. "What happened to the other girls, Nell?"

She starts to whimper like a wounded animal. "It wasn't my fault. It wasn't my fault!"

"Miss Hawkins . . . Nell, it is all right. I've seen them, in my visions. I've seen your friends. . . ."

She snarls at me then, with such a fury I am afraid she might kill me. "They are not my friends! Not my friends at all!"

"But they are trying to help."

She backs away from me, screaming. "What have you done? What have you done?"

Alarmed, a nurse leaves her post by the door, making straight for us.

"Miss Hawkins, please—I didn't mean—"

"Shhh! They're listening at keyholes! They will hear us!" Nell says, running back and forth, arms folded over her chest.

"There is no one, Miss Hawkins. It is just you and I. . . ."

She doubles back, crouching low at my knees, a feral thing. "They will see into my mind!"

"M-Miss Hawkins . . . N-Nell . . . ," I stammer. But she is lost to me.

"*Little Miss Muffet sat on a tuffet eating her curds and whey,*" she shouts, looking around as if speaking to an unseen audience in the airing yards. "*When along came a spider and sat down beside her and frightened Miss Muffet away.*"

With that, she jumps and runs to the waiting nurse, who

ushers her inside, leaving me alone in the cold with more questions than before. Nell's behavior, the sudden menace, has left me very troubled. I don't understand what she means or what has upset her so. I had hoped Nell would provide knowledge about Circe and the Temple. But Nell Hawkins, I must remember, is also living at Bedlam. She is a girl whose mind has been frayed by guilt and trauma. I don't know who or what to believe anymore.

Mrs. Sommers returns and sits beside me on the bench, smiling in her uncomfortable way. In the bald patches of her sparse eyebrows, the skin glows red.

"Is this all a dream?" she asks me.

"No, Mrs. Sommers," I answer, gathering my things.

"She lies, you know."

"What do you mean?" I ask.

Those plucked brows give Mrs. Sommers a disturbing appearance, like some demon unleashed from a medieval painting. "I hear them. They talk to me, tell me things."

"Mrs. Sommers, who talks to you and tells you things?"

"*They* do," she says, as if I should understand. "They've told me. She's not what she seems. Such wicked things she's done. She's in league with the bad ones, miss. I hear her in her room at night. Such wicked, wicked things. Watch yourself, miss. They're coming for you. They're all coming for you."

Mrs. Sommers grins, showing teeth too tiny for her mouth.

Shoving the newspaper clippings into my handbag, I back away and bolt inside, walking briskly through the halls, past the sewing classes and the tuneless piano and the squawkings of Cassandra. I pick up speed till I am nearly in a run. By the time I reach the carriage and Kartik, I am completely out of breath.

"Miss Doyle, what is the matter? Where is your brother?" he says, glancing nervously around.

"He says . . . to come back . . . for him," I say in bursts.

"What's the matter? You're flushed. I'll take you home."

"No. Not there. I need to speak with you. Alone."

Kartik takes in the spectacle of me, panting for breath and obviously shaken. "I know a place. I've never taken a young lady there, but it's the best I can think of at the moment. Do you trust me?"

"Yes," I say. He offers his hand, and I grasp it, climbing into the carriage, letting Kartik take the reins and my fate into his hands.

We travel across Blackfriars Bridge into the grimy, dark heart of East London, and I begin to have second thoughts about letting Kartik lead the way. The streets are narrow and rough here. Vegetable sellers and butchers scream out from their wagons.

"Potatoes, carrots, peas!" "Sweet cuts of lamb—no joint to speak of!"

Children crowd about us, begging for anything—coins, food, scraps, work. They compete for my attention. "Miss, miss!" they cry, offering "help" of every variety for a coin or two. Kartik pulls the carriage to a stop in an alley behind a butcher's shop. The children are on me, tugging at my coat.

"Oi!" Kartik shouts, using a Cockney accent I've never heard. "'Oo 'ere knows abou' the skull-'n'-the-sword, eh?"

The children's eyes go wide at this mention of the Rakshana.

"Righ'," Kartik continues. "So you be'ah well clear ou', if you know wha' Oi mean."

Instantly, the children scatter. Only one boy remains, and Kartik flicks him a shilling.

"Watch the coach, guv," he says.

"Right!" the boy answers, pocketing the coin.

"That was impressive," I say as we make our way over mucky streets.

Kartik allows himself one small, triumphant smile. "Whatever it takes to survive."

Kartik stays a pace ahead of me. He has a hunter's walk—all hunched shoulders and wary steps. We turn down one twisting street of dilapidated houses and then another. At last, we come into a short lane and stop before a small tavern sandwiched tightly between other buildings intent on crowding it out. We approach the heavy wooden door. Kartik knocks in a succession of short raps. A crude peephole in the door is opened from the inside, revealing an eye. The peephole closes, and we are let in. The place is dark and smells of the most delicious curry and incense. Big men sit at tables stooped over steaming plates of food, their dirt-stained hands wrapped around pints of ale as if they were the only possessions worth guarding. Now I see why Kartik has never brought a lady here before. From what I can tell, I am the only one here now.

"Am I in danger?" I whisper through clenched teeth.

"Not any more than I am. Just go about your business and don't look at anyone and you will be fine."

Why do I feel that this response makes Kartik very much like governesses who tell their charges grisly fairy tales before bed and then expect them to sleep peacefully through the night?

He leads me to a table in the back under a low, beamed ceiling. The whole place has a feeling of being underground, like a rabbit warren.

"Where are you going?" I ask frantically the moment Kartik starts to walk away.

"Shhhh!" he says, finger to his lips. "I shall surprise you."

Yes, that is what I'm afraid of. I fold my hands on the rough wooden table and try to disappear. In a moment, Kartik returns with a plate of food, which he puts before me with a smile. Dosa! I haven't had the spicy, thin cakes since I left Bombay and Sarita's kitchen. One bite has me longing for her kindness and the country I couldn't wait to leave, a country I wonder if I will ever see again.

"This is delicious," I say, taking another bite. "How do you know of this place?"

"Amar told me of it. The man who owns it is from Calcutta. You see that curtain there?" He points to a tapestry hanging on the wall. "There is a door behind it. It's a hidden room. If you should ever need me . . ."

I realize he is sharing a secret. It's a good feeling to be trusted.

"Thank you," I say. "Do you miss India?"

He shrugs. "My family is the Rakshana. They discouraged loyalty to any other country or customs."

"But don't you remember how beautiful the ghats looked at dusk, or the flower offerings floating on the water?"

"You sound like Amar," he says, biting into one of the steaming cakes.

"What do you mean?"

"He longed for India sometimes. He would joke with me. 'Little brother,' he would say, 'I'm going to retire to Benares with a fat wife and twelve children to bother me. And when I die, you can throw my ashes into the Ganges so I will never come back.'"

This is the most Kartik has ever said about his brother. I know we've pressing business to discuss, but I want to know more about him. "And did he . . . marry?"

"No. Rakshana are forbidden to marry. It is a distraction from our purpose."

"Oh. I see."

Kartik takes another dosa and slices it into neat, even pieces. "Once you've sworn an oath to the Rakshana, you are committed for life. There is no leaving. Amar knew this. He honored his duty."

"Was he very high in the ranks?"

A cloud passes over Kartik's still face. "No. But he might have been, if . . ."

If he had lived. If he hadn't died trying to protect my mother, trying to protect me.

Kartik pushes away his plate. He is all business again. "What was it you needed to tell me?"

"I think Miss McCleethy is Circe," I say. I tell him about the anagram and following her to Bedlam, about my mother's newspaper clippings and the strange visit with Nell. "Miss

Hawkins said that Circe tried to enter the realms through her but they couldn't do it. Nell could only see it in her mind. And when she couldn't . . ."

"When she couldn't?"

"I don't know. I've seen glimpses of it in my visions," I say. Kartik gives me a warning look, as I knew he would. "I know what you are about to say, but I keep seeing these three girls in white who were friends of Miss Hawkins's. It is the same vision, but a little clearer each time. The girls, the sea, and a woman in a green cloak. Circe. And then . . . I don't know. Something terrible happens. But I can never see that part."

Kartik drums his thumb softly against the table. "Did she tell you where to find the Temple?"

"No," I say. "She keeps repeating something about seeing the true path."

"I know you are fond of Miss Hawkins, but you must remember that her mind is not reliable."

"A bit like the magic and the realms just now," I say, playing with my gloves. "I don't know where to begin. It feels impossible. I'm to find something that doesn't seem to exist, and the closest I've gotten is a lunatic at Bedlam who keeps nattering on about 'stick to the path; follow the path.' I would be overjoyed to stick to a bloody path if I knew where it was."

Kartik's mouth hangs open. Too late I realize I've cursed.

"Oh, I'm dreadfully sorry," I say, horrified.

"You bloody well should be," Kartik says. He breaks out

with a boom of a laugh. I shush him, and soon we're both grinning like hyenas. An old man at another table shakes his head at us, certain we must be mad.

"I am sorry," I say. "It's just that I am so vexed."

Kartik points to my damaged amulet. "I can see that. What happened here?"

"Oh," I say, removing it. "That wasn't me. That was Miss Hawkins. The first time I visited her, she pulled it from my neck. I thought she meant to do me in. But she held it in front of her like this," I say, demonstrating.

Kartik frowns. "Like a weapon?" He takes the amulet from me and swipes at the air with it, as if it were a dagger. In the amber light of the tavern's lanterns, the metal glows golden warm.

"No. She cradled it like this." I take it back and move it in my hands as Nell had done. "She kept peering at the back of it as if she were looking for something."

Kartik sits up. "Do that again."

I move it back and forth once more. "What? What are you thinking?"

Kartik slumps down into the chair. "I don't know. It's just that what you're doing rather reminds me of a compass."

A compass! I pull the lantern close and hold the amulet beside its flickering light.

"Do you see anything?" Kartik asks, moving his chair so close to mine that I can feel the warmth of him, smell the air—a mix of chimney soot and spice—in his hair. It is a good smell, an anchoring smell.

"Nothing," I say. There are no markings that I can see. No directions.

Kartik leans back. "Well, it was a good thought."

"Hold on," I say, still looking at the amulet. "What if we can only see it in the realms?"

"Will you try it?"

"As soon as I can," I say.

"Good show, Miss Doyle," Kartik says, smiling broadly. "Let's get you home before I'm out of a job."

We leave the tavern and travel the two twisting streets back to where we've left our carriage. But when we come to that street, the little boy is no longer there. Instead, there are three men in the same cut of black suit. Two carry sticks that look as if they could do us harm. The third sits in the carriage, an open newspaper in front of his face. The street, which only a half hour ago was teeming with people, is deserted.

Kartik puts a hand out to slow my approach. The men see him and whistle. The man in the carriage folds his paper neatly. It's the man with the scar, the one who's been trailing me since I arrived in London.

"The Eastern Star is hard to find," the man with the scar says. "Very hard to find." I spy the sword-and-skull pin on his lapel. The others don't have one.

" 'Ello, mate," one of the burly men says, coming closer. He pats the stick against his palm with a thwack. "Remember me?"

Kartik rubs absently at his head, and I wonder what on earth they're talking about.

"Mr. Fowlson 'ere requires your presence at a business

mee'in' of sorts by the lady's carriage." He pulls Kartik hard. The other man escorts me.

"Fowlson," I say. "So you have a name."

The man scowls at the big hooligan for this.

"There's no need for pretense. I know you are Rakshana. And I'll thank you to stop following me about."

The man speaks in a low, controlled voice, as if he might be gently admonishing a wayward child. "And I know you are an impertinent girl with no regard for the seriousness of the business before you, else you should be in the realms searching for the Temple rather than dallying about London's seamier streets. Surely the Temple is not here. Or is it? Tell me, just where did this one take you?"

He doesn't know about Kartik's hiding place. Beside me, I feel Kartik holding his breath.

"Sightseeing," I say, standing a stone's throw from a slaughterhouse. "I wished to see these slums for myself."

The big man with the club scoffs at me.

"I assure you, sir. I am in earnest about my duty," I say to Fowlson.

"Are we, now, lass? The task is simple: Find the Temple and bind the magic."

"If it is so simple a matter, why don't you do it?" I answer hotly. "But no, you can't. So you will have to rely on me, an 'impertinent girl,' won't you?"

Fowlson looks as if he would like to hit me very hard. "For the present, it would seem so." He gives Kartik a cold smile. "Do not forget *your* task, novitiate."

He tucks his newspaper under his arm and motions to his men. The three of them back away slowly, vanishing at last around a corner. Kartik springs into action, practically pushing me into the carriage.

"What did he mean, do not forget *your* task?" I ask.

"I told you," he says, leading Ginger into the street. "My task is to help you find the Temple. That is all. What did *you* mean when you asked Fowlson to stop following you about?"

"He *has* been following me! He was at the train station the day I arrived in London. And then when I was out walking in Hyde Park with Grandmama," I say, purposefully avoiding Simon's name, "he rode by in a carriage. And I saw a woman in a green cloak with him, Kartik. A green cloak!"

"There are plenty of green cloaks in London, Miss Doyle," Kartik tells me. "They do not all belong to Circe."

"No. But one does. I am only asking if you are certain that Mr. Fowlson can be trusted?"

"He is one of the Rakshana, part of my brotherhood," he says. "Yes. I am certain."

He doesn't look at me when he says this, and I'm afraid that any trust we've begun to have has been frayed by my questions. Kartik takes his perch behind the reins. With a snap, we are off, the horse's blinders keeping her docile but her hooves kicking up a storm of dust on the cobblestones.

⌇⌇⌇⌇

In the evening, Grandmama and I take up our needlework by the fire. Each time a carriage passes by, she sits a bit straighter. At last I realize she is listening for our own carriage, for

Father's return from his club. Father has been spending a great deal of time there, especially in the evenings. Some nights I hear him coming home just before sunrise.

Tonight it is particularly hard for Grandmama to bear. Father left in a terrible temper, accusing Mrs. Jones of losing his gloves, practically tearing the library apart looking for them before Grandmama discovered them in his coat pocket. They'd been there the entire time. He left without so much as an apology.

"I'm sure he'll be home soon," I say, when another carriage clip-clops past our house.

"Yes. Yes, quite right," she says absently. "I'm sure he's simply forgotten the time. He does so enjoy being among people, doesn't he?"

"Yes," I say, surprised that she cares so much about her son. Knowing this makes it harder to dislike her.

"He loves you more than Tom, you know."

I am so startled I prick my finger. A tiny bubble of blood pushes its way through the flesh at the tip.

"It's true. Oh, he cares for Tom, of course. But sons are a different matter to a man, more a duty than an indulgence. You are his angel. Don't ever break his heart, Gemma. He has weathered too much already. That would finish him."

I'm trying not to cry, from the pinprick and the unwanted knowledge. "I shan't," I promise.

"Your needlework is coming along nicely, dear. Shorter stitches round the edge, though, I think," Grandmama says as if we've discussed nothing else.

Mrs. Jones enters. "Begging your pardon, Mrs. Doyle. This

came for Miss Doyle this afternoon. Emily took it and forgot to tell me." Though it's clearly intended for me, she offers Grandmama the box, which is beautifully wrapped with a pink silk bow.

Grandmama reads the card. "It is from Simon Middleton."

A gift from Simon? I am intrigued. Inside the box is a beautiful, delicate necklace of small amethyst stones that fan out along a chain. Purple, my favorite color. The card reads *Gems for our Gemma*.

"So beautiful," Grandmama says, holding them up to the light. "I do believe Simon Middleton is bewitched!"

It is beautiful, possibly the most beautiful thing anyone has ever given me. "Would you help me with the clasp?" I ask.

I remove my mother's amulet, and Grandmama secures the new necklace. I rush over to the mirror to see. The gems fall sweetly over my collarbones.

"You must wear it to the opera tomorrow evening," Grandmama advises.

"Yes, I shall," I say, watching the stones catch the light. They sparkle and shine till I hardly recognize myself.

⁂

I've a note from Kartik on my pillow: *There's something I need to tell you. I'll be in the stables.* I don't like that Kartik feels he can trespass in my room any time he likes. I shall tell him that. I don't like that he's keeping secrets from me. I shall tell him that, too. But not now. Now I am wearing a new necklace from Simon. Beautiful Simon, who thinks of me not as someone who can help him move up in the ranks of the Rakshana, but as a girl worthy of gems.

Gingerly, I lift the note from the pillow and twirl around the room with it stretched between my fingers. The necklace weighs against my skin like a calming hand. *Gems for our Gemma.*

I toss Kartik's note into the fire. The ends of the paper curl and blacken, and in an instant it is gone to ash.

CHAPTER
TWENTY-NINE

IF I AM ANXIOUS ABOUT THIS EVENING'S TRIP TO the opera, Grandmama is beside herself.

"I do hope those gloves will do," she tuts as a seamstress makes last-minute adjustments to my gown, a white duchess satin, the color young ladies wear to the opera. Grandmama has had my first opera gloves sent round from Whiteley's department store. The seamstress slips the pearl buttons through the loops at my wrist, shutting my naked arms away behind expensive kid leather. My hair has been artfully arranged away from my face with flowers in the chignon. And of course, I've put on Simon's lovely necklace. When I spy myself in the mirror, I must admit that I look quite lovely, like a true and proper lady.

Even Tom rises when I enter the parlor, shocked to see my transformation. Father takes my hand and kisses it. His own hand shakes a bit. I know that he was out until dawn, and he slept all the day, and I hope that he is not taking ill. He mops his sweaty brow with a pocket square, but his voice is merry enough.

"You are a queen, my pet. Isn't she, Thomas?"

"Not an embarrassment, to be sure," Tom answers. For an imbecile, he's rather elegant in his tails.

"Is that the best you can manage?" Father admonishes.

Tom sighs. "You look most presentable, Gemma. Do remember not to snore at the opera. It's frowned upon."

"If I have kept myself awake while you speak, Tom, I'm certain I can manage."

"The carriage has been brought round, sir," Davis, the butler, announces, saving us all from further conversation.

As we walk to the carriage, I catch sight of Kartik's expression. He stares, boldly, as if I am an apparition, someone he does not know. I'm oddly satisfied by this. Yes. Let him see that I am not some "impertinent girl," as the Rakshana henchman put it.

"The door, Mr. Kartik, if you please," Tom says tersely. As if pulled from a dream, Kartik quickly opens the carriage door. "Really, Father," Tom says when we are on our way. "I do wish you'd reconsider. Just yesterday, Sims made a recommendation on a driver—"

"The matter is closed. Mr. Kartik gets me where I need to go," Father says stiffly.

"Yes, that is my concern," Tom mutters under his breath, so that only I hear.

"Now, now," Grandmama says, patting Father's knee. "Let's be of good cheer, shall we? After all, it is nearly Christmas."

As the door to the Royal Opera House opens, I'm seized by panic. What if I look ridiculous, not elegant? What if something—my hair, my dress, my bearing—is out of place? I am so very tall. I wish I were shorter. Daintier. Brunette. Unfreckled. An Austrian countess. Is it too late to run home and hide?

"Ah, there they are," Grandmama announces. I spy Simon. He is so handsome in his white tie and black tails.

"Good evening," I say, curtsying.

"Good evening," he says. He gives me a small smile, and with that smile, I feel such relief and happiness that I could sit through ten operas.

We receive our programs and join the crowd. Father, Tom, and Simon are pulled into a conversation with another man, a portly, balding fellow sporting a monocle on a chain, while Grandmama, Lady Denby, and I stroll slowly, nodding and making our hellos to various society ladies. It is a necessary parade designed to show off our finery. I hear my name being called. It's Felicity with Ann. They are well turned out in their white gowns. Felicity's garnet earbobs shine against her white-blond hair. A pink cameo rests against the hollow of Ann's throat.

"Oh, dear," Lady Denby says. "It's that wretched Worthington woman."

The comment has Grandmama aflutter. "Mrs. Worthington? The admiral's wife? Is there some scandal?"

"You do not know? Three years ago, she went to Paris—for her health, they said—and she sent the young Miss

Worthington away to school. But I have it on good authority that she took a lover, a Frenchman, and now he's left her and she's back with the admiral, pretending that none of it ever happened. She is not received in the best homes, of course. But everyone attends her dinners and balls out of affection for the admiral, who is the soul of respectability. Shhh, here they come."

Mrs. Worthington strides over, the girls in tow. I hope the flush on my cheeks does not give me away, for I don't like Lady Denby's snobbery.

"Good evening, Lady Denby," Mrs. Worthington says, her smile radiant.

Lady Denby does not offer her hand but opens her fan instead. "Good evening, Mrs. Worthington."

Felicity gives a dazzling smile. If I didn't know her better I wouldn't recognize the ice in it. "Oh, dear. Ann, you seem to have lost your bracelet!"

"What bracelet?" Ann asks.

"The one the duke sent from Saint Petersburg. Perhaps you lost it in the dressing room. We must look for it. Gemma, would you mind awfully?"

"No, of course not," I say.

"Be quick about it. The opera is about to begin," Grandmama warns.

We escape to the dressing room. A few ladies preen at the mirrors, adjusting shawls and jewels.

"Ann, when I say you've lost your bracelet, play along," Felicity chides.

"Sorry," Ann says.

"I do loathe Lady Denby. She's a horrid woman," Felicity mutters.

"She isn't," I argue.

"You wouldn't say that if you weren't so besotted with her son."

"I am not *besotted*. He simply invited my family to the opera."

Felicity's raised eyebrow says she doesn't believe a word of it.

"Perhaps you'd like to know that I've discovered something about my amulet," I say, changing the subject.

"What is it?" Ann asks, removing her gloves in order to tend to her hair.

"The crescent eye is some sort of compass. That's what Nell Hawkins was trying to tell me. I think it may lead us to the Temple."

Felicity's eyes gleam. "A compass! We must try it tonight."

"Tonight?" I squeak. "Here? With all these people about?" With Simon, I almost say. "We couldn't possibly."

"Of course we can," Felicity whispers. "Just before intermission, tell your grandmother that you must be excused for the dressing room. Ann and I shall do the same. We'll meet in the hall and find a place where we can enter the realms from there."

"It isn't that simple," I say. "She won't let me go, not alone."

"Find a way," Felicity insists.

"But it wouldn't be proper!"

"Afraid of what Simon will think? It isn't as if you're betrothed!" Felicity tut-tuts.

The comment lands like a blow. "I never said anything of the sort."

Felicity smiles. She knows she's won. "So we are agreed. Just before intermission. Do not delay."

The plan in place, we turn our attention to the mirrors, positioning combs and smoothing dresses.

"Has he tried to kiss you?" Felicity asks in an offhand manner.

"No, of course not," I say, embarrassed. I hope no one has overheard her.

"I should be careful," Felicity says. "Simon has a reputation as a ladies' man."

"He's been the perfect gentleman with me," I protest.

"Hmmm," Felicity says, her eyes on her reflection, which is fetching, as always.

Ann's pinching her cheeks in vain, hoping to raise color there. "I hope I shall meet someone tonight. Someone kind and noble. The sort who likes to help others. Someone like Tom."

Two angry red welts crisscross near her wrist bone. The marks are new, perhaps a few hours old. She's cut herself again. Ann sees me looking and her freshly pinched cheeks pale. Quickly, she pulls her gloves on, covering the scars.

Felicity leads the way out, greeting a friend of her mother's near the door. I grab Ann's wrist and she winces.

"You promised me you'd stop doing that," I say.

"What do you mean?"

"You know very well what I mean," I warn.

Her eyes find mine. She wears a sad little smile. "Better that I hurt myself than be hurt by them. It stings less."

"I don't understand."

"It's different for you and Fee," Ann says, nearly crying. "Don't you see? I have no future. There's nothing for me. I'll never be a great lady or marry someone like Tom. I can only pretend. It's horrible, Gemma."

"You don't know what will be," I say, trying to soothe. "No one knows."

Felicity's noticed we're not beside her and comes back for us. "What is the matter?"

"Nothing," I say brightly. "We're coming." I take Ann's hand. "Things can change. Repeat it."

"Things can change," she parrots quietly.

"Do you believe that?"

She shakes her head. Silent tears trickle down her round cheeks.

"We'll find a way. I promise. But first, *you* must promise me you'll stop. Please?"

"I'll try," she says, brushing a gloved hand against her damp face and forcing a smile.

"Here is trouble," Felicity says as we rejoin the throng in the lobby. I see what she means. It's Cecily Temple. She stands beside her mother, craning her neck, looking this way and that in hopes that she will see someone of interest.

Ann's in a panic. "I'll be found out! Ruined! It will be the end for me."

"Stop it," Felicity snaps. But she's right, of course. Cecily can bring Ann's story of Russian nobility and distant peerage down like a house of cards.

"We'll avoid her," Felicity says. "Come with me. We shall

take the opposite stairs. Gemma, just before intermission. Don't forget."

"For the third time, I shan't," I say testily.

The house lights flicker in warning that the opera is to begin.

"There you are!" Simon says. He has waited for me. My stomach quivers. "Did you find Miss Bradshaw's bracelet?"

"No. She remembered that she'd left it in her jewelry box after all," I lie.

Simon's family has a private box quite high up that makes me feel as if I am the Queen herself, lording over all my subjects. We take our seats and pretend to read our programs, though no one's really paying any attention to *The Mikado*. Opera glasses are used to spy covertly on lovers and friends, to see who is wearing what, who has arrived with whom. There is more potential scandal and drama in the audience than there could possibly be onstage. At last, the lights are dimmed, and the curtain rises on a small Japanese village. A trio of sopranos in Oriental dress and black lacquered wigs sings of being three little maids at school. It is my first opera, and I find it delightful. At one point, I catch Simon watching me. Rather than look away, he gives me the most radiant smile, and I can scarcely imagine how I will tear myself away to enter the realms, for this too is magic, and I cannot help feeling resentful that my duty calls me.

Just before intermission, I spy Felicity through my opera glasses. She's looking at me impatiently. I whisper in Grandmama's ear that I must excuse myself to the dressing room. Before she can protest, I slip out the curtains that lead to the hall, where I greet Felicity and Ann.

"There is an unused box upstairs," Felicity says, taking my hand. A wistful aria floats through the opera house as we make our way silently upstairs. Ducking low, we push aside the heavy curtains and sit on the floor just inside. I reach for their hands. Eyes shut, we concentrate, and the door of light appears.

CHAPTER
THIRTY

THE SWEET SMELL OF LILAC GREETS US IN THE GAR-
den, but things look different. The trees and grass are a bit
wilder, as if they've gone to seed. More toadstools have popped
up. They cast long shadows across our faces.

"Why, you look lovely!" Pippa shouts to us from her perch
by the river. She races to us, her tattered hem flying in the
breeze. The flowers in her crown have gone dry and brittle.
"How beautiful! Where have you been in your finery?"

"The opera," Ann says, twirling in her fancy dress. "*The
Mikado* is still playing. We stole away!"

"The opera," Pippa says with a sigh. "Is it madly elegant? You
must tell me simply everything!"

"It is dazzling, Pip. The women drip with jewels. A man
winked at me."

"When?" Felicity says, disbelieving.

"He did! On the way up the staircase. Oh, and Gemma has
come with Simon Middleton and his family. She's sitting in
their box," Ann relates breathlessly.

"Oh, Gemma! I am so very happy for you!" Pippa says, giving me a kiss. Whatever misgivings I had about her have just melted.

"Thank you," I say, returning her kiss.

"Oh, it all sounds heavenly. Tell me more." Pippa leans against a tree.

"Do you like my dress?" Ann asks, twirling again for her inspection.

Pippa takes Ann's hands in hers, dancing with her. "It's beautiful! You are beautiful!"

Pippa stops twirling. She looks as if she shall cry. "I've never been to the opera, and now I never shall, I suppose. How I wish I could go with you."

"You would be the most beautiful of all, if you were there," Felicity says, making Pip smile again.

Ann runs to me. "Gemma, try the amulet."

"What's this?" Pippa asks.

"Gemma thinks her amulet is a sort of compass," Felicity says.

"Do you think it will show us the way to the Temple?" Pippa asks.

"We're going to find out," I say. I take the amulet from my handbag, turn it over. At first, there is nothing but the cold hard metal surface reflecting a distorted image of my face. But then, something changes. The surface grows cloudy. I move slowly in a circle. When I am facing two straight rows of olive trees, the crescent eye glows bright, illuminating a faint but obvious path.

"Stick to the path," I mutter, remembering Nell's words. "I think we've found the way to the Temple."

"Oh, let me see!" Pippa takes the amulet in her hands, watches it glow in the direction of the olive trees. "How splendid!"

"Have you been that way?" I ask.

Pippa shakes her head. A breeze whistles down the trail between the olive trees, carrying with it a handful of leaves and the scent of lilac. Using the amulet's shimmering glow as a guide, we duck into the cover of the trees, walking for what seems a mile, past strange totems with the heads of elephants, snakes, and birds. We reach an earthen passageway. The amulet flares.

"Through here?" Ann says, panting.

"I'm afraid so," I answer.

It is tight and not terribly tall. Even Ann, the shortest of us, has to stoop to pass through. The softness of the trail gives way to rockier ground. We come through the opening onto a path bordered on both sides by fields of tall reddish orange flowers that sway hypnotically. As we pass, the breeze bends them forward so that they brush gently across our faces and shoulders. They smell of fresh summer fruits. Pippa picks a bloom and tucks it into her fading crown.

Something flits past on my right.

"What was that?" Ann asks, standing close.

"I don't know," I answer. I can see nothing but the flowers rippling in the wind.

"Let's go on," Pippa advises.

We follow the amulet's bright glow till the path ends abruptly at an enormous wall of rock. It is tall as a mountain and seems to go on forever so that there is no way around it.

"What do we do now?" Felicity asks.

"There must be some way through," I say, though I haven't the vaguest idea how. "Look for a passage."

We press against the rocks till we are exhausted with the effort.

"It's no use," Pippa says, panting. "It's solid rock."

We can't have come all this way for nothing. There must be a way in. I walk along the wall, moving the amulet back and forth. It flares briefly.

"What's this?" I say.

I turn it again gently and it shimmers in my hand. When I look at the rock, there is the faint outline of a door.

"Do you see that?" I ask, hoping that I am not imagining it.

"Yes!" Felicity cries. "It's a door!"

I reach out a hand and feel the cold steel of a handle in the rock. With a deep breath, I pull on it. It's as if a great, dark hole has opened in the earth. The amulet's shine is strong.

"This would seem to be the way," I announce, though truthfully, I have no desire to step into that deep black well.

Felicity licks her lips nervously. "Go on, then. We'll follow."

"I'm not comforted by that," I say. Heart racing, half expecting to be swallowed whole by the rock, I step inside and wait for my eyes to adjust to the gloom. It's dank and smells of a freshly tilled garden. Paper lanterns of gold and rose hang from the stone walls, casting a weak light on the mud floors. It is difficult to see more than a few feet ahead, but I can feel that we're climbing, going up and around. Soon, our breathing is labored. My legs tremble from the effort. At last we come to another door. I turn the handle and we emerge to purple and red smoke billowing about us like clouds. A breeze pushes the colorful smoke away, and the scene opens up. We are high above the river. Far below us, the gorgon ship cuts silently through the blue water.

"How did we get so high up?" Felicity asks, trying to catch her breath.

"I don't know," I say.

Ann cranes her neck. "Gracious!" She stares openmouthed at the sensual goddesses carved into the cliff's side, at the curves of their hips and mouths, their dimpled knees, and the lush softness of their rounded chins. These stone women look down at us from so high, noticing but not bothering with us.

"I remember this," I say. "This is near the Caves of Sighs, isn't it?"

Pippa stops. "We shouldn't be here. The Untouchables live here. It's forbidden."

"Let's go back," Ann says.

But when we turn around, the door fades into rock. There is no going back that way.

"What do we do now?" Ann asks.

"I wish I'd brought my arrows," Felicity murmurs.

Someone is approaching. A figure appears in the thick smoke, a small woman with weathered skin the color of a wine cask. Her hands and face are painted in elaborate designs. But her arms and legs! The most hideous sores mark them. One leg is so swollen it is the size of a tree trunk. We turn away in disgust, unable to look at her.

"Welcome," she says. "I am Asha. Follow me."

"We were just leaving," Felicity says.

Asha laughs. "Where did you mean to go? This is the only way out. Forward."

As we can't leave by the way we've come, we follow. The path is crowded with others. They too are misshapen, bent, scarred.

"Don't stare," I admonish Ann quietly. "Just watch your feet."

Asha leads us around the cliff, through arched tunnels supported by pillars. The walls are painted with scenes of fantastic battles—the severing of a gorgon's head, the driving back of snakes, knights dressed in tunics painted with red poppies. I see the Forest of Lights, a centaur playing pipes, the water nymphs, the Runes of the Oracle. It is like a tapestry, with so many scenes I cannot count them all.

The tunnel opens out to another magnificent vista. We are quite high on the mountain. Pots of incense line the narrow path. Curls of magenta, turquoise, and yellow smoke tickle my nose, make my eyes sting.

Asha stops at the mouth of a cave. A crude carving of a chain of snakes marks the entrance. It looks less like a carving and more like something that has risen from the earth itself. "The Caves of Sighs."

"I thought you said this was the way out," I query.

"So it is." Asha steps into the cave and folds into the darkness. Behind us on the road, the others have formed a cluster five deep and ten across. There is no retreat.

"I don't like this," Pippa says.

"Nor do I, but what choice do we have now?" I say, ducking into the cave.

The moment I'm through, I understand why these caves have gotten this name. It is as if the walls themselves sigh with the bliss of a hundred thousand kisses.

"So beautiful." It's Ann. She's standing before a bas-relief of a face with a long flat nose and large, full lips. Her hands trace the curve of the upper lip, and I think immediately of Kartik. Pippa joins her, enjoying the feel of the stone.

"I beg your pardon, but we were following a path and it seems to have disappeared. Can you tell us the way back, please? We're in a dreadful hurry," Felicity demands sweetly.

"You seek the Temple?" Asha asks.

She has our attention now. "Yes," I say. "Do you know where it is?"

"What do you offer?" Asha asks, hands outstretched.

Am I to offer a gift? I've nothing to give. I couldn't possibly part with Simon's necklace or my amulet.

"I'm sorry," I say. "I've brought nothing with me."

Asha's eyes betray her disappointment. But she smiles anyway. "Sometimes we seek that which we are not yet ready to find. The true path is a difficult one. To see it, you must be willing to shed this skin like a snake. You must be willing to let go of that which is precious to you." She glances at Pippa when she says this.

"We should go," Pippa says.

I think she may be right. "Thank you for your trouble, but we must be getting back now."

Asha gives a bow. "As you wish. I can put you on the path. But you will need our help."

A woman whose face is painted a bright red with stripes of

deep green pours a clay mixture into a long tube with a hole at the end.

"What is that for?" Felicity asks.

"To paint you," Asha says.

"Paint us?" Ann nearly shrieks.

"It offers protection," Asha explains.

"Protection from what?" I ask warily.

"Protection from whatever comes looking for you in these realms. It hides what must be hidden and reveals what must be seen." Again, she gives that curious look to Pippa.

"I don't like the sound of this at all," Pippa says.

"Nor do I," Ann agrees.

"What if this is a trap?" Felicity whispers. "What if that paint is poison?"

The red-faced woman bids us sit and place our hands upon a large rock.

"Why should we trust you?" I ask.

"There are many choices to make. You are free to refuse," Asha answers.

The woman with the paint waits patiently. Should I trust Asha, an Untouchable, or take my chances in the realms unprotected?

I offer my hands to the woman with the painted face.

"You are brave, I see," Asha says. She nods to the woman, who squeezes the mixture onto my hands. It is cold on my skin. Is that the poison working its way into my blood? I can only close my eyes and wait, hoping for the best.

"Oh, look!" Ann gasps.

Fearing the worst, I open my eyes. My hands. Where the

clay mixture has dried it has turned a glorious brick red in a design more ornate than a spider's web. It reminds me of the brides of India whose hands are stenciled with henna in honor of their husbands.

"I shall be next," Felicity says, rushing to remove her gloves. She is no longer afraid of being poisoned, only of being left out.

In the deep recesses of the cave is a sheet of water smooth as glass that seems to rise and fall at the same time. The flow of it makes me drowsy. It is the last thing I see before I fall asleep.

〰〰〰

I am standing before a large well. The surface is alive with movement. It shows me things. Roses blooming fast on thick green vines. A cathedral adrift on an island. Black rock awash in fog. A warrior in horned helmet riding a fierce horse. A twisted tree against a bloodred sky. Asha's painted hands. Nell Hawkins. The green cloak. Something moves in the shadows, startling me, coming closer. A face.

I wake with a start. Felicity laughs merrily, showing off her hands, which have been painted in beautiful curlicues. She compares them with Ann's and Pippa's ornate designs. Asha sits across from me, her thick, scaly legs crossed.

"What did you see in your dreams?" she asks.

What did I see? Nothing that means anything to me. "Nothing," I answer.

Again I see disappointment in her eyes. "It is time for you to go."

She leads us to the mouth of the cave. The sky is no longer blue, but a deep, inky night. Have we been here so long? The pots of incense belch their rainbow of color. Torches line the path. The Hajin stand beside them, bowing as we walk.

When we once again reach the rock, the door appears. "I thought you said that the only way out was to go forward," I say.

"Yes. That is true."

"But this is the way we've come!"

"Is it?" she asks. "Take care on the path. Walk quickly and quietly. The paint will keep you hidden from sight." Asha places her palms together and bows. "Go now."

I don't understand at all, but we've wasted too much time already for more questions. We've got to get back to the path. In the glow of the amulet, I can see the delicate lines on my hands. It seems a scant protection from whatever may be looking for us, but I hope Asha is right.

THE GLOW OF THE CRESCENT EYE LEADS US AWAY from the mountain till we are on unfamiliar ground. The sky is not as dark here. It's suffused with the light of a dark red moon. We're surrounded by the gnarled bodies of giant trees. Their branches arch high over our heads, those bare, twisted fingers of bark intertwining in an eerie embrace. The effect is rather like being in one long cage.

"Did we come this way before?" Felicity asks.

"Where are we?" Pippa asks.

"I don't know," I say.

"It's a ghastly place," Ann says.

"I knew we shouldn't have trusted them. Filthy vermin!" Pippa says.

"Hush!" I say. In my hand, the amulet's glow has softened to a flickering glimmer, and then it's out like a candle snuffed. "It's gone out."

"Well, that's a fine thing! Now how will we get back?" Ann mumbles.

The red moon bleeds through the spindly, stripped branches, casting long shadows.

"We'll use the moonlight. Keep walking," I say. Why has the amulet stopped working?

"Gracious, what is that smell?" Felicity asks.

The wind moves this way, and I smell it too. A smell like disease and filth. A smell like death. A breeze pushes down the corridor of trees from behind us, rustling our satins and silks. It is more substantial than a puff of wind. It is an announcement. Something's coming.

Ann's got her hand to her nose and mouth. "Oh, that is truly beastly."

"Shhhh!" I say.

"What?" Pippa asks.

"Do you hear that?"

Riders. They're coming fast. A cloud of dust looms. They'll overtake us in a moment. The corridor ahead seems to stretch on for a mile. Can we squeeze through the spaces between the trees? The gaps are but slivers of light, too narrow to allow any of us to pass.

"Where've you gone?" Pippa asks, looking about.

"What do you mean? We're right here," Felicity says.

"I can't see any of you!"

The paint! It's keeping us hidden somehow. "The paint protects us. They can't see us."

"What about me?" Pippa asks, examining her hands, which are quite visible. "Oh, God!" She sounds desperate, and I don't know what to do to help her. The riders come into view—

skeletal wraiths twisted beyond whatever human form they once had. And behind them looms a figure of such terror—a hideous thing with giant, tattered wings and a mouth of long, pointed teeth. Flaps of flesh still cling to them in places. It has no eyes. But it sniffs the air, hunting for us. I know what it is, for I've faced one before. It's a tracker, the sort employed by Circe.

It sniffs in our direction. Its odor is enough to make me gag. I fight against it.

"You there," the dark spirit howls, and for a moment I think he has found us. "You have not passed, spirit?"

"M-me?" Pippa says. "I—I . . ."

The thing's mouth drools in slick, slimy ribbons. Oh, Pip! I want to save her but I'm frightened, unable to give up the safety of my invisibility. The horrid creature sniffs the air.

"Ah, I can smell them. Living things. The priestess has been here. Have you seen her?"

Pippa shakes. "N-no," she whispers.

The beast moves closer to her. Its voice is a growl laced with the despair of a thousand souls. "You would not lie to us, would you?"

Pippa opens her mouth but no words come.

"No matter. We shall find her eventually. My mistress is seeing to it. And when she has the Temple, the balance of power shall fall to the Winterlands at last." He moves closer to Pippa, showing a terrible grin. "Ride with us. You can share in our victory. Whatever you wish can be yours. Such a pretty pet. Ride with us."

That face is so very close to Pippa's lovely cheek. There's a rock beneath my boot. Carefully, I reach down and fling it across the lane. The tracker's massive head swivels in that direction. The wraiths howl and shriek.

"They are still near. They have some magic working for them. I can feel it. I'm sure we shall meet again, my pet. Ride!" With that, they race screaming into the corridor. We stand without moving or speaking until the ground has settled and the wind is no more.

"Are you all right, Pip?" Felicity cries.

"Y-yes. I think so," she says. "I still can't see you. I wonder why it didn't work on me?"

Yes, I wonder too. *It hides what must be hidden and reveals what must be seen.* Why would Pippa not need to be hidden, unless she already has protection in the realms? No, Pippa is nothing like that thing. That is what my head says. But in my heart is another, terrible thought: Soon, she might be.

"I want to leave this place at once," Ann says.

We walk quickly and quietly, as Asha advised. When we reach the end of the corridor, the amulet sputters to life in my hands.

"It's back!" I say. I move it about. It glows strongest on my left. "This way!"

Soon, we see the frayed edge of the golden sunset that marks the realm of the garden. By the time we reach the silver archway and the river, we're visible once more.

Pippa's shaking all over. "That creature . . . so horrible."

"Are you certain you're all right?" I ask.

She nods. "Gemma," she says, biting her lip, "what shall happen once you find the Temple?"

"You know what happens. I must bind the magic."

"And what will happen to me? Must I go?" Her voice is whisper thin.

It is the question I keep pushing away. But tonight, I have begun to realize—to see clearly, as Asha said—that this may not be forever. That Pippa might become one of those dark spirits herself if she does not cross. I can't bring myself to say it. I pick up a handful of dew from the ground. The drops gather in my fingers, becoming a silvery web that sticks them together.

"Gemma . . . ," Pippa pleads.

"Of course you won't have to go," Felicity says, storming past me. "We'll find a way to change things with the magic. The Order will help us."

"We don't know that," I say gently.

"But it's possible, isn't it?" Pippa asks, hope turning her eyes bright again. "Think of it! I could stay. We would be together forever."

"Yes, of course. We'll find a way. I promise," Felicity says.

I flash Felicity a warning look, but Pippa's crying tears of joy, wrapping her arms about Felicity's chest, cradling her in her arms. "Fee, thank you. I do love you so."

The paint on our hands has faded to nothing more than a shadow of lines and squiggles that disappear under the thin white lies of our gloves.

"You mustn't go just yet," Pippa begs. "I want to pretend that

I am also at the opera. And there is a ball after! Come on—dance with me!"

She runs out into the grass, sweeping her dress from side to side, kicking up her heels. Giggling, Ann runs after. I pull Felicity aside.

"You oughtn't to promise Pippa such things."

Felicity's eyes flash. "Why not? Gemma, she was lost to us, and now we have her back. There must be some reason for it, don't you think?"

I think of my mother's passing, of how keen the pain of her loss still feels, like a wound you think healed till you bump the fading bruise of it and feel the hurt anew. It is horrible. And yet . . . Asha's magic didn't work on Pip. Those dark spirits saw her. They courted her and hunted us.

"I do not know what we have, but it is not Pippa. Not our Pippa, at the least."

Felicity breaks away from me. "I won't lose her twice. You can see she isn't changed. She's still our Pippa, lovely as ever."

"But she ate the berries. She died. You saw her buried."

Felicity won't hear it. "The magic. That will change things."

"That isn't its purpose," I say softly. "Pip is a creature of the realms now, and she must pass before she is corrupted."

Felicity looks out to where Pippa and Ann frolic in the fresh grass, twirling like ballerinas. "You don't know that."

"Fee . . ."

"You don't know that!" She breaks into a run.

"Dance with me, Fee," Pippa calls, her smile radiant. She takes Felicity's hands in hers. Something passes between them that I cannot name. A tenderness. A togetherness. Just as if we were all gathered in Spence's grand ballroom, Felicity places her hands at Pippa's waist and pulls her into a waltz. They twirl and twirl, Pippa's ringlets catching the wind, wild and free.

"Oh, Fee. I do miss you so." She wraps her arm about Felicity's waist and Felicity does the same to Pippa. They could be Siamese twins. Pippa whispers something to Felicity, and she laughs. "Don't leave me," Pippa says. "Promise me you'll be back. Promise me."

Felicity lays her hands over Pip's. "I promise."

I need a moment to anchor myself. I walk to the river's edge to sit and think. The gorgon glides silently into view.

"Are you troubled, Most High?" she says in her slick voice.

"No," I grumble.

"You do not trust me," she says.

"I didn't say that."

She pivots her enormous green head in the direction of the garden, where my friends are dancing in the sweet grass. "Things are changing. You cannot stop the change."

"What do you mean by that?"

"You will have to make a choice, and soon, I fear."

I stand, brushing the grass from my skirt. "I know you helped slaughter members of the Order. You didn't warn us when the water nymphs were near. For all I know, you could be part of the Winterlands. Why should I listen to anything you have to say?"

"I was bound by magic to speak truth and do no harm to your kind."

Once.

I turn to leave. "As you said, things are changing."

∼∼∼∼∼

We return to the empty box of the Royal Opera House just as the curtain falls for the intermission. We're carrying magic with us. It clings to my body in a way that makes me aware of everything. The slow hiss of the gaslamp mounted on the edge of the private box roars in my head. The rising lights sting my eyes. And people's thoughts rush through me till I feel I'll go mad.

"Gemma? Are you all right?" Ann asks.

"Don't you feel that?" I gasp.

"Feel what?" Felicity says, irritated.

"The magic. It's too much." I put my hands to my ears as if that will stop things. Ann and Felicity do not seem bothered at all. "Try to do something magical—make a grasshopper or a ruby."

Felicity closes her eyes and holds out her palm. Something flickers there for a moment, but then it fades. "Why couldn't I make it happen?"

"I don't know," I say. I can scarcely catch my breath. "You try, Ann."

Ann cups her hands together and concentrates. She's wishing for a diamond crown. I can feel her wish surging inside me. In a moment she stops trying. "I don't understand," she says.

"It's as if all your magic is in me," I say, shivering. "As if I have it threefold."

Felicity peeks over the top of the lip of the box. "They've left their seats! They'll be looking for us! We've got to go to them. Gemma, can you stand?"

My legs are like a new colt's. Felicity and Ann flank me, our hands locked. We fall in behind a man and his wife. He's having an affair with her sister. He plans to meet her tonight after the opera. His secrets rush through my veins, poisoning me.

"Oh," I gasp, shaking my head to rid myself of his thoughts. "This is awful. I can hear and feel everything. I can't stop it. How shall I get through this evening?"

Felicity guides me down the stairs. "We'll get you to the dressing room and tell your grandmother that you are indisposed. She'll take you home."

"But then I shall miss my evening with Simon!" I wail.

"Do you want Simon to see you like this?" Felicity whispers.

"N-no," I say, tears slipping down my cheeks.

"Come on, then."

Ann's humming softly. It's a nervous habit of hers, but it's soothing somehow, and if I listen only to her voice, I find I can walk and look reasonably fit.

When we reach the bottom of the stairs and the grand foyer, Tom's there, looking for me. Ann stops humming, and I'm assaulted by the din of everyone's secrets. *Concentrate, Gemma. Turn them out. Choose one.*

Ann. I feel her heart beating in rhythm with mine. She's imagining herself dancing in Tom's arms, him looking adoringly at her. She wants it desperately, and I'm sorry I know it.

Here he comes, along with Lady Denby. And Simon. I lose

the thread that is Ann. Everything's rushing in again. I'm in a panic. All I can think about is Simon, beautiful Simon in his white tie and black jacket, and me, undone by the magic. He's striding over. For a moment, his thoughts push their way in. Fleeting images. His mouth on my neck. His hand removing my glove.

My knees buckle. Felicity pulls me up sharply.

"Miss Doyle?" Simon asks quizzically.

"Miss Doyle is a bit indisposed," Felicity says to my great embarrassment.

"I am sorry to hear it," Lady Denby says. "We'll send for the carriage at once."

"If you think it best, Lady Denby," Grandmama says, disappointed to cut her evening short.

"Lady Denby, how very nice to see you!" It's Cecily Temple's mother, marching our way with Cecily at her side. Cecily's eyes go wide when she spies Ann.

"Good evening," she says. "Why, Miss Bradshaw. What a surprise to see you here. Why are you not back at Spence with Brigid and the servants?"

"We are fortunate to have Miss Bradshaw with us for the holiday, as her great-uncle, the Duke of Chesterfield, was delayed in Russia," Felicity's mother informs her.

"Duke of Chesterfield?" Cecily repeats as if she hasn't heard quite right.

Mrs. Worthington recounts the tale of Ann's noble birth for Cecily and her mother. Cecily's mouth hangs open in astonishment, but cruelty corrects it, bending it into a malicious smile. Something cold and hard flows through me. It's Cecily's intention. She's going to do it. She's going to tell. Now Ann's alarm pummels me, mixing with Cecily's spite to make me woozy. Can't breathe. Need to think.

I hear Cecily's voice. "Ann Bradshaw . . ."

My eyes flutter. *Please stop.*

". . . is . . ."

Stop. Please.

". . . the most . . ."

Unable to bear it, I shout out, "*Stop!*"

A delicious relief fills me. There is utter and complete silence. No rush of thoughts. No crowd noises. No instruments being tuned. Nothing at all, actually. When I open my eyes, I see why. I've made everything stand still: the ladies gathering skirts, chattering. The gentlemen checking pocket watches. They are like the wax tableaus behind the giant glass windows of a department store. I had not intended for this to happen, but it has, and I must use it to our advantage. I must save Ann.

"Cecily," I intone, placing my hand on her rigid arm. "You will not say another word against Ann. You will believe everything we say, and what's more, you will treat Ann as if she were the Queen herself.

"Ann," I say, smoothing her hair away from her worried face. "You've no reason to fret. You deserve to be here. You are loved."

The man having the affair with his wife's sister stands near. I cannot resist. I slap him hard across the cheek. It is oddly satisfying. "You, sir, are a scoundrel. You will reform yourself immediately and devote yourself to the happiness of your wife."

Simon. How strange to see him standing at attention, those blue eyes open but not seeing. Very gently, I remove my glove and stroke the side of his jaw. The skin there is smooth, freshly shaven. My hand smells of his barber's balm. It will be my secret.

I pull on my glove and close my eyes, willing it all to be so. "Begin again," I say.

The world swings into action as if there's been no pause. The husband feels the sting of my slap. Simon puts his fingers to his jaw as if remembering a dream. Cecily's smug expression hasn't changed, and I hold my breath, hoping the magic has found its purpose as she opens her mouth. *Miss Bradshaw is the most . . .*

". . . charitable, dear girl in the whole of Spence," Cecily announces. "In fact, it is her modesty that prevented her from telling us about her royal blood. She is as good a girl as one could ever hope to meet."

I don't know who looks more thunderstruck—Ann or Felicity.

"Miss Bradshaw, I do hope I may have the pleasure of calling on you while you are in London," Cecily says with a new-found earnestness.

Tom pipes up. "Miss Bradshaw, you must do me the honor of attending the Christmas dance at Bethlem Hospital."

Has the spell extended to everyone? But no, I come to realize. The mere suggestion of fame and fortune casts a glamour all its own. It is rather alarming how quickly people will turn someone else's fiction into fact in order to support their own fictions of themselves. But seeing Ann's delighted face, knowing what's in her heart, I cannot help being glad for the illusion.

"I would be delighted," Ann says to one and all. She could have used the opportunity to gloat. I would have. But instead, she has proved herself worthy of royal blood.

"We should send the carriage round for Miss Doyle," Lady Denby says.

I stop her. "Please don't. I should like to stay for the rest of the opera."

"I thought you were ill," Grandmama says.

"I'm fine now." And I am. Using the magic has calmed me somewhat. I can still hear some people's thoughts, but they are not as urgent.

Felicity whispers, "What happened?"

"I shall tell you later. It is a very good story."

<hr/>

By the time I climb into bed, the magic is nearly gone. I'm exhausted and shaky. My forehead is warm when I place my hand there. I can't be sure whether it's the magic doing this or I'm actually falling ill. I only know that I desperately need sleep.

When they come, my dreams are not restful. They're wild kaleidoscopes of madness. Felicity, Ann, and I running through tunnels lit by torches, running for our lives, the terror clear on our faces. The Caves of Sighs. The amulet twirling. Nell Hawkins's face looms before me: "Do not follow the Eastern Star, Lady Hope. They mean to kill you. That is his task."

"Who?" I murmur, but she's gone, and I'm dreaming of Pippa outlined against the red sky. Her eyes are wrong again, horrible blue-white with pinpricks of black in the center. Her hair is matted with wildflowers gone to seed. Deep shadows ring her eyes. She smiles, revealing sharp, pointed teeth, and I want to scream, oh, God in heaven, I want to scream. She offers something in both hands, something bloody and foul. The head of a goat torn from its body.

Thunder rumbles through the reddening sky. "I saved your life, Gemma. Remember that. . . ." She blows a kiss to me. And then, swift as lightning, she grabs the goat's head and sinks her teeth into its neck.

CHAPTER THIRTY-TWO

IT IS DETERMINED BY OUR PHYSICIAN, DR. LEWIS, that I am suffering from catarrh and nothing more, and after several sneezes, I agree with his assessment. I am forced to stay in bed. Mrs. Jones brings hot tea and broth on a silver tray. And in the afternoon, Father spends an hour telling me lovely tales of India.

"So there we were, Gupta and I, traveling to Kashmir with a donkey who would not be moved for all the jewels of India. He saw that narrow mountain pass, bared his teeth at us, and simply lay down, refusing to go on. We pulled and pulled on the rope, and the more we pulled the harder he fought. I thought we were done for. It was Gupta's idea that saved us in the end."

"What did he do?" I ask, blowing my nose.

"He took off his hat, bowed to the donkey, and said, 'After you.' And the donkey moved on with us following."

I narrow my eyes at him. "You've made up that story."

Father puts his hand to his chest dramatically. "You doubt the word of your father? To the stocks with you, ungrateful child!"

This makes me laugh—and sneeze. Father pours me more tea.

"Drink up, darling. Don't want you missing Tom's dance with the lunatics this evening."

"I've heard Mr. Snow is fond of getting too familiar with his partners," I say.

"Lunatic or not, I'd have his hide if he dared," Father says, puffing out his chest and blustering like some retired naval officer. "Unless he's larger than I am. Then I'd need you to protect me, my dear."

I laugh again. He's in a happy temper today, though he's looking thin, and his hands still tremble at times.

"Your mother would have loved the idea of a dance at Bedlam, I can tell you. She did so love the unusual."

Silence descends. Father fiddles with the wedding band he still wears, turning it round and round. I'm torn between speaking honestly and keeping him here. Honesty wins. "I miss her," I say.

"As do I, pet." It is quiet again for a moment, neither of us knowing what to say to close the gap between us. "I know she'd be happy to see you at Spence."

"She would?"

"Oh, yes. It was her idea. She said that should anything happen to her, I was to send you there. Strange thing for her to say, now that I think of it. Almost as if she knew . . ." He stops, looks out the window.

This is the first I've heard of my mother's wanting me to attend Spence, the school that very nearly destroyed her and the school that introduced her to her friend-turned-enemy, Sarah Rees-Toome. Circe. Before I can ask Father more about it, he's up and making his goodbyes. The liveliness has been invaded by cold truth, and he cannot stay and make friends with it.

"I'm off then, my angel."

"Can't you stay a bit longer?" I whine, though I know he hates it when I do.

"Mustn't keep the old boys at the club waiting."

Why does it always seem that I have only the shadow of my father? I'm like a child constantly grabbing at his coattails and missing.

"Right," I say. I give him a smile, pretend to be his bright, shiny thing of a girl. *Don't break his heart, Gemma.*

"I'll see you for supper, pet."

He kisses my forehead and then he is gone. The room does not seem to miss him. He has not even made a dent on the bed where he was sitting.

Mrs. Jones bustles in with more tea and the afternoon's post. "Letter for you, miss."

I can't think of a soul who would send me a Christmas card, so I am surprised until I spy that it has come from Wales. Mrs. Jones spends an eternity tidying the room and opening drapes. The letter sits on my lap, taunting me.

"Will there be anything else, miss?" our housekeeper asks with no enthusiasm.

"No, thank you," I say with a smile. It is not returned.

At last, Mrs. Jones leaves, and I tear open the letter. It is from St. Victoria's headmistress, a Mrs. Morrissey.

Dear Miss Doyle,

Thank you for your inquiry. It is so very comforting to hear that our Nell has found a friend in one so kind. St. Victoria's did indeed employ a teacher by the name of Claire McCleethy. Miss McCleethy was with us from the fall of 1894 through the spring of 1895. She was a most excellent teacher of the arts and poetry and was very popular with certain of our girls, Nell Hawkins among them. Unfortunately, I seem to have no photograph of Miss McCleethy for Miss Hawkins to keep, as requested, nor do I have an address for her. When she left St. Victoria's, she was to take a post at a school near London where her sister is headmistress. I do hope this letter is of help to you and that you have the merriest of Christmases.

Yours sincerely,
Mrs. Beatrice Morrissey

So she was there! I knew it!

. . . she was to take a post at a school near London where her sister is headmistress . . .

A school near London. Spence? Does that mean Mrs. Nightwing is Miss McCleethy's sister?

I hear raised voices from below.

In a moment, Felicity barrels through my door with a sheepish Ann and furious Mrs. Jones just behind her.

"Hello, Gemma, darling. How are you feeling? Ann and I thought we'd come for a visit."

"The doctor said you should rest, miss." Mrs. Jones snips the ends of her words like an angry gardener.

"It's quite all right, Mrs. Jones, thank you. I believe a visit will do me good."

Felicity smiles in triumph.

"As you wish, miss. A *short* visit," she emphasizes, closing the door forcefully.

"Now you've done it. You've made Jonesy mad," I tease.

"How terrifying," Felicity says, rolling her eyes.

Ann examines the dress hanging just inside my cupboard. "You will be well enough to attend the hospital dance this evening, won't you?"

"Yes," I say. "I shall be there. Don't worry, *Tom* will be there. He's not taken my chill."

"I am glad to hear he's in good health," she says, as if she hasn't been waiting to hear that all along.

Felicity examines me. "You've a naughty look on your face."

"I have interesting news." I hand them the letter.

Felicity and Ann sit on my bed, reading silently, their eyes going wide.

"It's her, isn't it?" Ann asks. "Miss McCleethy is really Circe."

"We've got her," I say.

"When she left Saint Victoria's, she was to take a post at a school near London where *her sister is headmistress* . . . ," Felicity reads aloud.

"If that is true," I say, "Mrs. Nightwing is also suspect. We can no longer trust her."

CHAPTER
THIRTY-THREE

AFTER A HALF HOUR SPENT PACING, IT IS DECIDED
that we shall dispatch a note to the one person who may be of
help to us, Miss Moore. I wait impatiently for the messenger's
return, and just before I am to leave for the dance at Bethlem,
her reply arrives.

Dear Gemma,

*I too am troubled by these coincidences. Perhaps there is an
explanation for it all, but for the present, I advise you to be on your
guard. If she should show herself at Bethlem Royal, do what you must
to keep her from your Nell Hawkins.*

Your friend,
Hester Asa Moore

Father has not come home for supper as he promised. There
is no word. And he has Kartik and the carriage, so Tom and I
are forced to hire a cab to take us to Bethlem. The hospital has

been decorated nicely with holly and ivy, and the patients are dressed in their best, full of merriment and mischief.

I've brought flowers for Nell. One of the nurses takes me to the women's ward so that I might give them to her.

"What a beautiful corsage," the nurse says.

"Thank you," I murmur.

"Lucky day for our Miss Hawkins. That's twice she's gotten flowers."

"What do you mean?"

"She had a visitor today who brought her some nice roses."

A patient waltzes past with an imaginary partner.

"A visitor? What was her name?" I ask.

The nurse purses her lips in thought. "I can't remember, I'm afraid. It's been such a day! Mr. Snow's been in a very agitated state of mind. Dr. Smith told him if he didn't settle himself, he'd lose his privileges for the dance. Here we are," she says as we arrive at a small sitting room.

Nell is as disheveled as I've ever seen her. Her thin hair, splintered and broken, falls about her shoulders like a ruin. She's sitting alone, holding Cassandra's cage on her lap. The bird squawks to Nell, who murmurs sweet words in return. On the table beside her is a vase of bright red roses.

"Miss Hawkins," the nurse says. "Here's Miss Doyle to see you, and she's brought you a lovely corsage besides. Won't you say good evening?"

"Good evening! Good evening!" Cassandra chirps.

"I'll leave you to your visit, then," the nurse says. "You'll be needing to dress soon, Miss Hawkins."

"Nell," I say, when we are alone. "You had a visitor today. Was it Miss McCleethy?"

Nell flinches at the name, holding the cage so close that Cassandra hops about, flustered. "She led us to the rocks. She promised us the power, and then she betrayed us. It came up from the sea. Jack and Jill went up the hill . . ."

"She was your teacher at Saint Victoria's, wasn't she? What did she do to you? What happened?"

Nell reaches her tiny fingers through the bars of the cage, trying to touch Cassandra, who squawks and hops about, avoiding her grasp.

"Nell!" I grab her hands.

"Oh, Lady Hope," she says in a fierce whisper, her eyes filling with tears. "She has found me. She has found me and my mind is so troubled. I fear I cannot keep them out. They won't forgive me."

"Who won't forgive you?" I ask.

"Them!" she nearly shouts. "The ones you talk to. They are not my friends, not my friends, not friends."

"Shhh, it's all right, Nell," I murmur. I can hear distant violins tuning. The chamber orchestra has arrived. The dance is almost under way.

Nell rocks tightly. "I must flee soon. Jack and Jill up the hill, up the hill tonight. Tonight, I shall tell you where to find the Temple."

With a surprising agility and fierceness, Nell grabs hold of Cassandra's leg. The bird screeches in her grasp. But Nell's determined, her mouth set in a strange little smile.

"Nell! Nell! Let go of it," I say. I tug at her fingers and she bites my hand hard. A thin, jagged crescent of blood seeps up through my glove.

"Here now, what's all this ruckus?" A nurse marches over, all business. If she sees the bite, Nell will not be allowed to attend tonight's dance, and then I'll never know the location of the Temple.

"The bird pecked me," I say. "It frightened me."

"Cassandra, you're a bad girl, you are," the nurse clucks as she pries the cage from Nell's hands.

"Bad girl, bad girl!" Cassandra squawks.

"Tonight," Nell says hoarsely. "You must listen. You must see. It's our last chance."

My hand hurts like the devil. Worse, in the corridor, Mr. Snow waits, leering. He shouldn't be here in the female ward, and I wonder how he's slipped in. There's no debating it. I shall have to cross in front of him to get to the dance. Screwing my courage to the sticking place, I square my shoulders and stride past as if I own Bethlem Royal. Mr. Snow falls into step with me.

"You're a right pretty one, you are."

I keep walking, refusing to respond. Mr. Snow jumps before me, walking backward. I look about for help, but everyone is in the ballroom.

"Will you let me pass, sir?"

"Give us a kiss, then. A kiss to remember you by."

"Mr. Snow, remember yourself, please," I say. I try to sound firm, but my voice shakes.

"I've a message for you from them," he whispers.

"Them?"

"The girls in white." His face is so close I can smell the sourness of his breath. "She's in league with the dark ones. With the one who comes. She will lead you astray. Do not trust her," he whispers, giving that same sick leer.

"Are you trying to frighten me?" I say.

Mr. Snow puts his hands against the wall on either side of my head. "No, miss. We're trying to warn you."

"Mr. Snow! That will do!" At last one of the nurses appears and Mr. Snow slinks off down the hall, but before he does he calls to me, urgently.

"Careful, miss! Such a pretty little head!"

It isn't until I'm safely away from him that I remove my glove and examine the injury done to my hand. It isn't terrible. More like a deep scratch. But for the first time I've got my doubts about Nell Hawkins.

For the first time, I am afraid of her.

CHAPTER
THIRTY-FOUR

THE BETHLEM DANCE IS A VERY POPULAR AFFAIR. The hospital teems with people who have all arrived by invitation and by the purchase of a ticket allowing admission. Some have come for the music and dancing or out of a sense of charity; others for the curiosity of seeing the mad of Bedlam curtsying and bowing to one another, with the hopes that some strange, scandalous thing will occur, something they might repeat at this ball or that dinner. Indeed, two ladies watch discreetly as a nurse coaxes a tattered doll from the fierce grip of a patient, soothing the old woman with assurances that her "little girl" will be best served by a good night's rest in the "nursery." "Poor dear," the ladies murmur, and, "Breaks the heart," though I can tell from the light in their eyes that they've gotten a taste of what they've come for—a peek behind the curtain at despair, horror, and hopelessness, so that they may be happy to close it again and keep its taint far from the safe borders of their well-tended lives. I wish for them a long dance with Mr. Snow.

The dance is well under way by the time I spy Felicity

and Ann inching toward me through the throng. Mrs. Worthington has come as chaperone, but she's otherwise engaged, talking to the hospital's physician superintendent, Dr. Percy Smith.

"Gemma! Oh, what happened here?" Felicity says, seeing my bloodstained glove.

"Nell Hawkins bit me."

"How awful," Ann says.

"Miss McCleethy's been here already today. Nell's in a very distressed state. But she knows where to find the Temple, and tonight, she's going to reveal it."

"If she proves reliable," Ann says.

"Yes," I admit. "If."

Tom's suddenly beside me. He fiddles nervously with his tie. "I think it's proceeding rather well, don't you?"

"It is the best dance I've ever attended," Ann says. It is the only dance she's ever attended, but now hardly seems the time to mention it.

"I do hope tonight's performance is satisfactory," Tom says, looking in Dr. Smith's direction. "I've had some of the patients prepare a small program of entertainment for this evening."

"I'm certain it will be a delight to all," Ann says as if it were a matter of grave importance.

"Thank you, Miss Bradshaw. You are exceedingly kind." Tom offers a genuine smile.

"Not at all," Ann says before staring longingly at the dance floor.

Felicity pinches me lightly. She coughs delicately into her handkerchief, but I know she's trying desperately not to laugh at this forlorn exchange. *Come on, Tom,* I beg him silently. *Ask her to dance.*

Tom gives her a bow. "I trust you'll have a pleasant evening," he says, excusing himself.

Ann's face registers disappointment, and then shock. "She's here!" she whispers.

"Who?"

Ann opens her fan wide. From behind its protection, she points to the far side of the room. I see only Mr. Snow waltzing with the laughing Mrs. Sommers, but then my eyes find something familiar. I do not recognize her straightaway in her pale lavender dress and exposed neck.

It is Miss McCleethy. She has come.

"What should we do?" Felicity asks.

Remembering Miss Moore's letter, I say, "We must keep her away from Nell at all costs."

The orchestra has stopped its playing, and the lamps are dimmed to a cozy glow. People abandon the dance floor in pairs, moving to the sides of the room. Tom takes his place in the center. He goes to run his fingers through his hair—a nervous habit—and, remembering his gloves and the pomade, thinks better of it. There is an excessive clearing of the throat. I'm anxious for him. At last, he finds his voice.

"Ladies and gentlemen, if I may have your attention. Thank you for coming out on such a cold night. In gratitude, the Bethlem Royal players have prepared a small performance for you. And now, ah, well ... I give you the Bethlem Royal players."

Having acquitted himself well, Tom exits to polite applause. I find that I have lost Miss McCleethy in the crowd. A cold dread crawls slowly up my spine.

"I've lost Miss McCleethy," I whisper to Felicity. "Do you see her?"

Felicity cranes her neck. "No. Where are you off to?"

"To look for her," I say, slipping into the cover of the crowd.

As Mrs. Sommers plunks out a tune at the piano, I move quiet as fog through the room, searching for Miss McCleethy. Mrs. Sommers's playing is somewhat painful to hear, but the crowd claps for her anyway. She stands uncertainly afterward, bowing and smiling, her hand covering her mouth. When she begins to tear at her hair, Tom bids her gently to sit. The eerie Mr. Snow delivers a soliloquy from Shakespeare's *The Winter's Tale*. He has a voice trained for the stage and would be impressive if I could forget his performance for me earlier in the evening.

I've gotten through half the crowd, but I haven't spied Miss McCleethy again.

Nell Hawkins is introduced. Dressed in her best, her hair pulled back neatly at her neck, she seems a dainty doll of a girl. Pretty, like the laughing girl I've seen in my visions. The corsage has been pinned to her shirt. It nearly dwarfs her.

Nell stands staring at the crowd till they murmur with confusion: *What is she doing? Is this part of the performance?*

Her eerie, scratched phonograph of a voice rings out. "Jack and Jill went up the hill to fetch a pail of water. Jack fell down and broke his crown, and Jill came tumbling after."

A light sprinkling of low, polite laughter floats around the room, but I fear I shall cry. She promised me. And now I know that her promise was nothing more than another illusion spun from her disturbed mind. She does not know where to find the Temple. She is a poor, mad girl, and I could weep for both of us.

Nell grows animated, impassioned. It's as if she's a different girl.

"Where shall we go, maidens? Where shall we go? You must leave the garden. Leave it behind with a sad farewell. Down the river on the gorgon's grace, past the clutches of the slippery, nippery nymphs. Through the golden mist of magic. Meet the folk of the fair Forest of Lights. The arrows, the arrows, you must use wisely and well. But save one. Save one for me. For I shall have need of it."

A lady beside me turns to her husband. "Is this from *Pinafore*?" she says, confused, thinking it a Gilbert and Sullivan operetta.

I'm on fire. She does know! She has found an ingenious way of disclosing the Temple's location. For who, save us girls, could understand this gibberish? Miss McCleethy steps from behind a pillar, her left side showing, her right hidden in shadow. She too is listening intently.

"Offer hope to the Untouchables, for they must have hope. Travel on, far beyond the lotus blossoms. Follow the path. Yes, stick to the path, maidens. For they can lead you astray, away, with false promises. Beware the Poppy Warriors. The Poppy Warriors steal your strength. They will gobble you up. Gobble, gobble!"

This makes everyone laugh. Several of the patients repeat "Gobble you up" to amuse themselves. They are like chickens clucking until they are shushed by the nurses into quiet again. The hair at the back of my neck stands at attention. It is as if Nell is pantomiming for my benefit, speaking in a code I must decipher—or else she has slipped into total madness.

"Do not leave the path, for it is hard to find again once lost. And they will take the song to the rock. Do not let the song die. You must be careful with beauty. Beauty must pass. There are dark shadows of spirits. Just beyond the Borderlands, where the lone tree stands and the sky turns to blood . . ."

A few of the ladies flap their fans, uncomfortable with the mention of blood.

". . . in the Winterlands they plot and plan with Circe. They will not rest till the army is raised and the realms are theirs to rule."

There is unrest in the crowd, a sense that Nell has been indulged too long. Tom makes his way to the front. No! Not until she tells me where to find the Temple! Tom is already there.

"Thank you, Miss Hawkins. And now . . ."

Nell doesn't sit. She grows more agitated. "She wants in! She has found me and I cannot keep her out!"

"Nurse, if you would please . . ."

"Go where no one will, where it is forbidden, offer hope. . . . Jack and Jill went up the hill, the sea, the sea, came from the sea . . . go where the dark hides a mirror of water. Face your fear and bind the magic fast to you!"

"Come along now, Miss Hawkins," the nurse says, grabbing hold. Nell won't budge. She fights against the nurse with a brutal fierceness. Her shirt rips along the arm seam so that the whole of the sleeve pulls off in the nurse's hand. The crowd gasps. Nell's beside herself.

"She means to use me to find it, Lady Hope! She will use us both, and I will be lost, lost forever! Don't let her take me! Do not hesitate! Set me free, Lady Hope! Set me free!"

Two burly orderlies have arrived with a straitjacket.

"Come with us, miss. No trouble now."

Nell kicks and screams, showing that surprising strength again, but she is no match for them. One hooks her slender neck in the crook of a beefy arm, while the other forces Nell's grasping hands into the jacket's arms and tightens the laces at her back. Her body sags against the men, who half carry, half drag the limp girl till all that can be heard are her whimpers and the dull thud of her heels against the floors.

The crowd is loud with shock over the spectacle. Tom asks the musicians to resume playing. The music works to quiet the room, and soon some of the braver souls are at the dance again. I'm shaking all over. Nell's in danger, and I've got to save her.

I push my way to Felicity and Ann. "I've got to slip away and find Nell," I say.

"What did she mean, 'Beware the Poppy Warriors'?" Ann asks.

"It seemed like madness," Felicity adds, "what do you make of it?"

"I think it was a code for us, for finding the Temple," I say. "And I'm certain Miss McCleethy was listening too."

Felicity scans the crowd. "Where is she?"

Miss McCleethy is gone from her place near the pillar. She is not among the dancers, either. She has vanished.

Felicity looks at me, wide-eyed. "Go to her at once!"

I steal from the room as quickly as possible, running for the women's ward. I've got to reach her before Miss McCleethy does. *She has found me!* Right. Well, I'm not about to let her take you, Nell. Don't you worry.

The corridor is busy with the comings and goings of the nurses. When the last nurse leaves, I hike up my skirt and fly to Nell's room, as fast as I can.

Nell sits in a corner. They've taken off the straitjacket. The beautiful corsage has been damaged, the petals torn and flattened. Nell rocks back and forth, banging her head each time against the wall just slightly. I take her hands in mine.

"Miss Hawkins, it's Gemma Doyle. Nell, we haven't much time. I need to know the location of the Temple. You were just about to say it when they took you. It is safe now. You may tell me."

A thin stream of drool works its way out of the corner of her mouth. An odor like overripe fruit scents the tiny gusts of her breath. They've given her something to sedate her.

"Nell, if you do not tell me how to find the Temple, I fear we are lost. Circe will find it before us, and then there is no telling what could happen. She could rule the realms. She could do this to another girl and another."

From far below us, the music changes tempo as another dance begins. I do not know how long I can be gone before they begin searching for me.

"She'll never stop," Nell's raspy voice scrapes through the silence. "Never. Never. Never."

"Then we must stop her ourselves," I say. "Please. Please help me."

"It's you she wants, you she's always wanted," she slurs. "She'll make me tell her where to find the Temple, just as she made me tell her where to find you."

"What do you mean?"

A sound pricks at my ears. Footsteps in the hall, coming closer. I'm up at the door, peeking out. Someone comes. Someone in a deep green cloak. She stops to check each room in the gallery. I close the door gently.

"Nell," I say, my heart racing. "We've got to hide."

"Little Miss Muffet sat on a tuffet . . . frightened her away, frightened her away."

"Shhh, Nell. You've got to be quiet. Here, quickly, under the bed."

Nell is a small girl, but weighed down by the drug, she is hard to maneuver. We fall to the floor together in a heap. With effort, I manage to push her under the bed, then follow her. The footsteps stop at Nell's door. I've got my hand over her mouth as the door opens. I don't know what I fear more, that Nell will suddenly speak out and reveal our hiding spot or that the pounding of my heart will announce us.

There's a whisper in the dark. "Nell?"

Nell goes rigid against me.

The whisper comes again. "Nell, darling, are you here?"

The hem of her green cloak comes into view. Beneath it, I

can see the delicate lacings of polished, buffed boots. I feel certain I could see my own fear reflected in the high shine of them. Those boots come closer. I hold my breath; keep my hand on Nell's open mouth, where the saliva pools in my palm.

Beside me, Nell's so quiet I fear she may be dead. The boots turn away from us, and the door closes with a click. I scuttle out from under the bed and pull Nell out after. Nell clasps her hand on my wrist. Her eyelids flutter; her lips tighten into a grimace that lets only four words escape.

"See what I see. . . ."

We're falling hard and fast into a vision. But it is not my vision. It is Nell's. I see what she sees, feel what she feels. We're running through the realms. Grass licks at our ankles. But it's happening too fast. Nell's mind is a jumble, and I can't make sense of what I'm seeing. Roses pushing up through a wall. Red clay on skin. The woman in green, holding fast to Nell's hand by a deep, clear well.

And I am falling backward into that water.

I can't breathe. I'm choking. I fall out of the vision to find Nell's hand clamped around my throat. Her eyes are closed. She doesn't see me, doesn't seem to know what she is doing. Frantic, I pull at her hand, but it doesn't budge.

"Nell," I croak. "Nell . . . please."

She releases me, and I fall to the floor, gasping for air, my head aching from her sudden brutality. Nell has faded into her madness again, but her face is slick with tears.

"Don't hesitate, Lady Hope. Set me free."

CHAPTER
THIRTY-FIVE

TODAY IS CHRISTMAS EVE. ACROSS LONDON, THE shops and taverns are filled with people in high spirits, the streets bustling with this one carrying home a fragrant tree or that one selecting a fat goose for supper. I should be filled with the Christmas spirit and the urge to spread goodwill to my fellow man and woman. Instead, I am contemplating the puzzle that Nell Hawkins has left me to put together.

Go where no one will, where it is forbidden, offer hope. Go where the dark hides a mirror of water. Face your fear and bind the magic fast to you. It makes no sense. *Stick to the path. They will lead you astray with false promises.* Who? What false promises? The entire thing is a riddle wrapped inside another and another. I have the amulet to guide me. But I do not know where to find the Temple, and without that I have nothing. It vexes me till I want to pitch my washbowl across the room.

To make matters worse, Father is not home. He did not come home from his club last night. I am the only one who seems concerned about this. Grandmama is busy barking orders at the servants for our Christmas dinner. The kitchen is a flurry of cooks tending to puddings and gravies and pheasant with apples.

"He wasn't here for breakfast?" I ask.

"No," Grandmama says, pushing past me to yell at the cook. "I think we shall omit the soup course. No one bothers with it, anyway."

"But what if he's hurt?" I ask.

"Gemma, please! Mrs. Jones—the red silk will suffice, I should think."

⋏⋏⋏⋏⋏

Christmas Eve dinner comes and goes, and still there is no Father. The three of us set about opening our gifts in the parlor, pretending that there is nothing amiss.

"Ah," Tom says, unwrapping a long woolen scarf. "Perfect. Thank you, Grandmama."

"I am glad you like it. Gemma, why don't you open yours?"

I get to work on the box from Grandmama. Perhaps it is a beautiful pair of gloves or a bracelet. Inside are matching handkerchiefs embroidered with my initials. They're quite lovely. "Thank you," I say.

"Practical gifts are always the best, I find," Grandmama remarks with a sniff.

The unwrapping of gifts is over within minutes. Besides the handkerchiefs, I receive a hand mirror and a tin of chocolates from Grandmama, and from Tom, a jolly red nutcracker, who amuses me. I've given a shawl to Grandmama, and to Tom, a skull to keep in his office someday.

"I shall call him Yorick," Tom says, delighted. And I'm glad that I've made him happy. Father's gifts sit under the tree, unopened.

"Thomas," Grandmama says. "Perhaps you should go to his club and ask for him. Make some discreet inquiries."

"But I'm to go to the Athenaeum tonight as a guest of Simon Middleton," Tom protests.

"Father is missing," I say.

"He's not missing. I am certain that he will be home at any moment, probably laden with gifts he's traveled to get on a whim somewhere. Do you remember the time he arrived on Christmas morning like Saint Nicholas himself, riding an elephant?"

"Yes," I say, smiling at the memory. He'd brought me my first sari, and Tom and I had coconut milk, lapping it from bowls as if we were tigers.

"He'll be home. Mark my words. Doesn't he always turn up?"

"You're right, of course," I say, because I want desperately to believe him.

<hr />

The house falls into hushed tones of gasping fires and steady clocks, the lamps shushed to glowing murmurs of their former brightness. As it's after eleven o'clock, the servants have retired to their rooms. Grandmama is snuggled into her bed, and she thinks I am tucked safely in as well. But I can't sleep. Not with

Father gone. I want him to come home, with or without an elephant. So I sit in the parlor, waiting.

Kartik slips into the room, still dressed in his coat and
boots. He is out of breath.

"Kartik! Where have you been? What is it?"

"Is your brother at home?" He's very agitated.

"No. He's gone out. Why do you ask?"

"It's imperative that I speak with your brother."

I rise to my full height. "I've told you, he is not at home. You
may tell me."

He takes a poker and stabs at the brittle logs. They flare to
life. He says nothing, and I am left to imagine the worst.

"Oh, no. Is it Father? Do you know where he is?" Kartik
nods. "Where?"

Kartik cannot look me in the eyes. "Bluegate Fields."

"Bluegate Fields?" I repeat. "Where is that?"

"It is the dregs of the world, a place inhabited only by
thieves, addicts, murderers, and the like, I am sorry to say."

"But my father . . . why is he there?"

Again, Kartik cannot look at me. "He is addicted to opium.
He is at Chin-Chin's, an opium den."

It's not true. It can't be. I've cured Father. He's been better
since the magic, hasn't asked for a drop of laudanum. "How do
you know this?"

"Because he bade me drive him there last night and he hasn't
left since."

My heart sinks at this. "My brother is with Mr. Middleton at
his club."

"We must send for him."

"No! The scandal. Tom would be humiliated."

"Yes, wouldn't want to upset The Right Honorable Simon Middleton."

"You're too bold by half," I say.

"And you're lying about not wanting to humiliate Tom. You're saving yourself."

The hard truth of this stings me, and I hate him a little for saying it.

"There's nothing we can do but wait until your brother returns," Kartik says.

"Do you mean leave my father in that place?"

"There is no other choice."

"He's all I have," I plead. "Take me to him."

Kartik shakes his head. "It is out of the question. Bluegate Fields is not the sort of place for ladies."

"I am going whether you take me or not."

I walk swiftly toward the door. Kartik takes hold of my arm. "Do you know what could happen to you there?"

"I shall have to risk it." Kartik and I stand, opposing each other. "I cannot leave him there, Kartik."

"Very well," he says, relenting. He gives my figure a bold appraisal. "You will need to borrow your brother's clothes."

"What do you mean?"

"If you must go, you shall have to go dressed as a man."

I race up the stairs, hoping I do not wake Grandmama or the servants. Tom's clothes are a mystery to me. With difficulty, I manage to undress, taking off the many layers and my corset. I sigh with relief when free of it. I pull Tom's trousers over my woolen stockings and select a shirt and coat. They are a bit snug. I am tall but not slender as he is. Still, they will have to do. Securing my hair beneath his hat is a task, though. It threatens to spring from my head. And to wear Tom's shoes requires that I stuff the ends with handkerchiefs, as his feet are a full inch and a half larger than my own. It makes me walk like a drunk.

"How do I look?" I ask, coming down the stairs.

Kartik scoffs. "Like someone who shall be set upon by every hooligan in East London. This is a terrible idea. We'll wait until your brother returns."

"I will not leave my father to die in an opium den," I say. "Pull the carriage round."

ᜑᜑᜑᜑ

A light snow's begun to fall. It coats Ginger's mane in a thin gray powder as we pull slowly into the East London slums. The night is still and cold. Every breath is painful. Narrow, filthy alleys wind between ramshackle buildings that stand stooped as beggars. Crippled chimneys jut up from the sodden roofs, crooked metal arms asking the sky for alms, for hope, for some reassurance that this life is not all they can ever know.

"Pull your hat low over your face," Kartik warns. Even on this night and in the cold, the streets are crowded with people, drunk, loud, swearing. A trio of men in the open doorway of a gin house takes in my fine clothes, Kartik beside me.

"Don't look at them," Kartik says. "Don't engage with anyone."

A group of street urchins clusters about us, begging. This

one's got a sick baby sister at home; another offers to shine my boots for a shilling. Still another, a boy of no more than eleven or so, knows of a place where we can go and he will "be kind" to me for as long as I like. He does not smile or betray any feeling as he says this. He is as matter-of-fact as the boy offering to clean my boots.

Kartik pulls six coins from his pocket. They glisten in the black wool of his gloved palm. The boys' eyes grow wide in the dark.

"Three shillings for whoever watches this carriage and horse," he says.

Three boys are on him at once, promising all sorts of harm to whoever would bother such a fine gentleman's carriage.

"And three for the one who can escort us to Chin-Chin's without incident," he says.

They're quiet. A filthy boy in tattered clothes and shoes worn down to holes grabs the last of the coins. "Oi know Chin's," he says. The other boys look at him with envy and scorn.

"This way, gents," he says, taking us down a maze of alleys damp with the wind blowing off the nearby docks. Fat rats scuttle across cobblestones, poking at heaven knows what by the curb. Despite the raw wind and late hour, people are out. It is still Christmas Eve, and they crowd the gin houses and streets, some of them falling down with drunkenness.

"Roight 'ere," the boy says as we reach a hovel inside a tiny court. The boy pushes through the decrepit door and escorts us up steep, dark stairs that reek of urine and the damp. I trip over something and realize it's a body.

"That's jus' ol' Jim," the boy says, unbothered. " 'E's always 'ere."

On the second floor, we reach another door.

" 'Ere you go. Chin-Chin's. Give us a gin for the trouble, eh, guv?" the boy says, sticking out his hand in the hopes of more money.

I press another two shillings into his palm.

"Merry Christmas, guv." He disappears and I knock on the grime-thickened door. It creaks open to reveal an ancient Chinaman. The shadows under his hollow eyes make him seem more an apparition than a flesh-and-blood man, but then he smiles, showing a handful of teeth mottled brown as rotted fruit. He bids us follow him into the low, cramped room. Everywhere I look there are bodies. They lie about, eyes fluttering; some jabber on in long strings of sentences that mean nothing. They're broken by long pauses and the occasional weak laugh that chills the soul with its emptiness. A sailor, his skin the color of India ink, nods and sleeps in a corner. Beside him is a man who looks as if he might never wake.

The opium fumes make my eyes water and my throat burn. At this rate, it will be a wonder if we can escape the room without succumbing to the drug ourselves. I put my handkerchief to my mouth to keep from gagging.

"Mind the floor," Kartik says. Several well-to-do gentlemen are clumped together around an opium bowl in a stupor, mouths open. Above them, a rope stretches across the room, dingy rags hanging from it forming a rotted curtain that smells of sour milk.

"Which ship are you on, my boy?" comes a voice from the

darkness. A face moves into the glow from a candle. The man is Indian.

"I am not a deckhand. Or a boy," Kartik answers.

The Indian sailor laughs at this. There's an ugly scar snaking from the corner of his eye across his cheek. I shudder to think how he might have gotten it or what happened to the other man. He fingers his dagger at his side.

"You trained dog to English?" He points at me with the dagger. He makes a barking sound that tumbles into more laughter and then a terrible coughing fit that leaves blood on his hand.

"The English." He spits. "They give us this life. We are their dogs, you and I. Dogs. What they promise you cannot trust. But Chin-Chin's opium makes the whole world sweet. Smoke, my friend, and you forget what they do. Forget that you are a dog. That you will always be a dog."

He points the tip of his dagger into the sticky black ball of opium, ready to smoke his troubles away and float into an oblivion where he is no one's inferior. Kartik and I move on through the smoky haze. The Chinaman leads us to a tiny room and bids us wait a moment while he disappears behind the rags over the door. Kartik's jaw remains clenched.

"What that man said . . ." I stop, unsure of how to continue. "What I mean is, I hope you know that I do not feel that way."

Kartik's face hardens. "I am not like those men. I am Rakshana. A higher caste."

"But you are also Indian. They are your countrymen, are they not?"

Kartik shakes his head. "Fate determines your caste. You must accept it and live according to the rules."

"You can't really believe that!"

"I do believe it. That man's misfortune is that he cannot accept his caste, his fate."

I know that the Indians wear their caste as a mark upon their foreheads for all to see. I know that in England, we have our own unacknowledged caste system. A laborer will never hold a seat in Parliament. Neither will a woman. I don't think I've ever questioned such things until this moment.

"But what about will and desire? What if someone wants to change things?"

Kartik keeps his eyes on the room. "You cannot change your caste. You cannot go against fate."

"That means there is no hope of a better life. It is a trap."

"That is how you see it," he says softly.

"What do you mean?"

"It can be a relief to follow the path that has been laid out for you, to know your course and play your part in it."

"But how can you be sure that you are following the right course? What if there is no such thing as destiny, only choice?"

"Then I do not choose to live without destiny," he says with a slight smile.

He seems so sure, while I feel nothing but uncertainty. "Do you ever have doubts? About anything?"

His smile vanishes. "Yes."

I'd like to know what they are, but the Chinaman returns, interrupting our debate. We follow him, pushing aside the fetid rags. He points to a fat Englishman with arms the size of an elephant's legs.

"We're looking for Mr. Chin-Chin," Kartik says.

"Lookin' a' 'im," the Englishman says. "Took ofer from th' 'riginal proprietor t'ree years ago. Some cawls me Chin. Ofers cawls me Uncle Billy. Come fo' a tayste o' 'appiness?"

On a low table sits the opium bowl. Chin stirs the thick black goo. He pulls out a sticky, tarlike bead of opium and pushes it down into the wooden pipe. With horror I see that he wears my father's wedding ring on a string around his neck.

"Where did you get that ring?" I ask in a hoarse whisper that I hope passes as a young man's voice.

"Luv'ly, innit? Patron gimme it. Fair trade fo' me opyum."

"Is he still here? That man?"

"Don' know. Ain't runnin' a boardin'ouse, now, is I, guv?"

"Chin . . ." The voice, urgent but hoarse, comes from the other side of the ragged curtain. A hand pokes out. It shakes as it searches for the pipe. There's a fine gold watch fob dangling from the thin fingers. "Chin, take it. . . . Give me more. . . ."

Father.

I pull aside the filthy curtain. My father lies on the soiled, torn mattress in only his trousers and shirt. His jacket and coat adorn a woman who is draped across him, snoring lightly. His fine cravat and boots are gone—stolen or bartered, I do not know which. The stench of urine is overpowering, and I have to fight to keep from being ill.

"Father."

In the dim light, he struggles to see who is speaking. His

eyes are bloodshot, the pupils large and glassy. "Hello," he says, smiling dreamily.

My throat throbs with all I'm holding back. "Father, it's time to go home."

"Just one more. Right as rain. Then we'll go. . . ."

Chin takes the watch fob and pockets it. He passes the pipe to Father.

"Don't give him any more," I plead.

I try to take the pipe, but Father wrests it from my hand and gives me a hard shove in the bargain. Kartik helps me to my feet.

"Chin, the light. There's a good man. . . ."

Chin lowers the candle to the pipe. My father draws in the smoke. His eyes flutter and a tear escapes, making a slow track down his unshaven cheek. "Leave me, pet."

I can't stand another moment. With every bit of strength I've got, I push the woman off Father and pull him to his feet. The two of us stumble backward. Chin laughs to watch us, as if it were a night of cockfighting or some other sport. Kartik takes my father's other arm and together we maneuver him through the throngs of opium eaters. I am so ashamed that he should see my father in this state. I want to cry but am afraid if I did I would never stop.

We stumble on the stairs but somehow manage to make it to our carriage without further incident. The boys have been true to their word. The crowd has grown to about twenty children, who all clamber out of the seats and down from Ginger's back. The cold night air, an assault earlier, is a balm after the wretched opium fumes. I breathe in greedy gulps as Kartik and I help Father into the carriage. Tom's trousers catch in the door, tearing along the seam. And with that, I too rip apart. Everything I've held back—disappointment, loneliness, fear, and the crushing sadness of it all—comes rushing out in a torrent of tears.

"Gemma?"

"Don't . . . look . . . at . . . me," I sob, turning my face toward the cold steel of the carriage. "It is all . . . so . . . horrible . . . and it's . . . my fault."

"It is not your fault."

"Yes, yes, it is! If I hadn't been who I am, Mother wouldn't have died. He never would have been like this! I ruined his happiness! And . . ." I stop.

"And . . . ?"

"I used the magic to try to cure him." I'm afraid Kartik will be angry, but he doesn't say anything. "I couldn't bear to see him suffer so. What is the good of all this power if I can do nothing with it?"

This brings a fresh wave of tears. To my great surprise, Kartik wipes them away with his hand. "*Meraa mitra yahaan aaiye*," he murmurs.

I understand only a little Hindi, enough to know what he has said: *Come here, my friend.*

"I've never known a braver girl," he says.

He lets me lean against the carriage for a moment till my tears stop, and my body feels as it always does after a good cry—calm and clean. Across the Thames, the deep chimes of Big Ben sing two o'clock.

Kartik helps me into the seat next to my sleeping father.

"Merry Christmas, Miss Doyle."

⌇⌇⌇⌇

When we reach home, the lamps are lit, which is an ominous sign. Tom is waiting in the parlor. There's no way to hide what has happened.

"Gemma, where have you been at such an hour? Why are you dressed in my clothing? And what have you done to my best trousers?"

Kartik moves into the room, supporting Father as best he can.

"Father!" Tom says, taking in his semi-clothed, drugged state. "What has happened?"

My words rush out in a terrified torrent. "We found him in an opium den. He'd been there for two days. Kartik wanted you but I didn't want to scandalize you at the club and so I—I—I . . ."

Hearing the commotion, Mrs. Jones arrives, her night bonnet still on her head.

"Is anything the matter, sir?" she asks.

"Mr. Doyle has taken ill," Tom says.

Mrs. Jones's eyes say she knows it's a lie, but she immediately springs into action. "I'll fetch tea at once, sir. Should I send for the doctor?"

"No! Just the tea, thank you," Tom barks. He gives Kartik a hard look. "I can manage from here."

"Yes, sir," Kartik says. For a moment, I don't know whether to go to my brother or Kartik. In the end, I help Tom and Mrs. Jones get my father to bed. I change out of Tom's clothes,

• 379 •

scrub myself of the soot of East London, and dress in my own nightclothes. I find Tom sitting in the parlor, staring into the fire. He takes the twigs that are too small to be of any good, snaps them in half, and feeds them methodically into the angry flames.

"I'm sorry, Tom. I didn't know what else to do," I say. I wait for him to tell me how I've disgraced the family and that I shall never leave this house again.

Another twig lights. It screams in the fire and hisses down to cinder. I haven't any idea what to say.

"I can't cure him," Tom says so softly I have to strain to hear. "A medical student is a man of science. He is supposed to have the answers. I cannot even help my own father conquer his demons."

I lean my head against the wood of the doorframe, something solid to catch me should I slide right off this earth and keep falling. "You'll find a way, in time." I mean to be reassuring. I am not.

"No. Science is broken for me. It's broken." His head slumps forward into his hands. There's a strangled sound. He's trying not to cry, but he's helpless against it. I want to run across the rug and hold him tightly, risk his disdain to do it.

Instead, I turn the knob quietly and leave, letting him save face and hating myself for it.

CHAPTER
THIRTY-SIX

THE SOUND OF DISTANT CHURCH BELLS WAKES ME. It is Christmas morning. The house is quiet as a morgue. Father and Tom are still asleep after our long night, and Grandmama has chosen to stay in bed as well. Only the servants and I are awake.

I dress quickly and quietly and make my way to the carriage house. Sleep still hangs about Kartik in a sweet, charming way.

"I've come to apologize for last night. And to thank you for helping him," I say.

"Everyone needs help sometimes," he says.

"Except for you."

He doesn't answer. Instead, he hands me something ill-wrapped in a scrap of cloth. "Merry Christmas, Miss Doyle."

I am astonished. "What is this?"

"Open it."

Inside the cloth is a small blade the size of a man's thumb. Atop the blade is a small, crude totem of a many-armed man with a buffalo head.

"Megh Sambara," Kartik explains. "The Hindus believe that he offers protection against enemies."

"I thought you had no loyalty to any customs other than the Rakshana's."

Embarrassed, Kartik sticks his hands in his pockets, rocks on the heels of his boots. "It was Amar's."

"You shouldn't part with it, then," I say, trying to give it back.

Kartik jumps to avoid the blade. "Careful. It is small but sharp. And you may have need of it."

I hate to be reminded of my purpose here and now. "I shall keep it with me. Thank you."

I see there's another small bundle beside him. I would dearly love to ask if it is for Emily, but I can't bring myself to do it.

"Tonight is Miss Worthington's Christmas ball, yes?" Kartik asks, running fingers through his thick tangle of curls.

"Yes," I say.

"What do you do at these balls?" Kartik asks shyly.

"Oh," I sigh. "There is a great deal of smiling and talking of the weather and how lovely everyone looks. There is a light supper and refreshments. And the dancing, of course."

"I've never been to a ball. I don't know how this sort of dancing is done."

"It isn't so difficult to master for a man. The woman has to learn to do it in reverse without stepping on his feet."

Kartik lifts his hands into position as if holding an imaginary partner. "Like this?" He moves around and around.

"A bit slower. That's it," I say.

Kartik adopts a plummy tone. "I say, Lady Whatsit, have you had many callers since arriving in London?"

"Oh, Lord Hoity-toity," I answer, matching his tone. "Why, I've so many cards from the very best people that I've had to put out two china bowls to display them all."

"Two bowls, you say?"

"Two bowls."

"What an inconvenience for you and your china collection," Kartik says, laughing. He is so very lovely when he laughs.

"I should like to see you in black jacket and white tie."

Kartik stops. "Do you think I would look the grand gentleman?"

"Yes."

He bows to me. "May I have this dance, Miss Doyle?"

I curtsy. "Oh, but of course, Lord Hoity-toity."

"No," he says softly. "May *I* have this dance?"

Kartik is asking me to dance. I look about. The house is still shuttered with sleep. Even the sun is hiding behind the gray clouds of its bedclothes. No one's about, but they will be at any moment. My head whispers frantic warnings: *Mustn't. Improper. Wrong. What if someone should see us? What about Simon . . .*

But my hand makes the decision for me, pushing against the Christmas morning chill till it is joined with his.

"Ah, your, um, your other hand would be at my waist," I say, looking down at our feet.

"Here?" he says, resting his palm against my hip.

"Higher," I croak. His hand finds my waist. "That's it."

"What next?"

"We, we dance," I say, my breath coming out in shallow puffs.

He turns me round slowly and awkwardly at first. There is so much space between us that a third person could stand there. I keep my eyes on our feet stepping so close to each other, leaving patterns in the thin layer of sawdust.

"I think it would be easier if you weren't pulling away," he says.

"This is how it is done," I answer.

He pulls me closer to him, far closer than is appropriate. There is but a whisper of space between his chest and mine. Instinctively, I look around, but there is no one to see us but the horses. Kartik's hand travels from my waist to the small of my back, and I gasp. Turning round and round, his hand warm at my back, his other hand grasping mine, I am suddenly dizzy.

"Gemma," he says, so that I must look up into those magnificent brown eyes. "There is something I need to tell you. . . ."

He mustn't say it. It will ruin everything. I break away, my hand going to my stomach to steady myself.

"Are you all right?" Kartik says.

I smile weakly and nod. "The cold," I say. "Perhaps I should be getting back."

"But first, I need to tell you—"

"There's so much to do," I say, cutting him off.

"Well, then," he says, sounding hurt. "Don't forget your gift."

He hands me the charm blade. Our hands touch, and for an instant, it is as if the world holds its breath, and then his lips, those warm, soft lips, are on mine. It is as if I've been caught in a sudden rain, this feeling.

There's a sensation in my stomach like birds flapping as I break away. "Please don't."

"It's because I am Indian, isn't it?" he asks.

"Of course not," I say. "I don't even think of you as an Indian."

He looks as if he's been punched. Then he throws his head back and laughs. I do not know what I've said that is so amusing. He gives me such a hard look I fear my heart shall break from it. "So you don't even think of me as Indian. Well, that is a tremendous relief."

"I—I didn't mean it like that."

"You English never do." He walks into the stables with me on his heels.

I'd never thought of how insulting that might sound. But now, too late, I realize that he is right, that in my heart I have taken for granted that I have been so frank with Kartik, so . . . myself . . . because he is Indian and so there could never be anything between us. Anything I could say now would be a lie. I've made such a mess of things.

Kartik is gathering his meager possessions into a rucksack.

"Where are you going?"

"To the Rakshana. It is time for me to claim my place. To begin my training and advance."

"Please don't go, Kartik. I don't want you to go." It is the truest thing I've said all day.

"For that I am sorry for you."

The mews is coming awake. Servants have sprung into action like the tiny mechanized figures on a cuckoo clock.

"You'd best go in. Would you be so kind as to give this to

Emily for me?" he says frostily. He hands me the other gift, which opens just enough to reveal *The Odyssey*. "Tell her I am sorry I cannot continue teaching her to read. She'll have to get someone else."

"Kartik," I start. I notice he's left my gift to him from months ago leaning against the wall. "Don't you want to take the cricket bat?"

"Cricket. Such an English game," he says. "Goodbye, Miss Doyle." He hoists the rucksack upon his back and walks away, heading into the weak first light of morning.

BY NOON, THE STREETS OF LONDON ARE A CONCERT
of bells calling one and all to church. Grandmama, Tom, and I
sit on hard wooden pews, letting the reverend's words wash
over us.

"Then Herod, when he had privily called the wise men, in-
quired of them diligently what time the star appeared. And he
sent them to Bethlehem, and said, 'Go and search diligently
for the young child; and when ye have found him, bring me
word again, that I may come and worship him also . . .'"

I glance about the church. All around me, heads are bowed in
prayer. People seem content. Happy. After all, it is Christmas.

A light-dappled stained-glass window shows an angel deliv-
ering the annunciation. At his feet, Mary kneels, trembling as
she receives this fearful message from her celestial visitor. Her
face shows the awe and fear of that news, of the gift she has
not asked for but will carry nonetheless. And I wonder why
there is no passage to describe her terrible doubt.

"Then Herod, when he saw that he was mocked of the wise men, was exceeding wroth, and sent forth his men, and slew all the children that were in Bethlehem, and in all the coasts thereof . . ."

Why is there no panel showing women saying, *No, I'm sorry, I don't want this gift. You may have it back. I've sheep to look after and bread to bake, and I've no desire to be a holy messenger.*

That is the window I long to see.

A ray of light breaks through the glass, and for a moment, the angel seems to flare like the sun.

⁓⁓⁓⁓

I am allowed to spend the afternoon with Felicity and Ann, so that Grandmama and Tom may tend to Father. Mrs. Worthington is seeing to the outfitting of little Polly, which has put Felicity into a hateful mood to match my own. Only Ann is enjoying the day. It is the first Christmas she can remember in a real home with a ball to attend, and she's positively giddy about it, badgering us with questions.

"Should I wear flowers and pearls in my hair? Or is it too gauche?" she asks.

"Gauche," Felicity responds. "I don't see why we have to take her in. There are plenty of relatives more suited, I should think."

I sit at Felicity's dressing table running a brush through my hair, counting the strokes, seeing the hurt in Kartik's eyes with each swipe of the brush. "Sixty-four, sixty-five, sixty-six . . ."

"They fawn and fret over her as if she's a visiting princess," Felicity grumbles.

"She's a very pretty little girl," Ann says thoughtlessly. "I was thinking of wearing perfume. Gemma, does Tom find girls who wear scent too bold?"

"He is attracted to the smell of manure," Felicity says. "You might wallow in the stables to bring out the full flower of his love."

"You *are* in quite a mood," Ann grumbles.

I shouldn't have danced with him. I shouldn't have let him kiss me. But I wanted him to kiss me. And then I insulted him.

"Oh, it's all such a bother," Felicity harrumphs as she makes her way to the bed, which is awash in discarded stockings, silk, and petticoats. The whole of Felicity's cupboards, it seems, are splayed out for the world to see. And yet she can't seem to find anything that suits.

"I'm not going," Felicity blurts out. She's sprawled petulantly on a chaise in her dressing gown, woolen stockings pooled about her ankles. All pretense of modesty has been abandoned.

"It's your mother's ball," I say. "You must go. Sixty-seven, sixty-eight . . ."

"I've nothing to wear!"

I gesture grandly to the bed and resume my counting.

"Won't you be wearing one of the gowns your mother had made for you in Paris?" Ann asks. She's holding one of the dresses against her body, turning this way and that. She gives a slight curtsy to an imaginary escort.

"They're so *bourgeois*," Felicity snorts.

Ann runs her fingers over the water blue silk, the beadwork along the delicate neckline. "I think this one is lovely."

"Then you wear it."

Ann pulls her fingers back as if they burn. "I couldn't begin to fit into it."

Felicity smirks. "You could have if you'd given up those morning scones."

"It wouldn't make any d-d-difference. I would only insult the dress."

Felicity springs up with a sigh that borders on a growl. "Why do you do that?"

"Do what?" Ann asks.

"Belittle yourself at every opportunity."

"I was only making light of things."

"No, you weren't. Was she, Gemma?"

"Eighty-seven, eighty-eight, eighty-nine . . . ," I answer loudly.

"Ann, if you keep saying how unworthy you are, people will come to believe it."

Ann shrugs, returning the dress to the heap on the bed. "They believe what they see."

"Then change what they see."

"How?"

"Wear the dress. We could let it out on the sides."

"One hundred." I turn to face them. "Yes, but then it wouldn't fit you any longer."

Felicity's grin is feral. "Exactly."

"Do you really think that's a good idea?" I say. The dress is quite expensive, made in Paris to fit Felicity.

"Won't your mother be cross?" Ann asks.

"She'll be far too involved with her guests to notice what we're wearing. She'll only be concerned with what she's wearing, and whether it makes her look young."

It seems a bad idea, but Ann's already touching the silk again as if it were a treasured kitten, and I'm not going to be the one to spoil it for her.

Felicity jumps up. "I shall call Franny. For all her tiresomeness, she is a most excellent seamstress."

Franny is summoned. When Felicity explains what she wants done, the girl's eyes go wide with disbelief.

"Should I ask Mrs. Worthington first, miss?"

"No, Franny. It is to be a surprise for my mother. She will be so very happy to see Miss Bradshaw well turned out."

"Very well, miss."

Franny measures Ann. "It will be difficult, miss. I cannot say if there will be enough fabric."

Ann blushes. "Oh, please don't bother. I'll wear what I wore to the opera."

"Franny," Felicity says, making her name into a sweet lullaby, "you are such a skilled seamstress. I am sure that if anyone can do it, you can."

"But once I alter it, miss, I can't change it back again," Franny says.

"Leave that to me," Felicity says, pushing her out the door with the dress in her arms.

"Now, let's see to giving you a waist," Felicity barks.

Ann braces herself against the wall with both arms. She

starts to turn back to say something to me, but Felicity pushes her head forward again.

"You're not going to pinch me too terribly, are you?"

"Yes," I say matter-of-factly. "Now hold still." I give a sharp tug on her corset laces, cinching in Ann's waist as much as I possibly can.

"H-h-heavens," she gasps.

"Again," Felicity says.

I pull hard, and Ann straightens, panting for breath, tears pricking at her eyes.

"Too tight," she croaks.

"Do you want to wear the dress?" Felicity taunts.

"Yes . . . but I don't want to die."

"All right, no use having you faint on us." I loosen the laces a bit and color floods Ann's face.

"Here, sit," I say, guiding her to the chaise. She has no choice but to sit straight as a church steeple. She breathes as heavily as a worked horse.

"It isn't quite so bad once you're accustomed to it," Ann whispers, giving a weak smile.

Felicity throws herself on the chaise again. "Liar."

"What did you make of Nell Hawkins's performance? It was pure gibberish to me," Ann says, struggling for breath. "Tom looked very handsome, I think. He's so kind."

"I've not been able to make sense of it myself," I answer. "*Offer hope to the Untouchables; do not let the song die. Be careful with beauty; beauty must pass.*"

"*Do not leave the path.* What did that mean?" Ann wonders aloud.

"How about *the slippery, nippery nymphs?*" Felicity says, giggling. "Or *Beware the Poppy Warriors! They will gobble you up. Gobble, gobble!*"

Ann starts to giggle, but the corset cuts her merriment short. She can only smile and pant.

"She was trying to tell us something. I'm sure of it." I'm feeling quite defensive on this matter.

"Come now, Gemma! It was a nonsense poem. Poor Nell Hawkins is as mad as a hatter."

"Then how did she know about the gorgon or the Forest of Lights? Or the golden mist?"

"Perhaps you told her."

"I didn't!"

"She read it somewhere, then."

"No," I protest. "I believe she was speaking to us in a code, and if we can decipher it, we shall unlock the mystery of the Temple's location."

"Gemma, I know you wish to believe that Nell holds the key to all of this, but I must say, having seen her, that you are mistaken."

"You sound like Kartik." I instantly regret mentioning his name.

"What is it, Gemma? You're frowning," Ann inquires.

"Kartik. He's gone."

"Gone? Gone where?" Felicity asks, pulling on a stocking and examining it against the curve of her calf.

"Back to the Rakshana. I insulted him, and he left."

"What did you say?" Felicity asks.

"I told him I didn't even think of him as Indian."

"What is insulting about that?" Felicity says, not understanding. She removes the stocking and drops it on the floor. "Gemma, are we to go into the realms tonight? I want to show Pip my new gown and wish her a merry Christmas."

"It will be difficult to get away," I say.

"Nonsense. There are always opportunities to escape from the chaperones. I've done it before."

"I wish to enjoy the ball," I say.

Felicity fixes me with a mocking smile. "You wish to enjoy Simon Middleton."

"I was rather hoping to dance with Tom," Ann admits.

"We'll go tomorrow," I say, throwing Felicity a bone.

"I hate it when you're this way. Someday, I shall have my own power, and then I will enter the realms any time I please," Felicity huffs.

"Felicity, don't be mad," Ann pleads. "It's just one night. Tomorrow. Tomorrow we'll go into the realms again."

She walks away, dismissing us. "I miss Pip. She was always game."

<hr />

After Felicity's rude departure, Ann and I make small talk and spend time playing with ribbons. Then, as if nothing's happened at all, Felicity bursts through the doors along with Franny, who carries the blue silk dress gently across her arms.

"Oh, let's have a look, shall we?" Felicity exclaims.

Ann steps into the pooled fabric, snakes her arms through.

Franny loops the small pearl buttons at the back. It's lovely. Ann twirls in it as if she can't believe the girl in the mirror could be her own reflection.

"What do you think?" I say, holding Ann's hair off her neck for a grand effect.

She nods. "Yes. I like it. Thank you, Felicity."

"Don't thank me. It will be pleasure enough to watch my mother's face fall."

"What do you mean?" Ann asks. "I thought you said she wouldn't care."

"Did I?" Felicity says, feigning surprise.

I flash Felicity a warning look. She ignores me and pulls out a burgundy velvet gown from the pile on the bed. "Franny? You're such a brilliant seamstress, I'm sure it would be no trouble at all for you to make a tiny adjustment to this gown. Why, I'm certain you could do it within the hour."

Franny blushes. "Yes, miss?"

"It's just that the bodice on this dress is far too prim for a young lady going to such a grand party. Don't you agree?"

Franny examines the bodice. "I suppose I could lower it just a bit, miss."

"Oh, yes, please! Straightaway," Felicity says, pushing Franny out the door. She takes over my spot at the dressing table and breaks into a wicked grin. "This should be quite amusing."

"Why do you hate her so?" I say.

"I'm growing rather fond of Franny, actually."

"I meant your mother."

Felicity holds up a pair of garnet earbobs for inspection. "I don't care for her taste in gowns."

"If you don't wish to discuss it . . ."

"No, I don't," Felicity says.

Sometimes Felicity is as much a mystery to me as the location of the Temple. She is spiteful and childish one minute, lively and spirited in the next; a girl kind enough to bring Ann home for Christmas and small enough to think Kartik is her inferior.

"She seems quite nice to me," Ann says.

Felicity stares at the ceiling. "She has a lot invested in seeming nice—light and amusing. That's what's important to her. But don't make the mistake of going to her with anything that matters."

Something dark and hard flits across the surface of Felicity's face.

"What do you mean?" I ask.

"Nothing," she mutters. And the mystery that is Felicity Worthington deepens.

For fun, I slip into one of Felicity's frocks, a deep green satin. Ann fastens the hooks and a shapely waist comes into view. It is startling to see myself this way—the half-moons of my pale breasts peeking above the crush of silk and flowers. Is this the girl everyone else sees?

To Felicity and Ann, I'm a means into the realms.

To Grandmama, I am something to be molded into shape.

To Tom, I am a sister to be endured.

To Father, I am a good girl, always one step away from disappointing him.

To Simon, I'm a mystery.

To Kartik, I am a task he must master.

My reflection stares back at me, waiting for an introduction. *Hello, girl in the mirror. You are Gemma Doyle. And I've no idea who you really are.*

EVERY LIGHT IS ABLAZE AT THE WORTHINGTONS' grand home on Park Lane. The house glows in the softly falling snow. Carriages arrive in a long black line. The footmen help the ladies step gracefully to the curb, where they take the arms of their gentlemen and promenade to the front door, heads held high, jewels and top hats on display.

Our new coachman, Mr. Jackson, watches as the footman helps Grandmama from the carriage. "Mind the puddle, mum," Jackson says, noting the dubious wet pond on the street.

"There's a good man, Jackson," Tom says. "It's very lucky that we have you, as Mr. Kartik seems to have vanished without a trace. I certainly won't speak to his character, should his future employer contact me."

I wince at this. Will I ever see Kartik again?

Mr. Jackson tips his hat to me. He's a tall brute of a man with a long, thin face and a handlebar mustache that reminds me of a walrus. Or perhaps I'm being unkind because I miss Kartik.

"Where did you find Mr. Jackson?" I ask as we join the well-dressed couples parading to the ball.

"Oh, he found us. Came by inquiring whether we might have need of a driver."

"On Christmas Day? That is curious," I say.

"And lucky," Tom says. "Now remember, Father has taken ill and cannot attend this evening, but he sends his deep regrets."

When I say nothing, Grandmama takes hold of my arm, all the while smiling and nodding to others who are arriving. "Gemma?"

"Yes," I say with a sigh. "I shall remember."

⚡⚡⚡⚡

Felicity and her mother greet us as we arrive. Felicity's dress, tailored by Franny, shows a daring amount of décolletage that does not go unnoticed by the guests, the shock registering in their lingering glances. Mrs. Worthington's strained smile says all that she is feeling, but there's nothing for her to do but put on a brave face, as if her daughter weren't shaming her at her very own ball. I don't understand why Felicity goads her mother so, or why her mother endures it without much more than a martyred sigh.

"How do you do?" I murmur to Felicity as we exchange curtsies.

"Good of you to come," she says. We're both so formal that I have to fight a giggle. Felicity gestures to the man on her left. "I don't believe you've met my father, Sir George Worthington."

"How do you do, Sir George?" I say, curtsying.

Felicity's father is a handsome man with clear gray eyes and fair hair gone a muddy blond. He has the sort of strong profile one can imagine outlined by the gray of the sea. I can see him, arms behind his back as they are now, shouting orders to his men. And like his daughter, he has a charismatic smile, which is on display as little Polly enters the room in her blue velvet gown, her hair in ringlets.

"May I stay for the dancing, Uncle?" she asks quietly.

"She should go to the nursery," Felicity's mother says.

"Now, now, it is Christmas. Our Polly wants dancing and she shall have it," the admiral says. "I'm afraid I'm rather an old fool when it comes to indulging young ladies."

The guests chuckle at this, delighted with his merry spirits. As we move on, I hear him greeting people with great bonhomie and charm.

". . . yes, I'm off tomorrow to Greenwich to visit the old sailors at the royal hospital. Do you suppose they'll give me a bed? . . . Stevens, how's the leg holding up? Ah, good, good . . ."

On a side table, beautiful dance cards have been laid out. They are clever, ornamented with gold braid and a tiny attached pencil so that we may write the name of our partner beside the dance—waltz, quadrille, gallop, polka—that he requests to have with us. Though I should like to write Simon's name beside all of them, I know I am to dance no more than three dances with any gentleman. And I shall have to dance once with my brother.

The card will make a beautiful souvenir of my first ball, though truthfully, I am not yet "out of the schoolroom," since I've not made my debut and had my season. But this is a family party, and as such, I shall have all the privileges of a young lady of seventeen or eighteen.

Grandmama spends a tiresome amount of time visiting with various ladies while I am forced to trail behind, smiling and curtsying and generally saying nothing unless spoken to. I meet the chaperones—bored spinster aunts all—and a Mrs. Bowles promises Grandmama she will watch over me like a mother hen whilst Grandmama busies herself at cards elsewhere. Across the room, I spy Simon entering with his family, and my stomach flutters. I'm so absorbed in his arrival that I miss a question directed to me from a Lady Something-or-Other. She, Grandmama, and Mrs. Bowles stand looking at me, expecting an answer. Grandmama closes her eyes briefly in shame.

"Yes, thank you," I say, thinking it safest.

Lady Something-or-Other smiles and cools herself with an ivory fan. "Wonderful! The next dance is about to begin. And here is my Percival now."

A young man appears at her side. The top of his head reaches the bottom of my chin, and he has the misfortune of looking like a large fish, all bulging eyes and exceptionally wide mouth. And I've just agreed to dance with him.

I come to two conclusions during the polka. One, it is rather like being shaken for an eternity. Two, the reason Percival Something-or-Other has such an exceptionally wide mouth is from overuse. He talks for the whole of the dance, stopping only to ask me questions that he then answers for me. I am reminded of survival stories in which brave men were forced to amputate their own limbs in order to escape animal traps, and I fear that I shall have to resort to such a drastic measure if the orchestra does not stop. Mercifully, they do, and I manage to escape, while "regretfully" informing Percival that my dance card has been filled for the remainder of the ball.

As I hobble from the dance floor to return to the company of Mrs. Bowles and the chaperones, I see Ann coming out to dance with Tom. She could not look happier. And Tom seems charmed to be in her company. I feel quite warmed to see them together.

"May I have this dance, Miss Doyle?" It's Simon, giving me a small bow.

"I'd be delighted."

⚓⚓⚓

"I see Lady Faber trapped you into dancing with her son, Percival," Simon says while twirling me gently in the waltz. His gloved hand rests softly at my back, guiding me easily round the floor.

"He is a most careful dancer," I say, trying to be polite.

Simon grins. "Is that what you call it? I suppose it is a skill to be able to dance the polka and talk incessantly at the same time."

I can't help smiling at this.

"Look there," Simon says, "Miss Weston and Mr. Sharpe." He indicates a dour-looking young woman sitting alone in her chair, dance card in hand. She throws quick glances toward a tall man with dark hair. He's chatting with another young woman and her governess, his back to Miss Weston. "It is common knowledge that Miss Weston fancies Mr. Sharpe. It is also common knowledge that Mr. Sharpe doesn't know Miss Weston is alive. See how she longs for him to ask her for a dance. I'll wager she's kept her dance card free on the chance he'll ask."

Mr. Sharpe walks in Miss Weston's direction.

"Look," I say. "Perhaps he's going to ask her."

Miss Weston sits tall, a hopeful smile on her needle-slim face. Mr. Sharpe passes her by, and she makes a show of looking off into the distance, as if she is not bothered in the slightest by his rejection. It is all so cruel.

"Ah, perhaps not," Simon says. He offers quiet commentary on the couples around us. "Mr. Kingsley is after the widow Marsh's sizable trust. Miss Byrne is much larger than she was during the season in May. She eats like a bird in public, but I hear that in private, she can eat up the larder in the blink of an eye. Sir Braxton is said to be carrying on an affair with his governess. And there is the case of our host and hostess, the Worthingtons."

"What do you mean?"

"They are barely civil with each other. See how she avoids him?" Felicity's mother moves from guest to guest, giving them her attention, but she doesn't so much as look at her husband.

"She is the hostess," I say, feeling the need to defend her.

"Everyone knows that she lived in Paris with her lover, a

French artist. And the young Miss Worthington is baring too much skin this evening. It's already being gossiped about. She'll probably have to marry some brash American. Pity. Her father was knighted by the Queen, given the Knight Commander of the Order of the Bath for his distinguished naval career. And now he has even taken on a young ward, the orphaned daughter of a distant cousin. He's a good man, but his daughter is becoming a stain on his fine reputation."

What Simon says about Felicity is true, yet I don't like hearing him talk about my friend this way. It is a side of Simon I've not seen.

"She is simply high-spirited," I protest.

"I've made you angry," Simon says.

"No, you haven't," I lie, though I don't know why I pretend I'm not angry.

"Yes, I have. It was most ungentlemanly of me. If you were a man, I'd allow you a pistol to defend her honor," he says, with that devilish half smile of his.

"If I were a man, I should take it," I say. "But I would be sure to miss."

Simon laughs at this. "Miss Doyle, London is a far more interesting place with you in it."

The dance ends, and Simon escorts me from the floor, promising to ask for another when my card allows it. Ann and Felicity rush to my side, insisting I accompany them to the other room for lemonade. With Mrs. Bowles in tow, we pass through the rooms, arms linked, gossiping quickly and quietly.

"... and then she said I was far too young to wear my dress

so low and she might very well not have had me come at all if she knew I was to shame her in such a public fashion and the blue silk dress is ruined . . . ," Felicity babbles.

"She isn't angry with me, is she?" Ann asks, her face a picture of worry. "You did tell her I tried to stop you?"

"You needn't worry so. Your reputation is intact. Besides, Father came to my defense and Mother backed down at once. She'd never stand up to him. . . ."

The ballroom opens onto the room that has been set aside for refreshments. We sip our lemonade, which feels cool. Despite the winter chill, we are warm with dancing and excitement. Ann's looking anxiously toward the ballroom. When the music starts again, she jumps for her dance card.

"Is that the quadrille?"

"No," I say. "Sounds like another waltz."

"Oh, thank heaven. Tom has asked me to dance the quadrille. I wouldn't want to miss it."

Felicity is momentarily stunned. "Tom?"

Ann's beaming. "Yes. He said he wanted to hear all about my uncle and how I came to be a lady. Oh, Gemma, do you think he likes me?"

What have we done? What will happen when the ruse is discovered? I've an uneasy feeling about it. "Do you truly like him?"

"Very much. He is so . . . respectable."

I choke on the pulp in my lemonade.

"How are you faring with Mr. Middleton?" Felicity asks.

"He is a most accomplished dancer," I say. I'm torturing them, of course.

Felicity swats me playfully with her dance card. "That is all you have to say? He is a very accomplished dancer?"

"Do tell," Ann presses. Mrs. Bowles has caught up to us. Now she hovers near, hoping for a bit of conversation, a bite of scandal.

"Oh, dear, I've a rip in my gown," I say.

Ann angles her body to look at my skirt. "Where? I don't see one."

Felicity catches on. "Oh, yes. We must get you to the cloakroom at once. One of the maids can mend it. Don't mind us, Mrs. Bowles!"

Before our chaperone can say a word, Felicity spirits us away, down a flight of stairs till we're in a small conservatory.

"Well?"

"He is very lovely. It's as if I've known him all my life," I say.

"He doesn't care much for me," Felicity says.

Does she know what he's said to me about her? I blush thinking of how I could have come more to her defense. "Why do you say that?"

"He meant to court me. I refused him last year, and he's never forgiven me."

I feel as if I've been kicked hard. "I thought you had no interest in Simon?"

"Yes, exactly. I've no feelings for *him*. You didn't ask if *he* cared for *me*."

My good feelings have fallen to the bottom of my stomach, like confetti littering a dance floor. Has Simon been paying attention to me all this time as a way to goad Felicity? Or does he really care for me?

"I think we should return to the ball," I say, heading for the first floor, walking faster than is necessary, just enough to leave a gulf between Felicity and me. I don't feel like joining the happy crowd just yet. I need a moment to gather myself. At the far side of the room lies a pair of French doors that lead to a small balcony. I slip outside, gazing out at the wide expanse of Hyde Park. In the bare trees, I see Felicity, tempting in her low-cut gown, and me, the tall, gangly creature playing dress-up; the girl who is haunted by visions. Felicity and Simon. They could live an uncomplicated life together. They would be pretty and fashionable and well traveled. Would she understand his witty jokes? Would he even make them with her? Perhaps she would make his life a horror. Perhaps.

The cold air is a help to me. With each bracing breath, my head clears a bit more. Soon, I find I am recovered enough to be chilled. Below, the coach- and footmen have gathered about a coffee stall. They cuddle cups of the hot drink in their hands while pacing back and forth in the snow, trying to keep warm. These balls must be a misery to them. For a moment I think I see Kartik. But then I remember that he is gone.

✥✥✥✥✥

The evening plays on in dances and whispers, smiles and promises. The champagne has flowed freely, and people laugh merrily, forgetting their cares. Soon, the chaperones lose interest in guarding their charges, preferring to dance themselves or play whist and other card games in a room downstairs.

When at last Simon returns to the ballroom from his card game, I am all nerves.

"There you are," he says, smiling. "Have you saved me another dance?"

I can't help myself. "I thought perhaps you might be dancing with Miss Worthington."

He frowns. "A dance with the carnivorous Felicity? Why? Has she eaten all the other available gentlemen?"

I'm so relieved by this that I laugh in spite of my friendship with Felicity. "I shouldn't laugh. You're being horrible."

"Yes," Simon says, raising an eyebrow. "I'm very good at being horrible. Would you like to find out?"

"What do you mean?"

"Shall we take a walk?"

"Oh," I say, my fear mixed with a sliver of excitement. "I'll just inform Mrs. Bowles then."

Simon smiles. "It is only a walk. And look how she's enjoying a dance. Why should we disrupt her happiness?"

I don't wish to upset Simon, to make him think I'm such a bore. But it is improper for me to leave with him alone. I don't know what to do. "I really should inform Mrs. Bowles. . . ."

"Very well," Simon says. Smiling, he excuses himself. Now I've done it. I've pushed him away. But moments later, he returns with Felicity and Ann. "Now we are safe. Or at least, *your* reputations are secure. I don't know about mine."

"What is this about?" Felicity demands.

"If you ladies would care to join me in the billiards room, you shall find out soon enough," Simon says, taking his leave.

We wait a respectable length of time before making our way upstairs to the Worthingtons' billiards room. If I felt ill at ease about being alone with Simon, I feel doubly so about having Felicity with us.

"What have you in mind, Simon?" she asks. Hearing her use Simon's name so freely gives me a sick feeling in my stomach.

Simon walks to the bookcase and pulls a volume from the shelf.

"You intend to read to us?" Felicity wrinkles her nose. She pushes a white ball across the wide green felt of the table. It smashes into the neat triangle in the center, sending the other balls careening against the bumpers.

He reaches into the space behind the book and brings out a bottle of thick emerald green liquid. It is like no liquor I have ever seen before.

"What is that?" I ask, my mouth gone dry.

His lips curve into a roguish smile. "A bit of the green fairy. She's a most congenial mistress, I think you'll find."

I'm still confused.

"Absinthe. The drink of artists and madmen. Some say the green fairy lives in a glass of absinthe, and she spirits you away to her lair where all manner of strange and beautiful things can be seen. Would you like to try living in two worlds at once?"

I don't know whether to laugh or cry at this.

"Oh," Ann says, worried. "I think perhaps we should get back. Surely we have been missed."

"Then we shall say we were in the cloakroom having a tear in your dress mended," Felicity says. "I wish to try absinthe."

I *don't* wish to try absinthe. Well, perhaps a little bit—if I could be certain how it would affect me. I'm afraid to stay, but I don't want to leave the room now or let Felicity share this experience with Simon alone.

"I'd like to try it too," I croak.

"An adventurous spirit," Simon says, smiling at me. "That's what I love."

Reaching in again, Simon brings out a flat, slotted spoon. He pours himself half a glass of water from a decanter. He sets the glass on the table and places the strange spoon over the glass's opening. With graceful fingers, he reaches into his pocket and retrieves a cube of sugar, which he perches atop the spoon.

"What is that for?" I ask.

"To take away the bitterness of the wormwood."

Thick as tree sap, green as summer grass, the absinthe flows over the sugar, dissolving it on its relentless way. Inside the glass, a beautiful alchemy is taking place. The green swirls into a milky white. It is extraordinary.

"How does it do that?" I ask.

Simon takes a coin from his pocket, palms it, and shows me his empty hand. The coin has disappeared. "Magic."

"Let's see if it is," Felicity says, reaching for the glass. Simon holds it away, hands it to me.

"Ladies first," he says.

Felicity looks as if she could spit in his eye. It is a cruel thing to do, to goad her so, but I must be cruel myself because I can't help being satisfied that I'm the one chosen first. My hand shakes as I take the glass. I half expect this strange drink to turn me into a frog. Even the smell is intoxicating, like licorice spiced with nutmeg. I swallow, feel it burn my throat. The moment I finish, Felicity grabs it from me and drinks her share. She offers it to Ann, who takes the tiniest of sips. At last it goes to Simon, who takes his turn and passes it to me again. The glass makes its rounds thrice more, till it has been drained.

Simon uses his handkerchief to wipe the last of the absinthe from the glass and places everything behind the book to be retrieved at a later date. He moves closer to me. Felicity comes between us, taking hold of my wrist.

"Thank you, Simon. And now I suppose we'd best make that visit to the cloakroom to add truth to our story," she says, a satisfied gleam in her eye.

Simon isn't happy, that much I can see. But he bows and lets us get on our way.

"I don't feel much different," Ann says as we stand in the cloakroom, fanning ourselves, letting the maids search for imaginary tears in our gowns.

"That is because you didn't take more than a sip," Felicity whispers. "I feel quite fine."

There's a sweet warmth in my head, a lightness that makes it seem as if all is well and no harm can come to me. I smile at Felicity, no longer upset, just enjoying our indiscretion together. Why is it that some secrets can drown you while some pull you close to others in a way you never want to lose?

"You look beautiful," Felicity says. Her pupils are large as moons.

"So do you," I say. I can't stop smiling.

"What about me?" Ann asks.

"Yes," I say, feeling lighter by the second. "Tom will not be able to resist you. You are a princess, Ann." This makes the maid tending my dress raise her eyes to me for a moment but then she is back to it.

When we enter the ballroom again, it seems transformed, the colors deeper, the lights hazier. The green fairy melts to liquid fire that races through my veins like gossip, like the wings of a thousand angels, like a whisper of the most delicious secret I have ever held. Around me the room has slowed into a beautiful blur of color, sound, and motion; the *whisk-whisk* of the ladies' stiff skirts melting into the greens and blues, silvers and burgundies of their bejeweled bodies. They bend and sway into the gentlemen like mirror images that kiss and fly apart, kiss and fly apart.

My eyes feel wet and beautiful. My mouth is swollen as summer fruit, and all I can do is smile as if I know all there is to know but I cannot hold on to any of it. Simon finds me. I hear myself accepting a dance with him. We join the swirling throng. I am floating. Simon Middleton is the most beguiling man I have ever known. I want to tell him this, but no words will come. Through my blurry eyes, the ballroom has transformed into a sacred spiral dance of Whirling Dervishes, their white cassocks flying out like the first snow of winter, tall purple hats defying gravity atop their delicately spinning heads. But I know I cannot be seeing this.

With effort, I close my eyes to clear the scene, and when I open them again, there are the ladies and gentlemen, hands joined tentatively in the waltz. Over their downy white shoulders, the ladies communicate to each other with subtle nods and silent looks—"The Thetford girl and Roberts boy, a most suitable match, don't you agree?"—fates sealed, futures decided in three-quarter time under the glittering illusion maker of the chandelier throwing off diamond-hard prisms of light that bathe everything in a reflection of cold beauty.

The dance over, Simon guides me from the floor. Dizzy, I stumble slightly. My hand reaches for purchase in something solid and finds the broad expanse of Simon's chest. My fingers curl around the white petals of the rose on his lapel.

"Steady there. I say, Miss Doyle, are you quite all right?"

I smile. *Oh, yes, quite. I cannot speak or feel my body, but I am so absolutely lovely—please leave me here.* I smile. Petals fall away, twirling softly to the floor in their own spiral dance. The palm of my glove is stained with the sticky residue of the rose. I cannot seem to figure out how it got there or what to do about it. This strikes me as unbearably humorous, and I find I am laughing.

"Steady there . . . ," Simon says, applying a bit of pressure at my wrist. The pain brings me back to my senses slightly. He walks me past the large potted ferns near the doorway and behind an ornate folding screen. In its creases, I can see fractions of the ballroom whirling past. We are hidden but could be discovered here. I should be alarmed, but I am not. I don't care.

"Gemma," Simon says. His lips graze me just below my earlobe. They trace a moist arc down the hollow of my neck. My head is warm and heavy. Everything in me feels swollen and ripe. The room is still doing its swirling dance of lights, but the sounds of the party are muffled and far away. It's Simon's voice that floats inside me.

"Gemma, Gemma, you are an elixir."

He presses against me. I don't know if it's the absinthe or something deeper, something I can't describe, but I am sinking inside myself with no wish to stop.

"Come with me," he whispers. It echoes in my head. He's got my arm, leading me as if we were ready to dance. Instead, he walks me out of the ballroom and upstairs, away from the party. He brings me into a small attic room, the maid's room, I think. It is mostly dark, lit only by a candle. It's as if I have no will of my own. I sink onto the bed, marveling at how my hands look in the candlelight, as if they are not my own somehow. Simon sees me staring at my hands. He begins to unbutton my glove. At the opening, he kisses the tiny blue veins pulsing there.

I want to tell him to stop. The haze of the absinthe clears a bit. I am alone with Simon. He is kissing my bare wrist. We shouldn't be here. Shouldn't.

"I . . . I want to go back."

"Shhh, Gemma." He removes my glove. My naked skin feels so strange. "My mother likes you. We'd make a fine match, don't you think?"

Think? I can't think. He begins to remove the other glove. My body arches, goes tight. Oh, God, it's happening. It's happening. Over the rounded bow of Simon's back, I see the room shimmering, feel my body tensing with the vision I can't keep out. The last thing I hear is Simon's concerned voice saying "Gemma, Gemma!" and then I'm falling, falling into that black hole.

The three girls in white. They float just beyond Simon. *"We've found it. We've found the Temple. Look and see. . . ."*

I'm following them quickly through the realms, to the top of a hill. I can hear cries. Fast, we're going fast. The hill falls away, and there is the most magnificent cathedral I've ever seen. It shimmers like a mirage. The Temple.

"Hurry . . . ," the girls whisper. "Before they find it."

Behind them, dark clouds gather. Wind blows their hair about their pale, shadowed faces. Something's coming. Something's coming up behind them. It rises up and over them like a dark phoenix. A great black winged creature. The girls don't look, they don't see. But I do. It opens its wings till they fill the sky, revealing the thing inside, a churning horror of faces crying out.

And then I'm screaming.

"Gemma! Gemma!" It's Simon's voice I hear calling me back. His hand is over my mouth to stop my screams. "I am sorry. I meant no harm."

Hurriedly, he hands me back my gloves. It takes me a moment to come back into the room, to realize that Simon was kissing my bare shoulders and that he thinks the screams are over this. I am still woozy from the drink but now I feel as if I shall be ill. I vomit into the maid's washbasin. Simon rushes to bring me a towel.

I am mortified, and my head aches. I am also shaking all over, both from the vision and from what has happened between us.

"Should I send for someone?" Simon asks. He stands in the doorway, coming no closer.

I shake my head. "No, thank you. I wish to return to the ball."

"Yes, at once," Simon says, sounding afraid and relieved at the same time.

I want to explain to him, but how can I? And so we walk down the stairs in silence. At the first floor, he leaves me. The bell is rung for supper, and I simply fall in with the other ladies.

Supper is a long affair, and gradually, with food and time, I feel more like myself. Simon has not come to supper, and as my head clears, my embarrassment rises. I was foolish to have drunk the absinthe, to have gone with him alone. And then that horrific vision! But for an instant, I saw the Temple. I saw it. It's within our grasp. It is not the greatest comfort on this night, but it is some comfort, and I shall hold fast to it.

Mr. Worthington makes a toast to Christmas. Ann is introduced and asked to sing. She does, and the assembly applauds for her, none more loudly than Tom, who shouts, "Bravo!" The governess comes forth with a sleepy Polly, who clutches her doll.

Admiral Worthington beckons to the girl. "Sit upon my knee, child. And am I your own good uncle, then?"

Polly climbs up into his lap and gives a shy smile. Felicity looks on, a grim set to her mouth. I cannot believe she would be so childish as to be jealous of a little girl. Why does she do such things?

"What? Is that all the payment due unto uncles these days? Let's have a true and proper kiss for your uncle."

The child squirms a bit, her eyes darting from person to person. Each one gives her the same eager expression: *Go on, then. Give him a kiss.* Resigned, Polly leans in, eyes closed, and gives Admiral Worthington's handsome cheek a kiss. Murmurs of approval and affection float about the room: "Ah, well done." "There we are." "You see, Lord Worthington, the child does love you like her own father." "Such a good man."

"Papa," Felicity says, rising. "Polly should be getting to bed now. It is late."

"Sir?" The governess looks to Admiral Worthington for his orders.

"Yes, very well. Go on then, Polly dear. I'll be up to sprinkle fairy dust on you later, darling, to make sure you have beautiful dreams."

Felicity stops the governess. "Oh, do let me take our Polly to bed."

The governess gives a slight bow of her head. "As you wish, miss."

I don't like this. Why does Felicity want to be alone with Polly? She wouldn't harm the child, would she? Making excuses, I slip from the room in order to follow them. Felicity leads Polly upstairs to the nursery. I stand just outside the door, watching. Felicity's crouched low, her arms on Polly's slight shoulders.

"Now, Polly, you must promise me something. Promise me that you will lock your door before you go to bed. Promise?"

"Yes, Cousin."

"And you must lock your door every night. Do not forget now, Polly. It is very important."

"But why, Cousin?"

"To keep out the monsters, of course."

"But if I lock the door, Uncle can't sprinkle me with fairy dust."

"I will sprinkle you with fairy dust, Polly. But you must keep Uncle out."

I don't understand. Why would she be so insistent on keeping her own father out? What could the admiral do that could possibly . . .

Oh, God. The full horrible understanding rises in me like a great bird, the wings of truth unfurling slowly, casting a terrible shadow.

"You cannot go to her with anything that matters."

"No. No admirals."

"Do you suppose there is some evil in people that makes others do things?"

I move into the shadows as Felicity leaves Polly's room. She stands for a moment, listening for the click of the lock. She seems so small. At the stairs, I step out, surprising her.

"Gemma! You startled me. Is your head ringing? I shall never try absinthe again, I can tell you that! Why aren't you at the party?"

"I heard what you said to Polly," I say.

Felicity's eyes are defiant. But I'm not afraid of her this time. "Indeed? What of it?"

"Was there no lock on your door?" I ask.

Felicity takes a sharp breath. "I don't know what you are implying, but I think you should stop at once," she says. I place my palm on her hand, but she pulls away. "Stop it!" she spits out.

"Oh, Fee, I am so sorry. . . ."

She shakes her head, turns away from me so I cannot see her face. "You don't know how it really is, Gemma. It's not his fault. The blame is my own. I bring it out in him. He said so."

"Felicity, it most certainly is not your fault!"

"I knew you wouldn't understand."

"I understand that he is your father."

She looks back at me, her face streaked with tears. "He didn't mean it. He loves me. He said so."

"Fee . . ."

"That's something, isn't it? It's something." She's biting back the sobs, her hand against her mouth as if she can catch them, push them back down.

"Fathers should protect their children."

The eyes flash. The hand points. "Aren't you the fine expert on that? Tell me, Gemma, how does your father protect you in his laudanum stupor?"

I'm too shocked to answer.

"That's the real reason he's not here tonight, isn't it? He's not ill. Stop pretending everything's fine when you know it isn't!"

"It isn't the same thing at all!"

"You're so blind. You see what you want to see." She glares at me. "Do you know what it is to be powerless? Helpless? No, of course not. You're the great Gemma Doyle. You hold all the power, don't you?"

We stand there, staring each other down, neither saying a word. She has no right to attack me this way. I was only trying to help. At the moment, I can only think that I never want to see Felicity again.

Without another word, I start down the stairs.

"Yes, go on. Leave. You're always coming and going. The rest of us are stuck here. Do you think he'd still love you if he knew who you are? He doesn't really care—only when it suits him."

For a moment, I do not know whether she means Simon or my father. I walk away, leaving Felicity standing in the shadows at the top of the stairs.

⋌⋋⋌⋋⋌⋋

The ball is over. The floor is a mess. Gathering coats, yawning goodnights, the ballgoers step across the detritus on the floor—confetti, crumbs, and forgotten dance cards, the withered flower petals. Some of the gentlemen are red-nosed and tipsy. They shake Mrs. Worthington's hand with too much ardor, their voices too loud. Their wives pull them along with a polite but firm "Our carriage is waiting, Mr. Johnson." Others follow. Some leave with the flush of new love on their dreamy faces; others wear their dashed hopes and broken hearts in downcast eyes and trembling smiles.

Percival asks if he may call on us at home sometime. I do not see Simon. It would seem the Middletons have gone. He's left without saying goodbye.

I've made a mess of everything—Kartik, Simon, Felicity, Father. Merry Christmas. God bless us, every one.

But I have seen the Temple in a vision.

I only wish I had someone to tell.

CHAPTER
THIRTY-NINE

TWO MISERABLE, LONELY DAYS PASS BEFORE I FIND the courage to call on Felicity, under the pretext of returning a book.

"I shall inquire whether she is at home, miss," Shames, the butler, says, taking my grandmother's card, on which I have added my name in neat script. In a moment he returns my card to me—alone. "I am sorry, miss. It seems Miss Worthington has gone out after all."

On the walk, I turn back. Looking up, I see her face at the window. She immediately ducks behind the curtain. She is home and has chosen to snub me.

Ann comes out to me at the carriage. "I am sorry, Gemma. I'm sure she doesn't mean it. You know how she can be."

"That doesn't excuse it," I say. Ann seems agitated about more than this. "What is the matter?"

"I've received a note from my cousin. Someone's made inquiries about my claims to be a relation of the Duke of Chesterfield. Gemma, I'll be found out."

"You won't be found out."

"I will! Once the Worthingtons know who I am and that I've deceived them . . . oh, Gemma. I'm done for."

"Don't tell Mrs. Worthington about the note."

"She's already so very cross about the dress. I overheard her telling Felicity it was as good as ruined now that it's been let out for me. I shouldn't have let her talk me into it. And now . . . I'll be ruined forever, Gemma." Ann is nearly ill with her fear and worry.

"We'll remedy it," I say, though I have no idea how. Up at the window, I see Felicity again. So much to remedy. "Would you give Felicity a message for me?"

"Certainly," Ann moans. "If I am still here to give it."

"Would you tell her that I've seen the Temple. I saw it in a vision the night of the ball."

"You did?"

"The three girls in white showed me the way. Tell her whenever she's ready, we'll go back."

"I shall," Ann swears. "Gemma . . ." Not again. I cannot help her now. "You won't tell Tom about all of this, will you?"

If he finds out, I don't know whom he'll hate more for the deception, Ann or me. "Your secret's safe."

<hr>

I can't bear to return home. Father's deteriorating rapidly, crying out for laudanum or the pipe, some opiate to take away his pain. Tom sits outside Father's door, his long arms resting on the tops of his bent knees. He is unshaven and there are dark circles beneath his eyes.

"I've brought you tea," I say, handing him the cup. "How is he?"

As if in answer, Father moans from behind the door. I can hear the bed creaking under the weight of his thrashing. He cries softly. Tom puts his hands on either side of his head as if he could squeeze all thoughts from his skull.

"I've failed him, Gemma."

This time I sit beside my brother. "No, you haven't."

"Perhaps I'm not meant to be a doctor."

"Of course you are. Ann thinks you're going to be one of the finest physicians in London," I say, hoping to cheer him. It is hard to see Tom—impossible, arrogant, unstoppable Tom—feeling so glum. He is the one constant in my life, even if the constant is irritation.

Tom gives a sheepish grin. "Miss Bradshaw said that? She is most kind. And rich, as well. When I asked you to find me a suitable match with a small fortune, I was only joking. But you took me at my word, I see."

"Yes, well, about that fortune . . . ," I start. How do I explain this lie to Tom? I should tell him before things go much further, yet I can't bring myself to confess that Ann is no heiress, only a kind, hopeful soul who thinks the world of him. "She is rich in other ways, Tom. Remember that."

Father groans loudly, and Tom looks as if he will crawl out of his skin. "I can't take much more. Perhaps I should give him a little something—some brandy or—"

"No. Why don't you go out for a walk or to your club? I'll sit with him."

"Thank you, Gemma." He gives me an impulsive peck on

the forehead. The spot feels warm. "Don't give in to him. I know how you ladies are—too soft to be proper guardians."

"Go on, then. Away with you," I say.

Father's room is bathed in the purplish haze of dusk. He moans and writhes on the bed, twisting the linens into a wreck. The air smells of sweat. Father is drenched in it, his bedclothes plastered to his body.

"Hello, Father," I say, drawing the curtains and turning up the lamp. I pour water into a glass and put it to his lips, which are cracked and white. He takes halting sips.

"Gemma," he gasps. "Gemma, darling. Help me."

Don't cry, Gem. Be strong. "Would you like me to read to you?"

He grips my arm. "I'm having the most horrid dreams. So real I cannot tell if I am dreaming or awake."

My stomach twists. "What sorts of dreams?"

"Creatures. They tell me terrible stories about your mother. That she wasn't who she claimed to be. That she was a witch, a sorceress who did terrible things. My Virginia . . . my wife."

He breaks down sobbing. Something inside me falls away. *Not my father. Leave my father alone.*

"My wife was virtuous. She was a noble woman. A good woman." His eyes find mine. "They say it's your fault. All this is because of you."

I try to take a breath. Father's eyes soften. "But you are my darling girl, my very good girl, aren't you, Gemma?"

"Yes," I whisper. "Of course."

His grip is strong. "I cannot bear another minute of these things. Be my good girl, Gemma. Find the bottle. Before those dreams come back for me."

My resolve weakens. I'm no longer certain of myself as his pleadings grow more urgent, his tear-soaked voice a raw whisper. "Please. Please. Please. I can't bear it." A small bubble of spit floats on his cracked lips.

I think I shall go mad. Like Nell Hawkins's, my father's mind has been worn thin. And now those creatures have found him in his dreams. They will give him no peace because of me. This is my fault. I must remedy it. Tonight, I will go into the realms and not leave them until I have found the Temple.

But I will not let my father suffer while I do.

"Shhh, Father. I will help you," I say. Pulling up my skirts to an immodest length, I run to my room and find the box where I've hidden the bottle. I race back to my father's bedside. He's working the bed linens between his knuckles, rocking his head back and forth, writhing and sweaty.

"Father, here. Here!" I put the bottle to his lips. He drinks down the laudanum like a man parched.

"More," he pleads.

"Shhh, that's all there is."

"It's not enough!" he cries. "Not enough!"

"Give it a moment."

"No! Go away!" he screams, and pounds his head against the headboard.

"Father, stop!" I place my hands on either side of his head to keep him from injuring himself further.

"You are my good girl, Gemma," he whispers. His eyes flutter. His grip lightens. He settles into an opiate slumber. I hope I have done the right thing.

Mrs. Jones is at the door. "Miss, is everything all right?"

I stumble out. "Yes," I say, barely catching my breath. "Mr. Doyle is going to rest now. I've just remembered something I must do. Would you sit with him, Mrs. Jones? I shan't be long."

"Yes, miss," she says.

〜〜〜〜

It has begun to rain again. There is no carriage and so I take a cab to Bethlem Hospital. I want to tell Nell that I've seen the Temple in my vision and that it is within my grasp. And I want to ask her how I may find Miss McCleethy—Circe. If she thinks she can have her creatures torment my father, she is mistaken.

When I arrive, there is pandemonium. Mrs. Sommers scurries down the hall, wringing her hands. Her voice is high. She is in a very excited state.

"She's doing wicked things, miss. Such wicked things!"

Several of the patients have gathered in the corridor, anxious to see what is causing all the disturbance. Mrs. Sommers pulls at her hair. "Wicked, wicked girl!"

"Now, Mabel," a nurse says, pinning Mrs. Sommers's arm to her side. "What's all this carrying on about? Who's doing wicked things?"

"Miss Hawkins. She's a wicked girl."

There's a terrible squawking coming from down the hall. Two of the women begin a game of imitating it. The sound, everywhere at once, pierces me.

"Merciful heavens," the nurse exclaims. "What is that?"

We hurry past the squawking women, our footsteps echoing off the gleaming floors till we reach the sitting area. Nell's standing with her back to us. Cassandra's cage stands empty, the door ajar.

"Miss Hawkins? What's all the ruckus . . ." The nurse goes silent as Nell turns to us, the bird cradled in her small hands. Green and red feathers trail over her palms in a waterfall of color. But the head is all wrong. It lies at an impossible angle to the fragile body. She has broken its neck.

The nurse gasps. "Oh, Nell! What have you done?"

A crowd has gathered behind us, pressing in to see. Mrs. Sommers runs from person to person, whispering, "Wicked! Wicked! They said she was wicked! They did!"

"You cannot cage things," Nell Hawkins says flatly.

Horrified, the nurse can only repeat, "What have you done?"

"I've set it free." Nell seems to see me now. She gives a smile that would break the heart. "She's coming for me, Lady Hope. And then she will come for you."

Two burly men arrive with a straitjacket for Nell. They approach her gently and wrap her in it like a baby. She doesn't struggle. She doesn't seem to be aware of anything.

Only when she passes me does she scream. "They will lead you astray with false promises! Do not leave the path!"

CHAPTER
FORTY

BY LATE THE FOLLOWING DAY, FELICITY'S CURIOSITY
has overtaken her anger at me. She and Ann return my call.
Our days in London are dwindling. Soon we must return to
Spence. Tom greets Ann warmly, and she brightens. She's
grown more confident these past two weeks in London, as if
she believes herself worthy of happiness at last, and I worry
that it will end badly.

Felicity pulls me into the parlor. "What happened at
the ball, it must never be spoken of again." She won't look at
me. "It isn't what you think, anyway. My father is a good
and loving man and a perfect gentleman. He would never
harm anyone."

"What about Polly?"

"What about Polly?" she says, suddenly staring me
down. She can put such ice in those eyes when she has a
care to. "She's lucky to have been taken in by us. She'll have
everything she wants—the best governess, schools, clothes,

and a season to end all seasons. Better than the orphanage by far."

This is the price of her friendship, my silence.

"Do we have an agreement?"

Ann joins us. "Have I missed anything?"

Felicity's waiting for my answer.

"No," I say to Ann.

Felicity's shoulders drop. "Let's not be bothered by the horrors of holiday visits to home. Gemma knows where to find the Temple."

"I've seen it, I think."

"What are we waiting for? Let's go," Ann says.

ᴧᴧᴧᴧ

The garden is nearly unrecognizable to me. Weeds have sprung up thick and dry and tall as sentries. The carcass of a small animal, a rabbit or a hedgehog, lies opened in the brittle grass. Flies swarm it. They make an awful, loud buzzing.

"Are you sure we're in the garden?" Ann asks, looking around.

"Yes," I say. "Look, there's the silver arch." It is tarnished but there all the same.

Felicity finds the rock where Pippa's hidden her arrows and hoists the quiver onto her back. "Where's Pip?"

A beautiful animal steps out from the bushes. It is like a cross between a deer and a pony, with a long, glossy mane and flanks of a dappled mauve.

"Hello," I say.

• 430 •

The creature ambles toward us and stops, sniffing the air. She goes skittish, as if she's smelled something that alarms her. Suddenly, she breaks into a run, just as something leaps from the brush with a warrior's cry.

"Get away!" I shout, pushing the others into the heavy weeds.

The animal's wrestled to the ground, screaming. There is the sick sound of bone breaking, and then nothing.

"What was that thing?" Ann whispers.

"I don't know," I say.

Felicity grabs her bow, and we follow her to the edge of the weeds. Something's hunched over the animal's side where it has been ripped open.

Felicity positions herself. "Stop where you are!"

The creature looks up. It's Pippa, her face streaked with the animal's blood. For a moment, I swear I see her eyes go blue-white, a look of hunger passing over her usually lovely face.

"Pippa?" Felicity asks, lowering the bow. "What are you doing?"

Pippa rises. Her dress is tattered and her hair a mess. "I had to do it. It was going to hurt you."

"No, it wasn't," I say.

"Yes, it was!" she shouts. "You don't know these things." She walks toward us, and I instinctively move back. She pulls a dandelion from the ground, offering it to Felicity. "Shall we ride down the river again? It's so lovely on the river. Ann, I know a place where the magic is very strong.

We could make you so beautiful that you could have your heart's desire."

"I should like to be beautiful," Ann says. "After we find the Temple, of course."

"Ann," I warn. I don't mean to say it. It just slips out.

Pippa looks from Ann to Felicity to me. "Do you know where it is?"

"Gemma saw it in a vis—"

I interrupt Felicity. "No. Not just yet."

Pippa's eyes brim with tears. "You do know where it is. And you don't want me along."

She's right. I'm afraid of Pip, of what she's becoming.

"Of course we want you along, don't we?" Felicity says to me.

Pip demolishes the flower. She glares at me. "No, she doesn't. She doesn't like me. She never did."

"That isn't true," I say.

"It is! You've always been jealous of me. You were jealous of my friendship with Felicity. And you were jealous of the way that Indian boy, Kartik, used to look at me, as if he wanted me. You hated me for it. Don't bother denying it, for I saw your face!"

She's pierced me through with the truth, and she knows it. "Don't be ridiculous," I say. I can't catch my breath.

She fixes me with a stare like a wounded animal. "I wouldn't be here if it weren't for you." There it is, the thing that's been left unsaid.

"You—you chose to eat the berries," I sputter. "You chose to stay."

"You left me here to die in the river!"

"I couldn't fight Circe's assassin—that dark thing! I came back for you."

"Tell yourself whatever you wish, Gemma. But in your heart, you know the truth. You left me here with that thing. And if it weren't for me, you wouldn't have known . . ." She stops.

"Wouldn't have known what?" Ann asks.

"You wouldn't have known they were looking for you! I was the one who warned you, in your dreams."

"But you said you didn't know about that," Felicity says, sounding hurt. "You lied. You lied to me."

"Fee, please don't be cross," Pip says.

"Why didn't you tell me earlier?" I ask.

Pippa folds her arms. "Why should I risk telling you everything when you won't promise me anything?"

Her logic is a web expertly spun, and I am caught in it.

"Very well. If I cannot be trusted," Pippa says, turning her back, "then you may find the Temple without me. But don't come looking to me for help later."

"Pippa! Don't go!" Felicity calls after her. I've never seen Felicity beg anyone for anything. And for the first time, Pippa does not heed her call. She keeps walking till we can't see her anymore.

"Should we go after her?" Ann asks.

"No. If she wants to behave like a spoiled child, then let her. I shan't go after her," Felicity says, gripping her bow tightly. "Let's move on."

The amulet points the way, and we duck through the forest, past the thicket where the unfortunate ladies of the factory fire wait. We follow the path of the crescent eye on a long, winding trail until we reach the strange door that leads to the Caves of Sighs.

"How did we end up here again?" Felicity asks.

I'm terribly confused. "I don't know. I've lost my bearings completely, I'm afraid."

Suddenly, Ann stops, a look of fear on her face. "Gemma . . ."

I turn and see them, floating on the path.

Felicity goes for her arrows, but I stay her hand. "It's all right," I say. "These are the girls in white."

"The Temple is close," they whisper in those swarmlike voices. "Follow us."

They travel quickly. It is all we can do to keep them in our sights. The green of the jungle-like path opens onto rolling hills that become sandy patches. By the time we've descended a third hill, I no longer see them. They've vanished.

"Where are they?" Felicity asks. She takes down her quiver to rub her shoulder.

"I don't see them," I say, trying to catch my breath.

Ann sits on a rock. "I'm tired. Feels like we've been walking for days."

"Perhaps we'll see something if we climb up one of these hills," Felicity advises. "They said it was close. Come on, Ann."

Grudgingly, Ann rises, and we make our way up the rocky hill to our right.

"Do you hear something?" I ask.

We listen and there it is: a soft crying sound.

"Birds?" Felicity asks.

"Gulls," Ann says. "We must be near water."

We're close to the top of the hill. I offer Ann my hand, pulling her up.

"Criminy," Ann says, taking in the scene.

Before us, across an expanse of water, is a small isle. From it rises a majestic cathedral with a blue and gold painted dome. The seagulls we heard earlier circle it.

"That's it. That's the one from my vision," I say.

"We've found it," Felicity shouts. "We've found the Temple!"

In our mad haste to keep up, I have forgotten to look down at my amulet to check our course. When I do, I see that it has stopped glowing.

"We're off the path," I say, panicked.

"What does it matter?" Felicity says. "We have found the Temple at last."

"But it's not on the path," I say. "Nell said to stick to the path."

Exhaustion has made Felicity irritable. "Gemma, she was speaking gibberish. You're following the advice of a confirmed lunatic!"

I turn in a circle, moving the amulet up and down in an attempt to get some sort of signal from it. There is nothing.

Ann places her hands over mine. "It is true, Gemma. We've no idea if what she's telling us can be trusted. At best, she's a lunatic. At worst, she could be working with Circe. We don't know."

"How do you even know that amulet is reliable? Honestly, where has it led us? To the Untouchables? To those girls in the thicket? It nearly got us killed by those horrible trackers the night of the opera!" Felicity insists.

Ann nods. "You said yourself that the girls in white came to you in a vision. They showed you the Temple, and here it is!"

Yes, and yet . . .

It's off the path. Nell said we shouldn't be led astray. Nell, who strangled a parrot in a mad rage, who tried to strangle me as well.

Don't trust her, the girls in white said.

But Kartik said nothing from the realms could be trusted.

I don't know what to believe anymore.

The cathedral stands like something that has existed for many years. It has to be the Temple. What else could it be? Down on the shore, a small rowboat sits waiting, as if we have been expected.

"Gemma?" Felicity asks.

"Yes," I say, tucking the amulet away. "It must be the Temple."

With a yelp, Felicity runs sliding down the hill to the boat. In the distance, the magnificent cathedral beckons with a thousand lights burning. We untie the boat and push off from the shore, paddling toward the isle.

Out on the water, it grows foggy. Night rolls in suddenly. The cries of the gulls are all about us. The moat that separates us from the Temple is surprisingly wide. I look up through the haze and, for a moment, the towering church seems no more than a ruin. The yellowy moon bleeds through one of the cathedral's tall, hollow windows, glinting off the shards of glass that remain there like a beacon calling in a wayward ship.

I close my eyes, and when I open them again, it is still magnificent and whole, an enormous monument of stone and spires
and great Gothic windows.

"It seems deserted," Felicity says. "I can't imagine anyone
living there."

Or anything, I want to say.

We pull the boat ashore. The Temple sits high on the hill.
To get there, we'll have to take the steep stairs that have been
carved into the rock.

"How many do you think there are?" Ann says, peering all
the way to the top.

"There's only one way to find out," I say, and start climbing.
It is rough going. Halfway up, Ann has to sit to catch her
breath. "I can't do this," she huffs.

"Yes, you can," I say. "It's just a bit farther. Look."

"Oh!" Ann says, startled. A great black bird flaps close to her
face and takes a perch on the steps beside us. It's some sort of
raven. It caws loudly, making gooseflesh on my arms. Another
joins it. The pair seems to dare us to go on.

"Come on, then," I say. "They're only birds."

We push past them to the top of the steps, where we are
greeted by an enormous golden door. The most beautiful
flowers have been carved into it.

"How lovely," Ann says. She puts her fingers to the petals
and the door opens. The cathedral is vast, with ceilings that
soar high above us. Everywhere, candles and torches burn.

"Hello?" Ann says. Her voice echoes, *Hello, ello, lo.*

The marble floor tiles have been laid out in a pattern of red flowers. When I turn my head one way, the floor seems dirty and chipped, the tile broken in chunks. I blink and it is again shining and beautiful.

"Do you see anything?" I ask. *Anything, thing, thing.*

"No," Ann says. "Hold on, what's this?"

Ann reaches for something in the wall. That part of the stone crumbles away. Something skitters across the floor and lands at my feet. A skull.

Ann shudders. "What was that doing there?"

"I don't know." The hair at the back of my neck prickles in fear. My eyes are playing tricks on me, because the floor is going chipped again. The beauty of the cathedral sputters like the candles, flashing from majestic to macabre. For a second, I see another cathedral, a crumbling, broken shell of a building, the shattered windows above us looking eerily like the empty sockets of the skull.

"I think we should go," I whisper.

"Gemma! Ann!" Felicity's voice is high with fright. We run to her. She holds a candle close to the wall. And then we see. Embedded in it are bones. Hundreds of them. Fear screams inside me.

"This is not the Temple," I say, staring at the bones of a hand stuck fast in the crumbling stone. I'm chilled as I realize the truth. *Stick to the path, maidens.* "They led us astray, just like Nell said they would."

Above us, something scurries. Shadows run across the dome. Ann grabs my arm. "What was that?"

"I don't know." *Know, know, know.*

Felicity pats the quiver on her back. The scurrying comes from the other side. It feels close.

"We're leaving," I whisper. "Now."

Suddenly, there is movement all around. The shadows flit across the top of the golden dome like giant bats. We're almost to the door when we hear it: a high-pitched keening that turns my blood to ice.

"Run!" I shout.

We bolt for the door, our shoes clacking across the broken mosaic floor. But it is not enough to drown out the hideous screeching, growls, and barks.

"Go, go!" I scream.

"Look!" Felicity shouts.

The darkness of the vestibule is moving. Whatever was above us has gotten to the door before us, trapping us here. The keening dies down to a low, guttural chant. "Poppets, poppets, poppets . . ."

They step from the shadows, half a dozen or so of the most grotesque creatures I have ever seen. Dressed to the very last one in tattered, filthy white robes over ancient chain mail and sharp, steel-toed boots. Some have long, matted hair that trails over their shoulders. Others have shaved their heads bald, the cuts still fresh and bloody. One fearsome soul has but one long strip of hair in the center of his head, running from forehead to collar. His arms are ringed in bangles, and about his neck is a necklace made of finger bones. This one, the leader, steps forward.

"Hello, poppet," he says, smiling hideously.

He offers his hand. His fingernails have been painted black. There are deep black lines inked up his sinewy arms, thorny stems weeping tears of pitch. They end above his elbow, where fat red flowers bloom in a band around his arm. Poppies.

Nell's words swim back to me: *Beware the Poppy Warriors.*

CHAPTER
FORTY-ONE

THE SHADOWS MOVE. THERE ARE MORE OF THEM.
Many more. Far above us, they perch on railings and rafters
like a flock of gargoyles. One dangles a mace on its chain,
swinging it back and forth like a pendulum. I am afraid to
look at the man in front of me, but at last I do, into eyes that
are rimmed by black kohl in a diamond shape. It is like looking into a living Harlequin mask.

My throat's gone dry. I can barely stutter out a greeting.
"H-how do you do?"

"How do we do what, poppet?"

The others laugh at this, a sound that gives me chills.

He steps forward, closer. He's got a crude sword that he
uses like a walking stick, his hand clenched about the handle.
Every finger wears a ring.

"We're sorry to have intruded . . ." My mouth is too dry.
No other words come.

"We're lost," Felicity croaks.

"Aren't we all, poppet? Aren't we all. My name is Azreal. I am a knight of the poppy, as are we all. Ah, but you haven't told us your names, fair ladies."

We say nothing.

Azreal clucks his tongue. "Oh, that won't do at all. What have we here? Ah, I see you have made friends with the forest folk." He pulls the bow and arrow from Felicity and lays them on the ground. "Foolish poppet. What did you promise-omise them?"

"It was a gift," Felicity says.

The crowd breaks into a hiss of a chant. "Lies, lies, lies, lies . . ."

Azreal grins. "There are no gifts in the realms, poppet. Everyone expects something. What does such a sweet lass do with such a dreadful gift? Tell me, poppets, what were you looking for? Did you think this was the Temple?"

"What Temple?" Felicity says.

Azreal laughs at this. "Such spirit. 'Twill be almost a shame to break you. Almost."

"And if we were looking for this Temple?" I say, heart beating fast in my chest.

"Well, poppet. We'd need to keep you from it."

"What do you mean?"

"Have you bind the magic? No, poppet. Then we'd have none wandering near us. No one to play with."

"We're not here to bind the magic. We want what you do, a piece of it," I lie.

"Lies, lies, lies, *lies!*"

"Shhh," Azreal says, spreading his hands, wiggling his fingers. "The Poppy Warriors know why you've come. We know one of you is the Most High. We can smell the magic in you."

"But . . . ," I say, trying to find a way to reason.

He puts his finger to my lips. "Shhh, no negotiating. Not with us. Once we break you, we can suck the magic from your very bones. A sacrifice. 'Twill give us fierce power indeed."

"But it dooms you," Ann whispers.

"We are already doomed, poppet. No use crying over spilled blood. Now, which of you shall we offer first?" Azreal stops before Felicity. "Such games we could play together, poppet." He trails his sharp fingernail down Felicity's cheek, drawing a thin line of blood. "Yes. You would be such good sport, my pretty pet. We've found our first offering."

He grabs Felicity's arm and she falls to her knees, terrified.

"What can I offer you?" I shout.

"Offer us, poppet?"

"What do you want?"

"Why, to play our games, of course. We've no quests left to us, no crusades. Only games."

He claps, and two of the beasts grab hold of Felicity.

"Wait!" I shout. "This is hardly sporting, is it?"

Azreal stops the men. "Go on," he says to me.

"I propose a game."

Azreal grins, giving his face the appearance of a death mask. "I am intrigued, poppet." He snakes his hand around my neck, caressing it, as he whispers into my ear. "Tell me, what sort of game?"

"A hunt," I whisper.

Azreal steps back.

"What are you doing?" Ann warns.

I keep my eyes trained on Azreal's. If I can get us together, I can make the door of light appear, and we can escape the Poppy Warriors. Azreal claps again, breaking into a delighted cackle. The Poppy Warriors follow suit. Together, they sound like the birds we heard on our way across.

"A most sporting offer. Yes, yes, I like it. We accept, poppet. The hunt shall whet our appetites. Do you see that door?"

He points to an arched iron door at the far end of the cathedral.

"Yes," I say.

"It leads to the catacombs below, and five tunnels. One leads out and away. Perhaps you'll find it. That would be magic indeed, poppets. We'll let you start."

"Yes, but we shall need a moment to confer," I say.

Azreal waves a finger at me. "No time to wish for the door, Order priestess," he says, as if reading my mind. "Yes, I know all about it. Your fear lets us in." He shakes his hands over us, as if sprinkling fairy dust, his bangles jangling in an echo. "See if you can find the tunnel. Go now, poppets. Runrunrun." He chants it to us like a benediction. "Run. Run. Run."

The Poppy Warriors pick up the chant—*Run. Run. Run*— till it bounces off the cathedral's walls like a great roar. "*Rruuunnn! Rrruuunnn! Rrruuunnn!*"

As if shot from a cannon, Ann and I break for the door.

"Felicity!" I shout.

She's stopped to grab her bow and the quiver of arrows.

"Clever, poppet!" Azreal yells. "Such spirit you have!"

"Go!" she screams, catching up to us. We waste no time. We push through the heavy door into a long corridor lined with candles.

"Give me your hands!" I shout.

"Now?" Felicity screeches. "They're right behind us."

"All the more reason to leave at once!"

We join hands, and I try to concentrate. The most terrible, primal howls and screeches echo in the huge cathedral. They are coming after us. In seconds, they shall be through the door and we don't stand a chance. My whole body shakes with fear.

"Gemma, make the door of light! Get us away!" Ann screams, nearly hysterical.

I try again. A piercing shriek unnerves me, and I lose my train of thought. Felicity's face is wild with fear.

"Gemma!" she cries.

"I can't do it. I can't concentrate!" I say.

Azreal's singsong voice rings out. "There'll be no magic-agic here, poppet. Not when we've such games to play."

"They're keeping it from us. We're going to have to find another way out," I say.

"No, no, no!" Felicity whimpers.

"Come on! Look everywhere!" I shout. We stumble along the corridor, patting the walls, searching for some escape. It is gruesome work: my palms rub across chips of bone and teeth. A bit of hair pulls away in my fingers, and I gag with fear and revulsion. Ann screams. She's found a skeleton shackled to a wall, a warning of what's to come.

"Ready or not, poppets, we're coming for you!"

Oh, God. My trembling fingers find a handle. It is part of a small door that nearly blends into the wall.

"What's this?" I say. The door opens with a creak, and we come close to tumbling down a long rope of perilous steps. They snake around the wall, ending far below, where the room opens into five tunnels.

"This way!" I shout. Felicity and Ann step in and we push the heavy door closed, bolting it shut. Under my breath, I mutter a silent prayer that the wooden plank we've slid into place holds fast.

"Stay against the wall," I say, peering over the edge. Ann's boot sends a stone plummeting. It takes many seconds for it to hit the floor—a long way to fall. Quickly but carefully, we make our way down. It is like descending into hell. Torches cast an eerie glow on the wet, rocky walls. At last, we reach the bottom. We're in a circle that branches off into tunnels like a five-pointed star.

Tears streak Ann's face, mingling with mucus from her dripping nose. Her eyes are wide with fear. "What now?"

The shrieks of the Poppy Warriors drift through the crevices of the bolted door. They batter it mercilessly, the wood splintering in deafening cracks.

"We must find the tunnel that leads out."

"Yes, but which one?" Felicity says. The tunnels, lit by torches, flicker with shadows. Five tunnels. And we've no idea how long each one is—or what is waiting for us at the ends.

"We've got to separate. We'll each take a tunnel."

"*No!*" Ann wails.

"Shhhh! It's the only way. Each time we come back to the center. If you find the one, shout."

"I can't, I can't," Ann cries.

"We stay together, remember?" Felicity says, invoking the words we spoke in my room at Spence. It was only two weeks ago, but it feels a lifetime away.

"All right, then," I say.

I grab a torch from the grisly wall, and we enter the mouth of a darkened tunnel. The flame illuminates the few yards in front of us and nothing else. The light falls on the rats that scurry at our feet, and I have to stifle a scream. We push on until we reach a dead end.

"This isn't it," I say, turning back.

A high-pitched keening echoes off the walls. It bounces around the bones of the dead, those unfortunate playthings of the Poppy Warriors. I would give anything to escape that awful sound. Above us, the door has been battered, but mercifully, it still holds fast.

The great black birds we saw outside circle us in the catacombs. Some have perched on the steps. Others flutter to the ground, cawing. The second tunnel yields another dead end. Ann's sobbing openly by the time we have stumbled through the third tunnel, the weak light of the torch showing no way out.

Azreal's voice drifts down to us. "I can hear you, my pet. I know which one you are—you're the plump one. How will you run from me, my beauty bones?"

"Ann, stop crying!" Felicity shakes Ann, but it does no good.

"We're trapped," she sobs. "They'll find us. We'll die here."

The keening of the Poppy Warriors has turned to growls and squawks, like a reverse hunt in which the animals corner the humans. The sound makes my skin crawl.

"Shhh, we'll find it," I command, leading us back to the open circle. More birds have arrived. The air is thick with them.

"Only two tunnels left," Azreal calls out. How does he know that? He isn't at the door. Unless there's some other way in, a way only they know.

My heart beats wildly, and I fear I shall faint, when Felicity shouts, "Gemma, your amulet!"

It glows dimly beneath the fabric of my dress.

Ann stops crying. "It must be showing us the way out."

Dear God, yes, a way out! With frantic fingers, I pull at the necklace, but it's stuck on the lace of my dress. With one hard yank, I pull the amulet free. It sails through the air and skitters across the floor, landing somewhere in the dark.

"We've got to find it. Quick, help me look!" I shout.

The cavern is dark. We're down on hands and knees, hunting for anything shiny. My heart's a hammer swung hard and fast. I have never felt such fear. *Come on, come on. Find it, Gemma, that's a good girl. Keep the fear from your mind.*

Something glints in the dark. Metal. My amulet!

I rush to the spot. "I've found it!" I say.

My hand reaches down, but the metal doesn't come up in my hand. It is attached to something. A steel-toed boot. It takes shape under my fingers as a scream lodges in my throat. When I look up, I see Azreal glowing in the torchlight.

"No, pretty pet. I've found you."

CHAPTER
FORTY-TWO

THE GREAT BIRDS CAW. THERE IS A HUGE FLAP-
ping of wings as they leave their perches. As they fly down,
they change shape, becoming men, until they are the Poppy
Warriors, surrounding us, cutting off all escape.

Seeing my shocked expression, Azreal explains. "Yes, it was
the Order that cursed us so for our games. It's been so very
long since we've had such beauties to play with. So long
since we've been able to visit your lovely world and bring
back pets." He entwines my hair around his fingers like laces.
His breath is hot in my ear as he leans in close. "Such a very,
very long time."

My throat's dry as kindling, and my legs tremble.

"I don't think this will do you any good now," he says, dropping the lifeless amulet in my hand. "Now, who shall
we play with first?" Azreal stops in front of Ann. "Who
would miss you, pet? Would anyone sighedy-sigh over one
more lost maiden? Perhaps if she were the fairest of them

all. But this is no fairy tale. And you are not fair. Not fair at all."

Ann is so terror-stricken she's nearly in a trance.

"It would be a blessing if we took you, hmmm? No more burning inside while the others have all they could ever want and more. No need to cut into your own flesh. No more keeping your mouth closed tight around the scream that explodes inside while they mock you."

Ann nods in agreement. Azreal leans in to her. "Yes, we can end it for you."

"Stop it!" Felicity spits out.

Azreal moves to her, caresses her neck. "Such spirit, pet. How long would you last? If I broke and bled you? A week? Two?" He breaks into a slow grin. "Or . . . would you skitter away inside somewhere, as you did every time he touched you?"

Felicity's shame shows as a single tear coursing down her cheek. How does he know this about her?

"You be quiet," she whispers, her voice betraying her anguish.

"All those nights in your room. Nowhere to go. No one to trust. No one to hear you. Not such spirit, then, pet."

"Stop," Felicity whispers.

He licks her cheek. "You took it. And deep down, you told yourself, 'This is my fault. I made this happen. . . .' "

Felicity is so afraid. I can feel it in her. We all can. What was it he said? *We smell your fear. It lets us in.* Is there something about our fear that gives power to their magic?

"Fee, don't listen to him!" I shout.

"Do you know something, pet? I think you rather enjoyed it. 'Tis better than being ignored altogether, isn't it? That's what you truly fear, hmmm? That you are so very unlovable after all?"

Felicity's sobbing, unable to answer.

"You don't want to live with this anymore, do you, poppet? The shame. The heartbreak. The stain on your soul. Why don't you take this blade and do yourself in?"

Felicity reaches out and takes the dagger he offers.

"No!" I shout, but I'm restrained by one of the Warriors.

He coos to her sweetly as a mother with a babe. "That's it. Just end it. All that pain. Gone forever."

"Don't let them in," I say to Felicity. "They're using your fear against you. You must be strong. Be strong!" Strong. Strength. I'm reminded of something Nell said. "Felicity, Nell said the Poppy Warriors would steal our strength. Fee, you are our strength! We need you!"

I'm face to face with Azreal and his dead, kohled eyes. "What about *your* fear, poppet? Where should we begin? You can't even help your own father."

"I'm not listening to you," I say. I try to concentrate, abandon my fear. But it is so very hard.

Azreal continues. "All that power, yet you cannot do the one thing that matters."

A moment ago, the amulet began to glow, to show me the way out. I clutch it in my hand, secretly angling it toward the last two tunnels. Which is the one?

A hard slap stings my cheek. "Are you listening, poppet?"

Keep concentrating, Gemma. Do I imagine it, or does the amulet glow? It does! It is faint but real. The tunnel directly behind Azreal is the one. I've found the way.

"We visit your father from time to time," he says.

"What do you mean?" I say. My concentration is gone. The glow disappears.

"When he is under the drug's spell, his mind is most receptive to us. Such games, such games. We told him about you. About your mother. But he's getting weaker. And we're losing all our fun."

"You leave him alone."

"Yes, yes. For now. Let's play."

"Stop where you are!" Felicity stands poised on a rock, her bow drawn back, one eye squinting on the arrow that she aims in a sweeping arc, taking in the whole of the room. The Poppy Warriors caw at her. Her mouth curves into a hateful smile, a mimic of the bow's string.

"Put the bow down now, poppet."

Felicity trains the arrow on Azreal. "No."

His grin vanishes. "I'm going to eat you alive."

"I don't bloody think so," she says through tears.

With a great caw, he charges for her. Felicity's arrow flies hard and fast, piercing Azreal's neck just above the protection of his chain mail. His eyes widen as he sinks to his knees and falls to the dusty floor, dead. There is a moment of stunned silence, followed by pandemonium. The Poppy Warriors shriek in anger and grief. There is no time to lose.

"This way!" I shout, running for the tunnel the amulet has shown me. Felicity and Ann are on my heels, but so are the Poppy Warriors. We hadn't the chance to grab a torch. The tunnel is dark as pitch as we barrel through it, bumping into one another, feeling the rats tickle over our feet, hearing one another's desperate gasps and ragged breathing. And just behind us, there is the hideous cawing of those shape-shifting knights.

"Where is it?" Felicity cries. "Where is the way out?"

It is still too dark to see my hand. "I don't know!"

"Gemma!" Ann yelps. They are in the tunnel with us. I can hear them closing fast.

"Keep moving!" I shout.

The tunnel takes a sharp turn. Suddenly, I see it up ahead—an opening, and beyond that, the gray haze of fog. With an urgent burst of speed, we rush out into the thick air, breathing in deep gulps. We're on the shore.

"There's the boat," Felicity screams. It's sitting where we left it. Ann scrambles in and picks up the oars as Felicity and I push the boat away from the shore, wading into the murky water as we do. With effort, we climb in.

The birds come in a great black swarm of screeching.

Ann and I paddle against the current while Felicity takes aim against those terrible winged things. I close my eyes and row for all I am worth, hearing the sound of that awful cawing and Felicity's arrows slicing the air.

Something bumps the boat.

"What was that?" Ann asks.

"I don't know," I say, opening my eyes. I look around but see nothing.

"Keep rowing!" Felicity instructs, letting fly. Birds fall from the sky. They change into men and sink below the water.

"They're going back!" Felicity screams. "They're leaving!"

We give a cheer. Ann's oar is yanked from her hand. The boat is bumped so hard that we shake upon the water.

"What's happening?" Ann says, terrified.

With a great push, the rowboat goes over and we are pitched into the murky moat. I come up sputtering, wiping the water from my eyes with my fingers.

"Felicity! Ann!" I shout. There is no answer. I call out louder. "Felicity!"

"Here!" She pops up, sputtering beside me. "Where is Ann?"

"Ann!" I scream her name again. "Ann!"

Her blue hair ribbon floats upon the water, abandoned. Ann is gone, and all we see is the oily sheen of the water nymphs.

"Ann!"

We scream until we're hoarse.

Felicity dives under, comes up again. "They've got her."

Wet and shaking, we stumble onto dry land. In the distance, the hollow windows of the cathedral wink at me. The magical glamour cast off, it has reverted to its true self, a grand ruin. I put my head on my knees, coughing.

Felicity's crying. "Fee," I say, putting my hand on her back. "We're going to find her. I promise. It won't be like . . ." *It won't be like Pippa.*

"He shouldn't have said those things to me," she says in great hiccupping cries. "He shouldn't have said them."

It takes me a moment to realize that she is talking about Azreal and what happened in the catacombs. I think of her standing on that rock, piercing our tormentor with her arrow. "You mustn't be sorry for what you did."

She looks into my face, her sobs subsiding to a cold, tearless fury. She hoists the nearly empty quiver onto her shoulder.

"I'm not."

The walk back to the garden is long and hard. Soon I recognize the jungle growth of the place where we met the girls from the factory fire.

"We're close," I say. I can hear the factory girls talking.

"Where are we going?" one of the girls asks.

"With Bessie's friends. They know a place where we can be whole again," the other answers.

I pull Felicity down. We're crouched low behind a large fern. Now I see them. The three girls in white, the ones from my vision—they're leading the girls away from this spot in the jungle toward a direction we haven't yet been. *They will lead you astray with false promises. . . .*

Nell was right. Whoever these girls once were, they are dark spirits now, in league with Circe.

"Where are they going?" Felicity whispers.

"The Winterlands, I fear," I say.

"Should we stop them?" Felicity asks.

I shake my head. "We have to let them go. We have to save Ann, if possible."

Felicity nods. It seems a terrible choice, but it is made. And so we watch them go, some of them holding hands, some singing, all on their way to certain doom.

CHAPTER
FORTY-THREE

By the time we reach the familiar orange sunset of the garden, the silent, miserable walk in our soggy boots has worn blisters on our heels. They pinch and bite with each step. But I can't think about that now. We've got to save Ann—if she is still alive.

"Gracious, what happened to you?" It's Pippa. The blood has been washed from her cheeks. She no longer looks frightful but calm and beautiful.

"We've no time to explain," I say. "The water nymphs have Ann. We've got to find them."

"Of course, you wouldn't leave Ann," Pippa mutters. I let it go. "I told you not to come to me for help."

"Pip!" Felicity barks. "I swear to you that if you fail us now, I will never come back to see you as long as I live."

Pippa's startled by Felicity's sudden fury. "You would do that?"

"I would."

"Very well," Pippa says. "How do you propose we fight them? There are only three of us."

"Pip's right. We need help," I concede.

"What about the gorgon?" Pip asks. "She helped us once before."

I shake my head. "We don't know that she can be trusted just now. In fact, we do not know if any creature of the realms can be trusted."

"Who can be?" Pippa asks.

I take a deep breath. "I shall have to go back for help."

Felicity's eyes narrow to angry slits. "You said we wouldn't leave Ann behind. That it wouldn't be like . . . like last time."

Pippa looks away.

"I'm thinking of Miss Moore," I say.

Pippa's incredulous. "Miss Moore? What can she possibly do?"

"I don't know!" I snap, rubbing at the sides of my aching head. "I can't go to any of our families and tell them. I'd be locked away forever! She's the only person I can think of who would listen."

"Very well, then," Felicity says. "Bring her in."

⚘⚘⚘⚘⚘

It takes magic and concentration to make the door of light appear and to make my way fast and undetected through the London streets. I'm taking a terrible risk to do so, using a power that is unpredictable, but I've never been more desperate. The magic does nothing to shield me from the

London rain, though. By the time I reach Miss Moore's flat, I am dripping wet. Fortunately, Mrs. Porter is out, and it is my former teacher herself who answers.

"M-Miss M-Moore," I chatter, chilled to the bone.

"Miss Doyle! What ever is the matter! You're soaked. For heaven's sake, come in."

She leads me upstairs and into her rooms, putting me before the fire to warm myself. "I am sorry for this, but I must tell you something. It's urgent."

"Yes, all right," she says, hearing the fear in my voice.

"We need your help. Those stories we've told you about the Order? We haven't been completely honest. It's real. All of it. The realms, the Order, Pippa, the magic. We've been there. We've seen it. We've lived it. Every bit of it. And now the water nymphs have Ann. They have her, and we've got to get her back. Please. You must help us."

My words come out in a torrent to match the rain rattling the windows of Miss Moore's flat. When I finish, Miss Moore studies me for a moment.

"Gemma, I know you have been under quite a bit of strain, losing both your mother and your friend . . ." She places a hand on my knee.

I want to cry. She doesn't believe me.

"No! I am not telling tales for sympathy! It's true!" I wail. Two sneezes escape me. My throat is raw and swollen.

"I want to believe you, but . . ." She paces before the fireplace. "Can you prove it to me?"

I nod.

"Very well, then. If you can prove it to me here and now, I shall believe you. If not, I shall take you home immediately and speak with your grandmother."

"Agreed." I nod. "Hester . . ."

I waste no time. Grabbing her hand, I use the meager power I have left to make the door appear. When I open my eyes, it is there, the bright light illuminating the look of complete astonishment on Miss Moore's face. She closes her eyes and opens them again, but the door is still there.

"Come with me," I say.

Her hand in mine, I pull her through. It is an effort. I am growing weaker. I can barely feel the whoosh of blood in her veins fueling the heart that is even now accepting that logic is yet another illusion we create.

The garden shimmers into focus. There is the ground littered with purple flowers. Here is a tree whose bark curls into rose petals. There are the tall weeds and strange toadstools. For a moment, I am afraid the shock has proved too much for Miss Moore. She raises a trembling hand to her mouth and puts the other to the tree. She pulls away a handful of petals and lets them drop from her fingers while she wanders in a daze through the emerald green grass.

She sits on a rock. "I am dreaming. This is a delusion. It must be."

"I told you," I say.

"So you did." She touches one of the purple flowers. It becomes a garden snake that slithers up the tree out of sight. "Oh!"

Miss Moore's eyes grow wide. "Pippa!" Pippa and Felicity rush to meet us. Miss Moore reaches out a tentative hand to touch the silk of Pippa's hair. "It is you, isn't it?"

"Yes, Miss Moore. It is," she answers.

Miss Moore puts a hand on her stomach, as if trying to steady herself. "I'm really here, aren't I? I'm not dreaming?"

"No, you're not dreaming," I assure her.

Miss Moore stumbles through the garden, taking in everything. I'm reminded of my first journey here, how astonished I felt. We follow her under the tarnished silver arch and into the place where the runes once stood. She stares at the scorched earth there.

"That is where Gemma smashed the Runes of the Oracle, the binding on the magic," Pippa says.

"Oh," Miss Moore says, as if she is a thousand miles away. "That is why you were looking for your temple?"

"Yes," I say. "Still looking."

"You haven't found it, then?"

"No. We were trying to find it when we were led astray by some dark spirits. And then the water nymphs took Ann," I say.

"We've got to save her, Miss Moore," Felicity cries.

Miss Moore straightens. "Yes, of course we do. Where do we find these creatures?"

"They live in the river," I say.

"Is that their home?" Miss Moore asks.

"I don't know," I say.

Pippa speaks up. "The gorgon knows where they live."

Miss Moore's eyes widen. "There is a gorgon?"

"Yes," I answer. "But I am not certain she can be trusted just now. She was bound by the Order's magic to tell only truth and do no harm. But the magic is no longer as it was."

"I see," Miss Moore says. "Is there another way?"

"None that would be faster," Felicity argues. "We've no time. We have to trust the gorgon."

I do not like placing my faith in a creature of the realms, but Felicity is right. We must find Ann as quickly as possible.

The gorgon sits patiently on the river. When we approach, she swivels her hideous, writhing head in our direction. Miss Moore balks at the sight.

The gorgon's disturbing yellow eyes blink. "I see you have brought a new friend."

"An old friend," Felicity says. "Gorgon, may I present Miss Hester Moore."

"Miss Moore . . . ," the green, slithery head hisses.

"Yes. Hester Moore," Miss Moore replies. "How do you do?"

"As I have always done," the gorgon says.

The plank lowers, and Miss Moore walks onto the barge as if she expects the whole thing to evaporate at any moment.

"Gorgon," I say. "The day we visited the Forest of Lights, the water nymphs swam away in that direction." I point down the river. "Do you know where they live?"

"Yessss," the gorgon says, the snakelike eyes opening and closing slowly. "The lagoon is their home. But it is surrounded by black rock. I can only take you as far as that rock. From there, you must go on foot."

"That will be sufficient," Pippa says.

"Their song is great," the gorgon warns. "Can you resist the lure of it?"

"We shall have to try," I say.

We climb aboard, and the great barge turns for the journey down the river. I take my amulet into my hands.

"The crescent eye . . . ," Miss Moore says. "May I?"

I give it to her.

"It is a compass. Hold it like this."

She rocks it in her hands, but the amulet gives me no glow to guide us. We are off the path for certain now and completely on our own. The boat moves from the sunset of the garden into a green mist that makes it hard to see much of anything.

"How did you discover this place?" Miss Moore asks, looking around in pure wonder.

"My mother," I say. "She was a member of the Order. She was Mary Dowd."

"The woman from the diary?" she asks.

I nod.

"And you think your Miss McCleethy is the one who killed her?"

"Yes. I believe she's been traveling from school to school looking for me."

"And what will you do if she comes for you?"

I stare at the mist swirling into little funnels. "I'll make certain she never harms anyone ever again."

Miss Moore takes my hand. "I'm frightened for you, Gemma."

So am I.

It's growing warmer. Sweat trickles between my shoulder blades and plasters moist strands of hair to my forehead.

"This heat," Felicity says, wiping her brow with the back of her hand.

"It's horrid." Pippa lifts her hair, keeping it from touching her neck. But as there is no breeze to cool her, she lets go.

Miss Moore trains her eyes on the river, taking in every sight, every sound. Watching the water flow under and away from us, I wonder what has become of Mae and Bessie Timmons and the rest of the factory girls. Have they been swallowed up and enslaved by the dark spirits of the Winterlands? Did it happen quickly or did they have time to realize the full horror of what was happening to them?

I close my eyes against these thoughts and let the movement of the boat lull me.

"We're nearing the shallows," the gorgon says.

The river's begun to change color. I can see to the bottom. It's lined with phosphorescent stones and shoals that make our hands look green and blue. The barge comes to a stop.

"I cannot go farther," the gorgon says.

"We're on foot from here," I say. "Gorgon, may we take the nets with us?"

The gorgon nods her giant head. The others scramble to release them. The gorgon calls me to her. "Be careful you are not caught in a net, Most High," she says.

"I shall," I say, feeling uneasy.

But the gorgon shakes her head. The snakes hiss and writhe. "Some nets are difficult to see until you are thoroughly ensnared."

"Gemma!" Felicity calls in a loud whisper. I run to join the others. Felicity's got her arrows; Pip and Miss Moore have the nets and a rope. We step from the barge into ankle-deep water and onto land obscured by a cloud bank. The ground below us is hard and unforgiving. We have to hold hands to steady ourselves. The mist clears a bit, and I can see the desolate landscape of black, rocky hills. Small, steaming ponds lie here and there, carved into the rock. The mist rises from them in green, sulfurous whorls.

On hands and knees, we climb to the top of a jagged rock. Stretched out below is a deep, wide lagoon. The phosphorescent stones at the bottom of the lagoon give it a blue-green glow that leaks into the mist coming off the surface.

"I see her!" Felicity says.

"Where?" Miss Moore asks, surveying the horizon.

Felicity points to a flat rock at the far edge of the lagoon. Stripped to her chemise, Ann has been tied to the rock as if she is the figurehead on the bow of a ship. She stares straight ahead as if in a trance.

They will take the song, pin her to the rock. Do not let the song die.

"Do not let the song die," I say. "Ann is the song. That's what Nell was trying to say."

"Let's go," Felicity says, starting her descent.

"Wait," I say, pulling her back.

The water nymphs emerge from the depths, their shiny heads like polished stones in the glow of the water. They sing sweetly to Ann. The pull of their voices begins to work on me.

"They are like the sirens of old. Don't listen. Cover your ears," Miss Moore orders. We do except for Pippa. She is not susceptible to their lures, and I am reminded once again that she is no longer the Pippa we knew, no matter how much we'd all like to pretend otherwise.

Below, the water nymphs move some sort of sea sponge through Ann's tangled mop of hair, turning the strands a pearly green-gold. They stroke their webbed fingers across her arms and legs. She's covered in the light sheen of the sparkling scales they've left behind. They stroke the sponge over Ann's skin, making her shiver. Her skin turns the same shiny green-gold.

The nymphs have stopped singing.

"What are they doing?" I whisper.

Miss Moore's expression is grim. "If the legends are accurate, they are preparing Miss Bradshaw."

"Preparing her for what?" Felicity says.

Miss Moore pauses. "They're getting ready to take her skin."

We gasp in horror.

"That's what makes the water so beautiful and warm," Miss Moore explains. "Human skin."

Far across the lagoon, the mist grows brighter, taking form. One girl emerges, then another and another, till all three of the ghostly forms are present. The three in white. For a moment, they look in our direction with a curious smile, yet they do not betray us.

"Get down," I say, pulling at Miss Moore's skirt. She lies flat against the rock. "Those are very dark spirits. You don't wish to be seen by them."

The girls call to the nymphs in a tongue I do not know. When I peek over the rock, I see the girls leading the nymphs around a jetty and out of sight.

"Now," I say.

As quickly as we can, we scramble down the rocky cliff and out onto the near shore.

"Who shall go?" Pippa asks anxiously.

"I shall go," Miss Moore says.

"No," I say. "I shall. She is my responsibility."

Miss Moore nods. "As you wish."

She ties the rope around her middle. "If things should prove difficult, tug on the rope and we shall pull you to safety."

I take the other end and swim toward Ann on the rock. The water is surprisingly comfortable, but I shudder to think why it is so beautiful. As I get farther out, I find I have to close my eyes to keep going. At last I reach Ann.

"Ann?" I whisper, then more urgently, "Ann!"

"Gemma?" she says, as if briefly waking from a drugged stupor. "Is that you?"

"Yes," I whisper. "We've come for you. Hold still."

I loop the rope around Ann's waist and tie it tight. My fingers are slippery with lagoon water, but I am able to loosen the knots that hold her feet and hands. Ann slides into the water with a little splash.

"Gemma!" Felicity whisper-yells from the shore. "Don't let her drown."

I pull up on the rope and Ann bobs to the surface, coughing, awake. She thrashes about.

"Ann! Shush! You'll bring them . . ."

Too late. Across the lagoon, the nymphs have ended their meeting with the beastly girls in white. They see what I'm about. Angry and snarling, they let loose with a fierce screech that rips through me. They do not like that I've dared to take their pet. Then there is only the silvery bow of their backs as they dive under, one by one, swimming fast for us, hungry for our pretty skin.

I push off from the rock, towing Ann. I can feel Miss Moore drawing hard on the rope, but we're both struggling against Ann's dead weight.

"Come on, Annie, you've got to swim for it," I plead.

She does a groggy crawl, her arms thrashing about in the water, but we're no match for the furious nymphs coming our way.

I scream, no longer caring to keep quiet. "Pull! On the rope—pull hard!"

Felicity and Pippa rush to aid Miss Moore. Grunting and straining, they tug as hard as they can. We plow violently through the water. It's not enough.

"Use the nets!" I screech, taking in a mouthful of foul water so that I cough and gag.

Pippa runs for the nets. She hurls one out. It sails overhead and splashes into the water. The nymphs scream in rage. The net has frightened them, but only temporarily. They renew their efforts. This time, Pippa's net lands on four of the nymphs. There's a horrible scream as the net burns their skin. They bubble and blister until they are nothing more than sea foam.

The others fall behind, afraid to go farther. Felicity and Pippa lug us from the water onto the sharp shoals.

Miss Moore helps me to my feet. "Are you all right?"

Ann vomits onto the shoals. She is weak but alive.

We've cheated them of their prize. I can't help myself. I shout with glee and satisfaction. "Take our skin, will you? Ha! Take that!"

"Gemma," Miss Moore advises, pulling me back from the water. "Do not taunt them."

Indeed, the nymphs do not take kindly to my celebration. They open their mouths and begin to sing. The lure of it is like a net drawing me toward the water. Oh, that sound, like a promise that there need be no worry or want ever again. I could grow drunk on that tune.

Miss Moore places her fingers in her ears. "Don't listen!"

Felicity wades into the warm water to her ankles, then her knees, drawn by the song. Pippa runs to the edge, screaming her name. "Fee! *Fee!*"

Ann's begun to sing along. For a moment, I'm distracted by her voice. What am I doing in the water? I step out. Ann stops singing, and the nymphs flood me with their sweet promises again.

I'm vaguely aware of Miss Moore screaming, "Ann! Sing! You've got to sing!"

Ann finds her song again. It pulls me away from the water

and the nymphs enough to see what is happening. Felicity's swimming farther out.

"Sing, Ann!" I shout. My hands find the faint throb at her throat. "Sing as if your life depends on it."

Ann's song, thin at first, is no match for the temptation in Felicity's ears. But her voice gains strength. She sings more loudly and more powerfully than I have ever heard her sing, until she is the song itself. She stares at those creatures like a warrior warning of the battle to come. In the water, Felicity stops. Pippa rushes in after her.

"Fee, come back with me."

She reaches out her hand and Felicity takes it.

"Come on," Pippa says softly, luring her from the water. "Come on."

Felicity follows Ann's voice and Pippa's hand until she is back on solid ground.

"Pippa?" Felicity says.

Pippa embraces her, and Felicity holds so tightly I fear she will break Pippa.

The nymphs, realizing they have lost, screech in rage.

"Let's not wait around, shall we?" Miss Moore says. She gathers the rope onto her shoulder. I am so grateful for Miss Moore at this moment I could cry.

"Thank you, Hester," I say.

"It is I who should thank you, Gemma."

"For what?" I ask.

But there is no answer to that question. For the girls in white have returned. And they are not alone. They've brought the fearsome creature I've seen in my vision, the one who followed us back from the Caves of Sighs—a tracker. It emerges from behind them in the darkness, rising, spreading out till we are forced to look up at the vast, roiling expanse of it. The girls step inside it like children clinging to a mother's skirts.

"At last . . . ," it says.

Run. Get away. Can't move. The fear. Such fear. The wings unfurl revealing the horrible faces within. *The hate. The terror.*

Miss Moore pushes me out of the way, her voice strong. "*Run!*"

We tumble down the black rock. The slide is rough. It cuts my hands, but we reach the ground quickly.

"Get to the gorgon," Felicity shouts. She is in the lead, Pippa just behind. I'm pulling Ann, who can barely run. But where is Miss Moore? I see her! She appears in the sulfur green mist. The beast and the girls are close on her heels.

She waves us on. "Go! Go!"

Pulling Ann along, I run as fast as I can till I see the gorgon in the shallows. The four of us clamber onto the boat.

Miss Moore emerges, but the thing is quick. It blocks her path.

"Miss Moore!" I shout.

"No! Gemma, run!" she shouts. "Do not wait for me!"

With a mighty groan, the gorgon sets us back on course for the garden. I climb to the railing, but Felicity and Pippa pull at my arms. I'm fighting like a madwoman.

"Gorgon, stop this instant! I'm ordering you to stop!"

But she doesn't. We're slipping away from the shore, where that terrible creature towers over my friend.

"Miss Moore! Miss Moore!" I shout till my voice is raw, till I've no voice left. "Miss Moore," I croak, sliding to the deck of the boat.

⌇⌇⌇⌇⌇

We're back in the garden. My eyes are raw from crying. I'm exhausted and sick. I turn to the gorgon.

"Why didn't you stop when I ordered you to do so?"

That thick, scaly head rolls slowly toward me. "I am ordered first to bring no harm to you, Most High."

"We could have saved her!" I cry.

The head swivels away. "I think not."

"Gemma," Ann says gently. "You've got to make the door."

Felicity and Pippa sit together, arms intertwined, loathe to leave each other.

I close my eyes.

"Gemma," Ann says.

"Circe's creature got her, and I wasn't able to stop it."

No one has a comforting thing to say.

"I'm going to kill her," I say, my words hard as steel. "I'm going to face her, and then I shall kill her."

It takes tremendous effort to make the door of light appear. The others must steady me. But finally it shimmers into view. Pippa waves goodbye and blows kisses to us all. I'm the last to go through, and as I wait, I glance one last time at

Pippa. She's pulled something out from its hiding place behind a tree. It's the carcass of a small animal. She stares at it longingly before crouching low, sitting on her haunches like some beast herself. She brings the flesh to her mouth and feeds, her eyes gone white with hunger.

CHAPTER
FORTY-FOUR

MISS MOORE IS GONE. SHE IS GONE. I'VE NOT FOUND the Temple. The Rakshana were wrong to trust me with this task. I am not Nell Hawkins's Lady Hope. I am not the Most High, the one to bring back the glory of the Order and the magic. I am Gemma Doyle, and I have failed.

I am so tired. My body aches; my head feels stuffed with cotton. I should like to lie down and sleep for days. I am too tired even to undress. I lie across my bed. The room swirls for a moment, and then I am fast asleep and dreaming.

I'm flying over darkened, rain-slicked streets, through alleys where filthy children gnaw at mealy bread thick with buzzing insects. I fly on, till I'm floating down the halls of Bethlem and into Nell Hawkins's room.

"Lady Hope," she whispers. "What have you done?"

I don't understand. I cannot answer. There are footsteps in the corridor.

"What have you done? What have you done?" she shouts.

"Jack and Jill went up the hill; Jack and Jill went up the hill; Jack and Jill went up the hill."

I'm floating away on her ramblings, floating high above the corridor, where the lady in the green cloak sweeps down the darkened hall, unnoticed. I'm floating out into the inky night over St. George's when I hear Nell Hawkins's faint, stifled cry.

I do not know how late I have slept, what day it is, or where I am when I am awakened by an anxious Mrs. Jones.

"Miss, miss! You'd best dress quickly. Lady Denby has come to call with Mr. Simon. Your grandmother sent me to fetch you straightaway."

"I'm not feeling well," I say, flopping back on the pillows.

Mrs. Jones pulls me to a sitting position. "Once they've gone, you can rest all you like, miss. But for now, I'm to get you dressed and be quick about it."

When I descend, they're all assembled in the parlor, huddled tightly over teacups. If this is a social call, it is not going well. Something is amiss. Even Simon isn't smiling.

"Gemma," Grandmama says. "Sit down, child."

"I'm afraid I have some rather troubling news concerning your acquaintance Miss Bradshaw," Lady Denby says. My heart stops.

"Oh?" I say, faintly.

"Yes. I thought it strange that I wouldn't know of her family, so I've made inquiries. There is no Duke of Chesterfield in Kent. In fact, I was able to turn up nothing on a girl discovered to be of the Russian nobility."

Grandmama shakes her head. "It is shocking. Shocking!"

"What I did discover is that she has a rather vulgar cousin—a merchant's wife who lives in Croydon. I'm afraid your Miss Bradshaw is little more than a fortune hunter," Lady Denby says.

"I never cared for her," Grandmama says.

"There must be some mistake," I offer weakly.

"That is a kind assessment, my dear," Lady Denby says, patting my hand. "But remember that you too have been tainted by this scandal. And Mrs. Worthington, of course. To think that they opened their home to her. Of course, Mrs. Worthington isn't known for her sound judgment, if I may be so bold."

Grandmama gives her edict. "You are to have no further acquaintance with that girl."

Tom enters. His face is drawn and pale.

"Thomas? What is the matter?" Grandmama asks.

"It's Miss Hawkins. She took ill in the night with a fever. She will not wake." He shakes his head, unable to continue.

"I dreamed about her last night," I blurt out.

"Did you? What did you dream?" Simon asks.

I dreamed of Circe and Nell's stifled cry. What if that was no dream?

"I—I don't remember," I say.

"Oh, poor dear, you're pale," Lady Denby says. "It is very hard to hear that one has been duped by a supposed friend. And now your Miss Hawkins is ill. It must be a terrible shock."

"Yes, thank you," I say. "I'm not feeling well."

"Poor dear," Lady Denby murmurs again. "Simon, do be a gentleman and help Miss Doyle."

Simon takes my arm and escorts me from the room.

"I can't bear to think of Ann in such trouble," I say.

"If she misrepresented herself, she deserves what comes," Simon says. "No one likes to be deceived."

As I am deceiving Simon, letting him think me this uncomplicated English schoolgirl? Would he run if he knew the truth? Would he feel I had misled him? Keeping secrets is as much an illusion as acting out an elaborate charade.

"I know this is a horrible imposition, Mr. Middleton," I say. "But could you possibly delay your mother's visit to Mrs. Worthington until I've had a chance to speak with Miss Bradshaw?"

Simon gives me a smile. "I'll do my best. But you should know that once my mother sets her sights on something, there is little you can do to change the course of it. I think she's set her sights on you."

I should be flattered. And I am, in a small way. But I cannot shake the feeling that in order to be loved by Simon and his family, I shall have to be a very different sort of girl and that if they knew me—truly knew me—they would not welcome me so warmly.

"What if you were to be disappointed in me?"

"I could never be disappointed in you."

"But what if you discovered something . . . surprising about me?"

Simon nods. "I know what it is, Miss Doyle."

"You do?" I whisper.

"Yes," he says in earnest. "You have a hump on your back

that only appears after midnight. I shall take your secret to the grave."

"Yes, that is it," I say, smiling, blinking hard at the tears that sting my eyes.

"You see? I know everything about you," Simon says. "Now get some rest. I shall see you tomorrow."

~~~~~

I hear them in the parlor gossiping. I hear them because I am on the stair, soft as starlight. And then I am out the door, quiet as can be, and off to the Worthingtons' house to warn them. And after, I shall find Miss McCleethy, and she will answer for Miss Moore, my mother, Nell Hawkins, and the others. For this purpose, I tuck the blade Kartik left me into my boot.

~~~~~

Felicity's butler opens the door and I push my way inside, past his protests.

"Felicity!" I call out, not caring about manners or proto-col. "Ann!"

"In here!" Felicity answers from the library.

I barrel my way in with the butler on my heels. "Miss Doyle to see you, miss," he says, determined to return some sense of decorum to the proceedings.

"Thank you, Shames. That will be all," Felicity says. "What is it?" she asks, when we are alone. "Is it something about Miss Moore? Have you found a way to get her back?"

I shake my head. "We're found out. Lady Denby has made

inquiries. She's found your cousin, Ann. She knows we've been masquerading all this time." I sink into a chair. I am so very tired.

"Then everyone will know. You may be sure of that," Felicity says, looking truly terrified.

Ann pales. "I thought you said no one would be the wiser!"

"I hadn't counted on Lady Denby and her hatred of my mother."

Ann sits, trembling. "I'm ruined. And we shall never be allowed to see one another again."

Felicity's hand is a fist at her stomach. "Papa shall have my head."

"It was your idea," Ann says, pointing a finger at Felicity.

"You were only too happy to play along!"

"Please stop," I say. "We have to keep Lady Denby from telling what she knows."

"No one can keep her from that," Felicity says. "She is a very determined woman. And this is the sort of gossip that she lives for."

"We could come up with another story," Ann says, pacing.

"How long before she makes inquiries on that one as well?" I say.

Ann sits on the settee, lays her head on her arm, and cries.

"We could use the magic," Felicity says.

"No," I say.

Felicity's eyes flash. "Why not?"

"Have you forgotten last night? We shall need every bit of magic to find the Temple and face Circe."

"Circe!" Felicity spits. "Pippa was right. You only look after yourself."

"That isn't true," I say.

"Isn't it?"

"Please, Gemma," Ann blubbers.

"You've seen how the magic takes its toll upon me," I say. "I'm not myself today. And Nell Hawkins has fallen into a trance. Just last night I dreamed she'd been found by Circe."

Felicity's butler enters. "Is everything all right, Miss Worthington?"

"Yes, Shames. Thank you."

He leaves, but he does not take our anger with him. It hangs about the room in wounded looks and a hostile quiet. My head aches.

"Do you think it's true? Do you think Circe really has taken hold of Nell Hawkins?" Ann asks through her tears.

"Yes," I say. "So you see it is imperative that we go into the realms again tonight. Once we find the Temple and bind the magic, you may use it to make them think you are Queen Victoria herself if you wish. But first we find the Temple." And Circe.

Felicity exhales loudly. "Thank you, Gemma. I can keep Mother occupied and away from Lady Denby's clutches until tomorrow. Ann, you are about to become very ill."

"I am?"

"No one would dare to speak badly of an invalid," she explains. "Now, faint."

"But what if they can tell that I am pretending?"

"Ann, it is not terribly difficult to faint. Women do it all the time. You simply fall to the floor, close your eyes, and don't speak."

"Yes," Ann says. "Should I fall to the floor or here on the couch?"

"Oh, honestly, it doesn't matter! Just faint!"

Ann nods. With the finesse of a born actress she rolls her eyes back and crumples to the floor dramatically, like a soufflé falling in on itself. It is the most graceful fainting spell I've ever seen. It is a pity it has been wasted on us.

"Tonight," Felicity says, taking my hands.

"Tonight," I agree.

We push through the parlor doors as frantically as we can. "Shames! Shames!" Felicity calls.

The tall, icy butler appears. "Yes, miss?"

"Shames, Miss Bradshaw has fainted! I fear she has taken ill. We must call for Mother at once."

Even the placid Shames is disturbed. "Yes, miss. Right away."

As the house erupts into an excited frenzy—for everyone, it seems, loves the potential for disaster, a break in the numbing routine—I take my leave. I must admit that I find a savage delight in rehearsing what I will say to Grandmama about this visit. ". . . *and then Miss Bradshaw's kind, gentle spirit was so injured by these false accusations that she took ill and fainted.* . . ."

Yes, that will be a most satisfactory moment. If only I weren't so very tired.

Dusk has settled over London along with a bit of sleet. It's a raw evening, and I shall be glad to sit at my fire. I wonder what has happened to Miss Moore, if there is anything I can do to save her from her terrible fate. I wonder if I shall ever see Kartik again or if he has been absorbed into the shadows of the Rakshana.

Jackson's waiting patiently at the curb. That can only mean they've discovered me gone and come to the logical conclusion. I'm in for as much trouble as Felicity and Ann now. Most likely, Tom sits inside the carriage fuming.

"Evenin', miss. Your grandmother was very worried about you," Jackson says, opening the carriage door for me. He takes my hand to help me up and in.

"Thank you, Jack—" I freeze. It is not Tom or Grandmama waiting for me. Sitting in my carriage is Miss McCleethy. She is joined by Fowlson from the Rakshana.

"Get in, if you please, miss," Jackson says, exerting pressure on my back.

I open my mouth to scream. His hand presses hard against me, trapping the sound in my throat. "Oi know where your family lives. Fink on your poor dad, lyin' in the sickroom, all vulnerable like."

"Jackson," Miss McCleethy calls. "That will be enough."

Reluctantly, Jackson lets go. He closes the door behind me and swings up behind the horses. The lights of Mayfair fade away as the carriage lurches into the traffic heading for Bond Street.

"Where are you taking me?" I demand.

"Somewhere we can talk," Miss McCleethy says. "You are a very slippery girl to catch, Miss Doyle."

"What have you done to Nell Hawkins?" I ask.

"Miss Hawkins is the least of my concerns at the moment. We must discuss the Temple."

Fowlson douses a handkerchief with liquid from a small bottle.

"What are you doing?" I ask, the terror rising in my throat.

"We can't very well have you knowing how to find our hideaway," Fowlson says.

He looms over me. I fight back, turning my head left and right to avoid him, but he is too strong. The white of the handkerchief is all I can see as it floats lower, covering my nose and mouth at last. There is the inescapable, suffocating odor of ether. The last thing I see before succumbing to the darkness is Miss McCleethy popping a toffee into her mouth without a care in the world.

〰〰〰〰

I come to by degrees. First, there is the taste in my mouth, a foul, sulfurous thing that sits on my tongue and makes me gag. Then there is the blurred vision. I have to raise my arm to block the wobbly, dancing light. I'm in a dark room. Candles burn. Is there no one else? I can't see anyone, but I'm aware of others. I can feel them in the room. There's a rustling sound coming from the darkness above.

Two masked men enter the room, escorting someone in a blindfold. They remove the blindfold. It's Kartik! The other men back away, leaving us alone together.

"Gemma," he says.

"Kartik," I croak. My throat is dry. My voice cracks. "What are you doing here? Did they take you, too?"

"Are you all right? Here, have some water," he answers.

I take a sip. "I'm so very sorry about what I said that day. I didn't mean anything by it."

He shakes his head. "It is forgotten. Are you certain you're all right?"

"You must help me. Fowlson and Miss McCleethy kidnapped me and brought me here. If she has his loyalty, then we cannot trust the Rakshana."

"Shhh, Gemma. No one brought me here against my will. Miss McCleethy is part of the Order. She's working with the Rakshana to find the Temple and restore the Order to its full power. She's come to help you."

I lower my voice to a whisper. "Kartik, you know that Miss McCleethy is Circe."

"Fowlson says she is not."

"How does he know? And how do you know that he has not been corrupted as well? How do you know that you can trust him?"

"Miss McCleethy isn't who you think she is. Her name is Sahirah Foster. She's been on the hunt for Circe. She took the name McCleethy as a decoy, in hopes of calling the attention of the real Circe, as that was the name she took whilst she was at Saint Victoria's."

"And you believe this story?" I say with a sneer.

"Fowlson believes it."

"I'm certain Nell Hawkins could tell you differently. Don't you see?" I beg. "She is Circe! She murdered those girls, Kartik. She murdered my mother and your brother! I won't let her do the same to me."

"Gemma, you are mistaken."

He's been taken in by her. I can no longer trust him.

Miss McCleethy enters the room. Her long green cloak brushes the floor.

"This has taken entirely too long, Miss Doyle. You will take me into the realms and I shall help you find the Temple. Then we shall bind the magic and restore the Order."

From above, a deep voice rings out. "With access to the realms and the magic granted at last to the Rakshana." In the candlelight I can see only a masked face.

"Yes, of course," Miss McCleethy says.

"I know all about you," I say. "I wrote to Saint Victoria's. I know what you did to Nell Hawkins and the other girls before her."

"You know nothing, Miss Doyle. You only think you do, and therein lies the problem."

"I know Mrs. Nightwing is your sister," I announce triumphantly.

Miss McCleethy looks surprised. "Lillian is a dear friend. I have no sister."

"You're lying," I say.

The voice from above rings out. "Enough! It is time."

"I won't take you in!" I yell to one and all.

Fowlson grabs my arm roughly. "I've grown rather tired of your games, Miss Doyle. They've cost us too much time already."

"You can't force me to do it," I say.

"Can't I?"

Miss McCleethy intervenes. "Mr. Fowlson. Allow me a moment with the girl, if you please."

She pulls me aside. Her deep voice is but a whisper. "Don't worry, my dear. I've no intention of letting the Rakshana have any say in the realms. I'm only placating them with a promise."

"After they've helped you, you'll cut them off."

"Don't fret too much over it." She lowers her voice further. "They intended to take the realms for themselves. What words did they give you for binding the magic?"

"*I bind the magic in the name of the Eastern Star.*"

She smiles. "With those words, you give them the power of the Temple."

"Why should I believe you? Kartik told me—"

"Kartik?" She sneers in disgust. "Pray, did he tell you what his task is?"

"To help me find the Temple."

"Miss Doyle, you really are quite gullible. His task was to help you find the Temple so the Rakshana could take it over. Once they had all that power, do you really think they'd need anything further from you?"

"What do you mean?"

"You'd be nothing more than an annoyance at that point. A liability. And that brings us to his true task: to kill you."

The room grows smaller. I feel I can't breathe. "You're lying."

"Am I? Why don't you ask him? Oh, I don't expect that he will tell you the truth. But watch him—watch his eyes. They won't lie."

Do not forget your task, novitiate . . .

Was it all a lie? Was any of it true?

"So you see, my dear, we are stuck with each other after all."

I am too bitter to cry. My very blood is diseased with hate. "So it would seem," I say, fury a coiled snake in my belly.

"You possess extraordinary gifts, Gemma. Under my wing, you shall learn a great deal. But first, remember, you must bind the magic in the name of the Order." Miss McCleethy smiles, and I am reminded of a serpent. "I have waited twenty years for this moment."

I will die first. "I have to know the truth," I say.

She nods. "Very well. Fowlson!" she calls out. Moments later, he enters with Kartik. Above us, the chamber fills. The floor is alive with the soft sounds of discreet footsteps. Then, all is still in the room except for the flickering candlelight.

"Kartik," I ask, and my voice bounces off the walls. It is a smaller room than I realized. "What was your task from the Rakshana? Not the one about finding the Temple," I say, my voice filled with hate. "The other one."

"The . . . other one?" he says, stumbling over his words.

"Yes. Once I'd found the Temple. What was your task then?" I have never looked at anyone this way before, with a rage that could kill. And I have never seen Kartik frightened like this.

He swallows hard. His eyes glance upward to the faceless men in the shadows.

"Careful now, brother," Fowlson whispers.

"It was to help you find the Temple. There was no other," Kartik says. But he does not look me in the eyes as he says it, and now I know. I know that he is lying. I know that his task is to kill me.

"Liar," I say. This forces him to look at me, and just as quickly, he looks away. "I'm ready."

"Very well," Miss McCleethy says.

I take hold of Miss McCleethy's strong hands and close my eyes. *It's so easy to faint. Women do it all the time. They close their eyes and fall to the floor.*

"Ohhh," I moan, and do just that.

I am not as graceful as my friend Ann. Instead, I crumple forward, so that my hand is inches from my boot. My fingers find the hilt of the blade hidden in Megh Sambara. If ever I needed protection against my enemies, it is now.

"What now?" Fowlson sighs.

"She is masquerading," Miss McCleethy says, kicking me. I do not move. "I tell you, it's a deceit."

"Get her up!" the great voice booms out from above.

Kartik hooks his arms under mine and lifts me up, carrying me to the door, which opens for us.

"Fetch the salts," Fowlson orders.

"She's bluffing," Miss McCleethy snaps. "Don't trust her for a moment."

I keep my eyes lightly closed, peeking through narrow slits to see where Kartik is taking me. We're in a dim hall. From somewhere far above I hear men laughing, muffled talking. Is it a way out?

My fingers hold fast to my totem. I push Kartik away and pull the blade, threatening everyone.

"You won't get away. You don't know which door leads out," Fowlson says.

He's right. I'm trapped. Fowlson and Jackson step closer. Miss McCleethy stands waiting, looking as if she could cheerfully eat me for supper.

"No more of this foolishness, Miss Doyle. I am not your enemy."

Which door leads out? Kartik. I look to him. For a moment, he wavers. Then, his eyes travel to the door on my left. He gives a tiny nod, and I know he has betrayed them and shown me the way.

"Wha' are you abou' over there, boy?" Jackson shouts.

It is enough of a distraction that I am able to push through the door with Kartik on my heels. He shoves the door closed.

"Gemma! The blade—hurry! Through the latch there!"

I stick the blade through the iron latch, blocking the door. I can hear them banging and shouting on the other side. It will not hold forever; I can only hope it will hold long enough for us to get away.

"This way," Kartik says. We've come out onto a dark London street. Snowflakes mix with the black swirl of gaslit fog, making it hard to see very far. But there are other people out. I recognize this area. We're not far from Pall Mall Square and the most exclusive men's clubs of London. Those were the men's voices I heard!

"I'll hold them off until you can get away," Kartik says, breathless.

"Wait! Kartik! You can't go back," I say. "You can't ever go back."

Kartik bounces on his heels, his legs torn between standing

here and running back, the way a child runs to his mother to say *Sorry, sorry for what I did, now please forgive me*. But the Rakshana are not forgiving. Kartik's only just realizing what his rash act means. By helping me, he has thrown away any chance of joining them as a member in full. He has turned his back on the only family he knows. He is without patronage, without a home. He is alone, like me.

Fowlson and Jackson rush out onto the sidewalk, looking wildly left and right. They spot us. Miss McCleethy follows. Kartik still stands as if he doesn't know which way to turn.

"Come on," I say, looping my arm boldly through his. "We're going for a walk."

We do our best to blend in with the people bustling about on the streets, the men leaving their clubs after dinner, cigars, and brandy; the couples on their way to the theater or to a party.

Behind us, I can hear Fowlson whistling a military tune, something I've heard English soldiers sing in India.

"I wouldn't have done it," he says.

"Just walk, please," I say.

"I would have let you get away."

Fowlson's whistling, dishonestly pure, cuts through the street noise and traffic to chill my very bones. I glance behind us. They are getting closer. I face forward to see a greater horror: Simon and his father are just leaving the Athenaeum club. They must not see me here. I drop Kartik's arm and turn back.

"What are you doing?" he says.

"It's Simon," I say. "I can't be found out."

"Well, we certainly can't go that way!"

I'm in a panic. Simon steps out from under the watchful eye of the Athena statue atop the club's grand entrance. He is headed our way. His carriage waits at the curb. Someone steps from a hansom, paying the driver. Pushing another couple out of the way, Kartik opens the door for me.

"Duchess of Kent," he says, smiling at the outraged man and woman. "She's needed at once at Saint James's Palace."

The man sputters and shouts, drawing the attention of people on the street, including Simon and his father. I duck out of sight.

The furious man demands that I leave his cab. "I must protest, madam! It was rightfully ours!"

Please, please let me have it. Fowlson's sighted us. He's stopped his whistling and quickened his step. He'll be to us in a matter of seconds.

"What seems to be the trouble?" It's Lord Denby's voice.

"This young woman has taken our cab," the man sniffs. "And this Indian boy claims she's the Duchess of Kent."

"I say, Father, isn't that Mr. Doyle's former coachman? Why, it is!"

Lord Denby squares his shoulders. "Here, now, boy! What is the meaning of this?"

"Should we call for a constable?" Simon asks.

"If you please, miss," the man says imperiously, offering his hand through the window as I struggle to stay out of sight. "You've had your fun. I'll thank you to leave our cab at once."

"Come now, miss," the driver calls. "Let's not 'ave all this trouble on such a raw nigh'."

This is the end. Either I shall be found out by Simon and his father and my reputation shattered forever, or Fowlson and Miss McCleethy shall lead me away to who knows what.

My hand's on the door handle when Kartik suddenly jumps about like a madman, singing a jaunty tune and kicking up his heels.

"Is he drunk or mad?" Lord Denby says.

Kartik leans into the cab. "You know where to find me."

He throws his hands into the air and brings one down hard, slapping the horse's hide. With a loud whinny, the horse lurches into the street, the driver shouting, "Whoa, 'old there, Tillie!" to no avail. The best he can do is aim the beast away from the clubs and into the flow of traffic leaving Pall Mall. When I steal a last glance behind me, I see that Kartik is still acting the mad fool. A constable's arriving, blowing his whistle. Fowlson and Jackson pull back. They shan't get to Kartik for now. Only Miss McCleethy is nowhere to be seen. She has disappeared like a ghost.

"Where to, miss?" the driver calls down at last.

Where can I go? Where can I hide?

"Baker Street," I shout, giving Miss Moore's address. "And hurry, please."

CHAPTER
FORTY-FIVE

We've reached Baker Street in time for me to realize that I have no handbag. I have no means to pay the fare.

"'Ere you are, miss," the driver says, helping me from the cab.

"Oh, dear," I say. "I seem to have forgotten my handbag. If you will give me your name and address, I'll see that you are paid handsomely. I promise."

"And the Queen's me mum," he says.

"I'm in earnest, sir."

A constable makes his way down the opposite side of the street, the brass buttons of his uniform glinting in the gloom. My blood quickens.

"Tell it to the constable, then," he says. "Oi! Bob! Ofer 'ere!"

I make a run for it, the constable's whistle blowing sharply behind me. Quickly, I slip into the shadows of an alley and wait. The snow has turned to sleet. The tiny, hard ice bites at my cheeks, makes my nose run. The houses shimmer in the new sheen of frost and gaslight. Every breath is a painful rasp, a fight for air against the cold. But it is more than that. The magic has begun to wear me down. I'm feeling odd, as if I've a fever.

The constable's steps are sharp and close.

"And then he said she was the Duchess of Kent," the cabbie explains.

I flatten myself against the wall. My heart's thumping hard against my ribs; my breath is locked up tight as a criminal in irons.

"You might do well not to pick up odd women, mate," the constable says.

" 'Ow was I to know she was odd?" the cabbie protests.

Arguing on, they pass within inches of me without so much as a glance in my direction till their footsteps and voices are no more than faint echoes that are finally swallowed by the night. The breath I've been holding back comes out of me in a whoosh. I waste no time. I'm hobbling down the street and to Miss Moore's flat as quickly as I can move in my weakened state. The house is dark. I rap loudly, hoping I can devise a ruse that will get me inside. Mrs. Porter sticks her head out the top window, calling down irritably.

"Whachoo wont, then?"

"Mrs. Porter, I'm terribly sorry to disturb you. I've an urgent message for Miss Moore."

"She's no' a' 'ome."

Yes, I know, and it's all my fault. I feel I shall faint. My face is numb from the cruel pelting of the sleet. At any moment, the constable could come back. *I've got to get inside. I just need a place to hide, to think, to rest.*

" 'Ere, now, it's late. Come back tomorrow."

Footsteps echo on the slick cobblestones. *Someone is coming.*

"Dear Mrs. Porter," I say desperately. "It's Felicity Worthington. Admiral Worthington's daughter."

"Admiral Worthington's daw'er, you say? Oh, me dear chil', 'ow is the admiral?"

"Quite well, thank you. I meant, no, he's not well at all. And that is why I've come for Miss Moore. It's quite urgent. May I wait for her?" *Please, let me in. Just long enough to get my bearings.*

Down the street, I can hear the steady clip-clopping of the constable's shoes returning.

"We-uwll . . . ," Mrs. Porter says. She's already in her nightclothes.

"I wouldn't ask except that I know you are a good and kind soul. I'm certain that my father will wish to thank you personally, once he is able."

Mrs. Porter preens at this. "I won't be a minute."

The constable's lantern spreads fingers of light in my direction. *Please, Mrs. Porter, do hurry.* She's at the latch, letting me in.

"Evenin', Mrs. Porter," the constable calls out, tipping his hat to her.

"Evenin', Mr. John," she answers.

She closes the door. I steady myself with a hand against the wall.

"'Ow nice to 'ave comp'ny. So unexpected. Le' me take yer coat."

I pull my coat tight at my aching throat. "Dear Mrs. Porter," I croak. "Forgive me, but I'm afraid I must get to my business with Miss Moore and then return to Papa's bedside."

Mrs. Porter looks as if she's bitten into a piece of chocolate cake only to discover it has a pickled filling. "Hmph. 'S not right for me to admit you to 'er room. I run a honest establishment, see."

"Yes, of course," I say.

Mrs. Porter ponders her dilemma for a moment before emptying a vase on a side table and shaking the key to Miss Moore's rooms from its hiding place. "This way, if you please."

I follow her up the narrow staircase and to Miss Moore's door. "Bu' if she ain't back by 'alf past, you'll 'ave to leave," she says, jangling the key in the lock. The door opens and I step inside.

"Yes, thank you. Please don't trouble yourself to wait, Mrs. Porter. I feel a draft here, and if you were to catch cold on my account, I should never forgive myself."

This seems to mollify Mrs. Porter for the moment, and she leaves me, descending the stairs with a heavy step.

I close the door behind me. In the dark, the room is unfamiliar, ominous. I slide my fingers along the yellowing wallpaper till I find the gaslamp. It hisses into life, the flame flickering against the glass shade. The room wakes from its slumber—the velvet settee, the globe on its stand, the writing desk in its usual state of shambles, the rows of well-loved books. The masks seem gruesome in the evening gloom. I can't bear to look at them. I take comfort in Miss Moore's paintings—the purple heather of Scotland, the craggy cliffs near the sea, the mossy caves in the woods behind Spence.

I perch on the settee to calm myself, trying to make sense of everything. So tired. I want to sleep, but I can't. Not yet. I must think of what to do next. If the Rakshana are in league with Miss McCleethy, with Circe herself, then they cannot be trusted. Kartik was supposed to kill me once I found the Temple. But Kartik betrayed them to help me escape. The clock ticks off the minutes. Five. Ten. Pulling aside the curtain, I peek out at the street but see no sign of Mr. Fowlson or the black carriage.

A knock at the door nearly scares me to death. Mrs. Porter comes in with a letter.

"Dearie, you can stop waitin'. Seems I overlooked this. Miss Moore lef' it on me side tabuwl this mornin'."

"This morning?" I repeat. That isn't possible. Miss Moore is lost to the realms. "Are you sure?"

"Oh, yes. I saw her leave. 'Aven't seen 'er since, though. But I only jus' read the let'r. It says she's gone to be with family."

"But Miss Moore has no family," I say.

"Well, she does." Mrs. Porter reads aloud. " 'Dear Missus Por'er. Forgive the late no'ice, but I mus' leave at once as I'f accep'ed a position a' a school near London where moi sister is 'eadmistress. Oi shall send fer me fings as soon as possibuwl. Sincerely, Hester Asa Moore.' Hmph. Runnin' ou' on the rent is more like. She owes me two weeks' worth, Oi'll 'ave you know."

"A school? Where her sister is headmistress?" I ask faintly. I've heard that phrase somewhere before, in Mrs. Morrissey's letter from St. Victoria's. But she was speaking of Miss McCleethy.

"So it would seem," Mrs. Porter says.

Something horrible is fighting to take shape inside me. The paintings. Scotland. Spence. And that seascape is so very familiar, similar to the one from my visions. It could be Wales, I realize with a growing horror. Every place on Miss McCleethy's list is represented on these walls.

But Miss McCleethy is the one who taught at all those schools. *She* was the teacher looking for the girl who could take her into the realms.

Unless Miss McCleethy and Kartik were telling the truth. Unless Miss Moore is not Miss Moore at all.

"No sense in waitin' for 'er now, Miss Worthington," Mrs. Porter says.

"Yes," I croak. "Perhaps I'll just leave a note to go with her things."

"Suit yourself," Mrs. Porter says, leaving. "You could ask 'er for the balance due me. Never got me rent."

Scrounging about, I find a pen and a sheet of stationery and take a deep breath. Not Miss Moore. It can't be. Miss

Moore is the one who has believed in me. Who first told us about the Order. Who listened as I told her . . . everything.

No. Miss Moore is not Circe. And I shall prove it.

I write the words, big and bold: *Hester Moore.*

They stare back at me. Ann has already done an anagram for Miss Moore. It yielded nothing but nonsense. I stare at the note. *Sincerely, Hester Asa Moore.* Asa. The middle name. I cross it out and start again. With trembling fingers, I shift the letters of her name to make something new. *S, A, R.* At last, I put the remaining letters into place. *H, R, E.* The room falls away as the name swims before me.

Sarah Rees-Toome.

Miss Moore is Sarah Rees-Toome. Circe. No. I won't believe it. Miss Moore helped us rescue Ann. She told us to run as she battled Circe's creature. *Her* creature. And I took her into the realms. I gave her the power.

Things come back to me—Miss Moore's keen interest in Miss McCleethy. How she told us to keep her away from Nell Hawkins. The way the girls in white looked at her in the realms, as if they knew her.

When you can see what I see—that is what Nell said.

"I need to see. I want to know the truth," I say.

The vision comes down on me as fiercely as a sudden Indian rain. My arms shake, and I fall to my knees with the force of it. *Breathe, Gemma. Don't fight it.* I can't control it, and panic rises in me as I fall hard and fast.

Everything stops. There is calm. I know this place. I've seen bits and pieces of it before. The roar of the sea fills my ears. Its spray kisses the jagged cliffs and coats my hair and lips with its misty salt. The ground is cracked and worn, the skin of the rock splintering into thousands of tiny fissures.

Up ahead I see the three girls. But they are not ghostly specters. They are alive, happy and smiling. The wind catches their skirts. They flutter behind them like mothers' handkerchiefs. The first girl trips and wobbles, her shrieks turning to laughter when she rights herself.

Her laugh bounces round my head like a slow echo. "Come along, Nell!"

Nell. I am living this moment as Nell. I am seeing what she saw.

"She's coming to give us the power! We shall enter the realms and become sisters of the Order!" the second girl in white yells. She's beaming with the promise of it. I am so slow. I cannot keep up.

The girls wave to someone behind me.

Here she is, the woman in the green cloak, striding across the broken land. They call to her. "Miss McCleethy! Miss McCleethy!"

"Yes, I'm coming," she answers. The woman pulls the hood back from her face. But it is not the Miss McCleethy I have known. It is Miss Moore. And now I understand Miss Moore's shocked expression when we first mentioned that name, her rush to discredit our new teacher. She understood that someone from the Order was hunting her. And I've had it all wrong from the start.

"Will you give us the power?" the girls call out.

"Yes," Miss Moore says, her voice faltering. "Walk out on the rocks a little farther."

The girls clamber over the rocks, shrieking with a happy recklessness when the wind blows hard against them, making them feel mortal for a moment. I try to reach them.

"Nell!" Miss Moore shouts. "Wait with me."

"But, Miss McCleethy," I hear myself say. "They're getting ahead."

"Let them go. Stay with me."

Confused, Nell stands watching her friends out on the rocks. Miss Moore raises her hand. There is no snake ring on her finger. There never was, I come to realize. I told Miss Moore about the ring I'd seen, and the girls in white made me see what she wanted me to see.

Miss Moore mumbles in a tongue I cannot hear. The iron gray sky comes alive, twisting and turning. The girls sense the change. Their faces show alarm. The creature rises from the sea. The girls scream in terror. They try to run, but the great phantom stretches out like a cloud. It races over them and descends, swallowing the girls whole as if they had never existed. The creature sighs and groans. It unfurls its great wing-arms, and I see the girls trapped inside, screaming.

Miss Moore's hand shakes. She shuts her eyes.

The creature turns its hideous head in our direction. "There is one more, I see," it hisses. The sound makes my blood go cold.

"No," Miss Moore says. "Not this one."

"She cannot bring you in. Why do you care if she is sacrificed?" it screeches in that doomed voice.

"Not this one," Miss Moore repeats. "Please."

"We decide who shall be spared, not you. It is your misfortune if you come to care for them." The thing expands to fill the sky. The skeletal face is large as the moon. The mouth opens to reveal jagged teeth.

"Run!" Miss Moore screams. "Run, Nell! Keep running! Block it from your mind!"

I do. In Nell's body, I'm running as fast as I can, slipping over rocks. My heel catches in a crevice, and my ankle gives way with a sharp twist. Wincing in pain, I hobble on, down the cliffs, the thing hunting me.

The creature shrieks in rage.

The fear is overwhelming. I shall die from fright. Have to keep it from my mind. "Jack and Jill went up the hill to fetch a pail of water. Jack fell down and broke his crown and Jill came tumbling after."

I'm out on the slippery rocks. The sea grabs at my ankles, soaking me through. It's coming. Oh, God, it's coming for me. "Jack and Jill, Jack and Jill, Jack and Jill . . ."

It's so close. I let go, falling into the restless sea. I'm sinking. Lungs ache for breath. Bubbles race for the surface. I'm fighting the current. I shall drown! I open my eyes. There they are: the three of them. Such pale faces! The dark hollows beneath their eyes. My scream is buried underwater. And when I'm pulled from the depths by a pair of fisherman's hands, I'm still screaming.

The pressure's back. The vision's ending, and I find myself once again in the yellow light of Miss Moore's flat.

I know the truth. I try to stand and my legs give way. With effort, I stand. When I leave, I don't even bother to shut the door. The stairs shift before me. I go to put my foot on one and fall.

"You awl righ'?" Mrs. Porter asks. I cannot answer. Must get outside. Air. I need air.

Mrs. Porter comes after me. " 'D'you ask 'er 'bout me rent?"

I stumble out into the night air. I'm shaking all over, but it isn't from the cold. It's the magic taking hold of my body, wearing me down.

"Miss Moore!" I scream into the darkness. My voice isn't much more than a raw cry. "Miss Moore!"

They're at the bend in the street, waiting for me, those awful girls in white. Their shadows grow taller, long dark fingers creeping across the wet cobblestones, closing the distance between us. The familiar voice skulks out.

"Our mistress is in. We have the seer. She shall show us the Temple."

"No . . . ," I say.

"It's almost ours. You've lost."

I try to swipe at them, but my arms barely move. I fall to the wet street. Their shadows reach across my hands, bathing me in gloom.

"Time to die . . ."

The constable's shrill whistle rings in my ears. The shade recedes.

"Easy there, miss. We'll get you home."

The constable carries me down the street. I hear the percussive clicking of his shoes on cobblestones. Hear the whistle blowing, the voices. I hear myself mumbling over and over like a mantra, *"Forgive me, forgive me, forgive me . . ."*

CHAPTER
FORTY-SIX

SOMEONE DRAWS THE CURTAINS. THE ROOM GROWS
dusty dark. I cannot speak. Tom and Grandmama are at my
bedside. I hear another voice. A doctor.

"Fever . . . ," he says.

It's not a fever. It's the magic. I try to tell them that, to say
something, but I cannot.

"You must rest," Tom says, holding my hand.

In the corner of the room, I see the three girls waiting, those
silent, smiling apparitions. The dark hollows under their eyes
remind me of the skeletal face of that thing on the cliffs.

"No," I say, but it comes out as no more than a whisper.

"Shhh, sleep," Grandmama says.

"Yes, sleep," the girls in white whisper sweetly. "Sleep on."

"Something to help with that . . ." The doctor's voice is tinny.
He brings out a brown bottle. Tom hesitates. Yes, good Tom.
But the doctor insists, and Tom puts the bottle to my lips. No!
I mustn't drink. Mustn't go under. But I've no fight left. I roll
my head, but Tom's hand is strong.

"Please, Gemma."

The girls sit, hands in their laps. "Yes. So sweet. Drink and sleep. Our mistress is in now. So go to sleep."

"Sleep now," Tom's voice advises from far away.

"We'll see you in your dreams," the girls say as I fall under the drug's spell.

I see the Caves of Sighs, but not as they were. This place is no ruin, but a magnificent temple. I'm walking through the narrow tunnels. As I brush my fingers over the bumpy walls, the faded drawings come alive in reds and blues, greens and pinks and oranges. Here are paintings of all the realms. The Forest of Lights. The water nymphs in their murky depths. The gorgon ship. The garden. The Runes of the Oracle as they once stood. The golden horizon across the river, where our spirits must journey. The women of the Order in their cloaks, hands joined.

"I've found it," I murmur, tongue thick with opiate.

"Shhh," someone says. "Sleep now."

Sleep now. Sleep now.

The words drift down a tunnel into my body, where they become rose petals blowing across my bare feet on the dusty ground. I prick my finger on a thorn stuck through a crack in the wall. Drops of blood spiral down into the dust at my feet. Fat green vines push through the cracks. They crisscross rapidly around the pillars in designs as intricate as the Hajin's mendhi. Deep pink roses bud, bloom, and open, wrapping themselves around the pillars like lovers' fingers intertwined. It is so beautiful, so beautiful.

Someone comes. Asha, the Untouchable. For who better to

guard the Temple than those no one suspects of having any power at all?

She greets me, pressing her palms together and touching them to her forehead as she bows. I do the same. "What do you offer?"

Offer hope to the Untouchables, for they need hope. Lady Hope. I am the hope. I am the hope.

The sky cracks open. Asha's face is filled with worry.

"What is it?"

"She senses you. If you stay, she will find the Temple. You must leave this dream. Break the vision, Most High. Do it now!"

"Yes, I'll go," I say. I try to get myself from the vision, but the drug is taking hold. I cannot make myself leave.

"Go! Run into the realms," she says. "Cloud your mind to the Temple. She will see what you see."

I'm heavy with the drug. So heavy. I cannot make my thoughts obey. I stumble out of the cave. Behind me the paintings lose their color, the roses pull back into buds, and the vines slip back into the cracks. When I come out of the cave, the sky has grown dark. The incense pots send their colorful plumes up to the clouds like a warning. The smoke parts. Miss Moore stands before me with poor Nell Hawkins, her sacrifice.

"The Temple. Thank you, Gemma."

✦✧✦✧✦

I open my eyes. The ceiling, sooty from the gaslight, comes into view. The curtains are drawn. I do not know what time of day it is. I hear whispering.

"Gemma?"

"She opened her eyes. I saw her."

Felicity and Ann. They rush over and sit on the bed beside me, taking my hands in theirs.

"Gemma? It's Ann. How are you feeling? We were so worried about you."

"They said you had a fever, so naturally they wouldn't allow us to come until I insisted. You've been asleep for three days," Felicity says.

Three days. Still so tired.

"They found you in Baker Street. What were you doing there, near Miss Moore's rooms?"

Miss Moore. Miss Moore is Circe. She has found the Temple. I have failed. I have lost everything. I turn my head to the wall.

Ann prattles on. "With all the excitement, Lady Denby hasn't had a chance yet to tell Mrs. Worthington about me."

"Simon has been here every day, Gemma," Felicity says. "Every day! That must make you happy."

"Gemma?" Ann says, concerned.

"I don't care." My voice is so small and dry.

"What do you mean you don't care? I thought you were mad for him. He's mad for you, it seems. That is happy news, isn't it?" Felicity says.

"I've lost the Temple."

"What do you mean?" Ann asks.

It is too much to explain. My head throbs. I want to sleep and never wake. "We were wrong about Miss McCleethy. About everything. Miss Moore is Circe."

I won't look at them. I can't.

"I took her into the realms. She has the power now. It is over. I'm sorry."

"No more magic?" Ann says.

I shake my head. It hurts to do it.

"But what about Pippa?" Felicity says, starting to cry.

I close my eyes. "I'm tired," I say.

"It can't be," Ann says, sniffling. "No more realms?"

I don't answer. Instead, I feign sleep until I hear the bed creak with their leaving. I lie there, staring at nothing. A crack of light peeks through the drawn curtains. It is day after all. Not that it matters to me one whit.

⌁⌁⌁⌁

In the evening, Tom carries me into the parlor to sit by the fire.

"You've a surprise visitor," he says.

With me in his arms, he pushes open the parlor doors. Simon has come without his mother. Tom puts me on the settee and covers me with a blanket. I probably look a fright, but I can't seem to care.

"I'll have Mrs. Jones bring tea," Tom says, backing out of the room. Though he leaves the doors open, Simon and I are on our own.

"How are you feeling?" he asks. I say nothing. "You gave us all quite a scare. How did you end up in such a dreadful place?"

This Christmas tree has dried out. It's losing its needles in clumps.

"We thought perhaps someone wished a ransom. Perhaps

· 510 ·

that fellow who followed you at Victoria wasn't a figment of your imagination after all."

Simon. He looks so worried. I should say something to comfort him. I clear my throat. Nothing comes. His hair is exactly the color of a dull coin.

"I've something for you," he says, coming closer. He pulls a brooch from his coat pocket. It is decorated with many pearls and looks quite old and valuable.

"This belonged to the first Viscountess of Denby," Simon says, holding the feather-light pearl brooch between his fingers. He clears his throat twice. "It's over one hundred years old and has been worn by the women in my family. It would go to my sister, if I had a sister. Which I don't, but you know that." He clears his throat again.

He pins it to the lace of my bed jacket. I understand vaguely that I am wearing his promise. I understand that things have changed greatly with this one small gesture.

"Miss Doyle. Gemma. May I be so bold?" He gives me a chaste kiss, very different from the one the night of the ball.

Tom returns with Mrs. Jones and tea. The men sit speaking jovially, while I continue to stare at the pine needles drifting to the floor, sinking into the settee, the weight of the brooch holding me down.

⌁⌁⌁⌁⌁

"I thought we might pay a visit to Bethlem today," Tom announces at lunch.

"Why?" I say.

"You've been in your bedclothes for days. It would do you good to get out. And I thought perhaps it might change Miss Hawkins's status if you were to visit."

Nothing will change her status. A part of her is trapped in the realms forever.

"Please?" Tom asks.

〜〜〜〜

In the end, I relent and go with Tom. We've another new driver, Jackson having disappeared. I cannot say that I am surprised by this.

"Grandmama says that Ann Bradshaw is not any relation to the Duke of Chesterfield," Tom says, once we are en route. "She also says that Miss Bradshaw fainted when told of these accusations." When I neither confirm nor deny this, he continues. "I don't see how it could be true. Miss Bradshaw is such a kind person. She's not the sort who would mislead someone. The very fact that she fainted proves that her character is too good to even entertain such an idea."

"People aren't always what you want them to be," I mumble.

"Beg your pardon?" Tom says.

"Nothing," I say.

Come awake, Tom. Fathers can willfully hurt their children. They can be addicts too weak to give up their vices, no matter the pain it causes. Mothers can turn you invisible with neglect. They can erase you with a denial, a refusal to see. Friends can deceive you. People lie. It is a cold, hard world. I do not blame Nell Hawkins for retreating from it into a madness of her own choosing.

The halls of Bethlem seem almost calming to me now. Mrs. Sommers sits at the piano, plunking out a tune filled with wrong notes. A sewing circle has been set up in a corner. The women work their pieces intently, as if they are sewing their salvation with each careful stitch.

I'm taken to Nell's room. She's stretched out upon her bed, her eyes open but not seeing.

"Hello, Nell," I say. The room is quiet. "Perhaps if you left us," I say to Tom.

"What? Oh, right." Tom leaves.

I take Nell's hands in mine. They are so very small and cold.

"I am sorry, Nell," I say, the apology coming out like a sob. "I am sorry."

Nell's hands suddenly grip mine. She is fighting against something with every bit of strength she has left. We are joined, and in my head, I can hear her speaking.

"She . . . cannot . . . bind it," comes her whisper. "There . . . is still . . . hope."

Her muscles relax. Her hands slip from mine.

"Gemma?" Tom asks as I bolt from Nell's room and head straight for the carriage. "Gemma! Gemma, where are you going?"

⋏⋏⋏⋏⋏

It is fifteen past five o'clock when I secure a cab. With luck, I shall make it to Victoria Station before Felicity and Ann can board the five forty-five train to Spence. But luck is not on my side. The streets are congested with people and vehicles of all sorts. It is the wrong time of day for hurrying.

Big Ben chimes the half hour. I poke my head out the side of the cab. Stretched ahead of us is a sea of horses, wagons, cabs, carriages, and omnibuses. We're perhaps a quarter mile from the station and hopelessly stuck.

I call out to the driver. "If you please, I should like to get out here."

Darting between snorting horses, I step quickly across the street to the sidewalk. The walk to Victoria is short, but I find I am weak from my days in bed. By the time I reach the station, I have to lean against the wall to keep from fainting.

Forty minutes past five o'clock. There is no time to rest. The platform is awash in people. I shall never find them in this chaos. I spy an empty newspaper crate and stand upon it, searching the crowd, not caring about the scowls I receive from passersby who find my outrageous behavior insulting to ladies everywhere. At last I spy them. They're standing on the platform with Franny. The Worthingtons haven't even bothered to come see their daughter off with a kiss and a tear or two.

"Ann! Felicity!" I shout. More black marks against my character. I hobble over to them.

"Gemma, what are you doing here? I thought you weren't to leave for Spence for days," Felicity says. She's wearing a smart traveling suit in a flattering mauve.

"The magic isn't hers," I explain breathlessly. "She hasn't been able to bind it."

"How do you know?" Felicity asks.

"Nell told me. She must not have enough power on her own. She needs me to do it."

"What should we do?" Ann asks.

A whistle blows. The train to Spence sits on the track in a haze of smoke. It is ready. The conductor stands on the platform calling passengers to board.

"We're going in after them," I say.

I see Jackson and Fowlson have arrived. They see us too. They're coming straight toward us.

"We've company," I say.

Felicity spies the men. "Them?"

"Rakshana," I say. "They'll try to stop us, control it all."

"Then let's give them the slip," Felicity says, boarding the train.

CHAPTER
FORTY-SEVEN

"THEY'RE BOARDING THE TRAIN TOO!" ANN
says, panicked.

"Then we shall have to get off," I say. We're almost to the
doors when the train lurches into motion. The platform disappears behind us, the well-wishers waving through first one
window, then the next and the next, until they cannot be seen
at all.

"What do we do now?" Felicity says. "They'll surely discover us."

"Find a compartment," I say.

We search left and right until we find an unoccupied cabin
and pull the door shut. "We shall have to work quickly," I say.
"Take my hands."

What if I can't summon the door? What if I am too weak or
the magic has been compromised in some way? *Please, please let
us in once more.*

"Nothing's happening," Felicity says.

Down the corridor, I hear the opening of a door, Fowlson's voice saying, "Terribly sorry, not my cabin after all."

"I'm too weak. I need your help," I say. "We must try again. Try harder than you've ever tried at anything in your life."

We close our eyes again. I concentrate on breathing. I can feel the soft, fleshy warmth of Ann's hand beneath her glove. I can hear the brave thumping of Felicity's wounded heart, sense the heavy stain upon her soul. I can smell the earthy nearness of Fowlson in the corridor. I can sense a deep well of strength opening inside me. Every part of me is coming alive.

The door appears.

"Now," I say, and we step through into the realms once again.

The garden is wild. There are more toadstools. They've grown to nearly six feet or more. Deep black holes have been eaten away in their fat, doughy stems. An emerald green snake slithers from one of the holes, dropping into the grass.

"Oh!" Ann screams as it narrowly misses her foot.

"What has happened here?" Felicity marvels at the change.

"The sooner we get to the Temple, the better."

"But where is it?" Ann asks.

"If I'm right, it has been under our noses the entire time," I say.

"What do you mean?" Felicity asks.

"Not here," I say, looking around. "It's not safe."

"We should find Pip," Felicity says.

"No," I say, stopping her. "No one is to be trusted. We go alone."

I'm braced for an argument, but Felicity gives me none. "Fine. But I shall bring my arrows," she says, searching for the hiding place.

"You mean arrow," Ann corrects. Felicity has used all but one.

"It shall have to do," she says, pulling it from the quiver. She slings the bow over her shoulder. "I'm ready."

We follow the path through the jungle growth till we reach the base of the mountain. "Why are we going this way?" Felicity asks.

"We're going to the Temple."

"But this is the way to the Caves of Sighs," Felicity says, voice filled with disbelief. "Surely you're not suggesting . . ."

Ann is astonished. "But it is just caves and some old ruins. How can that be the Temple?"

"Because we haven't seen it the way it really is. If you wanted to hide your most valuable possession, would you not hide it in a place where no one would think to look? And why not have it guarded by those everyone assumes have no power?"

"*Offer hope to the Untouchables, for they must have hope,*" Ann says, repeating Nell's words.

"Exactly," I say. I point to Felicity and then to Ann. "Strength. Song. I am Hope. Lady Hope. That's what she kept calling me."

Felicity shakes her head. "I still don't understand."

"You will," I say.

We make our way up to the narrow, dusty road that leads to

the top of the mountain, where the Caves of Sighs wait. I have to stop along the way to rest.

Felicity steadies me against her shoulder. "Are you all right?"

"Yes. Still weak, I'm afraid."

I look up, shading my eyes with my hand. It seems so far to the top.

"Gemma! Felicity!" Ann shouts. "Over there!" She points down to the river. The gorgon barge is making speed toward us. Pippa's climbed up into the crow's nest. The wind whips her black hair behind her like a silken cape.

"Pippa!" Felicity calls, waving.

"What are you doing?" I say, pulling her arm down.

Too late. Pippa's spotted us. She waves back as the gorgon glides to the riverbank.

"If we are going to bind the magic, Pip should be here," Felicity says. "And perhaps there is a way . . ." She trails off.

Strength. Song. Hope. And Beauty. *Be careful of Beauty; Beauty must pass. . . .*

"You know that I cannot promise that, Fee. I cannot say what will happen."

She nods, tears welling in her eyes.

"Ahoy!" Pippa yells, making Felicity smile bitterly.

"The least you can do is to let us say a proper goodbye, then. Not like last time," she says softly.

I watch Pippa tripping merrily through the brush to the sandy passage up. She seems so alive.

"She's coming," Ann says, looking to me for a response.

"We'll wait for her," I say at last.

It doesn't take long for Pip to reach us. "Where are you going?" she asks. Her daisy crown is gone. There are only a few dried flowers in her tangled hair.

"We've found the Temple," Felicity says.

Pippa is astonished. "This place? You can't be serious."

"Gemma says it's an illusion, that we don't see it as it truly is," Ann explains.

"This is the place where the magic is born?" Pippa asks.

"And where it can be contained," I say.

A cloud passes across Pippa's face.

I get to my feet. "We've waited too long. We must go on."

The incense pots fume in reds and blues as we enter the long hall of faded frescoes. The wind blows dried rose petals into a spiral that rises and falls. For a moment, I am besieged with doubt. How could this wreck of a place possibly be the source of all magic in the realms? Perhaps my vision was wrong, and I am looking in the wrong place once again. Asha steps forward like a mirage. She places her hands together and bows. I return the gesture. She smiles.

"What do you offer us?" she asks.

"I offer myself," I say. "I offer Hope."

Asha smiles. It is a most beautiful smile. "I am your servant."

"And I am yours," I answer.

"Are you ready to bind the magic?"

"I think so," I say, suddenly afraid. "But how?"

"When you are ready, you must step through the waterfall to where the well of eternity waits."

"What happens then?"

"I cannot say. There you will face your fear and perhaps come through the other side."

" 'Perhaps' come through?" I say. "It isn't certain?"

"Nothing is ever certain, Lady Hope," she says.

Perhaps. It is such a thin shield of a word.

"And if I do come through?"

"You must choose the words for the binding. Your words direct the course it will take. Choose them well."

"I should like to begin," I say.

Asha leads me to the strange waterfall that seems to fall and rise at the same time. "When you are ready, step through without fear."

I close my eyes. Take one breath and another. I can feel the Temple coming alive around me. The roses pushing through the cracks in the walls. The air, fragrant with their smell. The frescoes blooming with color. The soft sighs become distinct voices, many languages, but I can hear them all. The thrumming of my heart joins this chorus.

I am ready.

I step through the sheet of water to embrace my destiny. The well of eternity is a perfect circle of water so smooth there is nary a ripple. Its surface shows me everything at once. It shows me the realms, the world, the past, present, and perchance the future, though I cannot be certain. Does my destiny lie in those waters? Or is it only possibility? I stare into them, thinking of the form I wish the binding to take, the words I shall need.

I'm distracted by a sound. There is movement in the shadows of the cave.

There you will face your fear and perhaps come through the other side.

Something is coming. Miss Moore steps into the light, the captive Nell beside her.

"Hello, Gemma. I've been waiting for you."

CHAPTER
FORTY-EIGHT

I LOOK BACK AT THE SHEET OF WATER THROUGH which I've entered. Clear as a picture, I can see the worried faces of Felicity, Pippa, and Ann. Only Asha betrays no emotion. I want to run back through the waterfall to safety. But safety is another illusion. I can only move forward.

"You can't actually touch the magic, can you? That's why you needed Nell. Why you need me. You can only control the magic through someone else."

"You are the Most High. It wants your words after all," she says. "Gemma, together, you and I can restore the power and the glory of the Order. We can do good things—glorious things. You have more magic in you than anyone in the history of the Order. There is no limit to what you and I could do." She offers her hand. I do not take it.

"You don't care about me," I say. "Your only desire is to control the magic and the realms."

"Gemma—"

"You have nothing to say to me that I want to hear."

"Will you please just listen to me?" she pleads. "Do you know what it is to have your power taken from you? To forever surrender to someone else? I held power in my hands, I controlled my own destiny, and they took that away from me."

"The realms didn't choose you," I say, keeping the well between us.

"No. That is a lie they tell. The realms gifted me. The Order denied me. They chose your mother over me. She was the more compliant. She was willing to do as they asked."

"Leave my mother out of this."

"Is that what you want, Gemma? To be a faithful servant to them? Would you fight their battles, secure the Temple, bind the magic, and then hand it all over to them to administer as they like? What if they choose to leave you out? What if all this is taken from you now? Have they promised you anything?"

They haven't. I've not questioned anything. I've done as they've asked.

"You know I'm speaking the truth. Why have they offered no aid? Why did they not bind the magic themselves? Because they couldn't do it without you. But once you bind the magic and there is no more danger, they will ask you to bring them in. They will take over. And you will be of no value to them unless you do exactly as they say. They won't care for you as I do."

"As you cared for Nell. As you cared for my mother." I practically spit the words.

"She promised to help me. She sent me a letter from Bombay and said she'd had a change of heart. Then she betrayed me to the Rakshana."

"So you killed her."

"No. Not me. The creature."

"It is the same thing."

"No, it isn't. You know very little about the dark spirits, Gemma. They will eat you alive. You need my help." She gives a last appeal. "Without the magic, I cannot rid myself of my bond to these creatures, Gemma. You can save me from this wretched existence. I've spent years searching for the one, for you. Everything I've done, I've done for this moment, for this chance. We can form a new Order, Gemma. Just say the words. . . ."

"I saw what you did to those girls."

"It's horrible. I won't deny it. I have made many sacrifices for this," Miss Moore says. "What sacrifices will you be willing to make?"

"I will not do what you have done."

"You say that now. Every leader has blood on her hands."

"I trusted you!"

"I know. And I'm sorry. People will disappoint you, Gemma. The question to ask is whether you can learn to live with the disappointment and move on. I'm offering you a new world."

I cannot live with it.

"They were right to deny you. Eugenia Spence was right."

Her eyes flash. "Eugenia! You do not know what she has become, Gemma. She has been with the dark spirits all this time. How will you fight her if you must? You will need me in the time to come. I promise you that."

"You're trying to confuse me," I say.

"You cannot cross!" It's Asha's voice.

Pippa has rushed through the wall of water.

"Pip!" Felicity runs after her. Ann wavers for a moment but follows.

"What is happening?" Pippa asks.

Felicity raises her bow. "I've one arrow left."

"If you shoot me, I take with me all the secrets I know about the dark spirits and the Winterlands. You'll never know."

"Do you know how to use the magic to keep a spirit here and free?" Pippa asks uncertainly.

"Yes," Miss Moore says. "I can find a way to give you what you want. You will not have to cross over. You can stay here in the realms forever."

"She's lying, Pippa," I say.

But I see the aching desire in Pippa's eyes already. So does Miss Moore.

"I wouldn't have to leave you, Fee," Pippa says. Of Miss Moore she asks, "Will it hurt terribly much?"

"No. Not at all."

"And will I remain as I am?"

"Yes."

"Don't believe her, Pip."

"What have you promised me, Gemma? I helped you and what have you done for me?"

She steps around the well and takes Miss Moore's hand. "So we can be together, Fee. Just like before."

Felicity's hand wavers on the bow. The string loosens.

"Felicity, you know it can't be," I whisper.

"Shoot her," Ann whispers. "Shoot Circe."

Felicity takes aim, but Pippa moves in front of Miss Moore, protecting her like a shield. I do not know what would happen to Pippa, a spirit, if she were to be killed inside the realms.

Felicity stands, muscles straining from the weight of the taut bow and the ruthless task. At last she lowers the bow. "I can't. I can't."

Pippa's smile is heartbreaking in its love. "Thank you, Fee," she says, running to embrace her.

I grab the bow and hold it fast. I'm not the shot Felicity is, and there is only one arrow.

Miss Moore holds Nell in her arms. "I could offer Nell right now as a sacrifice. Join me, and I shall let her go peacefully."

"You've given me an impossible choice," I say.

"But it's a choice, nonetheless, which is more than you've given me."

Nell leans against Miss Moore like a lifeless doll. Whatever spark flashed in her eyes once is gone, buried beneath layers of pain. I can spare Nell, join with Miss Moore and share the Temple with her. Or I can watch her offer Nell to the creature and use that power to do as she pleases.

Nell turns her anguished eyes to me. *Don't hesitate. . . .*

I let go. Fleet and straight the arrow flies, piercing Nell Hawkins through the throat. With a small gasp, she slumps to the ground. As a sacrifice, she is useless now.

Miss Moore looks up with a mix of fury and shock in her eyes. "What have you done?"

"Now I have bloodied my hands," I say.

Miss Moore races for me. There is no time to follow the rules. I shall have to make new ones. Closing my eyes, I race forward toward the well. But Miss Moore is fast. She grabs hold of my hand. I'm caught off balance, and we fall together, arms locked in battle, into those great, eternal waters.

I can feel Miss Moore's breathing, hear the mad thumping of her heart as it discharges blood, that necessary messenger. Smell the faint scent of London chimney soot and lilac powder and something else. Beneath the skin, there is fear. Pain. Remorse. Yearning. Desire. A fierce longing for power. All of this. We are joined. It is as if we live in the center of a great storm. Around us the world of the realms revolves like a giant kaleidoscope, images refracted again and again. So many worlds! So much to know.

Yes, Miss Moore seems to say inside my head. *So much you do not know.*

I'm being stretched by it all. I can feel every bit of me spreading out till I am part of everything I see. I'm the leaf as it turns into a butterfly, and I'm the river polishing the stones on the bank. I'm the charwoman's hungry belly, the banker's vague disappointment with his children, the girl's yearning for excitement. I want to laugh and cry at the same time. It is so much, so much.

A frozen wasteland comes into view. We're soaring over craggy mountains under a savage sky. Below, an army of spirits, a thousand strong, howls at the emptiness. I can feel them inside me. The fear. The rage. I am the fire. I am the monster who destroys. I have no wish to stop the cruel fight. It is the fight that keeps me alive.

I feel Miss Moore's arms tighten around mine. She will not be denied a second time. I'm aware of nothing but our struggle now. Only one of us can emerge from the well. As if she can read my thoughts, Miss Moore pushes hard against me. She wants to win, wants it with all her heart.

I also want to win.

You must reflect on the course you wish to take, the form of the binding. I must think of a way to contain the magic, but it is difficult in the midst of this desperate fight. All I can see is Miss Moore, my teacher, my friend, my enemy. And suddenly, I know what I must do, how I must bring this to an end.

With one great push, I kick away from Miss Moore, sending her flying backward. Her eyes grow large. She knows what is in my mind, what I aim to do. She lunges for me, but this time, I am made quick by my determination. I climb up and over the top of the well, emerging slick and shiny as a newborn babe. I hold my hands over the surface of the water and say the words I hope shall restore the balance.

"I place a seal upon the power. Let the balance of the realms be restored and let no one disturb their majesty. I bind the magic in the name of all who shall share the power one day. For I am the Temple; the magic lives in me."

There is a sudden burst of brilliant white light. I feel as if I'm being split wide open by the force of it. This is the magic. The binding is using me as its pathway. It rushes through me like water. And then it is done. I'm on my knees, gasping.

But the cave is drenched in color. The frescoes are vibrant once more. The roses bloom, and the great statues seem alive.

"What happened to Miss Moore?" Ann asks.

"I have done as she asked—I have saved her from her wretched existence and bound her in a place where she can do no more harm."

"So it's done, then?" It's Pippa's voice.

Ann gives a small gasp as Pippa steps from behind a rock. With the magic no longer wild, the glamour has begun to fade. Atop her curls, the flower crown is now freshly in bloom, but Pippa is not the Pippa we have known and loved. The creature before us is changing. The teeth a bit jagged, the skin thinner, showing the faint blue of her veins. And her eyes . . .

They've gone a muddled white with pinpricks of black.

"Why are you looking at me that way?" she asks, fearful.

None of us can answer.

"It's done, but I'm still here," she says. She smiles, but the effect is chilling.

"It's time to leave us, Pip," I say softly. "To let go."

"No!" she wails like a wounded animal, and I feel as if my heart shall break. "Please, I don't want to go. Not yet. Please, don't leave me! Please! Fee!"

Felicity's crying. "I'm sorry, Pip."

"You promised you'd never leave me. You promised!" She wipes her tears with her arm. "You'll be sorry for this."

"Pippa!" Felicity calls, but it's too late. She's left us, running for the only place that will shelter her. Someday, we will meet again, not as friends, but as enemies.

"I couldn't use the magic to keep her here. You understand, don't you?"

Felicity won't look at me. "I'm tired of this place. I want to go home." She marches off down the mountain till she's lost in the colorful smoke of the incense pots.

Ann slips her hand into mine. It is her way of saying that she forgives me, and I'm grateful for it. I can only hope that Felicity will also forgive me in time.

"Look, Lady Hope!" Asha calls.

Across the river, I see them—thousands crossing over to the world beyond this one, ready at last to make that journey. They stream past us, oblivious. They want only their rest. I hope against hope that I shall see Bessie Timmons and Mae Sutter among their number. But I do not. They've reached the Winterlands, then, as Pippa will soon. But that is another fight for another day.

"Lady Hope!"

I turn and see Nell Hawkins waving dreamily to me from the shore. She is as I remember her from my visions, a tiny, happy thing. I feel a stab of remorse. My hands will forever be stained by the blood of Nell Hawkins. Have I done the right thing? Will there be others to follow?

"I'm sorry," I say.

"You cannot keep things caged," she answers. "Goodbye, Lady Hope." With that, she wades into the river, goes under, and emerges on the other side, walking toward the orange sky until I do not see her at all.

⌁⌁⌁⌁⌁

The gorgon waits for us in the river.

"Shall I take you to the garden, Most High?" she asks.

"Gorgon, I release you from your bondage to the Order," I say. "You are free, as I suspect you have been since the magic was first loose."

The snakes dance upon her head. "Thank you," the gorgon replies. "Shall I take you to the garden?"

"Did you hear? You are free."

"Yesssss. Choice. It is a fine thing. And I choose to take you back, Most High."

We float downstream on the gorgon's back. Already, the air feels lighter. Things are changing. I cannot say how or what form they shall take eventually, but the change is the thing. It is what makes me feel that all things are possible.

The forest folk have gathered on the shore below the Caves of Sighs. They line the riverbank as we pass. Philon hops up on a rock, shouting at me. "We shall expect our payment, priestess. Do not forget."

I clasp my hands together and bow as I have seen Asha do. Philon returns the gesture. We are at peace, for now.

I cannot say how long the peace shall last.

"You tried to warn me about Miss Moore, didn't you?" I ask the gorgon once we are on the open river. Above us, white clouds spread out in grainy streaks, like sugar spilled across the floor of the sky.

"I knew her once by another name."

"You must know a great deal," I say.

The gorgon's hiss comes out as a sigh. "Someday, when there is time, I shall tell you stories of the days past."

"Do you miss them?" I ask.

"They are but days my people lived," she says. "I am looking forward to the days to come."

⌁⌁⌁⌁⌁

Father's room is dark as a tomb when I finally return home. He sleeps fitfully on sweat-drenched sheets. It is the first time I will use the magic since binding it. I pray I shall make better use of it. The first time I tried to heal him, but I've come to think it doesn't work that way. I cannot use the magic to control another. I cannot make him whole. I can only guide him.

I place my hand over his heart. "Find your courage, Father. Find your will to fight. It is there still. I promise you."

His breathing grows less labored. His brow smooths. I think I even see a hint of a smile. Perhaps it is only the light. Perhaps it is the power of the realms at work through me. Or perhaps it is some combination of spirit and desire, love and hope, some alchemy that we each possess and can put to use, if we first know where to look without flinching.

CHAPTER
FORTY-NINE

IT IS MY FINAL DAY IN LONDON BEFORE RETURNING to Spence. Grandmama has agreed to send Father to a sanitarium for a rest. Tomorrow, she will leave for the country and a rest of her own. The house is a flurry of servants covering furniture with sheets. Trunks are packed. Wages are settled. London is emptying its fashionable houses until April and the season.

Tonight we are to dine one last time with Simon and his family. But first, I've two calls to make.

He is surprised to see me. When I sweep into his room through the little door behind the drape he once showed me and pull the hood from my face with bold fingers, he stands softly at attention, like a child awaiting either the strap or a kiss of forgiveness. What I've brought is not quite either. It is my own compromise.

"You remembered," he says.

"I remembered."

"Gemma—Miss Doyle, I—"

Three gloved fingers is all it takes to silence him.

"I shall be brief. There is work to be done. I could do with your help, if you are willing to offer it freely and without obligation to another. You cannot serve both our friendship and the Rakshana."

His smile catches me unawares. It flutters about the soft boughs of his lips, a broken bird unsure where to settle. And then the dark eyes fill with tears that he blinks away with a desperate concentration.

"It . . ." He clears his throat. "It seems a necessary point that I am no longer wanted by the Rakshana. Therefore, it may do your cause no favor, being championed by one so disgraced."

"It shall have to do, I suppose. We are rather a ragtag crew."

His eyes clear. His voice strengthens. He nods to no one in particular.

"It seems you've changed your destiny after all," I say.

"Unless it was my fate to do so," he responds, smiling.

"Well, then," I say, pulling my hood forward again. I am nearly to the door unscathed, but he cannot keep from saying one last thing.

"And allegiance to the Order . . . is that the only fealty you require of me?"

Why does this one question have the power to push the breath from me?

"Yes," I whisper, without turning around. "That is all."

In a rustle of velvet and silk, I am through the door, trailing the scent of juniper, the silence, and a shadow of a whisper: *For now . . .*

Miss McCleethy's rooms are in Lambeth, not far from Bethlem Royal.

"May I come in?" I ask.

She lets me in with a pretense of friendliness. "Miss Doyle. To what do I owe this surprise visit?"

"I've two questions for you. One concerns Mrs. Nightwing; the other, the Order."

"Go on," she says, settling into a chair.

"Is Mrs. Nightwing among our number?"

"No. She is simply a friend."

"But you quarreled at the Christmas party, and again in the East Wing."

"Yes, about repairing the damage to the East Wing. I argued that it was time to rebuild. But Lillian is so very frugal."

"But she accepted you as Claire McCleethy, though that is not your real name."

"I told her I had taken a new name to escape a love affair gone wrong. That is something she understands. And that is all there is to it. What is your other question?"

I cannot be sure if she is telling me the truth or not. I move on.

"Why has the Order never shared its power?"

She fixes me with that unsettling glare. "It is ours to have. We've fought for it. Sacrificed and shed blood for it."

"But you've hurt others as well. You've denied them any chance to have a part of the magic, to have a say."

"I promise you they'd do the same. We look out for ourselves. This is the way of things."

"It is an ugly business," I say.

"Power is," she says without regret. "I was not happy when you left me with the Rakshana. But I understand that you thought I was Circe. It is of no consequence now. You kept Circe from the Temple and the magic. You have done well. Now we can reestablish the Order with our sisters, and—"

"I think not," I say.

Miss McCleethy's mouth wants to smile. "What?"

"I am forging new alliances. Felicity. Ann. Kartik from the Rakshana. Philon of the Forest. Asha, the Untouchable."

She shakes her head. "You can't be serious."

"The power must be shared."

"No. That is forbidden. We don't know if they can be trusted with the magic."

"No. We don't. We shall need to have good faith."

Miss McCleethy fumes. "Absolutely not! The Order must remain pure."

"That's worked out well, hasn't it?" I say with as much venom as I can muster.

When she sees that she is getting nowhere, Miss McCleethy changes course, speaking to me as gently as a mother soothing an anxious child. "You may try to join hands with them, but chances are, it won't work. The realms guide who shall become part of the Order. We have no power over that. That is the way it has always been."

She attempts to stroke my hair, but I break away.

"Things change," I say, taking my leave.

Abandoning decorum, Miss McCleethy calls after me from her window. "Do not make enemies of us, Miss Doyle. We shall not give up our power so easily."

I do not turn back to look at her. Instead, I keep my eyes straight ahead, looking for the entrance to the Underground. A framed advert on the wall extols the virtues of the coming revolution in travel. They have already begun electrifying the tracks in some stations. Soon, all trains shall run on the invisible power of that most modern invention.

It is indeed a new world.

⅄⅄⅄⅄

Dinner with the Middletons is bittersweet. It is hard to keep my mind upon polite conversation over soup and peas when I've so much to do. When it is time for the men and women to retire to separate quarters, Simon spirits me away to the parlor, and no one objects.

"I shall miss your company," he says. "Will you write me?"

"Yes, of course," I say.

"Did I tell you Miss Weston made a fool of herself chasing after Mr. Sharpe at a tea dance?"

I don't find the story amusing. I only feel sorry for poor Miss Weston. I feel as if I can't breathe suddenly.

Simon's concerned. "Gemma, what is it?"

"Simon, would you still care for me if you discovered I was not who I say I am?"

"What do you mean?"

"I mean would you still care for me, no matter what you came to know?"

"What a thing to ponder. I don't know what to say."

The answer is no. He does not need to say it.

With a sigh, Simon digs at the fire with the iron poker. Bits of the charred log fall away, revealing the angry insides. They flare orange for a moment, then quiet down again. After three tries, he gives up.

"I'm afraid this fire's had it."

I can see a few embers remaining. "No, I think not. If . . ."

He sighs, and it says everything.

"Pay me no mind," I say, swallowing hard. "I'm tired."

"Yes," he latches onto that excuse. "Still recovering. You'll put this all behind you soon enough and everything will be like it was."

Nothing will be as it was. It is already changed. I am changed.

The maid knocks. "Begging your pardon, sir. Lady Denby asked for you."

"Very good. Miss Doyle—Gemma, will you excuse me? I won't be long."

When I'm alone, I take the poker and strike at the smoldering logs again and again till one catches and a small fire blazes to life. He quit too soon. It only needed a bit more tending. The stillness of the room closes in around me. The carefully grouped furnishings. The portraits looking down with passive eyes. The tall clock measuring the time I have left. Through the open doors, I can see Simon and his family, smiling, content, not a care in the world. Everything is theirs—not for the taking but for the having. They do not know hunger or fear or doubt. They do not have to fight for what they want. It is simply there, waiting, and they walk into it. My heart aches. I would so very much like to wrap myself in the warm blanket of them. But I have seen too much to live in that blanket.

I leave the pearl brooch on the mantel, grab my coat before the maid can give it to me, and walk out into the cold dusk. Simon will not come after me. He is not the sort. He'll marry a girl who is not me and who will not find the brooch heavy in the slightest.

The air is crisp and biting. The lamplighter ambles up the street with his long stick. Behind him the lights burn. Across Park Lane, Hyde Park rolls out, the shroud of winter covering its eventual spring. And beyond that, Buckingham Palace stands, governed by a woman.

All things are possible.

Tomorrow I shall be back at Spence, where I belong.

CHAPTER
FIFTY

SPENCE, THAT DOUR, IMPOSING LADY EAST OF LON-
don, has grown a friendly face in my absence. I've never been
so happy to see a place in all my sixteen years. Even the gargoyles have lost their fierceness. They are like wayward pets
who haven't the sense to come in from the roof and so we let
them live there, glaring but cheerful.

The rumors surrounding the night the constable found me
in Baker Street have already run rampant through the school.
I was kidnapped by pirates. I lay at death's door. I nearly lost a
leg—no, an arm to gangrene! I actually died and was buried
only to pull the bell rope with my toe, giving the poor
gravedigger a fright when he had to release me from the coffin
in the nick of time. It is astonishing the stories girls will con-
coct to relieve their boredom. Still, it is nice to have everyone
offering to do things for me, to have them part when I enter a
room. I shan't lie; I am enjoying my convalescence immensely.

Felicity has taken it upon herself to give the younger girls archery lessons. They adore her, of course, with her Parisian hair combs and status as one of the older, fashionable girls. I suspect that they would follow her like the Pied Piper of Hamlin no matter how nasty she chose to be. And I suspect that Felicity is aware of this and rather enjoys having a crowd of adorers.

As I am under strict orders from Grandmama and Mrs. Nightwing to do no exercise until I am well again, I sit under a mound of blankets in a large chair that has been brought out especially for me. It is, I find, the best way to exercise, and I shall try to extend this for as long as possible.

Out on the great lawn, the targets are in place. Felicity instructs a passel of ten-year-olds in the proper technique, correcting this one's form, chiding that one for giggling. Admonished, the giggling girl stands straight, closes one eye, and shoots. The arrow bounces along the ground and sticks in a lump of dirt.

"No, no," Felicity sighs. "Pay attention. I shall demonstrate proper form again."

I open the morning's post. There is a letter from Grandmama. She doesn't mention anything of Father until the end. *Your father is making progress at the sanitarium and sends his warm regards.*

There is also a small parcel from Simon. I am afraid to open it, but eventually curiosity wins out. Inside is the small black box I returned to him by messenger along with its original note: *A place to keep all your secrets.* That is all. He has surprised me. Suddenly, I am not at all sure of what I am doing, of whether I have done the right thing by letting him go. There is something so very safe and comforting about Simon. But it's a bit like the false-bottomed box, that feeling. I know only that something in me senses I might eventually fall through the bottom of his bright affection and find myself trapped there.

I've been so absorbed that I haven't noticed Mrs. Nightwing behind me. She takes in the sight of the girls with bows and arrows and clucks in disapproval.

"I am not at all certain about this," she says.

"It is nice to have choices," I say, the box in my hand. I'm trying not to cry.

"In my day, there were not such choices. Such *freedom*. There was no one to say, 'Here is the world before you. You have only to reach for it.' "

At that moment, Felicity's hand springs open, releasing the arrow. It cleaves the air in two and finds its target directly in the center, a solid bull's-eye. Felicity cannot contain herself. She shrieks with the joy of victory in a most natural and unladylike fashion, and the girls follow suit.

Mrs. Nightwing shakes her head and raises her eyes briefly to heaven. "No doubt the fall of civilization is at hand."

A faint smile escapes, and just as quickly, she stifles it. For the first time, I notice the lax skin at Mrs. Nightwing's jaw, the fine down that lies upon her cheek like the imprint of a child's hand, and I wonder what it must be like watching yourself soften under the years, unable to stop it. What it's like measuring your days in perfecting girls' curtsies and drinking nightly glasses of sherry, trying to keep up with the world as it pulls you spinning into the future, knowing you are always one step behind.

Mrs. Nightwing glances at the box in my hands. She clears her throat. "I understand you've decided against Mr. Middleton."

I see other rumors have spread as well.

"Yes," I say, fighting back the tears. "Everyone thinks me mad. Perhaps I am mad." I try to laugh, but it comes out a small sob. "Perhaps there is something the matter with me that I cannot be happy with him."

I wait for Mrs. Nightwing to confirm that this is the case, that everyone knows it, that I should dry my eyes and stop acting the fool. Instead, her hand comes to rest on my shoulder. "It is best to be sure, through and through," she says, keeping her eyes steadfastly on the girls running and playing on the lawn. "Else you could find yourself one day coming home to an empty house, save for a note: *I've gone out.* You could wait all night for him to return. Nights turn into weeks, to years. It's horrible, the waiting. You can scarcely bear it. And perhaps years later on holiday in Brighton, you see him, walking along the boardwalk as if out of some dream. No longer lost. Your heartbeat quickens. You must call out to him. Someone else calls first. A pretty young woman with a child. He stops and bends to lift the child into his arms. His child. He gives a furtive kiss to his young wife. He hands her a box of candy, which you know to be Chollier's chocolates. He and his family stroll on. Something in you falls away. You will never be as you were. What is left to you is the chance to become something new and unsure. But at least the waiting is over."

I'm scarcely breathing. "Yes. Thank you," I say when I manage to find my voice again.

Mrs. Nightwing gives my shoulder one small pat before taking her hand away to straighten her skirt, smoothing the waistband of its creases. One of the girls shouts. She's found an orphaned baby bird that has somehow survived the winter. It cries in her hands as she runs to Mrs. Nightwing with it.

"Oh, what madness is this?" our headmistress mutters, springing into action.

"Mrs. Nightwing, please . . . may we keep it?" The young girl's face is open and earnest. "Please, please!" the girls chirp like the eager little chicks they are.

"Oh, very well."

The girls erupt in cheers. Mrs. Nightwing shouts to be heard. "But I shall not be responsible for it. It is your charge. You keep it. I've no doubt I'll come to regret this decision," she says with a sniff. "And now, if you'll excuse me, I should like to finish my book, alone, without the presence of a single ringleted girl to disrupt me. If you should come for me at dinner and find me in my chair, gone to the angels at last, you shall know that I died alone, which is to say in a state of utter bliss."

Mrs. Nightwing marches down the hill toward the school. At least four girls stop her along the way to ask about this or that. They besiege her. At last, she gives up and, with a gaggle of girls in tow, heads into Spence. She will not read her book until this evening, and somehow I know this is what she wants—to be needed. It is *her* charge.

It is her place. She has found it. Or it has found her.

⊹⊹⊹⊹⊹

After dinner, when we have gathered round the fire in the great hall, Mademoiselle LeFarge returns from her day in

London with Inspector Kent. She's beaming. I've never seen her so happy.

"*Bonjour, mes filles!*" she says, sweeping into the room in her handsome new skirt and blouse. "I've news."

The girls make a mad dash for her, barely allowing her time to sit by the fire and remove her gloves. When she does, we immediately note the presence of a small diamond on the third finger of her left hand. Mademoiselle LeFarge has news indeed.

"We are to be married come May," she says, smiling as if her face could break from joy.

We fawn over the ring and our teacher, peppering her with questions: How did he ask for her hand? When will they marry? May we all attend? It should be a London wedding— no, a country wedding! For luck, will she wear orange blossoms? Will she wear them in her hair or embroidered upon her dress?

"It is remarkable to think that even an old spinster such as I can find happiness," she says, laughing, but then I catch her straightening the third finger of her left hand. She's looking at the ring without wanting to seem as dazzled by it as she is.

On the first Wednesday of the new year, we make our pilgrimage to Pippa's altar. We sit at the base of the old oak, watching for signs of spring, though we know they are months away yet.

"I've written Tom and told him the truth," Ann says.

"And?" Felicity prompts.

"He did not like being misled. He said that I was a horrible girl to have pretended to be someone I'm not."

"I am sorry, Ann," I say.

"Well, I think he is a boor and a poor sport besides," Felicity claims.

"No, he's not. He had every right to be cross with me."

There is nothing I can say to this. She is right.

"In books, the truth makes everything good and fine. The good prevail. The wicked are punished. There is happiness. But it's not like that really, is it?"

"No," I say. "I suppose it only makes everything known."

We lean our heads back against the tree and look up at the puffy, white clouds.

"Why bother with it at all, then?" Ann says.

A cloud castle floats lazily by, becoming a dog in the process.

"Because you can't keep up the illusion forever," I say. "No one has that much magic."

For a long while, we sit, saying nothing. No one attempts to hold hands or tell a merry joke, to talk of what has happened or what is to come. We simply sit, our backs to the tree, our shoulders grazing one another. It is the lightest of touches and yet it is enough to weight me to the earth.

And for a moment, I understand that I have friends on this lonely path, that sometimes your place is not something you find, but something you have when you need it.

The wind picks up. It sends the leaves scurrying for cover until a softer breeze blows through, settling them down again as it to say, *Shhh, there, there, it's all right.* One leaf still dances in the air. It spins higher and higher, defying gravity and logic, stretching for something just out of reach. It shall have to fall, of course. Eventually. But for now, I hold my breath, willing it to keep going, taking comfort in its struggle.

Another gust blows. The leaf is carried toward the horizon on the wind's powerful wings. I watch till it becomes a line and then a speck. I watch until I can't see anything, until the path it has traveled is erased by a sudden flurry of new leaves.

ABOUT THE AUTHOR

LIBBA BRAY's first novel, *A Great and Terrible Beauty*, was a *New York Times* bestseller. She likes saying that, especially on bad hair days. She lives in Brooklyn, New York, with her husband, their son, a cat, and two goldfish. When she's not writing, she's often thinking about writing, which can be a problem on the subway stairs. She'd love it if you drop by her Web site: www.libbabray.com. But she understands if you're busy.